THE KILLING ROOM

CHRISTOBEL KENT'S previous books include *A Darkness Descending, The Dead Season, A Fine and Private Place, A Time of Mourning, A Party in San Niccolo, Late Season* and *A Florentine Revenge.* She lives near Cambridge with her husband and five children.

Also by Christobel Kent

The Sandro Cellini Novels

A Darkness Descending

The Dead Season

A Fine and Private Place

A Time of Mourning

Christobel
Kent

THE KILLING ROOM

Published in trade paperback in Great Britain in 2014
by Corvus, an imprint of Atlantic Books Ltd.

10 9 8 7 6 5 4 3 2 1

A CIP catalogue record for this book is available from the British Library.

Trade paperback ISBN: 978 0 85789 330 7
E-book ISBN: 978 0 85789 331 4

Printed in Italy by Grafica Veneta S.p.A.

Corvus
An imprint of Atlantic Books Ltd
Ormond House
26–27 Boswell Street
London
WC1N 3JZ

www.corvus-books.co.uk

For Laura, with love

THE POWDERY RESIDUE DUSTED Nieddu's hair white: it sat in his eyebrows and on his lashes, but even beneath it the stonemason was ghost-pale. He pushed his way out through the PVC sheets they'd hung to protect the rest of the Palazzo from the excavation's fallout. The other man – no more than grunt labour, a Romanian on day rates – followed him anxiously until they reached the long doors that opened into the imposing building's garden. Pulling roughly at his mask on the threshold, the mason gulped the damp, cool air as if he'd been underwater.

Below them three men were talking under umbrellas on the terrace, and beyond them the great city spread out in the drizzle. The boss in his tight-buttoned coat turned to look up at the workers and, seeing something, held up a hand to stay his interlocutors.

It was the boss and the architect out there in the rain; the third man was a prospective client. The boss had introduced the client to Nieddu, when they'd passed through the cellar excavations, as a man of science: a bit of showmanship that was really a warning to be on best behaviour. The hand the man had held out to him had trembled and stalled in mid-air, and the mason had felt something in the atmosphere then, a vibration. Afterwards it seemed to him the client's reluctance foreshadowed what was to come.

Nieddu had not long worked out there was something back there: the little rivulet of crumbling plaster at the first probing was the telltale sign of a long-gone rush job. It hadn't been the time to mention it. They'd waited until the men were out of earshot before starting in with the Kango and the big sledgehammer. It had taken no more than fifteen minutes to get through, then another five for the dust to settle.

A man of science. The stonemason was a practical type himself but even he knew science didn't explain everything. It didn't explain what they had found.

'There's a whole other room down there,' he said to the Romanian, his breathing still irregular. 'It must have been bricked up.'

'Bricked up?' The labourer repeated the words in his thick accent, still struggling to understand Nieddu's pallor, the haste with which he'd backed out of the excavation site. The two men hardly knew each other, but the air between them had turned nasty. Something had seeped out from the place they had disturbed.

'Years ago. Decades. Maybe centuries, I don't know.' Nieddu shook his head and the dust shifted. There were spots of colour now in his cheeks, streaked with dirt. 'The boss needs to know about it.'

Bottai was walking up towards them. The architect stared after him uncertainly: he would do what he was told, anyway.

The smile the stonemason had seen fixed on the boss's face from day one, for the benefit of the prospective clients, had been replaced with a look of grim determination.

'I don't like it,' said Nieddu, to himself. 'It's more than bad luck.'

Chapter One

THE SUIT HUNG ON the heavy-fronted wardrobe, souring the evening before it had begun. It had been put there by Luisa who, by the time Sandro saw it, was in the bathroom applying her make-up.

'Just put it on,' she said, without looking round.

Standing next to her now, at sunset on the steep cant of the Costa San Giorgio, Sandro surreptitiously worked a thumb into his waistband. The woman ahead of them in the line to get in – a Marchesa di Something or Other, Luisa whispered – had already given him a look of disdain.

'You could get it let out,' Luisa had said dubiously in the bed-room, walking round him, tugging here and there. Loosening something off. The suit had been made by a tailor in Prato more than twenty years earlier and Sandro had remembered the man saying through the pins in his mouth, *It'll see you out. Room for another five kilos.*

Which, to the tailor – a wiry little smoker of cheroots, an unmarried man who sat under fluorescent light at his cutting table in a grimy Prato backstreet until late into the night – must have represented a wild over-estimate of what a man of stature could expect to gain in his middle years.

He couldn't remember why he'd had it made. It seemed a ridiculous extravagance from this end of a life, though much had been made at the time of the bargain he was getting. A wedding? A funeral was more likely, even then, even when he'd been little more than forty. In their prime, policemen attended funerals like most people went to christenings.

'Why are we even going?' he'd said grumpily, gingerly pulling the sides of the jacket together. 'Why were we even invited.' It was more a lament than a question.

'She's an important customer.'

'Who is?'

'She's called Alessandra Cornell.'

And now Alessandra Cornell was standing just inside the carriage entrance to a *palazzo* on the steep southern bank of the Arno, a slender blonde in a nicely cut cocktail dress Sandro assumed Luisa had sold her. A barrel-chested man Sandro distantly recognised stood beside her, leaning down to clasp the hand of the Marchesa.

Alessandra Cornell had a name badge. 'Welcome to the Palazzo San Giorgio,' she said, fixing him with her attention. She spoke in English to him too, as though by passing through the flawlessly restored doorway of the palace they had left Italy behind them.

'She's . . . what is she?' Luisa had said from behind his back in their bedroom, uncharacteristically vague. 'She spends plenty in the shop. I think her card says "attaché", or something.

She's basically going to be running the place.'

'The place' being the newly consecrated Palazzo San Giorgio, a luxury residence overlooking the glittering expanse of Florence from the privileged slopes of the Oltrarno. Sandro had looked at the brochure Luisa had brought home a week or so back. A new concept in leisure, a revolution in lifestyle choices. He had no idea what that meant. As far as he knew, it was serviced apartments. And attaché? For the love of God.

Four storeys high and five vast windows across, the wide, handsome frontage of the palace was visible from Fiesole, on a clear day. For decades it had stood decaying and unrestored while its multiple owners haggled with sitting tenants, bickered with their children and their cousins and their wives over whether it should be sold and for how much, and then over how the spoils should be divided.

'Ah,' said Alessandra Cornell, holding on to Sandro's hand a fraction longer than he would have liked and looking, not at Luisa, which would, given their connection, have been both the polite and the natural thing to do, but at Sandro, and too intently at that. 'So this is the famous Sandro.'

Sandro flinched, but did not turn accusingly, as he would have liked to have done, on Luisa.

'Am I?' he said weakly.

Cornell frowned a little and turned to the man at her side. 'This is our Director,' she said. 'I'm sure you already know of him. Gastone Bottai.'

Looking over Sandro's shoulder, the man offered him a limp hand. No warm clasping for Sandro.

'Yes,' said Sandro. 'Of course.'

A pampered son, a PR man. Bottai's gaze rested on him, supremely indifferent. They might have been introduced half a dozen times, but it wouldn't be worth his while remembering a policeman. Ex-policeman. He supposed the title *Director* must mean Bottai was the boss. In which case, God help them.

And abruptly he found himself moved on, past Bottai and Cornell and into the high vaulted space of the entrance where a waiter stood, already glazed with boredom, holding out a tray. 'Luisa,' he heard Cornell say behind him, airily familiar, 'I'll catch up with you later. Enjoy.'

Enjoy. Sandro reached for a glass of champagne. It was going to be one of those evenings. He remembered that thought, later.

'Behave yourself,' said Luisa, into his ear. They followed the couple in front of them around a corner and found themselves in the garden.

There were candles everywhere, gleaming in the clipped hedges, in deep glass jars standing on the low walls, flickering on small tables. Sandro didn't understand candles outside a church – secular, domestic candles, scented candles, candles in the bathroom, nightlights in special holders. The young woman in the building opposite them in Santa Croce burned tealights every evening, a little votive row along her windowsill.

Below them on the garden terraces people moved in the flickering light, the night filled with murmuring voices. A good turn-out: between them Cornell and Bottai must have used the big guns. Why Sandro had been invited remained an uneasy mystery to him.

A tall, fair man with a high forehead stood immediately in front of them, talking to a younger, stockier one with a chiselled jaw. Just to the side, a very handsome woman with auburn hair and a lot of gold at her neck was looking bored. The younger man appeared to be listening earnestly: the tall one was stooping slightly and talking, as far as Sandro could tell, about seaweed. 'The figures are what are interesting,' he was saying. 'Costs barely anything to generate. Of course there are environmental concerns—'

'Darling,' said the handsome woman, interrupting, her eyes sliding over the young man, pausing, moving on. Sandro made a guess at her age: forties. Strong. After fifty that tends to go. 'I'm sure I can see the Flemings.' Now she was looking at Luisa, pondering.

Luisa nodded just barely. The woman nodded back and turned away.

'Who was that?' said Sandro, his interest piqued despite himself.

'Customer. One of their . . . residents. Scardino. He's English, but Italian some way back, a professor of something. She's the wife. Polish.' Luisa wore an expression he knew of old: concentrated dignity, which she assumed when confronted with bad-mannered foreigners. Out of the corner of his eye he saw the back of the woman's neck, the glint of gold, the shining hair. He heard her laugh, low. Luisa smiled just faintly. 'Third wife.'

'And not the last?'

Her smile warmed, rewarding him. I love my wife, he thought.

'You should mix,' she said, giving him a little push at the elbow. 'It's what we're here for.'

Sandro stood his ground, and she looked at him. 'Don't you understand,' she said, 'this is what you have to do. It's called networking.' She lowered her voice. 'Cornell's got clout. She might not know it yet, but she needs someone like you.' And then she was waving. 'Signora Artusi,' she called, and she turned her back on him, the woman she'd hailed already swivelling round to size her up with narrowed eyes. 'Marina!'

It was all right for Luisa, she knew what these occasions were for, she just got down to work. He'd been cut loose.

*

Marina Artusi was a prize bitch – mostly on the subject of her only son and his foreign fiancée – but unlike most of the Florentine nobility at least she was entertaining. She didn't waste any time on the usual insincere praise, and within five minutes Luisa had heard her scathing opinion of her future daughter-in-law's fashion sense, fat English legs and performance in bed. 'I can hear them at it!' Marina said, outraged. 'She spends all the time bossing him about.'

Guiltily Luisa tried and failed not to be amused, looking around to make sure that Sandro was not in earshot. This kind of conversation would have him squirming in shame.

To her mixed feelings he seemed to have disappeared. When she turned back, Marina Artusi was practically on tiptoe as she strained to get sight of something. Catching Luisa's surprise, she drew herself back down.

'Looking for someone?' said Luisa, and an expression she hardly recognised appeared on Marina's face: a soft, flushed look. Luisa glanced from the glass in the woman's hand – still full – across to the heads where her gaze had been directed.

'Oh, someone I knew years ago,' Artusi said, as if trying to catch her breath and affect composure at the same time. 'You know we were in Damascus? Carlo and I. Oh, twenty-five years back at least.'

'Yes?' said Luisa, who had not known that. She was trying to find a face worthy of Marina's besotted expression. All she could see was a sea of middle age, but then twenty-five years was a long time.

'I heard he'd signed up for this place,' said Marina. Then, carelessly, 'With his wife, of course. I knew her too.' Her aristocratic nose wrinkled.

Luisa looked up at the façade: they'd done a good job, no expense spared. For as long as she could remember, the palace had sat there crumbling away above the city, a blighted place. And – oddly, because Luisa wasn't one prone to shivery intimations – she felt the creep of fine hairs rising at the nape of her neck, as though a draught had escaped from the building's cellars and found its way to her.

'There! There he is!' Marina's hand was on her arm, the other one pointing.

The man Luisa saw – stocky, square-shouldered, sixtyish – looked completely unexceptional to her. But he did have a full head of hair at least, even if it was grey, and she grudgingly admitted that most men looked good in a dinner suit. The James Bond effect. He leaned down a little to listen to something someone concealed from view on his other side was saying.

Marina Artusi let out a little sigh. 'Martin,' she said. 'Martin

Fleming. I believe he has one of those British honours now.' She spoke lightly, but Luisa wasn't fooled. Marina had obviously been stalking the man. 'A *cavaliere*? Sir Martin. He was something at the British Embassy. I never found out what he actually did, but we went to an awful lot of cocktail parties there. That English restraint.' Her eyelids quivered. 'Carlo couldn't stand him, of course.'

Of course. Marina's husband Carlo had been a stranger to restraint: he had died of a heart attack in the arms of another woman ten years earlier. As they looked, a woman stepped out from behind Sir Martin, a small person with chopped-off grey hair and a sallow complexion – and Luisa saw that he was holding her hand. The snort of impatience that escaped Marina Artusi then was much more characteristic of her.

'He got away then?' said Luisa, before she could check herself.

Marina Artusi turned, a look of narrowed derision on her face. 'They were childhood sweethearts,' she pronounced, contemptuous. Then, with satisfaction tinged with shock, 'My God, she's aged.'

At that moment, almost as though despite the hubbub he might have heard the exchange, the man glanced in their direction. To Luisa's dismay, Artusi immediately raised a hand. At her age, thought Luisa (meaning, our age). *No, no.*

But immediately the man – this Martin Fleming – smiled back. He even took a step towards them. Marina Artusi took several steps in his direction, tugging Luisa behind her, and they were brought up close.

'Marina,' he said. 'After all this time.' And, addressing his wife, 'You remember Marina, darling?'

What struck Luisa first was that after twenty-five years he had remembered Marina's name without hesitation. But then he turned to Luisa and, seeing his smile, his crinkled eyes close to and focused on her, she couldn't help but smile back, and she abruptly understood exactly what Marina Artusi meant. Charm, or something. Luisa turned hastily away and found herself looking instead at Martin Fleming's wife, the small grey-haired woman whose hand he still held. She seemed distinctly amused.

Beside Luisa, Marina Artusi cleared her throat in annoyance.

*

Out of sight of Luisa and feeling quite adrift, Sandro turned with a start when a hand fell on his shoulder. The young man with the big jaw who'd been listening to the Professor was now flashing a broad smile that did not quite distract Sandro from the bulge of trapezoid muscle pushing the line of his expensive suit out of shape at the shoulder.

'Sandro Cellini?' said the young man, the smile earnest and widening. '*The* Sandro Cellini?'

Sandro laughed with disbelief. 'I don't know about that,' he said warily. 'It's my name.'

'How modest,' said the man – not much more than a boy, he seemed to Sandro, for all his muscle. There was an eagerness about him, like a well-trained schoolboy. 'You tracked down that English girl, a couple of years back. And wasn't there a fraud case? The murdered bank manager? Not to mention that political sabotage business.' He held out his hand. 'Giancarlo Vito.'

'You're well informed,' said Sandro. 'It's not always so eventful.' The days spent staring out of the window, or recording a young wife's visits to the hairdresser, for her paranoid husband.

'I know,' said Vito, clasping his hands behind his back, standing to attention like a cadet. The stance made his shoulders look impossibly broad, and made Sandro feel like his grandfather. He straightened. 'I'm in the same business,' said Vito. 'So it's kind of a professional interest, you might say. Not that I'm my own boss, like you.' He almost bowed. 'I work for the Stella d'Argento.'

The investigations agency whose emblem was a sheriff's badge, advertised on billboards out towards the airport and in all the professional circulars.

'Mostly cybercrime, the bread and butter stuff,' he went on apologetically. 'I'm sat behind a computer. Not very exciting.' Vito looked around with a young man's hunger, the glitter of the evening reflected in his eyes.

Sandro opened his mouth to ask what he was doing there, then closed it again. One superannuated old-school detective with rounded shoulders, one handsome young cyber-expert standing to attention.

'And you've got an elegant wife, so I hear,' said Vito, turning back to Sandro politely. 'You see, you're ahead of me there, too.'

All this self-deprecation was beginning to niggle. What was he after? Sandro was aware of the charm, the open smile, throwing up a smokescreen, but it worked all the same. The boy got away with it.

'Yes,' said Sandro, looking around for her. 'I'm a lucky man. Five years married by the time I was your age. At least.' But turning back he caught the first sign on Giancarlo Vito's face of something underneath the charm: a fleeting sly look of pleasure and calculation, of the anticipation of conquests.

On the terrace below them someone was tapping on a microphone, ascending a podium. A crowd was gathering. Without looking, Sandro knew that the speaker would be Bottai.

'Better get down and show willing,' said Vito, patting Sandro on the shoulder. 'Catch you later, perhaps? I'd love to hear your stories.' And he and his smile were gone, leaving behind them the whiff of doubt, and Sandro's mood sinking like a pricked balloon.

His stories, indeed. What had that been about? Sandro shifted on his feet, the warm champagne glass in his hand. With the boy's disappearance the evening felt like a net drawing tighter around him in the dark, all these wealthy people in their satin-lapelled dinner suits and their jewels nothing more than shiny fish. That draught from the cellars had been the start.

It came back to him that the builders had found something during the works on this place, a piece of gossip that had dissipated almost as soon as it appeared. Bones? Sandro doubted it. Human remains weren't easily hushed up. Something archaeological, maybe. You couldn't put a spade in the ground here without turning up a Roman brothel.

Turning away, Sandro saw a bar which had been set up under some bougainvillea beneath the illuminated façade, and headed straight for it. Feeling the champagne sour his stomach, he asked for a beer. A big dishevelled man, so ungroomed he might have been a gatecrasher, stood at the other end of the long zinc counter. He was talking to a young woman Sandro recognised as part of the well-bred rent-a-crowd. The man's big paw came to rest on her slender knee; she looked down at it, debating her next move. Before she could make it, Sandro reached between them, setting his glass down on the bar. They looked at him, united in affront.

'Sorry,' said Sandro. The girl adopted the faintly bored expression she probably reserved for the bumbling elderly. Sandro turned to the big scruffy man. 'Sandro Cellini,' he said, holding out his hand. 'I'm so sorry. I'm not used to these occasions. Formal occasions.' He grimaced apologetically. At his shoulder the girl evaporated.

'Thanks for that,' said the man, offering neither his hand nor his name as he watched her go.

'I'm so sorry,' said Sandro, affecting innocence. 'I'm sure she'll be back.'

The bearded man grunted sourly. 'There'll be another one,' he said, then groaned. 'Christ, here they come,' he muttered, and, sliding heavily off his stool, gestured to the barman, who handed him a beer without a word.

He must belong here, then. Sandro looked to see who had ousted him. A middle-aged couple, certainly foreign, were making their way up the steep path that led up the side of the garden from the lower levels. The man, climbing doggedly in the candlelight, was wiry, with the lined skin of an Anglo-Saxon who has spent too much of his life in the sun. The woman was pale and unmade-up: she had a country look about her, standing there awkwardly brushing at her silk dress as if she'd just taken off an apron. Sandro turned to look back after the big man, glimpsed him lumbering down through the garden. Maybe it's me, thought Sandro, with dour pleasure.

'I'm damned if I'll listen to that PR rubbish,' the new arrival was saying tersely, oblivious to Sandro, though it seemed to him the wife, if wife she was, was trying to catch his eye. 'He's got my money, hasn't he?' The man was talking in English, with an accent. American? No, thought Sandro, Australian. Paid-up residents. 'I'm not boring myself to tears into the bargain, I've listened to enough bullshit in my time. They're not our sort.' The woman murmured, distressed, but the husband just turned his back on her and called the barman impatiently.

These people were so wealthy: why were they so discontented? Only a young man like Vito would hanker after what they had.

Down below them on the terraces the booming voice had stopped. Sandro peered down. From the far side of the stage a camera flashed, and Sandro blinked. He hoped there wouldn't be a picture of him in *La Nazione* tomorrow. He rubbed his eyes. He saw the usual faces, the Florentine nobles and freeloaders, and distinct from them the incomers, the foreigners. Prospective residents of the Palazzo San Giorgio. A big woman, very old but still imposing, with cropped fine white hair and a strong profile; and a handful of couples. Average age early sixties: on the cusp of retirement, he supposed, although he knew the wealthy often got there early.

Sandro watched as the Professor ducked his high forehead to dodge the trailing jasmine above him on the pergola and raised a hand. Had they opened the floor for questions already? Maybe the end was in sight.

'What kind of get-out clauses are you offering, Gastone?' The Professor spoke drily, familiarly. At his elbow his wife smiled a little, provocative. Her hair, Sandro thought, momentarily fascinated, was extraordinary, dark red-gold. There'd been something in the way she'd looked at that young man with the broad shoulders. Vito. She put a hand to her hair as if she knew Sandro was watching. A titter ran along the back

'It's all in the literature, Professor Scardino,' Bottai said smoothly. 'Why? Has your lovely wife already spent it all in the Via Tornabuoni?' The titter faded, then resurfaced, and Sandro looked for the woman. Her head was thrown back, her mouth open in a full-throated laugh. Men were staring at her.

Behind Sandro at the bar the Australian wife's sniffling became audible and he turned. Feeling the husband's pale eyes settle on him, Sandro held out his hand. 'Welcome to Florence,' he said in English. 'Sandro Cellini. I'm a . . . I'm here with my wife.' As if that explained everything. He tilted his head, looking at the woman. 'Are you . . . is everything all right?' He felt the husband looking at him with flat hostility.

'Marjorie Cameron,' she said, holding out a limp hand. 'From Melbourne. We're here for a year. My husband – this is my husband, Ian – he'll be retiring soon, and we thought it would be a nice base for me. He works all over the world, you see, an engineer. Something in my eye.'

The non-sequitur took Sandro aback until he realised she was explaining her pink-eyed look. 'There's a lot of pollen, too,' he said and gratefully she began to talk about allergies. She'd been pretty once, he registered as she brightened.

'I would never have chosen Italy,' said the engineer, interrupting her. Looking at his tough, lined face, his gingery eyebrows, Sandro reflected reluctantly that the Anglo-Saxons often seemed rude to start with. You couldn't condemn them straight off. 'But the ladies like it.'

Sandro was about to consider that statement when a noise started up somewhere far down the garden, a shrill yelping overlaid with a woman's cries of distress: a sound of panic and fear. It reverberated through the evening; heads turned, the tenor of the conversation changed. And then a man's voice, raised and blustering. Sandro took advantage of the diversion to edge away from the Camerons and head downhill, following the sound.

At the lower edge of the terrace a young woman – black-haired and pale with shock, but beautiful – was holding up a small, soaking-wet dog under her chin, murmuring to it. Gastone Bottai was trying to soothe her while the other man – her husband, Sandro would have said, from the body language – blond and brick-faced, was shouting, in American-accented English. 'For Christ's sake,' he was saying. 'A well? What kind of a Third World outfit is this, Bottai? Why didn't it have a – a – some kind of a cover on it? I mean, Jesus, Therese might have gone down after him.'

The woman's head was lowered, her white cheek pressed against the shivering dog. The fine fabric of her evening gown was soaked where she held the animal against her. Therese.

Bottai was murmuring, all apologies and disclaimers, evading responsibility already. Sandro could hear him. And then another man was there among them, his hand on the woman's shoulder. Therese, thought Sandro again, mesmerised by her welling blue eyes. Then he saw that the third man, his broad hand so familiarly placed on the beautiful woman's back, was Giancarlo Vito.

Experiencing an odd kind of shock at the sight, Sandro sidestepped, moving on, down to where they'd come from, an instinct propelling him into the dark below. And if it hadn't been for the presence of another man already there, he might have walked into the well himself.

'Jesus,' he exclaimed, teetering on the edge of a circular void, perhaps a metre in diameter. He was grateful for the stranger's arm holding him back.

'Right,' said the man, in accented Italian. 'Lethal, huh?' Another American: tallish, dark, lean.

Sandro stepped back; the American let him go, and they both looked down. You couldn't see the water but you could smell it, cold and mineral and mossy.

'There must be a cover,' said Sandro, kneeling. The American turned, bent down and tugged at something. It grated and Sandro leaned across to help. It was heavy; it took the two of them to shift it.

'Negligent, at the least, wouldn't you say?' The American's voice was light. 'It's not like they were showing the thing off, it's not illuminated. This isn't any wishing well.' The man sat back on his heels.

'I don't know,' said Sandro, warily.

The American held out a hand. It was his night for formal introductions, thought Sandro, looking around as his eyes adjusted to the light. Why *had* the well been uncovered?

'John Carlsson,' said the man, the hand still proffered.

Sandro took it. 'Cellini,' he said, hoping for anonymity.

'The detective,' said Carlsson. 'Sandro Cellini, right? Business or pleasure?'

Sandro's shoulders dropped. 'It's certainly not pleasure,' he said. 'I don't know what I'm doing here, to tell the truth.' Rising to his feet, he tugged at his collar, stifled, and feeling his balance go in the dark, took a step back.

The American stood too, and looked up towards the candlelit façade. 'I'm supposed to be writing the evening up,' he said. 'Our Miss Cornell will be sweet-talking me before you know it, not to mention this little incident.' Sandro looked at him blankly. 'I'm a journalist,' said Carlsson. 'This was only meant to be a nice puff piece.'

'And now you're going to write about a dog falling in the well?'

The man gave him a sardonic look. 'And the rest,' he said. 'If I was of a mind to cause her trouble.'

'Such as?' Despite himself, Sandro was caught.

'Like that room they found, digging out their gym, or whatever.' Sandro drew himself up, attentive, but the man had moved on. 'And as for this lot. You go along thinking, well, free champagne, all these charming wealthy people.' He clapped Sandro on the shoulder. 'Only, when you look closely at them, some of them turn out to be not so charming after all; they've made their money in pretty unglamorous places, or doing rather ugly things. And they buy themselves a nice cover story and an attaché and private security.'

Sandro wondered what his game was, all these hints, nothing concrete. 'Room?' he said, dogged. Too old to follow hares, whoever set them running. 'What room did they find?'

Carlsson snorted. 'You're very thorough, aren't you, Sandro Cellini? The room's not really my point.'

'All the same,' said Sandro. 'Humour me.'

'It had been bricked up in the foundations. A – a chamber.' The journalist was looking up the hill. 'You've seen the exhibition, Mediaeval Instruments of Torture? It's very popular with the tourists: the Virgin of Nuremberg, all that. The chamber was empty when they found it, more or less, and it's God knows how old, centuries, though no doubt down the generations it found its uses.'

The cold metallic smell of the water from down in the earth was still in the air, and Sandro felt queasy, his stomach still sour. He took a step back. 'So are you going to do something about it?' he asked. 'All these dubious characters. Are you that kind of journalist?'

In the dark beside him Carlsson's teeth flashed in a broad grin. 'We all start out wanting to be that kind of journalist,' he said. 'We grow up, we take the money instead. That's the theory anyway.'

And then he heard Luisa's voice, calling him. Turning to look up, he saw her, stepping daintily down the path in her party shoes, his saviour.

'Where on earth did you get to?' she said, coming breathlessly to a halt. 'We've been looking for you.'

'Can we go now?' Sandro said, more loudly than he intended. Luisa groaned. 'What?' he said.

'I do hope we're not keeping you,' said Alessandra Cornell, emerging into view from behind Luisa.

Sandro turned to look for John Carlsson, but he had disappeared.

Chapter Two

IT HAD TAKEN LUISA a good twenty-four hours to forgive him. With not a single client since February, Sandro needed all the contacts he could get; he could live without managing to antagonise the rich and well connected.

The morning after, Luisa hadn't been surprised, and she told him as much. 'I don't know why I bother,' she said. 'Why couldn't you have just been civil? If you accept someone's hospitality,' and he'd grunted at that, because they both knew he'd like to have been given the opportunity not to accept any such thing, 'you should be gracious about it. Just because they're wealthy doesn't make them bad people.'

And before he'd had a chance to wonder at her vehemence, she'd gone to work without her coffee.

So the wealthy residents of the Palazzo San Giorgio had settled discreetly into their first few weeks of cocooned luxury. John Carlsson had written his puff piece for a foreign newspaper – Sandro knew that because Luisa had brought it home from work. Scanning the article, he found it only anodyne, so he assumed the hunt must have gone elsewhere. Once or twice Sandro did think of Giancarlo Vito too, with his charming smile and his cybercrime expertise, and he wondered. But the last thing Sandro needed was a reminder that he was down to his own last coffee-spoonful of testosterone and more ignorant of hard drives than the average eight-year-old, so he pushed the thought away. And by the time they heard from Alessandra Cornell again it was halfway through a scorching May, and the evening had turned into the fading memory of one more social occasion on which Sandro had shown his wife up and sabotaged his own professional chances.

So there was something shamefaced as well as gleeful about the way Luisa marched in to the kitchen, dropped her handbag on the table and announced, more than a month after what they both viewed as a debacle, 'Guess who dropped by the shop this evening, asking for you?'

Sandro knew better than to say anything. He smiled warily.

'Alessandra Cornell.' She sat down, and Sandro could see the glow of the day's heat in her cheeks. 'The woman from the Palazzo San Giorgio.'

'The attaché,' said Sandro. 'Asking for me? I have an office, don't I?'

Luisa gave him a sidelong look. 'And you were there all day, were you?'

Sandro shifted uneasily, then stood up to go and stir the sauce he was making: tuna and olives. He'd never been known to even reheat a pizza, but after a month of idleness at the office, of watching Luisa coming home from work, the sole breadwinner, and straight away putting on her apron, he'd decided that perhaps he'd better get his act together. Luisa had needed to bite her tongue a couple of times when he'd got it wrong, but she had surrendered the ground once or twice a week.

He switched off the gas and went back to the table. 'I might have nipped out for a coffee. To the market.' He gave in. 'She came to the office?'

Luisa smiled; she was good at regaining the high ground. She shook her head. 'Phoned. I said you'd have been out on a job and would have the mobile off.'

So Alessandra Cornell had been looking for him. He thought of her expensive vanilla-pale hair, and her condescension, and had to admit to being gratified.

'You're going to see her at ten tomorrow morning,' said Luisa, which wiped the smile off his face.

Chapter Three

THE MAN WAS NAKED. He was kneeling like one of the very devout or a beggar, his face between his knees, his great shoulders humped and his arms out. His head was down between his knees, his hands were palms uppermost and he was dead. Twelve hours, or thereabouts: there was mottling and discolouration where the fluids had collected, and in the late-spring heat the tissues had begun minutely to bloat and swell. Where his face was pressed sideways against the rug, it was stained darkish.

'It's all mine,' she said from the doorway, arms folded, her mouth turned down in disgust. The *carabiniere* lifted his head from his examination of a lividity at the back of the man's neck to look at her, a woman old enough to be his grandmother. You wouldn't want a grandmother like this one. 'The rug,' she said. 'He took it fully furnished. Who'll pay for the damages? God knows what he's done to my bathroom. I can hear everything that goes on, you know.'

'And what did you hear?'

She peered down unashamed at the pale soles of the man's feet, the shadow of his genitals between them.

'I thought he'd gone away on holiday,' she said. 'I saw him go yesterday afternoon. He must have come back.'

'You didn't see him last night? Hear him?'

'I was out,' she said. 'I went to see my sister.' Outraged at the missed opportunity: spying on her tenant better than the telly, no doubt.

But thinking him away, she'd let herself in to snoop this morning, early.

The dead man would have been roughly the *carabiniere*'s own age, late twenties, a good fifteen kilos heavier but all of it muscle, stiffened now into dead meat. There was a stink in the room, pungent, unmistakable, of a body in extremis. The young *carabiniere* sat back on his heels a moment, waiting for his stomach to settle. He didn't want to throw up in front of the old woman. He looked at the bookshelf – a couple of fat dog-eared paperbacks on it and a cheap-looking trophy on its side – registered the dusty blinds, the stale smell from the kitchen. She probably charged through the nose for this dump.

There was a crosstrainer in the corner of the room, Lycra training gear over the back of the dingy armchair. If he'd walked past this man in the street, would he have felt a twinge of envy at the outline of perfectly worked muscle? He could hear his partner downstairs, on the radio talking to forensics. They'd been and gone, would be coming back again. The bathroom needed a closer look.

The dead man's landlady was waiting.

'You'll have taken a deposit?' he said, and her mouth set in a line.

'Not enough,' she said. 'If I'd known what – what kind he was, I'd have taken double.'

'We don't know what he was,' said the *carabiniere*. They both looked down at the traces of powder scattered on the rug; there was other stuff in the bathroom. Steroids, as far as he could tell, and a modest few grams of coke. She'd been in with her passkey, and had a good sniff around. Not for a second did she seem to register that the stiffened thing on the rug had once been human.

'I'm sorry,' he said gently. 'We're going to have to ask you to stay out of the apartment until we're done.' Shutting the stable door, but still. 'And of course we'll need your prints.'

'This is my house,' she spat.

'Yes,' said the *carabiniere*, quite calm. 'And this is a crime scene.'

After a long moment, she turned away. Before she'd got to the bottom of the stairs, he had his head in the scale-encrusted toilet bowl and was silently throwing up his coffee.

*

The bastard.

It was bad enough, Elena thought, having to remember him before she opened her eyes, having to groan at the memory of the messages – four, five? – she'd sent before she'd finally come to her senses. Loving, then anxious, then angry, then desperate, then . . . drop it. Never send a message to ask if the first message arrived, because it always has. He's not answering because it's over. How many times had she been through it? Move on.

Bad enough, without this. Beyond the window a large vehicle was making a lot of noise, again. There'd been comings and goings all night, it felt like. Yet another delivery to the splendid new development that was the Palazzo San Giorgio.

Elena Giovese wasn't the only one who objected. Residents up and down the steep street, even those with charmed family lives and stable careers, had put in official complaints about deliveries at all hours of the day and night. What might it be this time? She could hear the cranking of some kind of hydraulic lift: it would be a bath carved from a single piece of crystal, perhaps, or a gold-plated statue, or four tonnes of polished Carrara marble.

She opened her eyes and saw his CDs by the door and groaned, audibly.

The persistent complainers, Elena was sure, the ones who threatened legal action and letters to the *comune*, had got paid off. She hadn't been down that route herself. She wanted a quiet life, in all senses of the word. She wanted to get up at nine, go downstairs and unlock the workshop; she wanted to make a cup of coffee for her uncle when he turned up and she wanted to settle down peacefully to a specific task. Sanding a piece of two-hundred-year-old wood, regilding a cornice, scraping off damaged paintwork.

Only her uncle was in the hospital: a heart attack a week ago. He's doing well, they said, cautiously. But he was still in intensive care at Santa Maria Nuova. Three days with tubes in him and at last he was sitting up, talking, even if he did look like a ghost. They said the first week was crucial.

Elena looked down from the bedroom window at the building opposite and something horrible rose inside her. He used to stand right here, having climbed naked out of her bed, and look down. She felt a tightening, like fear, in her chest, and she didn't know why.

Standing still a moment as her heart raced, Elena told herself she might as well take advantage of having been woken at six. She dropped John's CDs into the waste bin on her way out of the door to the hospital. It was a start.

Chapter Four

SANDRO WAS AT THE Palazzo San Giorgio at a quarter to ten. He was wearing his suit, and he hadn't had any breakfast. A mistake – two mistakes, connected by a tight waistband – because it was never a good idea to attend an interview with discomfort and hungry bad temper seething just under the skin.

The beautiful doorway beneath which they'd lined up for the party, with its high wide arch through which carriages would once have rolled, was open – but blocked. A truck bearing a huge padded packing case (Sandro found himself thinking, the Trojan Horse?) had somehow got wedged while attempting to reverse through the gates. It seemed to have been there some time. As Sandro skirted it there was an alarming hiss and bounce as it tried to move, then stopped again. There was no room to fit past it. A man in a hard hat leaning on the bumper talked lazily into a walkie-talkie; Sandro tried to catch his eye but he turned his back. He looked around, trying to work out which was the Palazzo's official entry point, and eventually the man in the hat directed him further up the hill.

Waiting to be admitted, Sandro watched as a girl walked doggedly up towards him, her small strong body leaning in to the angle of the hill. A tangled knot of black hair was twisted up on her head. She turned and let herself in to a workshop opposite the truck. He just caught her look of weary exasperation directed at the truck as she pushed through the door.

The Palazzo's regular entrance was a smaller arched doorway. A doorman of late middle age wearing a striped waistcoat and tails stood guard over its plate-glass inner doors and hushed foyer. He led Sandro down a softly lit, pale corridor in ostentatious silence. Observing the man from behind, Sandro saw that he had a bald patch and his uniform was too big for him on the shoulders.

The carpeted corridor was very quiet, as if soundproofed, and they saw no one until they walked past the open door of a vast room with book-filled alcoves, round tables and a bar at one end. The waistcoated barman – small, dark, alert – raised his head as they passed the doorway. Sandro glimpsed a couple drinking coffee from a silver pot at one table. Therese – no Alzheimer's yet, he thought, as the name jumped into his head – Therese with the dog, and her sandy-haired husband.

A figure was coming towards them down the corridor now, moving slowly. Sandro had plenty of time to observe her. The white-haired woman with that high forehead and warrior's nose, statuesque even in motion, leaning heavily on a cane, her very pale, very intelligent blue eyes raised to his. She paused, and out of deference Sandro couldn't help doing the same.

'Who's this, Lino?' she said, in ringing, English-accented Italian, with the fearlessness of the very old.

The doorman gaped. 'I . . . this is—'

'Sandro Cellini,' Sandro said, holding out his hand.

'I saw you at the launch,' she said, letting her own large-boned hand rest in his. Her hair was so fine and so white it was almost transparent, but the effect was oddly beautiful. 'With a handsome woman. Was that your wife? You talked to the Camerons.' Her eyes narrowed. 'I thought you looked like an off-duty policeman.'

Startled, Sandro let out a laugh. 'Once upon a time,' he said, 'you would have been right, Signora . . . ah . . .'

The doorman Lino shifted on his feet, but Sandro could not have got past the old woman without pressing himself against the wall, and he wasn't prepared to do that.

'Athene Morris,' she said, and let his hand drop at last. 'You've come to see our Mr Bottai? She tilted her head. 'No. You've come to see Alessandra. Would you like me to tell you why?'

'Signora Morris,' said Sandro, 'I don't know myself yet. You have a gift, clearly.' He saw pleasure light her pale eyes.

'I'm just nosy,' she said, leaning on her stick. 'Not many vices left, at my age.' And she smiled conspiratorially. 'I happen to know there's a vacancy.'

Lino cleared his throat, and with a tiny creak of discomfort Athene Morris stepped back, just enough to allow them past. 'I expect I will see you later, Mr Cellini,' she said.

As she answered the door, at first sight Alessandra Cornell looked as impeccable as she had on the evening of the palace's launch; pale, blonde, flawless. Stepping inside, Sandro reminded himself that he was not the petitioner here: she had come to him.

The attaché's office was on what was nominally the palace's ground floor, although with the steep slope of the gardens falling away it felt as grand and light as a *piano nobile.* After the dim padded corridors Sandro was momentarily dazzled. There was a big rosewood desk, a bookshelf, low modern white armchairs; the vaulted ceiling was decorated with a very freshly – and pinkly – restored fresco of garlands and babies. Clearly a very great deal of money had been spent here.

Sandro felt Cornell watching for his reaction, and he was careful not to show it. 'It's beautiful,' he said, trying for humility and awe. He wondered if she might have to surrender it to one of the fractional owners, for the right price.

She inclined her head, and indicated that he should sit down. He lowered himself gingerly into an armchair.

There was a silver-framed photograph on the desk, of a man's face, and Sandro only had time to register the corporate dullness of the smile, the bland neatness of the shirt and tie that made it hardly worth putting in a frame, before Cornell turned it away.

It was safe to say they hadn't hit it off at the launch. In the candlelight, with Sandro irritable from the champagne, she'd quizzed him sharply about his work, his clients, the reasons for his departure from the police, and, resentful at being subjected, without warning or explanation, to what seemed to be an interview, he'd answered her curtly. Rudely, Luisa had said. If there'd been a job going, it had gone to some one else.

'Thank you for coming.' She sounded weary, suddenly. The pallor lost its lustre. She leaned back against her desk.

'Of course, it is a pleasure,' said Sandro, with stiff pity. 'I had the impression I had failed the first interview. If it was an interview.'

'Ah,' she said. 'Well. Perhaps the conditions weren't ideal.' Sandro waited, and Alessandra Cornell sighed. 'It's a delicate matter,' she continued, slowly. 'At least, now it is.'

The door opened abruptly and a voice said, 'I understand you've spoken to the lawyers? Was that strictly necessary? There are ways of getting rid—' Gastone Bottai had not bothered to look into the room he was entering until it was too late. Seeing Sandro, he stopped, put out.

'Gastone!' There was panic, thought Sandro, as well as exasperation in Alessandra Cornell's voice. 'Do you never listen to anything I say?'

Bottai looked at her, something childishly discontented in his expression, and Sandro pondered the hierarchy. He's her boss, but she's smarter than him. He liked her fractionally better.

'This is Sandro Cellini,' she went on, her voice levelling as she held Bottai's gaze. 'We were to talk, do you remember?'

'I know who he is,' said Bottai, huffily, put out at having to make the acknowledgement. 'As long as it is merely preliminary. Clearly I am also involved in any recruitment decisions.'

She inclined her head, effectively dismissing him.

'I'm sorry,' said Alessandra Cornell, her unease still apparent even after Bottai had closed the door behind him.

The words preliminary and recruitment were not cheering Sandro; the only thing keeping him in his seat, little did Cornell know it, was his curiosity about Bottai's indiscretion. Lawyers?

She put her hands on the table. 'At the launch I wasn't sure we even needed a full-time security consultant here,' she said. 'It was still at the early stages.' Was she pleading?

'That's the thing,' Sandro said, sitting back in his chair. 'I mean, what is that – in a place like this? Security consultant. Did you want him to talk closed-circuit monitoring, set up proximity technology?' He was aware of being bullish, but what did he have to lose? 'Or is it more like nursemaiding? Keeping the guests happy? My guess is, a bit of both.'

She looked startled. 'We got input from clients, from management,' she said, faltering. 'And we found a man we thought was suitable for the position.'

Smoke-filled rooms then: the usual bartering. Sandro could imagine his CV being pushed to one side. Too old, too bad-tempered. But it was back on the table now. He leaned forward.

'Because I have to say, Miss Cornell.' He was in earnest now. 'I can keep an eye on a security camera with the best of them, but I'm not an expert on technology, nor am I much of a nursemaid.' He held her gaze. 'Too rough round the edges. So if that's the brief—'

'It didn't work out,' said Cornell, blunt at last, looking down. 'Two days ago I had to let him go. I'm eager to replace him straight away, so as to reassure the clients.'

He looked at her, taking his time, making sure he remembered the name right. 'It was Giancarlo Vito, wasn't it,' he said, and her eyes widened. 'I expect he looked like just the man for the job. But you fired him. What did he do, exactly, that was so . . . indelicate?'

Two spots of colour appeared on Alessandra Cornell's cheeks, and she compressed her lips.

'He wasn't up to it,' she said, and at last he heard frankness, saw the poise broken down. 'He allowed things to happen. It got beyond his control.'

He looked into her eyes and he saw something else. Alessandra Cornell was frightened.

'I need someone I can trust.'

Chapter Five

'JUST SAY YES.'

Giulietta Sarto sighed into her mobile. She was supposed to be at work in half an hour. Say yes? There was something about Luisa Cellini that made it hard to say anything else.

'It's not forever,' Luisa said. 'Just to tide him over. So he feels he's not abandoning the business.'

Eyes closed, Giulietta shook her head, just slightly.

'It's just absolutely not the right time,' she said, steeling herself. 'Things are shaky enough at the Women's Centre. They only took me on as a paid employee last year, and now they're laying people off. If I ask to cut back the hours – or take a leave of absence – I mean, it's probably just the excuse they need.' She inhaled. 'And it's not like the private detective business is booming.'

There was a silence, that lengthened.

'All right,' she said. 'All right, when he asks me, I'll say yes.'

She heard Luisa breathe out: it sounded like genuine relief. A pause. 'Did you say you had news?'

Giuli had forgotten her news. Was that a bad sign? 'Oh, yes,' she said reluctantly. 'Enzo and I have set a date.'

'A date?'

'To get married.'

They'd been engaged close to two years, so it shouldn't have come as a surprise to anyone. Daft though it might seem, Giuli had barely given a thought to it. She hadn't had the kind of history that ended in marriage, as a rule. Her mother had worked as a prostitute in the southern suburbs of Florence before overdosing; abused, anorexic and drug-addicted Giuli had ended up in prison for killing her abuser, and until Luisa and Sandro had come into her life, she'd assumed she was several times more likely to be dead by the age of fifty than married.

She was forty-four this year. What should a forty-four-year-old woman be? She had no clue.

'Oh, Giuli,' said Luisa.

Hearing the catch in her throat, and knowing Luisa was as a rule not one to give in to emotion, Giuli said gruffly, 'Don't. And don't start on the wedding dress.' Little did Luisa know.

'All right,' said Luisa, recovering herself. 'All right. I just wanted . . . well, anyway. I've just come off the phone with him. With Sandro. I wanted to get to you first.'

Hanging up, Giuli stared at the row of chiffon and lace in front of her, and broke out into a sweat. Mistake. Huge mistake. She backed towards the door; the saleswoman, who'd been standing looking at her with undisguised impatience even before she answered her mobile, didn't move to detain her.

On the street, Giuli looked back at the shop window. A dummy gazed out at some point above her head, an expression of idiot bridal rapture on its face, not at all what Giuli would have considered appropriate for a woman who'd been trussed up in twenty metres of pearl-studded satin – namely something closer to outrage.

Mistake. And if she were to let Luisa loose on it – those high standards, after thirty years in the business of dressing women, that infallible taste, the pursed lip, not to mention the unmanageable emotion this particular wedding was going to dredge up – the mistake would turn tsunami.

Giuli stared down at the phone in her hand. She thought maybe she should call Sandro. Luisa had forgotten to ask her the actual date, after all that, which was just as well as it was only two weeks away. Cue all-out wedding-dress campaign, no thank you.

And on top of all that, Sandro was going to ask her to go full-time manning the office for him. Because something had come up.

'It's such an opportunity for him,' said Luisa. 'They've already had a bad experience, I gather. The first guy didn't work out. But the money's good, and it's regular. It'll start on a trial basis, I imagine, but . . . it's a real job.'

Giuli tapped her teeth with the phone. What if Sandro didn't work out either? And what if she burned her boats with the Women's Centre? She'd come to love the place. It might be contraception advice and battered wives and grubby feral kids, it might harbour one too many reminders of her old life, but it was home.

Then again, working for Sandro did something for her nothing else did, and it gave her a pang to hear Luisa say, of this fancy house-detective deal, *a real job*. Like their little office wasn't, with its battered computer and filing cabinet with the drawer that stuck, and her three mornings spent exchanging gossip with Sandro and listening to him moan about the modern world while weeding out his inbox. People were beginning to hear about them, too, not just Sandro but her as well. And what about the old ladies who wanted them to find a long-lost grandson, last heard of washing up in Treviso, or catch their neighbour putting down poison for the cat?

Plus, she needed a distraction. Turning her back to the window display of Dream Bride, Giulietta Sarto set off south, towards the Centre and an afternoon of wrangling women who'd turned crazy for one good reason or another. There'd be a solution.

*

Sandro paused at the foot of the Costa San Giorgio, where it came out on to the river through a wide, low arch. He'd left the attaché's office above him on the hillside but he couldn't shake the feeling he'd had in that bright room, of things unsaid, whispers and secrets, just out of earshot. He put his phone away in his pocket and leaned there, looking. On the opposite bank the lofty elegance of the Uffizi's arcaded frontage was thronged with people, and underneath it the bright fluttering flags danced on the souvenir stalls in the noon sunshine. He pushed himself off the rough stone of the arch's pillar and set off down the Borgo San Jacopo towards San Frediano, and the office.

He hadn't told Luisa the full story, just that the job was his, if he wanted it. She could hear him keeping something back, of course, but Luisa was a strategist, she was biding her time.

Was she pleased? He'd known his wife since they were nineteen and twenty-one, but Sandro Cellini still found it hard to second-guess her reaction to anything, even something she'd engineered herself. And now the boot was on the other foot; now he might find himself talking *her* into it, once she knew this wasn't exactly the smart suit and sinecure she wanted for him. More like a poisoned chalice.

Alessandra Cornell was so discreet it had seemed to cause her physical pain to give him any information at all about the circumstances under which the job was suddenly his, and the fear had still been there, in the way she hadn't been able to keep her hands still.

'I need to know the situation here, that's all,' Sandro had said, soothingly. 'I need to know if I'm the man for the job, and what I'm walking into. You understand? If I'm to help. Perhaps you could start from the beginning. When did he start?'

Alessandra Cornell sat up, her shoulders taut. He felt sorry for her.

'We were all agreed, he was just what we . . . the Palazzo needed.' She spoke hurriedly. 'He fitted the image, he was young, smart, eager, and he said he could start straight away.'

Sandro cleared his throat, aware of his own distinct lack of eagerness. 'His agency was okay with that?'

She looked surprised. 'As far as I know. You know them? The Stella D'Argento. It must have been okay because he was in the next day. And the clients all seemed to like him.'

'How many are there?' Sandro got to his feet and she looked up, startled. He took a step towards the long windows, then another. He could see out. A maid was setting out loungers on a lower terrace. 'In residence? Let's say, since Vito arrived.'

'Well, when we roll out, we hope there'll be at least twice as many—' She caught his eye. 'But just now, there are four couples and one single, two if you count our artist in residence. They were all at the launch.'

Mentally Sandro made a quick tally. The Australians. The tall Professor and his big-spending wife, who liked men to look at her – Scardino? Therese, whose name he still hadn't forgotten, her little dog, and her brick-faced husband. So there would be another couple he hadn't identified, plus the singles. Athene Morris would be one.

'I met the Camerons,' said Sandro mildly, pondering the other single. Artist in residence. It could only be him: the big guy at the bar, whose chat-up routine Sandro had walked into. 'So what went wrong?'

She frowned down at her hands. 'Small things,' she said. 'To begin with, anyway. Small unpleasant things. Spiteful. A bracelet of Miss Morris's disappeared from her room, she was very upset.'

Sandro tried to imagine the fierce old woman upset: it was an oddly painful thought.

'Sentimental value, she said. The maid resigned, Giancarlo seemed quite sure she'd done it, but the bracelet wasn't found. Dog's mess smeared on skirtings and on a door. The steam room was locked with a guest inside. A child's tricks, although they got worse.'

'How much worse?'

She raised her head. 'The dog,' she said. 'We never should have allowed the dog. We made an exception—' She faltered.

'What happened to the dog?'

'We don't know,' said Cornell, fidgeting, looking down. 'It – he – the dog disappeared.'

He felt it then: the little surge in the blood. Not dead yet, said some little ticking in the prostate. That dog had been the start of it, at the launch. That young woman's distress – holding the soaking animal heedless of her expensive dress – had been the only real thing there. Disappeared.

'The dog,' he said. 'At the launch, wasn't there . . . didn't something happen to the dog at the party? Fell down a well?'

She frowned. 'Yes,' she said. 'But that was . . . we sorted that out. The gardening team we'd had in the day before, they admitted they'd neglected to secure the cover. Well, eventually they did. It was an accident.'

An accident. 'You checked the well when the dog went missing?'

She drew herself up. 'Of course.'

Sandro turned, thinking, found himself gazing through the long window and almost immediately stepped back. A couple in late middle age, a stocky man and his grey-haired wife, were walking slowly to the terrace under Cornell's window. The diplomat Marina Artusi was besotted with, Sandro guessed. Luisa had filled him in. Based in the Middle East, she'd said; he must have seen some action, these past twenty years. As Sandro watched, the man leaned down, solicitous, to help his wife sit, and she looked back up at him. Even from this distance her smile transformed her thin face. She looked almost transparent in the sunshine: a lifetime away from any kind of home clearly took its toll.

He turned back to Alessandra Cornell, feeling like a voyeur.

'Four couples, two singles, then,' he said. 'And what about staff? The domestic staff? How many are there?'

Again the spots of colour appeared on her cheeks. 'Well, at the moment we're working on minimal staffing—'

'It's all right,' he said patiently, 'I'm not a client.'

'A doorman – Lino – eleven till midnight, with breaks of course, but the guests have their keys, this isn't a hotel. We're looking for a second doorman.' She hurried on. 'There's a barman. Again, we will eventually need a second, but Mauro is very capable.' Sandro felt a pang for Lino with his thin shoulders, not so capable. 'Two maids, mornings only unless we have a function. Last night, for example, they were serving drinks, and the same tonight.'

Sandro nodded, feeling the numbers settle in his head. Out on the terrace the maid straightened, turned and looked back up, shading her eyes. Italian, for which he was relieved. In a place like this they might well employ exclusively foreigners, and he was already worn out speaking another language.

'All trustworthy, naturally?' He smiled. 'Except the girl who resigned, I suppose.' He spoke mildly. 'Although of course the incidents continued after her departure, so perhaps . . .' He shrugged. 'And Vito couldn't work out what was going on?'

Cornell twisted her fingers together. 'He never seemed to take it very seriously. His approach was to go around talking to guests, smoothing things over, but he didn't actually get to grips with why or how these things were happening. It was unsettling. Even I found it so. But Giancarlo just played it down.'

'And you – you gave him an ultimatum?'

She shifted uneasily. 'Not exactly,' she said. 'Gastone supported him, said his approach was the right one. We let him go because one of the guests put in a complaint about him.'

She fidgeted. He waited. Eventually she said, 'There was a woman. A woman was . . . brought in, by one of the guests.' She took a breath. 'A prostitute. Giancarlo took no action; he was even seen at the door with her as she left.'

'Seen by whom?'

'Mr Cameron made the complaint,' she said.

Cameron. The Australian who bullies his wife. 'Do you know which guest she was – ah – visiting?'

Alessandra Cornell's face looked frozen. Silently she shook her head. 'I was under the impression I was interviewing you, Mr Cellini,' she managed eventually.

'Look,' said Sandro, feeling sorry for her. 'Signorina Cornell. I don't know if that means you want me to take over. All I can say is, I don't believe in ghosts. Or poltergeists, or evil spirits, or for that matter in smoothing things over. It seems more practical to look for answers in the real world.'

She gazed back at him, wanting to believe she'd found her saviour.

'I'm sure we can sort this out,' he said, and cursed himself.

So he was going to accept. The traffic of the Via Maggio behind him was heading for the bridge and he paused, enjoying the cool the Via Santo Spirito always harboured, perpetually oblique to the fierce sunlight as it was. He felt in his pocket for his phone, but didn't remove it. *Call Giuli,* Luisa had said.

If Sandro had to pick a street where he felt Florence was fully itself – and therefore fully his – it would be this one. Big silent palaces, the ancient possessions of the Frescobaldi and the Capponi and the rest; their discretion, unlike the ersatz, bought-in version Alessandra Cornell was installing at the Palazzo San Giorgio, was absolute. Centuries of iron will, taste, ruthlessness and money, these palaces opened their doors only to their own: their shutters were closed, their gardens were hidden. Could she manage that for her clients? She could try.

It had only occurred to him as he was leaving to ask where he would actually be working. 'I mean, did Vito spend all day patrolling the premises?' They were standing in the doorway to Cornell's office. 'Or is there somewhere I can sit down, now and again?' He cursed himself for sounding like an old man, and added, 'Do – ah – paperwork?'

Wearily apologetic, she had taken a little bunch of keys from her drawer – a couple of brass ones, a Yale, a plastic card, a bigger silver key – and led him to a tiny corner room beyond the library. She'd unlocked it and held the jingling bunch out to him by the key she'd used, the Yale. A gesture of faith. Taking them, he was agreeing, and he knew it.

The room was barely big enough to accommodate the desk and narrow bed it contained, with a single slit-window looking on to another wall. He saw Cornell glance quickly around as if looking for something, but the room was empty except for a brochure on the desk about the Palazzo. Sandro had picked it up, registered Cornell watching him. 'May I?' She had nodded, unresisting, and he had put it in his briefcase.

Locking the door behind him, he'd had a sudden urge to run, down the corridor and into the daylight and the fresh air; he'd had to force himself to shake her hand and walk away. He could feel her eyes on his back all the way.

Now Sandro walked on, deeper into the silence of the Via Santo Spirito, savouring the air of the streets, a breeze off the river. Enough. It would be interesting. His mobile was still in his pocket; there'd be no point in dialling Giuli's number because there was no signal here, nor anywhere along the canyoned streets he'd walked that ran parallel to the river on the south, from the Via San Niccolò to the Borgo San Frediano. Perhaps that was why he liked them; unlike most of his countrymen, Sandro had never embraced the mobile phone, not even the new one Luisa and Giuli had talked him into having, with internet and all that. He didn't see it as a boon but a ball and chain. While his phone couldn't make contact with its mothership, he was hidden here, as protected as the satisfied *borghesi* behind their massive doors.

What was it Giuli had told him, just the other day? That with the clever phone, the magic phone with its touchscreen and Bluetooth and global positioning, they knew where you were. And not only that, but from the moment you first turned it on, a file was created, tracking your movements, stacking up numbers, co-ordinates, transactions, spooling them out endlessly in cyberspace. She'd had to stop him chucking the thing into the river on the spot. Since when did Giuli get so trusting?

'It's good,' she'd insisted, looking at him wide-eyed. 'Information's always good, right?' It might have been Luisa speaking, whom tough-talking streetwise Giuli covertly worshipped; his honest wife who had nothing to fear because she knew she was both innocent and right, who had fought off the cancer in her breast because she believed in staring information in the face. And he was just paranoid, with his 'they'.

Phone still in hand, he turned down the Via Maffia, brighter, warmer, wider, lined with carriage entrances. The Via Maffia was where the great families had kept their stables, and every façade was dominated by a massive arched doorway, wide enough to admit a coach and four, vast iron rings at regular intervals along the street front. Here he could use the mobile, but he didn't. Sandro kept walking as the streets grew sunnier, the houses grew humbler, and the squawking of neighbours arguing across their balconies announced San Frediano, district of fishwives and thieves and artisans.

He stopped halfway down the Via del Leone on the eastern side and looked at the brass nameplate that he'd only just got around to paying for, after four years operating out of this shabby street. Fishwives, thieves, artisans – and *Sandro Cellini, Investigations.*

*

Am I being selfish? thought Luisa Cellini, waiting at the table her boss had booked at the small restaurant behind the straw market.

Life's too short, sometimes. She imagined the two of them out there in the city, her husband, her not-exactly child, Giuli. Shoving them into things was second nature; she knew this would be good for Giuli – but for Sandro? There was the significant possibility that he'd hate every minute of it. She wondered what he'd think, for example, of the charming Martin Fleming. Sir Martin, although he'd refused to allow them to call him that. There was also the possibility that Sandro was, as he was always complaining, too old – too old for change, and too old to be someone else's employee. However charming.

It was a risk. That her feeling – the feeling that had kept her with him through close to forty years of obstinacy and silences and bad temper, the feeling that her husband could actually do anything he put his hand to – was a misguided notion born of stupid romantic longing. Wanting something, as Luisa knew as well as almost anyone, did not make it so.

But what if Luisa, after a whole working life walking a shop floor in the service of other people, was the one who was too old to be someone else's employee?

He was late, but then Enrico Frollini, handsome, *affascinante*, seventy-two-year-old owner of the chain of shops that bore his name, was never less than twenty minutes late. It was a matter of principle. It was a good job that Sandro, who'd never – to Luisa's amusement and irritation – trusted her boss to keep his hands off her, didn't know his wife was about to have lunch with Frollini. Particularly, perhaps, a lunch where she would announce that their relationship was about to cease to be a professional one.

In a two-thousand-euro grey suit – summer wool, end-on-end weave, just a shade flashy – he breezed through the door. She imagined that even on his deathbed Enrico Frollini would look immaculate.

'Enrico,' she said. She didn't stand up. He took her hand and kissed the air a centimetre above her knuckles. 'Madame,' he said in an exaggerated, ridiculous French accent. 'What a pleasure this is.'

Chapter Six

OUT ON THE RINGROAD near Firenze Sud – no more than a kilometre or two from the Palazzo San Giorgio but a world away – the unmarked van pulled out of the villa's dusty parking lot and joined the traffic on its way north to the mortuary. The oleanders dividing the four lanes of traffic were ruffled by a light breeze; the sky was a brilliant blue. It was a beautiful day.

Simpering, the landlady had introduced herself to the returning forensics officer, to whom she'd taken a shine: 'Valeria Maratti.' She'd offered him a coffee. And at least that had got rid of her, temporarily, the three men – two in uniform, one in the hooded white forensics suit – had silently agreed, as the angular figure disappeared into the gloom of her downstairs apartment.

He died between eleven and midnight, was the preliminary conclusion. Blunt trauma to the skull. Death more or less instantaneous, which would be just as well for the killer, as the victim was more than equipped to fight back. No signs of a forced entry.

The body had been removed. The name he'd given the landlady had checked out, they'd taken away a computer. The apartment contained not much more than a wardrobe of ironed shirts and sharp suits, big in the shoulder. No clue as to next of kin, nothing personal, no photographs, the drawers of the cheap desk empty except for a single folder of paperwork. Tax forms, employment contracts, one signed only a month previously. Valeria Maratti insisted he had a mother, but there were no letters, no pictures. No doubt he'd invented her, to please the old woman or to get her off his back.

The sporting trophy on the chipped lacquer of the bookshelf said: *Iron Man Genova 2008, 3rd Place.* A single one-kilo handweight. 'Don't these usually come in pairs?' the young *carabiniere* said to Captain Sandrino, lifting it in a latex-gloved hand.

This was only the third time they'd been out together, and his superior's taciturn indifference still unsettled him. They found the other dumbbell in the garden, in the long grass: a skinny cat had been sniffing around it, high-bounding off when they approached. There were traces of blood and hair on one end.

The *carabiniere* had had to explain to the forensics boys that he'd thrown up in the toilet, had contaminated the scene. The older of the two officers, benign as a child's entertainer in his white hooded outfit, had rested a gloved hand on his shoulder briefly. 'It happens,' he said. 'Not just to the young ones. You'd be surprised.' He bent over the shower tray, an old deep one that doubled as a hip bath, and delicately probed around the plughole with a fine metal scraper. The young *carabiniere* saw his nostrils flare.

'Might have to look in the drains,' he said, sitting back on his haunches.

*

The truck wedged in the vehicular entrance to the Palazzo San Giorgio had fallen silent by around twelve and at the back of the workshop Elena, absorbed in the task of removing blistered gilding from a tiny, fire-damaged Renaissance mirror, had forgotten all about it. But when she stood up from her work around two, unexpectedly hungry, she saw that it was still there. She strolled out into the sun.

'Yes?'

She didn't know where the bark had come from but it was gruff, irritated. Had someone heard her? Elena stepped back into the shadows of the shop. She watched as a man emerged from around the side of the truck, silhouetted against the sunlight. A bulky, untidy shape, grunting with exertion as he squeezed himself, undignified, across the truck's wheel arch and into the road. '*Cazzo*.' The standard muttered obscenity. He looked up and down the empty street, ready to be offended, then, scratching the back of his shaggy head, at the truck.

'*Cazzo*,' he muttered again, then turned, eyed her with interest.

'What is it?' she said. He looked at her, baggy-eyed with a hangover. Elena looked back at him, refusing to be intimidated. 'That thing, on the truck. Do you know?'

As he regarded her from under his heavy eyebrows she couldn't tell if he was annoyed or interested. 'It's a sculpture,' he said.

'Are you in charge?' she asked. 'Of getting it in there?' He looked amused; there was something familiar about him with the smile.

'In charge? I suppose.'

The way he was looking at Elena began to unsettle her: penetrating, curious. Forward, for a workman. 'What?' she said defensively.

'You don't know who I am, do you?' he said, watching her.

'Should I?' She hugged herself, irritated.

He put out a big hand, hairy at the wrist. 'Danilo Lludic.'

She did know the name, dimly. 'Elena Giovese,' she said.

He turned and nodded at the shrouded object on the trailer. 'I made it.'

'Right,' she said. 'If you say so.'

Then he laughed. 'You've heard of me, right?' She made a comic helpless face, and his voice turned a little sulky. 'I did have something at the Biennale last year. Christ, Italy's so parochial.'

'I'm just a worker,' she said stubbornly. 'I haven't heard of anyone.' But then she relented. 'You lived in New York,' she said, watching his expression. What else? 'Something to do with garbage? You make sculptures out of—'

'Detritus,' he said, still surly. 'Garbage, yeah.'

Arrogant. There'd been some scandal or other, she dimly remembered: in one of the magazines, *Oggi* or *Gente*, his bear-like figure holding a hand up to shield his face from the photographers. A woman had accused him of something. 'So it's one of yours.'

He couldn't disguise a look of crafty delight, like a boy having pulled off an outrageous scam, and she thought he seemed closer to forty than fifty years old.

'It is,' he said. 'Part of the deal. Specially commissioned.' He stepped towards her, inspecting her.

Elena stood her ground. 'Part of the deal?'

'D'you want a coffee?' he asked.

She jerked her head back towards her workbench. 'I've got a lot on,' she said. 'Short-handed.' He looked over her shoulder into the recesses of the workshop. 'Some of us have to work for a living,' she said.

Danilo Lludic's eyes narrowed, preparing to sound off at her, but instead he laughed, a gust of tobacco and coffee on his breath. 'I've seen you,' he said, his interest growing. 'You were at the launch, right? Not like them to invite a mere worker. Were you with someone?'

She felt her cheeks burn, her throat close up. 'You have a deal with them?' she said, arms folded. Not answering the question.

'I'm to be a resident, too,' he said, shrugging. 'I believe I add colour. Artist in residence.'

'Nice work if you can get it.'

He passed a hand over his forehead and his face fell, just a little. 'Jesus,' he said. 'But I'm beginning to wonder if it's worth it.' He tugged at his hair. 'And they're beginning to make noises about the bar bill. I've only been there a month.' He let his hair fall back, smiled wryly. 'They don't understand the artistic temperament. It's like . . . like . . .' He looked at her. 'Have you ever been to Dubai?'

'Dubai?' She laughed disbelievingly. She'd seen pictures: skyscrapers and shopping centres and artificial islands; she'd rather take a holiday on an industrial estate. 'No thanks.'

'Yeah,' Danilo Lludic said. 'Well, I was paid to go there, too, but that was just a week. Not a bloody life-sentence. What is it about big money? I mean, really big money. It's not that they're boring, exactly.' He looked up at the façade. 'You know how you get so rich? You have to have . . . a one-track mind. You have to go for it, grab it, hang on to it. They're monsters.'

Looking back down at her, he laughed, hugely. '*We're* monsters.'

And in that moment, his big mouth open red in the shaggy-bearded head, he looked it: alarming, voracious.

'I wouldn't know,' Elena mumbled, turning away from the sight, her head full of confused thoughts about that night, the night of the launch. She'd tried her best; she'd even had an interesting conversation, with an English scientist. He'd asked her about early varnishing techniques and had told her about his work, which had something to do with algae as far as she could remember. The scientist's wife had been talking to John; when she found out he was a journalist, she'd dragged him over to meet her professor husband, ousting Elena with no more than a glance. Elena was getting used to it: journalists were useful. The wife had been unnervingly attractive. Finding herself looking at the back of the woman's glossy head, she had left. John had come in late, smelling of scent. Whether it was the glossy woman's, she had no way of knowing.

'Come over, why don't you?' Lludic was talking to her back. 'I mean, assuming these arseholes manage to get the thing into position. Six o'clock. Champagne reception. The grand unveiling.'

'Yeah,' said Elena. Anything to get rid of him. 'I'll dig out my ballgown.'

But he'd turned away: in the street someone was shouting and he was shouting something in reply.

And for a stupid second she wished him back.

*

Giuli sat outside Dr Massini's office, waiting. She didn't know why she was so nervous, but it had something to do with the speed with which her boss had agreed to see her. In the reception area Giuli had glimpsed someone she didn't recognise until a heartbeat too late, by which time she was already headed on down the corridor; her nervousness had something to do with that too. They popped up, these faces, looking a hundred years older, scarred and lined, bloated and breathless. Drugs and disease.

She'd hoped for some breathing space; like with the wedding, she felt like she was being hustled into something.

'It won't be for long,' Sandro had said, in the warm corner of the *trattoria* where he'd bought her lunch. He seemed distracted. 'At least, I hope not. I've got to show willing, you know. With Luisa.'

'That's marriage,' she'd said, dubiously. 'And Enzo tells me I've got to eat.' To look halfway decent in the wedding dress. Enzo knew her: a week of this stress and she'd be back to skin and bone, and at her age, that wasn't a good look.

'Delighted to hear it,' said Sandro, lifting a finger for the waitress. Giuli could see his eyes on her. He'd ordered *pecorino e baccelli*, sheep's cheese with young broad beans, olive oil and lots of pepper. Beef stew. Bread. He wasn't going to mention the wedding, and she was grateful enough for that.

He pushed the beans towards her, and grudgingly she began to stab at them with her fork. 'So,' he'd said cautiously, watching every mouthful. 'If you could take, say, a month's leave. Could you call it compassionate? Someone's died?'

It wasn't just distraction, she decided: he was excited. She hadn't seen Sandro like that in ages. A nervous energy.

'I think they need me, actually,' he'd said, almost apologetic. 'At the San Giorgio.' First-name terms already, thought Giuli. 'I mean, it could turn out to be just nannying, but . . . there's something wants sorting out there. There's some sort of event this evening I've got to turn up for, to meet the inmates. The previous guy—' And he laughed drily. 'Well, it would appear he let the wrong sort of woman in. Among other things.'

Giuli had gazed at him, wondering if he no longer thought of her that way. It had been seven years; maybe now she could stop being an ex-hooker, ex-junkie, ex-anorexic. Wrong sort of woman. She'd really had that thought, even now.

He had leaned down and fished something out of his briefcase: a big glossy brochure. He pushed it across the table to her and she opened it, to show willing. A lot of photographs of terraced gardens, roses, four-poster beds, cute little modern kitchenettes. Something fell out and she picked it off the floor. A piece of paper with some drawing on it. It looked like a floorplan. Sandro tilted his head to get a look and she held it out to him.

'My predecessor,' he said. 'Trying to get his bearings, I imagine.' He laughed uncertainly. 'It's a bit of a maze inside.' Frowning, he folded it and put it in his pocket, looked back at her. 'So?'

'I suppose I could use the wedding as an excuse,' she said grudgingly, knowing she'd already agreed.

He'd relaxed then, settling back into the padded booth, and had helped himself to a large portion of beef stew. And Giuli had thought, well, Sandro's pleased, Luisa'll be pleased, even Enzo won't be upset. Her husband-to-be had his reservations about her work at the clinic. That at least was the right decision.

But now, waiting in the empty clinic corridor, she wasn't so sure. So much depended on the goodwill you'd built up, didn't it? They could just come down hard if they didn't value you, and that was what she didn't want put to the test. The door opened with a jerk, and Massini was there, staring down at her through thick horn-rims.

Not good. She knew that straight away.

The Clinic Director stood stiffly away from her as Giuli passed inside the room, her hand held out straight to indicate the chair.

'I'm glad you've come to see me, Ms Sarto,' she said. 'Giulietta.' She didn't sound glad. 'Something's come up.'

'I – I . . .' Giuli felt her face frozen into a mask as she stammered. Lunch had solidified into an indigestible lump inside her. 'I wanted to ask . . . a favour,' she said, wanting to forestall it, whatever it was.

Massini took off her glasses. 'I'm afraid this isn't the time,' she said stiffly. Giuli had always thought she was one of the good guys. Something had changed.

'There's no nice way to put this, Giulietta,' she said.

*

By the time she turned to go, Giuli felt as though she was sleepwalking back out through the door. This wasn't real. This wasn't happening. She felt like flailing, thrashing, shouting, beating the white walls. Passing the cleaner in the corridor, she felt the good-hearted old woman's eyes on her. Did she know? Out in a daze through reception, empty now save for Sandra, the bad-tempered Englishwoman behind the desk, who watched her go as if she knew too, and into the sun of the Piazza Tasso. She walked on around and behind the vast city wall that formed one side of the square and she didn't stop until she was on the *viale* and hidden by the brick bulk.

With shaking hands she took out her mobile.

Who? Her head buzzed with it. Who would do that? Who would say that? And it wasn't in outrage or disbelief, it wasn't that she couldn't imagine who. It was more that she'd always known this was coming; it was that the world – the lovely city, its high stone walls, its shitty parks and needle-strewn corners, its dodgy bars – was full of them. Enemies. Only she'd let down her guard, she'd started to think she was free. You were never free.

She'd have to tell Enzo.

But she dialled Luisa instead; the number went straight to answerphone. She'd be busy, of course she would, she'd be with a customer. Giuli hung up without leaving a message, staring at the little screen. Sandro? He'd be in the office, wouldn't he? She walked the hundred or so steps around the corner halfway down the Via del Leone, stopped in front of the brass plate, lifted her finger to the bell-push and burst into tears.

It was where Sandro found her ten minutes later when he slipped out for a coffee.

'To hell with them,' he said, when she managed to blurt it out in some kind of comprehensible form. 'To hell and back with the bastards.' And as he patted her helplessly on the shoulder she started crying all over again.

*

'But it's not true?' said Luisa, into the phone, and immediately cursed herself. Of course it wasn't true. She thought of the four years she'd known Giuli, and tried to convince herself that was long enough, to know a person inside and out. Hadn't Luisa always shied away from that maxim, one day at a time? The catechism of the recovering addict: you're never cured. You can never relax. Luisa had somehow thought that Giuli was different, hadn't she? The rules didn't apply. And they'd all relaxed.

Sandro didn't dignify it with an answer. 'I'm keeping her here with me for the afternoon,' he said. 'I'll take her this evening, when I go to be introduced. Cornell said I'd have to do that, she's keen to get things started. But I can tell them she's my second in command.'

'They won't have heard?' And cursed herself again. It wasn't like anyone at the Palazzo San Giorgio cared about some bit of office politics in a San Frediano health clinic. The two worlds could hardly be more different.

'They won't have heard a thing,' he said. 'Damn the lot of them.'

Chapter Seven

BELOW HER IN THE street Sandro was pacing, talking urgently on his mobile. Whoever had called him had something more pressing to talk to him about than her problems: he'd jumped like a scalded cat and headed back outside. The signal was better out there – but there was more to it than that. She was getting in the way.

She couldn't expect him to save her life, not again. She had to deal with this herself.

There's been an allegation,' Dr Massini had begun, and Giuli had felt her life coming down around her like a falling building, in slow motion.

Someone had walked into one of the treatment rooms to come upon Giuli shooting up in there. 'The person said there could be no mistake. Came straight back out again, but . . .' Massini had used the feminine ending, faltered. A woman.

Giuli had found she could hardly breathe. The words, when they came out, were jumbled, wrong. 'What? What? Which room?' Trying to think the last time she'd actually been in a treatment room.

'In the Addictions Clinic,' Massini began, then checked herself.

Was that the wrong question? Was she incriminating herself? Giuli had started again. 'Who says they saw me?'

'I can't tell you that just now, Giulietta,' Massini had said, a rebuke in her voice, and Giuli's face had burned, with the shame. 'The person came to me in confidence and until an inquiry is initiated, legally . . .'

An official complaint had been made. Other testimony was being investigated – whatever that meant.

In the street below, Sandro came to a halt and looked up at her, worried.

She made herself smile. Sandro's first reaction had been a visible effort not to ask her if it was true. He'd help, he'd know the questions to ask – only just now he had his hands full. His head was bent back over the phone now.

Who?

A woman: Giuli's solitary piece of evidence. Well, the place was full of women. And that very morning she'd seen someone from her past, hadn't she? Waiting in reception. Giuli squeezed her eyes shut and her life before Sandro – on the streets and in squalid walk-ups – was thronging and alive suddenly, in the blood-dark behind her eyes; faces she'd trained herself to forget materialising out of the shadows. Why hadn't she fought back? Massini would never know what it was like, to have a past.

Sandro had gazed at her. She could tell what he was thinking. *Shit.*

'She said, she had to follow procedure. She said I'd be laid off on full pay while an official investigation was under way. The details of the allegation would be revealed to me – or to my lawyers.' Lawyers. They'd know Giuli had no money for lawyers. Wordlessly Sandro had handed her another tissue. She saw him calculate: how much?

'And the official investigation will clear you,' he said stoutly. 'In the meantime, *I* need you.' Then, more recklessly, 'Look, I need you, full stop. I'm . . . well, I'm not thinking of retirement quite yet, but the plan has always been that you would take over. Even before this came up.'

And then his phone had gone off.

On the other end of the line a woman's voice had been audible, high-pitched. Luisa? Not Luisa.

'Miss Cornell?' Sandro's voice had gone straight to alert. 'All right,' he said. High alert. 'It's all right.' And he'd shot out of the door.

Below her now he folded the phone, paused a moment in contemplation. Across on the opposite pavement, movement caught Giuli's eye: Maria. The Centre's ancient cleaner, bent and toothless in her forty-year-old raincoat, was scuttling as if to get past before she was seen. Only she couldn't resist looking up, and their eyes met. *No*, the old woman's were saying, clear as day. *Don't ask me.*

Don't ask me what?

Sandro was in the doorway, breathing heavily after the stairs. He needs to get some weight off, thought Giuli with a pang as she turned to look at him. 'I've got to go,' he said. 'Will you be all right?'

'I'll be all right,' she said mechanically. Maria knows something.

'My new employers,' he said, hesitating in the doorway. 'I said I'd get over as soon as . . . well. They've got a problem.'

'Sure,' she said, refocusing. He's not telling me what she said on the phone.

The thought must have appeared in her eyes because he said, 'I trust you with my business, Giuli, and I'd trust you with my life, you know that.'

'I know,' she said, weary.

Sandro cleared his throat. 'You're part of my team,' he said. 'They need to know that, at the Palazzo, you're involved. I was going to introduce you. Things have changed, and she needs me there right now. But – maybe this evening. There's some do on—'

Giuli felt the heat rise in her cheeks again. 'Sure,' she said uncomfortably. 'Whenever.'

'I'll call you.'

'Go,' she said. And he went.

*

'It wasn't an accident,' Cornell said. 'A violent death. Giancarlo.'

Lino the doorman had silently stood aside this time, and let Sandro pass. He hadn't needed to say who he'd come to see.

Alessandra Cornell was almost talking to herself, pacing the carpet in the big room. The shutters were half-closed and the whole Palazzo seemed deserted. Lino had sent him in alone and the library had been empty as he'd hurried past. Sandro wondered if they all knew already, guests, staff and all. The staff, you bet they knew: it was one advantage of being lower down the food chain, information moved more freely.

'We've got to keep this . . . under control,' she said urgently. 'We've got to keep it quiet. You understand that? They'll be here – they'll be here—' Cornell put her hands to her face, then dropped them. 'The *carabiniere* asked if this afternoon would be convenient.'

The attaché looked almost dishevelled. Her collar was skewed and something was smudged in the corner of her eye, as though she'd rubbed at it, hard. Sandro didn't think she'd been crying, but he couldn't be sure.

Carabinieri case. If it had been the Polizia di Stato, in which Sandro had served for thirty years, this would have been an awful lot more friendly. He might have left the State Police under something of a cloud, but he had a lot of allies there still, not least his old partner Pietro. He *had* worked on a case with the Carabinieri – the Military Police – since his retirement, which had worked out okay, so there were people he might talk to— *Hold on,* he told himself, don't call in any favours just yet. Let's see where this is going.

'Why don't you sit down,' he said, and abruptly she obeyed. 'Now, tell me again.'

'Giancarlo was found dead in his apartment this morning,' she stated stonily, staring straight ahead. 'His landlady found him. They didn't say how he died, but they said they were investigating it, so it couldn't have been . . . an accident. Could it? He'd been dead,' and Cornell looked crazed for an instant, 'since last night. They're saying midnight.' She put a hand to her head as if it hurt her.

He knew she was trying not to think of what that meant because even after three decades' experience he was doing the same himself. Even twelve hours – in this heat. Rigor then dissolution, humanity gone.

'I fired him two days ago,' said Cornell, staring. 'Could he have killed himself?'

'I wouldn't have thought he was the type,' said Sandro. 'How did he react, when you fired him? Was he . . . distressed?'

She frowned. 'Not exactly. He was . . . well, first of all, actually, he laughed. As if he couldn't believe it. Then he was angry. He said how was he to know the – the woman, the prostitute—' She fumbled. 'How was he to know she wasn't a visitor? He said he wanted to talk to Gastone, but Gastone wasn't around.' Never there when you need him, thought Sandro. That kind of guy. She went on. 'He was. . .' and her lips clamped as if on an unpleasant memory, 'he was aggressive.'

Sandro nodded, thinking.

'You can't always tell, with these macho guys,' he said mildly. 'The *carabiniere* didn't ask about his state of mind?'

'He wanted to know if Giancarlo took drugs.' Sandro registered her use, once again, of the man's first name. Would Vito have been her type? Something began to tick in the recesses of his old policeman's brain.

'He wanted to know if that was the reason we let him go.' She looked up at Sandro, pleading. 'I said no. He said they'd need to talk to us.'

'Did you tell him why you *did* fire him?'

Slowly Cornell shook her head. 'I panicked,' she said, and swallowed. 'I said . . . he was coming to the end of a trial period and it wasn't really working out.'

It was Sandro's turn to put his head in his hands. 'Okay,' he said. 'Well, that wasn't exactly a lie.' He looked her in the eye. 'You can't actually lie to the Carabinieri, you do know that?' She gazed back at him, saying nothing. 'There were no drugs? You're sure?'

Cornell sat up. 'If I'd had any suspicion he was a drug-user, I'd never have employed him, I'd have fired him on the spot.' She frowned. 'It would have been easier if it was drugs, wouldn't it?'

Sandro reflected that she was right, interestingly. If the question had been asked, they'd have a reason for it. Substances at the scene – they wouldn't have toxicology results quite yet.

'What can I say to them? I can't risk this . . . getting out. We can't.' She held his gaze a moment then went around behind her desk, and, opening a drawer, pulled out a stapled sheaf of papers. 'This is the job, Sandro: damage limitation. You've got to help me. This is your contract.' She set the document down on the desk between them. 'But our loyalty is to the Palazzo. We have to protect our guests. This is the job, if you want it.'

She folded her arms, chin jutting, and Sandro almost felt sorry for her.

'Alessandra,' he said gently. 'Miss Cornell. Don't you think it is possible that you need me more than I need you, at the moment? Please.'

The attaché sat down again, eyes gleaming. Was it an act? He didn't think so.

'I'll try to help you,' he said, and sighed. 'First we work out what we tell the Carabinieri, then we work out what we tell the . . . clients.' He eyed the contract. 'But me – you tell me the truth. And I need a free hand, with the guests, with my investigation. If I need to talk to someone, inside or outside, I can talk to them. If I need to involve a – a colleague, I can do that. My partner, Giulietta Sarto.'

She began to shake her head, eyes wide. 'I can't – Gastone simply wouldn't allow it.'

Sandro stood up, put on his jacket. 'All right,' he said, thinking of his freedom. Luisa would be mad as hell but he could be out of here. 'So those nasty little mishaps were just a series of accidents. Vito's death . . . well, I'm sure the Carabinieri will solve that in five minutes. Accidental overdose would be my guess; not too much blowback – if you're lucky. Sure, you still need a house detective but maybe you could train the doorman up? And keep your fingers crossed.'

It was a long time since Sandro had taken a stand; it coursed in his veins like euphoria. He turned to the door.

'No,' she said, very quietly behind him, and he turned back, grimly. 'You're right,' she said. 'I'll deal with Gastone. But please—' And Alessandra Cornell stopped, her knuckles white as she gripped the back of the chair, so used to keeping control she didn't know how to surrender it.

'You'll have to trust me,' he said wearily. 'You have no option.'

An intercom buzzed on the desk. Rigid, she stared at it as if it might bite her, and Sandro leaned down and picked up the handset. 'Miss Cornell's office,' he said. It was Lino the doorman, affronted at hearing Sandro's voice. They were here.

'Would you tell the officer Miss Cornell will be free very shortly?' he said, and heard Lino's intake of breath. 'Send him along in five minutes.'

He took the contract from the desk. 'I'll need to show that to my wife before I sign anything,' he said. 'So. We haven't got long.'

As he left, the *carabiniere* in the familiar dark uniform was walking towards Sandro down the corridor, young and upright but pale under the southern tan. On impulse Sandro turned on to the stairs, just so as not to have to hold the man's gaze. The young *carabiniere* passed behind him – and something followed him, tainting the air.

There was a smell to it. Death.

*

Giuli knew where to find Maria. You could tell the time by the old bird: at the Centre cleaning until three-thirty, home to prepare her husband's dinner, out for a brandy in the Dolce Vita in the Piazza del Carmine before he got back. Five sharp, like clockwork.

It was impossible to tell how old Maria actually was. Born in the hills up near Poppi, she had the lined, dark skin of a *contadina* and had probably lost her teeth by the time she was forty. She might have been married fifty years, thought Giuli, quailing at the thought.

A text came in from Sandro as Giuli was locking the office door behind her. *I need you onside tonight, six sharp Palazzo San Giorgio. I've cleared it.*

The old Giuli would have said, you can stuff it. No thanks. I don't need any of you. But Luisa and Sandro – and now Enzo too – had softened her up. Taught her that sometimes people meant what they said, and that it took guts to ask for help. All the same, she didn't go overboard replying.

Okay. And headed out.

When she saw Giuli, old Maria seemed to shrink down even smaller at the Formica bar, clutching her precious glass. She was watching the TV over the barman's head, the *telegiornale* announcing some politician resigning, a tickertape commentary running along the bottom: Lotto announcements, a sex scandal and a fall in export figures. And then a girl in plunging sequins and plastic boobs introduced a gameshow. At random Giuli ordered fruit juice, one of the little bottles of apricot nectar Luisa always forced on her.

Maria had edged away, her little shoulders hunched, looking anywhere but at Giuli.

'Does everyone know?' Giuli said, eyeing the sickly liquid in her glass. Who was she kidding, feeding herself up for a wedding dress? But she swallowed it down like medicine all the same. 'Do they know who it is, too? Telling lies about me.'

'I don't know. I don't know what you mean,' mumbled Maria, but Giuli saw her leathery cheeks redden. She'd pinned her thin hair back in a sparkly barrette, incongruous against the ancient raincoat, and Giuli felt a pang of guilt at the sight; this glass of brandy would be the cleaner's only break in a day of slog.

'I'm sorry,' she said, patting the raincoated shoulder. She gestured to the barman to refill the old woman's glass, put down a note and headed out. But she hadn't got as far as the door when she sensed something pulling at her, a small snuffling presence at her elbow, and there was Maria, glass in hand, pointing at the back room.

'Does everyone think it's true?' Giuli said when they were seated. The room had no windows; the only other occupant was an old man muttering over a dog-eared paper in the corner. A smell of unwashed layers rose off him.

Maria curled her fingers round the glass. 'Not everyone,' she said. 'Maybe half and half.' And she looked at Giuli, nervous of having said the wrong thing.

Fifty per cent. 'And which half are you?' Giuli said.

The toothless old mouth collapsed in on itself, mumbling. Then she spoke up. 'You're a good girl, Giulietta,' she said, and gingerly she sipped at her brandy. 'No children, me, what do I know? But you're always on time, never bugger off early like some, and you don't complain. About what life's dealt out to you.' It amounted to a speech, by the old lady's standards.

'Has Farmiga been back?' Last year a case of Sandro's had got a doctor sacked for her ties to a right-wing group; if Giuli had to pinpoint her most definite enemy, it would be Nicoletta Farmiga. She had no idea where she'd gone.

But Maria shook her head. 'Haven't seen hide nor hair. She wouldn't have the nerve, anyway.'

Giuli wouldn't put anything past Farmiga. 'So who?'

The old man's head was lifted, scenting something across the room, and Maria looked around anxiously. 'I dunno, honest,' she said.

'You know something, though,' said Giuli, patient.

The old woman took a quick swig, then she spoke hurriedly. 'The Director did have someone in with her yesterday. A patient. I've seen her once or twice, but usually . . . well. Usually she doesn't see the Director, let's say. She's in—' And she jerked her head as if they were back in the Centre and she was pointing down a corridor. 'Down there. Comes in for the methadone.'

Addictions, then. Massini had let that slip.

Maria went on. 'You can't say I told. I'll be out too if they know, won't I?'

'It's all right,' said Giuli. 'Has someone told you not to talk to me?'

Maria looked down into her drink. 'They might clear you anyway, mightn't they? Why would they believe her over you?' Giuli said nothing, and the cleaner took another sip. 'Anyway, it was after that the rumours started going round. About you. Yesterday afternoon.'

Her day off: probably no coincidence. If you want to stick the knife in, wait until your victim's back is turned. Massini would have made a big fuss about confidentiality but she had a secretary, didn't she? People liked to talk. And only the week before they'd all been clustering around her cooing at her engagement ring. Gold with diamond chips: all Enzo could afford, but nobody said how small the stones were. In the stuffy back room, aware that there were questions Maria wasn't answering, conscious of the crazy old man peering over his paper, Giuli struggled with paranoia.

She took a deep breath. 'You know her name? The methadone junkie.'

The old woman shook her head. 'They're always trying to get her children off her. The *comune* are. And she knows you – so maybe you know her.'

Giuli felt her forehead prickle with sweat as the name came to her. 'Rosina.'

The woman she'd seen in reception that very morning, eyes sliding away as Giuli looked, with her skin blotched from drugs and her skinny limbs. The woman Giuli would have turned into if she'd stayed on the streets. Reluctantly Maria nodded.

'She still living out in Galluzzo then?' Giuli said softly, very softly, as the old man's filmy eyes swept the room. 'A *casa popolare*, wasn't it, last I heard?

Hunched over her glass, Maria stared, saying nothing, and Giuli had the sense of the woman's used-up body being a cage of bones, inside her chest a tired old muscle that didn't know when to give up.

'I think she was evicted last time they found drugs,' she whispered at last. 'She's probably back with the mother. For as long as it lasts.'

They both knew what that meant. 'She takes them to school every morning,' Maria said. 'To show them she can be a mother. The big *elementare* in the Via della Chiesa.'

Giuli nodded. Maria's worn old hand crept across the table to rest on hers.

'You be careful, Giulietta,' she said. No one called her Giulietta any more.

'What have I got to lose?' she said.

As she came out on to the street she heard a *motorino*'s engine start up somewhere behind her, but she didn't turn around.

*

They'd been gossiping up in menswear all afternoon, Giuseppina and Beppe. Luisa had only gone up to challenge them after the woman had been in with her husband – the woman from the Palazzo who already did bad things to Luisa's blood pressure. Dislike was like poison in the bloodstream: you could try to neutralise it, but sometimes people were just too hateable. Magda Scardino.

He had sat oddly stiff in an armchair, reading something, while Luisa brought cocktail dresses, which Magda Scardino wanted tight, to the cubicle, and she talked through the curtain at him as though Luisa wasn't there.

'I expect you're delighted, are you?' she said, invisible. 'You never liked him.'

The man hardly raised his head from his sheaf of papers, but when his wife emerged from the changing room, barely contained by a red dress, he cleared his throat. 'I don't know about that, my sweet,' he said. 'I do what I'm told, you know that. I know you like to introduce an element of competition into these things. I certainly wouldn't have wished a violent death on him.'

Luisa turned the words over in her head, feeling a stir of unease. Who were they talking about?

Professor Scardino spoke mildly, as if he was only talking about what to have for lunch. Perhaps she'd heard wrong. And as he spoke he was eyeing his wife's body in the swathed silk, not with love, exactly. With a clinical sort of look, Luisa thought. And as she wondered what it must be like to be married to a scientist, his words sank in. *Competition*. Then she blinked. *Violent death?*

Over their heads, Beppe and Giusy had been talking about it too.

'How did you hear about it, by the way, darling?' the Professor said, head back down over his papers, as his wife looked at herself approvingly this way and that in the mirror. 'Your ear to the ground?'

'Oh, one of the servants,' she said airily. 'They were gossiping. Someone's aunt knew his landlady, or something. You know how these people are.'

Magda Scardino's eye flickered to Luisa in the mirror, then in a kind of challenge. Luisa stepped forward. 'You might want it just nipped at the shoulder,' she said, placing thumb and forefinger on the beautiful fabric from behind and pinching it into place.

Their eyes met a moment in the mirror before Magda Scardino said, already turning away, 'I want something in gold.'

She chose three dresses, all to be taken in by that very evening – more, Luisa thought, for the pleasure of putting others to trouble than because they needed adjusting. The husband paid with one of those credit cards only available to the very wealthy, Giusy at the till looking nervously at Luisa over his shoulder.

She and Beppe hadn't got Luisa in on it, Giusy said staring when the door closed behind the Scardinos, because they assumed she knew already. Of course.

'Bottai called on Mr Frollini this afternoon, too. It must be connected,' said Giusy, enjoying every minute. 'Not good publicity for the place.'

Sandro had not thought to tell her, though. That the man he'd been hired to replace had been found dead by his landlady.

Luisa thought of bluffing it out with them, but in the end it was beneath her dignity. 'It won't have occurred to you,' she said drily, watching Giusy's face, 'that the reason they've hired Sandro is precisely because he's not a blabbermouth. You think he's the kind of man who calls his wife up every five minutes to give her the inside story?' She watched Giusy pout like a smacked child and almost believed it herself.

There already seemed to be all sorts of theories: they'd come tumbling from Giusy's over-excited mouth before she caught Luisa's expression and pulled herself up. Auto-erotic asphyxiation, sex games gone wrong, drugs, a hit – the more lurid the better. Luisa was old enough not to believe any of it right off, because people loved to make up stories, and Giusy more than most. She didn't need more than a hint to spin out a whole tabloid scandal.

'They're lucky they've got Sandro,' she said stoutly.

'Of course,' said Beppe, coming down the stairs behind Giusy. But Luisa saw the glance they exchanged. 'Why don't you get off early, Luisa?'

Chapter Eight

SANDRO SAT ON ONE of the white loungers on the lower terrace in the evening sun; he had eaten a handful of nuts from the bowl on the low table beside him, and his hand was greasy. He could see the backs of the houses below and as he watched an old woman moving slowly on her balcony, watering plants. He felt a pang of envy: she was on the outside. She leaned over a pale-blue trailing thing; Luisa would have known what it was called. Why did women know about plants? He was nervous. Focus, he thought. He could hear them now, voices on the upper terrace, and soon he would have to stand up and shake their hands and make polite conversation.

There were no napkins. Surreptitiously he wiped his palm on the side of one of the lounger cushions – it was that or his own trousers. He wondered where the maid had got to. Alice, she was called. He reached into his pocket and took out the piece of paper he'd found there half an hour earlier. Vito's floorplan.

It had been a mistake, trying to explore – or snoop. Alice had caught him at it. Calculating that the Carabinieri would be in with Alessandra Cornell for forty minutes at least, Sandro had slipped upstairs, and got lost.

He had never thought of himself as the claustrophobic type, but he had found himself pulling at his collar as he stepped out into a long corridor, wall to wall cream carpet stretching all the way to the end. He had sent Giuli a text telling her to come to the unveiling of the sculpture that evening, and now he felt like he might never find his way back out to meet her.

He'd seen the housekeeper's trolley outside the furthest door, stacked with bottles and cloths, had leaned against the wall, and breathed. That was when he'd felt something crackle in his pocket. As he pulled out Vito's floorplan, he had heard a noise, though he couldn't have said whether it came from above or below him. It had sounded like a woman crying.

He laid out the piece of paper now on the low table on the terrace. There was a floorplan on one side, on the other a crude sketch of the palace's façade, with initials over the windows. BVV, IC on the first floor, the *piano nobile*; AM, DL on the floor above, Athene Morris next door to the artist. Vito had underlined one set of initials three times: MS/DS. The Professor and his wife: Magda and David Scardino. On the top floor, their suites a little smaller, and their neighbours the Flemings. MF/JF. Very cosy.

He hadn't looked at it earlier because as he'd stood there in the corridor, far off the sound of crying had wavered, risen and subsided, then started up again. He lifted his head to listen, but maddeningly he still couldn't locate it. Not furious, angry tears but a whimpering, apologetic, monotonous sound, the kind that drove men to battery.

'Hello?' The voice was sharp. 'Can I help you?' He looked up and there was a young woman in a maid's pale striped tabard, already halfway down the corridor towards him.

'I'm the new house detective,' he said. 'Did she tell you? Sandro Cellini.'

The girl had folded her arms across her chest. 'He's dead, isn't he?' she said. 'I heard that.'

'Vito?' said Sandro. 'Yes. You all know, then.'

She nodded. In the silence he listened, but the sobbing had died right down. Had it finished? The maid was listening too, her ear cocked.

'You hear that?' he asked.

She shrugged. 'We're paid not to hear anything,' she said. She hesitated, head still raised, but there was nothing. 'It's most likely the Australian woman. Always at it.' Something at the maid's throat caught his eye: a tiny crucifix. 'It's her husband,' she said, and pursed her lips.

'Marjorie Cameron,' said Sandro. The first time he'd seen her he thought she'd been crying. 'What does her husband do to her?' he asked gently.

'He didn't like the way she looked at Mr Vito, for starters,' she said. 'But any excuse will do, won't it? With that sort. My mother told me, never marry a bully.'

'He hits her?'

The girl hunched her shoulders. 'If you ask me. Or she does it to herself.' She made scratching gestures at her wrists, her forearms. 'I've seen the marks.'

'I thought it was teenagers did that,' he said. 'Self-harm.' She shrugged, not much more than a teenager herself. 'What's your name?' he asked.

'Alice,' she said, arms still tight across her chest.

'Did you like Mr Vito, Alice?' said Sandro. 'Giancarlo. Was he a popular guy?'

She stared, hostile.

'It's all right,' said Sandro. 'You can say what you think.'

'He got Mariaclara fired,' she said. 'He said he'd seen her take the old lady's bracelet.'

'I thought she resigned,' said Sandro.

'That's what they call it,' said Alice. 'She had no choice, once she was accused of it. He had no proof so they gave her a decent reference. Trade-off. They always blame you, when things go wrong. He tried to say I locked the steam room when Signora Cameron was in it, too – he had no idea.'

'Who let Mrs Cameron out, by the way? Of the steam room?'

Alice looked at him curiously. 'One of the other women,' she said, with a shrug. 'I don't remember. The key was on the floor outside the steam room. I don't think Vito even knew that, he never asked, anyway.' She drew herself up. 'But then he wasn't a real detective.'

'What do you mean by that?' said Sandro.

'Nothing,' she said, obstinate. 'But detectives are supposed to find stuff out, aren't they? When bad things are happening. Only he wasn't bothered at all, he'd just make something up, blame one of us. Too busy sucking up. Finding out what guests wanted and giving it to them.' And having delivered her speech, stiffly she turned, a hand to the crucifix at her neck. He put a hand on her arm. She looked down at it in panic.

'What bad things happened?' he said. 'Do you know who did take the bracelet? Who locked the steam room?' He should go down there, it was in the basement, he knew. But the thought was unpleasant: it was suffocating enough up here. She had just stared at him.

'Did Mariaclara get another job?' he asked. 'Where is she now?'

'I've got to go,' she said. 'I'm serving drinks in ten minutes. I only came up because they said . . .'

'Said what?'

She compressed her lips. 'Mess to clear up. Again. You'd think with the dog gone—' Somewhere far off a little bell tinkled. 'I've got to go.'

As he followed her down the stairs, it had come to him that she was afraid.

On the terrace now something bit Sandro on the ankle, and he swiped at it. 'Bastard,' he muttered under his breath. Mosquitoes, he supposed, had coexisted with man for as long as man had lived here, and man still hadn't worked out either how to eliminate them, nor yet to live with them. Sandro himself would never be reconciled to their existence, that thin whine, the itch, the way the evening air would thicken and spoil with them. There were countries without mosquitoes, imagine that, and for a moment he closed his eyes and allowed himself to wonder if it would be worth it, leaving this city of warm stone and stagnant water for one of those dim, cool, foggy places.

'Mr Cellini,' said a voice at his shoulder, and he started to his feet, hastily stuffing the floorplan back in his pocket. It was Athene Morris: for a big woman, and at her age, she was surprisingly quiet on her feet. Coming down the path behind her was Therese Van Vleet, stepping daintily on the gravel in heels, and her husband; she raised her head and he saw big dark blue eyes fixing on him in silent appeal. He could almost hear Luisa's tut.

'I said we'd meet again, didn't I?' said Athene Morris. The English had little tolerance of emotion, as far as Sandro understood. 'So, how did it go with Miss Cornell? Are you now our new . . . ah—'

'Head of Security,' he supplied hastily, wondering if that would do.

She leaned a little towards him and said, lowering her voice, 'I expect you know what happened to the last one?' Was that almost a smile? 'Poor Therese, she's so upset. A tender soul. She and her husband—'

She straightened, and her voice was loud again. 'Therese,' she said, reaching out with a ringed hand, surprisingly elegant, Sandro noticed. She took the young woman's and drew her close. 'My dear. And Brett. Have you met Mr Cellini? Our new Head of Security.' She turned to Sandro. 'Brett and Giancarlo got on like a house on fire.' Then as if as an afterthought, 'So sad. Such a shock.'

Brett Van Vleet cleared his throat. 'He was a good guy,' he said, uneasy.

'It's an army thing,' said Therese. 'They talked about military service. Brett was in the Marines for ten years.'

Sandro frowned. He'd have thought Vito would have been too young for compulsory military service, but before he could complete the necessary calculation Athene had chipped in.

'Brett is in – what do you call it in America? – real estate, or so he tells us. Or is it that you've made so much money you've retired? How's that gorgeous car of yours?'

'Athene,' protested Therese Van Vleet, uncertain, tearful – or was she actually crying?

Sandro felt a surge of pity. 'Mrs Van Vleet,' he said. 'It's a pleasure.'

She took his hand gratefully and turned towards her husband, who was still looking uncomfortable. She was not yet thirty, calculated Sandro. He would be ten years older, his ruddy complexion turning from tan to brick against the sandy hair.

Sandro offered his hand again. 'Mr Van Vleet.' The handshake was surprisingly diffident for a big man; Sandro wasn't sure if his own was sweating or still greasy.

'You English,' said Van Vleet awkwardly, letting Sandro's hand drop. 'Athene's just being funny, sweetheart.' He turned to Sandro. 'I was in real estate, yes, over in Florida. And I had my car shipped over, sure.'

'It's vast,' supplied Athene Morris, with evident pleasure. 'It actually doesn't fit in the garage.'

'And if I'd known how narrow the streets are . . .' said the American, with a flash of ill-temper. Then, casually, 'I may just have it shipped back.'

Sandro saw Therese Van Vleet give him a quick, anxious look. He wondered how much it would cost to ship a big American car halfway across the world and back.

'I'm so looking forward to the unveiling,' Therese said, flushing.

'Oh, yes,' said Athene, turning back to Sandro. 'I do want to see Martin's face when Mr Lludic's masterwork is revealed. All that reticence, will he be able to keep it up?' All the time her pale blue eyes were still on Sandro's face, roaming, he felt, looking for something. It came to him that she was a mischief-maker.

'You know Sir Martin?' As if Sandro would; he just smiled mildly. 'He's our diplomat. Sir Martin and Lady Fleming – Juliet Fleming as was, though anyone less like a Juliet you couldn't imagine, she never was pretty, not even as a young woman. Never the romantic heroine.' The light, teasing tone was gone, replaced with something colder, harsher, and she raised her head, looking up towards the great house with its windows.

On the upper terrace another small group had gathered. Sandro could see the tall Professor, leaning down to talk to the Australian, and there was the maid Alice, moving between them with a tray, head down. Sandro felt a kind of claustrophobic dread. Jesus. He was bringing Giuli into this lot, with all the baggage she'd accumulated today. And he still hadn't phoned Luisa.

'Really, Athene,' Therese Van Vleet was saying. 'Juliet's not well, you know.'

'Will you excuse me a moment,' he said, marvelling that the panic he felt had not found his way into his voice. 'There's someone . . . there's something I have to do.' And stumbling on the gravel, he tried not to run from them.

Chapter Nine

'I SAW YOUR BEAUTIFUL NECK,' John had said afterwards. 'Like a painting, like a Vermeer through the window.' How he found her.

As Elena looked through the greasy window of the workshop, the light of late afternoon beyond it low and hazy, the memory sent her in search of detergent, to distract herself.

She'd go and see her uncle again tomorrow. It had cheered him up, the nurses had said. He's not going home any time soon, they confided. It'll be a long haul. The implication being, if he goes home at all he'll be lucky.

She'd sent John a message about the heart attack. That had been the first sign, looking back. Because they'd got on well enough: her uncle always looked up with his funny old smile when he appeared at the window, and John would shake his hand, every time, with comedy vigour. But John had sounded strained and distant when he called back, which hadn't been until the following day, a week ago now. *Poor old thing. Well, how is he? Poor old thing. I must visit him.* But all vague. Other things on his mind. Other people. It had been the last time she'd spoken to him.

Other people: the idea made her feel sick. She didn't want anything to do with other people. The unveiling ceremony suddenly looked like a bad idea. Danilo Lludic just after another scalp. She scrubbed harder at the window and then, sitting back on her heels to wipe a drip of dirty water from her cheek, she became aware of someone walking up the street and stopping at the door to the Palazzo San Giorgio.

Her uncle had said something when Elena had seen him that morning, sitting up on the pillows and pale as paper. 'I thought your guy might have come to see me.' She'd just smiled weakly. Then he'd gone on. 'He was always looking out of the window, wasn't he? Never could work that out.'

Funny that it had struck her uncle too. But then she remembered that John would stand looking out through the workshop window as well, while she and her uncle worked. Just watching.

'He's gone, hasn't he?' her uncle had said then, and he'd laid his head back on the pillow, too tired for any more talking.

Elena stood up with the bucket, half turning just as the woman across the road half turned too. Short spiky hair, bare arms, on the thin side. Not expensively dressed enough for that place, not by a long way. Something about her visible unease drew Elena's attention, and then . . . the profile, and those skinny arms.

I know her, thought Elena, and as if in response the woman turned to look at her full on. And then the doorman beckoned her in and the door was closing behind her.

Giulietta Sarto. My God, thought Elena. God in heaven. The last person, the very last person she'd expect to see going in there.

Giulietta Sarto had been in her final year at middle school when Elena had arrived. She had a reputation for being wild and furious, and she was terrifyingly thin. No one went near her – except a certain kind of boy – for fear of being mauled. But for a period Elena had been bullied by a girl a couple of years older and Giulietta Sarto had taken her on, almost at random. Coming upon Elena cornered by the girl, Sarto had pulled the girl back off her by the hair, a clump of it coming out in her hand, and the bully had left Elena alone after that. Giulietta Sarto had never spoken to her, not then, nor afterwards.

And then of course, some twenty-five years later – and five years back now – she'd been in the news. Maybe if you hadn't been at school with Giulietta Sarto, you'd have forgotten all that by now.

Still, thought Elena. Perhaps I will go. I'll go to that unveiling.

*

At his post in the orchid-scented foyer, his hands behind his back, the doorman turned to meet Sandro as he emerged from the corridor.

'Lino,' said Sandro with weary sympathy, clapping him on the shoulder. 'All right if I hang around here? I'm expecting someone.'

Lino nodded: not much older than him, but ground down. No muscle under the coat.

He had sent Luisa a text. It wasn't enough, he knew that. Particularly as it only said, *Home late, don't wait up.*

'You married, Lino?'

The man shook his head. 'Widowed. Ten years.'

The doors stood open and both men contemplated the view in silence. Ten years, thought Sandro with horror.

'At least you get a sight of the outside world,' he said. Opposite was a wall whose stucco had gone in places, and an unruly plant had rooted in the mortar. It had little white flowers; by comparison the orchid looked like it was made of plastic. Sandro could smell someone's dinner cooking, heard a clatter of pans from across the street and felt an itch to be out of here. Home.

'Long day for you,' he said. 'Eleven in the morning till midnight, Ms Cornell told me.' Would a widower – Sandro shrank from the word – even have anything to go home to?

'I can manage,' said Lino.

Sandro skated over the prickliness of the reply. 'All these events,' he said. 'Last night, for instance. Some talk on, wasn't there?'

'Renaissance medicine,' said Lino, still looking out into the street. 'Dottoressa Tassi, a lady from the university. A colleague of the Professor's.'

An old man was leading a small fat dog. As they watched, it manoeuvred itself into defecating position, hindquarters quivering over the kerb. The owner affected not to notice, just gave the lead a tug and they walked on. Sandro thought of the maid upstairs cleaning mess off a door. The dog was gone, but the shit was still around. A man was dead.

'Do they eat here, after?' said Sandro casually. 'Cook for themselves?'

Lino gave him a scornful look. 'You must be kidding,' he said. 'They're out every night.'

'And you can't really relax until you've seen them all off the premises, I suppose. Or signed them back in.' Sandro spoke nonchalantly, but Lino gave him a sharp look.

'They have their own keys,' the doorman said. 'It's not a prison.'

'I expect they like to have the door held open for them, though,' said Sandro. The smell of cooking was irresistible: his stomach emitted a little growl.

Despite himself, Lino cracked a wintry little smile. 'Who you waiting for, then? Whoever it is, I can send them along to your office if you like.'

'My palatial accommodation,' said Sandro.

'I've got a chair in a cupboard,' said Lino, nodding towards a door cleverly concealed in some panelling. Sandro pulled at the handle, curious: it was indeed a cupboard, with a narrow padded bench barely big enough for an adult to lie on. He closed it again and behind him Lino sighed. 'But you're right. When they come back from the restaurant in their cabs they like the taxi driver to see a doorman.'

'Last night, for example?'

Lino frowned. 'Last night, last night, I don't know. Why d'you . . .' Something dawned, and he gave an uneasy laugh. 'Giancarlo? You think someone here . . .' He shook his head slowly. 'You've got a screw loose. It was a drugs overdose, I heard.' He turned to look out through the long glass doors to the garden at the back of the foyer, where the guests were congregating on the terrace under Cornell's window. Sandro could see Magda Scardino practically on tiptoe, trying to get her husband's attention. 'This lot? They wouldn't know how, would they?'

'Oh, you'd be surprised,' said Sandro. 'Just humour me, though. I'm interested. Best to be prepared, if the Carabinieri come back again.'

'All right,' said Lino stiffly. 'Let's see. The talk ended at eight, eight-thirty. Dottoressa Tassi, very, ah, very nice,' and he smiled wistfully. 'She said she'd be back tonight for the unveiling, colleague of the Prof's. They came out in dribs and drabs afterwards, heading off for their dinners.' He had brightened. 'Miss Morris never goes out, not too nifty on her feet and she feeds herself off the freebies anyway. Nuts and that, and she's not rich like the rest. She's up later than most, just pottering around – she likes to come down and say goodnight, for example. Up and down in the lift, never locks her door. Hoping for visitors.'

'Lonely,' said Sandro.

Lino nodded. 'The others – well, the Camerons were first out, they're early eaters. I heard them come back around eleven. Then the Flemings and the Scardinos, they seem to get on . . .' He paused, ruminative, eyebrows raised.

'You're surprised?' Sandro put in lightly.

'She's high-maintenance, that one,' Lino said, his mouth turning down. 'The Prof's wife. Just the thought wears me out.' Sandro smiled, and the doorman went on doggedly. 'The couples came back separately. The Flemings on the back of the

Camerons, as far as I remember. And Sir Martin likes to smoke a cigar on the doorstep before he comes in.'

He had relaxed now. Witnesses, in Sandro's experience, needed to do that before you could rely on what they were telling you.

'The Americans are the late birds. Mr and Mrs Van Vleet – Therese.' He shot Sandro a glance. 'She's a good person. I was sorry about the dog, she loved that little thing.' He smiled a touch sadly. 'Once said to me – she looked at me and you could see how she'd have been as a little girl – said she could imagine living without her husband, but not the dog.'

He frowned then. 'I swear it never got past me. She was always letting it off the leash in the garden, and some of the others didn't like that – the Prof's wife for one, complained of the mess. But hearing it yapping, like it was having some fun . . . well, this place needs some of that.'

'Yes,' said Sandro, more heartfelt than he'd intended. 'Did they blame you?'

Lino shrugged, uneasy. 'I told him, ask the old lady down below, it could have got out down at the bottom of the garden. Dogs can be very determined, and you can hardly blame the thing, stuck in here. A terrier, too, bred for rabbit holes. But he wouldn't lower himself. Vito. Oh, he smiled and held her hand but he didn't do a blind thing to find it.'

Sandro took a step to the threshold and breathed the sweet evening air. He thought of the old lady down below, watering her plants. 'You were saying. The Van Vleets were out late last night?'

'They didn't go out till ten. I didn't see them get back in. I often don't. He likes the nightlife.'

So, the Van Vleets not accounted for. 'And Lludic?' Arrogant, lazy, predatory were the words that sprang to mind when he thought of the sculptor, sitting at the bar during the launch party, waiting for women. 'I suppose it's like the old lady, you don't go out to eat on your own.'

'Oh,' said Lino slowly. 'Oh.' And his hands came out from behind his back.

'What?' said Sandro.

'He did go out,' said the doorman, and cleared his throat. 'But he didn't come back. At least, not until nine or so this morning.'

In the window of the workshop opposite, Sandro saw a girl's face swim out of the darkness, looking out into the street. There were footsteps and then Giuli was there in the doorway.

*

Luisa dropped her bag inside the door of their apartment; she didn't look at her phone.

She could have done without Frollini turning up as she'd come up from the storeroom buttoning her old coat. That hadn't escaped him: Enrico Frollini could tell if a suede shoe had been finished in France or in Italy, never mind what he thought of a coat already five years old with a button missing at the neck.

It had only given him a moment's pause though. Full of plans. Telling her he'd been talking to people – to that windbag Gastone Bottai, he meant – and that he thought there was a nice solution to her – what had he called it? – her *downsizing needs*. Rubbing his hands together, but he wouldn't tell her his solution. 'Tomorrow morning, nine-thirty sharp.'

Men, she thought, fuming. It's all plans and meetings and programming this and scheduling that – and who does the actual work?

And she could have done without Marina Artusi ambushing her as she'd walked through the Piazza Santissima Annunziata, shoving her arm through Luisa's as she entered the big tranquil space framed by loggias, the route home Luisa always chose when she needed calming down.

Behind them the Piazza San Marco, buses endlessly circling, an army barracks opposite a monastery and permanently occupied by tourists and soldiers. Ahead of them the huge, gloomy Piazza d'Azeglio, where the roar of the ringroad competed with the din of the children's playground. And in the middle . . . this. Always empty, the long portico of the Ospedale degli Innocenti always soothing. Not this evening, though.

'I don't know anything about it,' she'd said crossly in the dingy bar on the corner of the Via della Colonna. She'd been manoeuvred into having a coffee, but she had refused to sit down. 'You're asking the wrong person, Marina.' She downed the little cup, and picked up her bag. 'I'm sure it's nothing to do with the place, anyway. A lot of very respectable people. The man had just been fired, he just went on a – a binge. An accident.'

Marina Artusi snorted. 'Accident? That's not at all what I hear. And as for respectable. Well, that's a matter of opinion. I heard some of the residents are having a little trouble actually coming up with their payments, having to draw in their horns, somewhat. Send things back to the shop, if you understand me. And old Athene Morris. A *grande horizontale*, if ever there was one – you know what that means, Luisa?'

Luisa stared at her stonily, but she couldn't help but think back with a saleswoman's reflex. Professor Charles Scardino's transaction had gone through straight away, not even a security check, even though the dresses had come to more than five thousand euros. So if anyone was in financial trouble, it wasn't them.

Marina Artusi carried on gaily. 'But I'm sure Martin knows the ins and outs, anyway; tell Sandro to ask him. There was a big extortion case in Damascus when we were there – blackmail, a man found hanging from a dam – and Martin told me, oh, months before it came out, that a certain government minister would be implicated.'

Back home now, Luisa pushed open the windows. Sandro said he'd be back late.

'You just tell Sandro to get Martin Fleming on his side. Martin knows everything.'

Luisa had slapped down her money then, buttoned her old coat, and thanked Marina Artusi with elaborate courtesy.

The woman had caught up with her at the door. 'It's always a pleasure, Luisa,' she said. 'And if you would just find out from Sandro if it's true? That Juliet Fleming isn't well. Not well at all. Of course, they call it an illness, these days, don't they?'

Luisa had left her standing.

Sandro's message had come in as she put her key in the apartment door. A long shower, she thought, hanging up her coat.

Chapter Ten

THERE WAS A MURMUR, non-committal, uncertain, then firming up into hesitant approval. Oh God, thought Giuli, with the heart-sinking certainty of her own ignorance as the veil dropped. What is it?

They were in a courtyard at the back of the Palazzo San Giorgio. On the podium now, the blonde woman who had introduced herself as Alessandra Cornell was holding up a hand for quiet. Giuli darted a pleading glance at Sandro: how long was this going to go on? They hadn't had a chance to talk yet, he'd just hurried her through, apologetically explaining her presence to a succession of stiffs along the way.

It was a big chunk of marble, was what it was, maybe five tonnes of the stuff. Smoothed on one side, as smooth as a pebble from the sea, with a soft indentation in its side, a hollow you wanted to put your hand in. On the other side it was as jagged as though it had just broken away from the rockface. The sculptor just stood there, looking surly.

There was a spatter of polite applause and Giuli looked

around covertly, wondering which of this lot had brought the hooker in. Middle-aged men: could be any of them. The tall pale one with the high forehead and the bitch for a wife? Professor Something. She had given Giuli a filthy look as Sandro led her inside, which made Giuli think she wouldn't be up for a threesome, somehow.

Someone stepped up to her from behind.

'Ah, just a quick word.' Alessandra Cornell seemed nervous all of a sudden, tapping too loudly on her microphone. 'You all know Giancarlo Vito left us at the weekend.' Giuli saw her fix on Sandro, the Bottai guy glaring at her. 'And now perhaps some of you do not know but . . .' She faltered, then pulled herself together. 'We are not sure of the circumstances, but it seems Giancarlo met with an unfortunate . . . an accident, or possibly . . .' She cleared her throat. 'He passed away last night.'

So that was what Sandro hadn't told her.

There was an anxious murmuring, but not, Giuli thought, any great shockwave: they already knew, or most of them. An ageing woman with grey-blonde curls clutched at her husband's arm, the bitch-wife stood up taller, chin in the air. Sandro shot Giuli an apologetic glance. It came to her that she hadn't told Enzo her own bad news yet either.

Alessandra Cornell was hurrying on. 'However, we have a new Head of Security in Mr Sandro Cellini, a man much respected in the community and among his ex-colleagues in the Polizia di Stato. I am sure he will make himself known to all of you.' And she stepped down, flushed.

'So there's upstaging for you.' The voice was a woman's, ironical. Half turning, Giuli caught a thick tangle of black hair tied in a knot, creases around the eyes. She doesn't belong here, either. Shorter than Giuli, maybe five years younger. Was it her Giuli had felt step up behind her?

'Mr Lludic won't be too happy about that.' The woman tipped her head on one side. 'What d'you think of the piece? Do you like it?'

'It looks like he didn't get around to finishing it,' Giuli said, defiantly. There was something about the way the younger woman was looking at her, wary conspiracy, old knowledge shared. So when she spoke, Giuli knew what was coming.

'It's Giulietta, isn't it? Giulietta Sarto?'

Behind her – all around her – Giuli could feel eyes on her.

'You don't know me,' she said, before she could think about it.

*

Bottai had shifted as many of them as he could bully into the library. Giuli, white-faced and in conversation with the girl from over the road, had stood her ground outside, dismissing Sandro's pleading glance with a stiff shake of the head. Once inside, Sandro had stationed himself at one end of the bar, to give himself as low a profile as he could while still able to see and be seen.

Sir Martin Fleming was at the far end of the long bookcase with a patient expression on his face and a tall glass in his hand; he was being talked to by the Australian engineer. The Van Vleets were standing with Magda Scardino: she had her hand on Therese Van Vleet's arm, proprietorially. Athene Morris, leaning on her stick, was managing to loom over Marjorie Cameron in the middle of the room. Cameron had certainly been pretty once, Sandro registered for a second time, in a soft sort of way: those fair curls, hazel eyes. Now she looked blurred, with unhappiness perhaps. Her nose was red even at this distance and he saw her dab at it. The Professor was talking to a woman Sandro hadn't seen before, in angular glasses, and for the first time since Sandro had arrived, he looked happy.

He should have told Giuli about Vito. Never mind talked to her about her own troubles, only the very thought of the Women's Centre filled him with a sense of doom. A nest of vipers – but then this place wasn't much better. Sandro could see Magda Scardino eyeing him speculatively, her hand now on Therese Van Vleet's waist.

Sandro already hated this room. Although large and notionally elegant, with a wall full of leather-bound books, alcoves, panelling and the long, gilded bar, it managed also to be claustrophobic. It was like a shuttered barn, a place for herded animals. He felt the barman looking at him.

'You're Mauro,' he said.

The barman gave a little bow. All this discretion was giving Sandro a stomach-ache, and he'd drunk two glasses of Ferrari Brut that weren't helping. 'Could I have a glass of water?' he said. Sardinian, he calculated, from Mauro's small stature and dark looks.

'Stepping into a dead man's shoes,' the barman said, pushing the glass across to him. 'Are you up to it, Mr Cellini?'

Not so discreet after all. 'You didn't like him,' Sandro said, with a flash of insight.

Mauro looked down, passing a cloth over his bottles. 'Nope,' he said. 'He wasn't much of a detective. Or at least, not unless there was something in it for him.'

Sandro leaned forward a little. 'So I hear,' he said. 'The maid that – ah – resigned. I don't suppose you know where she went?' He held his breath.

Mauro raised his head and looked at him thoughtfully. 'Mariaclara? She's at the Excelsior,' he said slowly. 'They gave her an excellent reference. She's a cocktail waitress in the Terrace Bar.'

Sandro nodded, half turned to watch the room. Sir Martin Fleming was making his way between the tables towards them. Sandro lowered his voice and spoke quickly. 'And what about the hooker? The one who got Vito fired?'

Mauro said nothing.

'You know who she was brought in for?'

The barman began to shake his head, very slowly. 'Oh, no,' he said. 'You'll get *me* fired that way.'

Fleming had been intercepted by Athene Morris. She represented a formidable obstacle, one hand on his shoulder.

'*Giancarlo* might not have been much of a detective, Mauro,' Sandro said, taking advantage of the breathing space. 'But my wife tells me it's about the only thing I *can* do.' The barman almost smiled. 'You're a clever guy,' Sandro said, easily. 'Do you really think there's no connection between this place and Giancarlo's death?'

Mauro's face closed up again. 'I would leave it, if I were you,' he said. 'These are powerful people. They'll leave you alone if you leave them alone.'

'You know what you're talking about,' said Sandro. 'Am I right?'

'I worked at the Algerian Consulate and then the French Embassy in Rome for a while,' said the barman. He folded a glass cloth and set it down. 'Seven years, as a matter of fact.'

'Ah,' said Sandro, nodding. 'Yes. The French kept you that long? You must be good. Special skills required.'

'Let's just say, I know a spy when I see one.' And the Sardinian smiled.

Fleming had moved on; Athene Morris was staring after him, her colour higher than usual.

Sandro had Mauro's attention now, and he leaned in. 'Something's wrong here, has been for weeks, don't tell me you don't know. Nasty tricks. And rather than solve it, Giancarlo had been sticking his nose in other people's business. Feathering his own nest.'

Mauro hesitated, then sighed. 'Lino recognised the hooker,' he said quickly. 'Quite a classy one. He said he used to see her working the Granduca lobby most evenings when he had a job there. Of course, if you look close. . . But you have to have a sharp eye to know a whore from a wealthy wife, sometimes.'

At that Sandro saw that Giuli had come into the big windowless room and was talking to the Australian engineer: the man who could spot a whore at twenty paces. She was looking longingly at the door.

'Indeed,' said Sandro.

'Long black hair,' said Mauro. 'Tiny star tattoo under her left ear. Calls herself Bruna.'

Then someone was at the bar. Sandro turned and saw to his surprise that it wasn't Sir Martin Fleming, but the woman Professor Scardino had been talking to. She was fortyish, thick hair streaked with grey and green eyes behind the rectangular glasses. Handsome.

Mauro bowed to her. 'Dottoressa Tassi,' he said, and bent over her hand, lips hovering in the Sardinian way. He straightened, and without being asked set a glass in front of the woman and began to busy himself with a cocktail shaker. 'You came back for the sculpture? This is Mr Cellini, our new detective. The Dottoressa gave us a talk on Renaissance medicine last night. A colleague of the Professor's.' The one Lino had mentioned, then; the one he had a soft spot for.

The woman examined Sandro wearily. She looked unhappy to him, and he wondered why she'd come. She lifted the glass Mauro slid across to her in salute.

And then smoothly Mauro went on, 'Sir Martin. Your usual?' Because the Englishman had arrived at Sandro's other side.

'Juliet would like another whisky,' said Sir Martin Fleming, and held out a hand to Sandro. 'Mr Cellini. I don't think we've met properly.'

His eyes were faded grey, slightly bloodshot in the weathered face, and his handshake was warm. *I like him*, thought Sandro, to his own surprise.

*

The sun was dipping behind the railway station of Santa Maria Novella and the air, oily with exhaust fumes, was still warm.

Traffic circled the roundabout below, the rough sleepers were unrolling their grimy sleeping bags on the sparse grass and a handful of Albanians were talking business by the taxi rank.

The couple nearest to the coach bays, four or five dogs curled on and around their bodies, seemed to have been sleeping there for days, at least since the police had last come round, the week before. They're not even old, thought Donato, climbing out of the driver's seat of his coach – the Airport Express, misnomer if ever there was one, given the traffic and the roadworks on the Firenze-Pisa-Livorno *superstrada*. He was waiting for his courier Joe, who'd gone for a coffee inside the station. It got a bit rank in the bus once the weather warmed up.

He'd seen the faces of the rough sleepers that morning, a man of twenty-five or so with dreadlocks and the girl not much more than a teenager. What kind of a life was that? Donato felt old. Maybe they thought driving a coach up and down the Fi-Pi-Li five times a day wasn't much of a life, either. Maybe it wasn't.

An hour until the next pick-up, the last of the day, and Donato lit up, to clear the air. Something smelled off, for sure, but it was tough to say what exactly, what with the dogs and the traffic and the unwashed humanity. Once someone had left a cheese in the bus's overhead rack and it had been a good week of building stench before they noticed it. The couriers were supposed to check the bus inside and out, but they were paid peanuts just like him; who could blame them for scurrying off at the end of the day.

He saw Joe weaving his way back through the taxi rank, suspiciously bright-eyed and nodding to all the drivers. You could get more or less anything in and around Santa Maria Novella station, and Joe looked like he hadn't stuck to coffee.

'Hey,' Donato said. 'When d'you last check the racks?' He threw his cigarette on to the tarmac and, setting a foot on the coach's step, registered the dreadlocked man in his sleeping bag raising himself up and yawning. Sleep all day, come awake when the sun goes down. Not safe here in the dark, those Albanians circling like hyenas.

'Or the hold? Something stinks.' Donato hauled himself back in, sat in his seat and pressed the buttons overhead that operated the hydraulic doors to the luggage compartments.

Joe had climbed on and was doing a manic sweep down the aisle. 'Nothing here,' he said, coming back, arms raised like a gladiator asking for his accolade. 'And they always get in touch if it's a suitcase they've left behind. Like, without fail.'

They heard the hiss and groan of the luggage compartment opening. On the sidewalk at the top of the station ramp a girl had come up, pulling a wheeled suitcase. She was eyeing them tentatively. Joe stood in the doorway, a hand on either side of the frame. Below them the bodywork panels were sliding out and up along the coach's side, and from his seat Donato saw the courier's face flatten in distaste.

'Yeah,' Joe murmured, stepping on to the tarmac, and Donato was there after him, a hand held up to the waiting girl.

'A moment please,' he said. They bent down.

'It's a big one,' said Joe. 'Excess baggage right there.'

It sat at the centre of the compartment, as though its owner had thrust it as far in as possible. You couldn't see it unless you leaned right down and looked in: it might have been there for days. Joe climbed in, his nose pressed into his arm, and gave it a tug that brought it into the lights of the station forecourt. A tag dangled from the handle, stained with something.

Donato started as the girl appeared at his shoulder, peering in with them. 'Gee,' she said, in a light, childish voice. 'Something sure smells bad.'

Chapter Eleven

THE SUN HAD GONE down. Elena had stood and watched its last rays shining silver down the length of the river below and wondered about Giulietta Sarto. The blue-grey dusk was settling over the city and lights were beginning to go on along the embankments. A woman came and stood beside her. In the gathering dark the huge sculpture loomed, concealing them from the Palazzo.

'I've seen you,' she said, startling Elena. 'Just like a Vermeer, through the window.' She held out her hand. 'My name's Juliet Fleming. We were at the embassy in Amsterdam for a while, have you ever been?' Her Italian was very correct, although accented, but Elena just stared.

'That's how John described me,' she said, before she could think.

The woman sipped at her glass of whisky; her husband had brought it out to her and slipped away again. 'John?'

'My . . . I came with him. To the launch. Weeks ago.'

'I see.' Juliet Fleming was looking at her with such calm

understanding, Elena felt as though she had worked the whole story out.

A girl came past with a tray of champagne glasses and recklessly Elena took one. Juliet Fleming's tumbler seemed to be empty already and she set it on the tray. 'Could you bring me another?' she said, smiling gently at the maid, who bobbed. 'Medicinal,' she said.

'Maybe you know him,' said Elena, emboldened by the drink, and the smile. Why should she? 'He's a journalist. John Carlsson.'

'Oh, John,' said the Englishwoman straight away. 'Oh, yes.' Her gaze had settled on Elena, thoughtful. 'He's your lover,' she said. Elena said nothing.

'I haven't seen John in a day or two,' said Juliet Fleming, reaching for the glass the returning maid had brought her. 'He does seem to find us all so interesting, goodness knows why.' Her voice was thoughtful. 'Anyone who wants to talk to Ian about his bridges . . .' She tailed off. 'He's been away somewhere,' she said.

'Yes,' said Elena. Because that was what he'd told her, too. *I'll tell you about it when I get back*, was all he'd said on the phone, forestalling her questions. And never did.

But it seemed he hadn't minded telling Juliet Fleming. 'Down south, he said. Researching something. Bari?' The Englishwoman held the glass against her teeth a moment. 'But he's back, isn't he? He was here, when, Monday? The day Giancarlo went. Looking for someone.'

'A woman?' Elena wished her voice hadn't sounded so small.

Juliet Fleming turned back to look at her. 'Ah, I see,' she

said, and for a brief moment she sounded tired, and kind. 'No,' she said. 'I don't think that was it.' Her hand rested, light as dry leaves, on Elena's, then was gone. 'Oh, my dear,' she said. 'Journalists. Everything for the story, you know. They're not a good bet. Never.'

Elena smelled the whisky and it made her feel sick, a little anxious tick-tick behind the thumping of her heart: he'd been in here. Had she been asleep, had she been at the hospital? Or had he come in the dark, so as not to be seen?

'I haven't seen him in more than a week,' she said.

Small and grey in the dusk, Juliet Fleming cradled her glass. 'He's probably just . . . you know. Following a scent,' she said. 'I'm sure . . .' She hesitated. 'I'm sure there's nothing wrong.'

Only there was. Juliet Fleming's whisky-softened gaze told her so.

It was then that Elena felt Danilo Lludic rather than saw him: smelled the tobacco and chemicals and felt the big bulk at her shoulder. Momentarily giddy with the drink, and her heart pounding from having just been talking about John, she leaned into him. Mistake.

*

No message from Enzo. She should have called him, not sent a text. Better still, she should have gone straight to find him and told him, face to face. Maybe Sandro was right, the world was going to hell in a handcart, and it was sending a text message as it went.

If she got a message from Enzo, Giuli thought, saying, it's

okay – though she couldn't have said what form of words, exactly, would work – then it would matter less. All of it. But as she waited, she felt like . . . she could hardly describe it. Like she wanted to scratch all her skin off, from shame. She could hear Sandro's voice saying, stoutly, *What have you to be ashamed of? You've done nothing. It's a lie.* But didn't he understand? It wasn't what you'd done, it was what you *were.*

She'd seen the girl off. Not a girl any more, but school fixed you; if someone was four years younger than you then, they were forever a kid. Elena: they'd overlapped maybe for a year. She remembered a girl with scuffed shoes and tangled hair. Giuli didn't know what she'd done – or not done – for the girl to remember her. She had been a different person then – she hoped she had. Were you allowed to change?

Why had she said it? *You don't know me.* If anything was suspicious, that was. Elena had backed off, startled: *I'm so sorry, I must be mistaken.* But Giuli had seen the look in her eyes. Without thinking, she let out a long breath, like a sigh.

The man who was talking earnestly to her about a bridge he had built somewhere in the Middle East, forty years ago, paused at the sound, then resumed. His name was Ian Cameron, he was Australian, and he had retired last year. This much Giuli had managed to register, despite his English, despite his unfamiliar accent; there was even something soothing about how little what he was saying meant to her. Perhaps there was less to this small-talk business than she thought. She concentrated on his face: freckled northern skin, pale eyes, thin-lipped.

'And why have you come to Florence?' she put in as he paused, just for something to say.

He looked momentarily nonplussed, as if he couldn't remember, or didn't understand the point of the question. 'My wife,' he said vaguely, lifting his head and turning, scanning the heads. 'She thought it would be a good idea. Art, culture, you know. Food.'

'So you have done it for her,' she said. 'That's nice.'

Again he looked at her with those pale eyes as though he didn't know what she could mean. 'It really doesn't matter to me,' he said, 'where we live. I've always travelled, you see. And there's consultancy, now I'm retired.' He looked towards the door. 'I think I'm in Bahrain next week, as a matter of fact.'

'Your wife doesn't mind being alone.'

Giuli thought she really should stop this: this was the last place for recklessness. 'Sorry,' she said hastily. 'I am being too curious.'

'She had the children,' he said slowly, distant. 'This little jaunt won't last. Marjorie's a country girl, you see; it was more or less bush where we lived in Australia. Drove a pick-up when the children were small, spent the day barefoot, knew how to look after herself then. There was none of this . . . gadding about.' His thin mouth curled in disapproval, and something changed.

'Ian!'

The woman had moved in on them silently, although when Giuli shifted to see who'd spoken, she saw she was the most imposing woman in the room, the sort who arrived like a liner, spreading turbulence.

'Who's this? Won't you introduce us?'

She was elderly, twenty years at least on Ian Cameron, but

the way she spoke to him was flirtatious and commanding, with the certainty of a woman in her prime.

'Athene Morris,' said Ian Cameron, unbending, with no sign of the awe Giuli felt; tension was more like it, resistance. 'This is Giulietta Sarto.'

She held out a hand, croaked, 'It is a pleasure, Mrs Morris.'

Athene Morris laughed unexpectedly, almost a cackle but full-throated. 'I'm a *signorina*, strange though that may seem at my age. Or do all old women become *signora* in Italy, by default? Is there no Ms, in this country? I don't believe there is.'

'But we keep our name here, when we get married,' said Giuli. The woman was right though. It was all nonsense. Why did they need to get married?

'And what is your connection?' said Athene Morris. Giuli felt them both turn and focus on her, the old woman and the engineer, like she was prey. 'Why are you here?'

'I'm a colleague of Mr Cellini,' she said bravely.

'Ah,' said Athene Morris. 'Yes.' Giuli saw her glance across the room. 'I must have a proper word with him.' She put her hand on Ian Cameron's forearm, and he stiffened visibly. 'Our new Head of Security,' she said, and laughed. 'I don't think Brett's going to like him quite as much, somehow. Don't you get the feeling he can see through us all, already?'

Cameron pulled his arm out from under hers, not a violent movement, but across the room Giuli saw Sandro's head turn towards them.

'You're a troublemaker, Athene,' Cameron said shortly, giving Giuli a cold glance, transparently wishing for her to disappear.

'Just having fun, Ian,' said Athene Morris. 'Isn't it rather a strain, behaving so well all the time? Being sensible. Life's too short.'

'And you're old enough to know better.' His Australian accent was harsh, suddenly, and with a quick, graceless movement he extracted himself from her grip. 'I'm going to find my wife.'

They looked at his back.

'He's a bore,' said Athene Morris, in Italian, with a surprisingly good accent. 'Worse than a bore. Men so often are, as they get older. Women less so, I find. No, marriage never tempted me, even if love did, once upon a time.' She paused. 'Oh, I'm glad I'm past all that.' But she turned a little from Giuli as she said it, looking over the crowd, her eyes moving, pausing, moving on.

'Your Italian is beautiful,' said Giuli, liking her. 'Have you lived here for a long time?'

'I have lived a long time, full stop,' said the old woman, and there was something weary in her voice. 'I lived in Rome for ten years once, an age ago. I was in love with a man much younger than myself.'

Then she looked back at Giuli, and lowered her voice. 'If I were to tell you—' But then there was a shift, and a shuffling in the room, and Athene Morris pulled back, pressed down on her stick and raised her head to see what was going on. Whatever she had been about to say was suspended.

Pompously, Bottai, whose voice Giuli had off and on been able to hear in the room, had managed to elevate himself above the crowd – did he carry a podium with him? – and was urging them all to accompany him to dinner somewhere.

In her pocket Giuli felt the silent thrum of her phone and

her heart leapt. A message. Athene Morris had turned back towards her, bearing down on her, about to speak again, but Giuli pulled out the phone and offered it by way of explanation.

'Sorry,' she said to Athene, whose face had abruptly stiffened, turned old. 'It's work, I'm so sorry.'

As Giuli turned and moved away, the old woman's expression was still there in her head, like the negative image imprinted on the retina after over-exposure to bright light. It would still be there the next morning. But in the moment she couldn't help herself, it was an instinct – she needed to get away, fast, to get out, not just to regain the phone signal, nor just to get away from these people, not even the urgent need to read what Enzo had said in privacy. It was this place.

Almost at the doorway she remembered Sandro and turned back to locate him. He was standing at the bar next to a woman with glasses. Giuli raised a hand to him, pointing at the telephone – but she didn't get off that easy. The woman behind him was gesturing to the barman for another drink, but Sandro was already halfway across the room. He caught up with Giuli at the door.

'Right,' he said, breathless. There was something just a little bit reckless about him; it was the drink, Giuli realised. Sandro wasn't an aperitif man, as a rule. 'Okay. You have a choice: hooker at the Granduca, or cocktail waitress at the Excelsior Terrace.'

She stared at him stonily. 'Are we talking future employment?' She folded her arms. 'Because I'm a bit long in the tooth for either of those.'

Sandro's shoulders sagged. 'Sorry,' he said sheepishly. 'That didn't come out right.'

She listened in silence while he explained. 'I'll take the hooker,' she said.

The Granduca was a dump but the Excelsior probably wouldn't let her through the door, all that marble and all those tasselled concierges.

'You want me to do it on my way home?' Uneasily, Sandro shrugged, yes. 'You get back to your lady friend, now,' she said. She felt cheerful: sod it. Sod them.

The doorman turned in the doorway, in the act of tipping his hat to her, as she looked down at her phone. She read the message, looked up and saw the same message in the doorman's eyes.

I'm outside. The doorman spread his arm and there, through the doorway, standing on the steeply sloping street with his hands in his pockets, was Enzo.

She held on to him, tight. He stood patiently in her arms, all his questions unasked.

'There's one errand I've got to run,' she said. 'For Sandro. 'Then we can talk.'

*

Sandro was having some difficulty getting his key in the lock, and he hadn't even made it to the tricky apartment door yet. He was still out on the street, although as it was close to two in the morning there were no passers-by to observe his fumblings. Sandro hadn't been up this late since he was in the force, and he'd never had trouble with his own front door before. He staggered slightly.

As the possibility dawned on him that he might have had a little too much to drink, the key slid into its rightful place and Sandro toppled into his hallway. At the top of the stairs he focused, breathed deep. Belched, a hand over his mouth to stifle it. Luisa. Mustn't know.

There was a woman, he thought, leaning against the wall and waiting for the world to steady itself. Or was there another? Beautiful woman, gorgeous woman. Place was full of them. Therese Van Vleet was one. She was just lovely, those big blue eyes. He felt suddenly mournful at the thought, how she'd looked at him, asking for his help, and then mournful turned to a yawn. Too old to help. Sleep.

They'd started offering him drink. The scientist had done it. He'd been quite happy talking wives and English literature with Fleming, and she'd had to put herself between them. Green eyes behind those glasses. Tassi, her name was, Lauren Tassi, half-American, half-Italian, living with her mother, came here to work with Professor Scardino. Had he got that right? He had to drink with her, she said, or was he the kind that escorted women like her off the premises? Women. Weren't fair to him. How did you say no?

Still, he'd have been fine if it had been just that. He would. Miss Cornell watching him from across the room, eyes fixed on the glass in his hand. Which he'd set down carefully, only half drunk. *Dottoressa Tassi, I'm so sorry, I need to speak to the attaché.* Sandro tried to repeat the words now, only they didn't come out in the right order. What *was* an attaché?

Briefcase: where was it? His hands empty. There it was, on the floor, at his feet. Slowly he bent down, taking it easy at his age, and straightened with the briefcase clasped to his chest. He had an office in that big place, he needed to remember that. He'd collected the briefcase from his office. Miss Cornell had given him the piece of paper, though he couldn't quite remember now what the paper had been or why he'd wanted it. He'd put it in the briefcase. Certainly he had. He patted the briefcase tenderly. Luisa had bought it for him when he'd started the agency.

He still would have been fine. If he hadn't had to go up in that lift. Excelsior Terrace. Where the next lovely woman was waiting for him, with her cocktail menu and her row of bottles and those long-stemmed glasses. Candles on the tables and everyone turning to examine him when he came in. He'd looked around and seen his city through the glass, the Cestino's little dome, churches and velvety gardens spreading up the hills and floodlit towers rising out of the dark city. Mariaclara, tall and haughty as a film star and much too beautiful ever to have been a hotel maid, was wearing a little dicky-bow outfit and standing behind the bar.

What had she told him? That when they'd been digging out the cellars of the Palazzo San Giorgio they'd found a room where people had been killed, long, long ago. Tortured and killed. A woman, they said, left there to starve to death for adultery. She'd turned away from him then, her long hair swinging, to pour something into a glass. He didn't catch what she said then, until she turned back. 'Him? I wasn't his type, *caro*.' And that wide sweet mouth smiling at him. 'There's a name for boys like him. And they often come to no good.'

Perhaps, he thought, leaning against the wall again, it would be easier if he closed his eyes and felt for the lock this time; miraculously it turned out to be so.

He tripped, taking off his trousers, so he didn't bother with anything else, slid into bed beside Luisa, set the briefcase on his chest, folded his hands on top of it and once the room stopped spinning, he was asleep.

Chapter Twelve

DONATO WAS SMOKING HIS twentieth cigarette of the night in silence outside the police pound where they'd confined the bus for the foreseeable. The pound was out to the dark west of the city, between the red-rusted pylons of the Viadotto dell'Indiano and the bulrushes and shanty towns beyond the Isolotto. He looked to the east: above the hills of the Casentino the night sky was turning grey at the edges.

The police had long since said he could go home, they'd be in touch, but Donato wasn't ready to leave his bus yet. It occurred to him, listening to his heart bumping away, that one of these days he'd need to get himself checked out. Freaked. Not quite as freaked as Joe, mind, who had kept rubbing his hands against his sides, as if he had got something on them. He probably had.

The company ran on a shoestring; they'd had to get another bus down from Amerigo Vespucci to sort out the passengers left grumbling on the station forecourt. Eventually Donato had herded them inside to the bus company's ticket booth, just because it had to be bad for business, four policemen, then five, the light blue uniforms clustered around the luggage compartment. A van from the morgue at close to midnight, though the passengers had gone by then.

'Don't open it,' Joe had said in a panic as Donato had leaned down to try the locks, not even thinking yet, though Joe had been, of what must be inside. It was locked. He'd looked at the tag, found it blank and then he'd realised that his fingers were sticky.

Joe had run into the station in a panic to the little Polizia di Stato post inside the station and the police officers had come sauntering out, expecting a fuss over nothing. They'd soon changed their tune when they'd seen the staining on the big cheap suitcase, and then the air in the bus's underbelly had hit them.

They'd opened the suitcase in the back of the police van in the end. Donato heard sounds coming from inside the vehicle and a man had climbed out grey-faced. The case was big and very heavy: it had slid out of their hands and hit the pavement with a crunch when they'd lugged it out.

He had no idea how long it might have been in the compartment. When they'd asked him the question, Donato had thrown a sidelong glance at Joe, and answered truthfully. Joe just gibbered. Might have gone on at Pisa, at Vespucci, or here at Santa Maria Novella. People walked up with their suitcases, put them on, hung about smoking and chatting, then got inside when the bus was ready to leave. Some made a fuss about positioning their luggage, others just shoved it in. Their business.

Donato had seen the dreadlocked guy, with his dogs and his teenage girlfriend wriggling up beside him, all the while sitting there rolling a cigarette as cool as a cucumber as the policeman leaned down to ask him questions.

He might have been driving around for three, four days with it in the hold. Leaning against the long fence around the pound, in the flickering yellow of the streetlight, his bus sitting somewhere in there in the dark, Donato lit another cigarette.

*

It had seemed like a good idea at the time. At the first shafts of thin grey dawn, Elena turned over in the stuffy bedroom and groaned.

In the growing light Elena rolled over in her bed and buried her face in the pillow. It had seemed like a good idea at the time, but somewhere in the night the tide had turned, hadn't it? At two in the morning, not yet able to sleep, it had still seemed exhilarating, the things she had said entertaining enough to make her smile in the dark. But around three-thirty, in her sleep, perhaps even dreaming, her body, or some deep cortex of the brain, informed her that she'd behaved like a fool.

'It's all right,' Lludic had said. 'I don't intend to take advantage of you.' And then in the next breath, 'But come and see my room, why don't you?' And his broad face split in a grin. 'Just to give the old biddies something to gossip about?'

It had seemed like a good idea at the time.

The pillow still smelled unfamiliar and suddenly Elena sat bolt upright in the gloom, pulling at the sheet. No. No. Straining to see.

Her heart slowed: she was in her own bed. She climbed out of it, one hand to her forehead to stave off the dull throb behind her eyes. She pushed at the shutters, letting in a crack of soft grey light; the streetlights must have blinked off, the air was misted and the pavement slick with the night's rain. Had it all been a dream? Not all.

He had kissed her: that much really had happened. At least he hadn't done it in front of all those stuffed shirts in the library, though he might as well have done, parading her through their midst as they pretended not to watch. Standing back as he pressed the button to the lifts, making sure they could see.

Standing at her window now, Elena turned her face into her shoulder and smelled him on her skin – along with something else. Her head ached. On the threshold of his rooms he'd kissed her too hard, she hadn't liked it. But then he'd let her go, abruptly, and had turned to flick on the lights.

You could just about see that his apartment had started out all white and cream like the rest of the place, a lot of tasteful reproduction furniture, a vast bed and some floor-to-ceiling swagged curtains across two long windows. But the pale good taste of the place was pretty much obscured by around fifty unframed canvases stacked around the walls, oil abstracts that might have been lines or skies or horizons or breaking waves, of varying colours both muted and violent. She stared, putting a hand to her mouth to feel where his mouth had been. She could taste blood.

'Don't tell me what you think of them, please,' he said roughly. He was at a small table in a corner of the room and she heard a chink and splash as he poured.

She thought they were beautiful. She had said nothing. Now at her own window she leaned a little forward on the windowsill and breathed in the moist grey morning air.

He'd given her a glass of something strong; she thought it was something like whisky only sweeter. She'd hardly drunk it, did little more than feel the burn in the back of her throat, but she'd stood as close to the door as she could with the glass in her hand.

He watched her a minute then suddenly, like the sun coming out, he grinned broadly again, back to the man he'd been earlier: a bit of an idiot, a bit of a show-off, sheepish with it. 'Sorry,' he said. 'Bad habit, I suppose. Just in case someone might be passing, you have to give them a show.'

He meant the kiss. Elena looked at him, trying to work him out, but the smile got her in the end. She turned to shut the door behind them.

'You don't paint them in here?' she said, thinking of the mess. They stood on spattered dustsheets, but she could see that the spilled paint was largely dry flakes.

'They're for show,' he said, downing his drink and pouring another one, holding out the decanter to her across the room.

'For girls like me,' she said, shaking her head.

'You're not a girl,' he said. 'You're a woman.' She couldn't tell if he was insulting her or praising her: she concentrated on keeping her expression indifferent.

'Are they recent?'

'Some of them,' he said. 'Do you want to talk about art? Really?' He went to the window and pushed it open. 'Maybe you want to go?' He sounded suddenly weary, and a little unhappy. Perhaps he was a tortured artist, after all. The pictures at least were real.

'Walk back past that lot in the library on my own?' She'd

crossed the room to stand beside him in the window. 'Let's give it an hour or so.' And he'd put an arm around her shoulders, light for all his bulk, and brotherly.

Nothing happened. As if she was explaining herself to her uncle – or to John. *We just talked.*

What they'd mostly done was gossip, or rather, she'd listened to him, idly.

'Athene's next door,' he'd said, pointing along the façade. 'The old woman – I mean, the very old woman. She was a poet, did you know that? Very well known. A hundred lovers, she told me. She said she'd asked to be put in the apartment next to me, because she's not easily shocked. A hundred lovers, and I don't know if she's ready to call it a day, either.' He'd poured himself another glass.

Elena had craned her neck. The old woman's windows were open and light flooded out, but there was nothing to see. What a life, she thought. Did a hundred lovers make you happy?

On the terrace people were talking, low and civilised. It was late now, they must have come back from their dinner. Somewhere further off someone was having an argument, hissed furious words: the Australian and his wife.

Further down, a figure occupied the canvas lounger. All that was visible of her by the light of the candle almost guttered down to nothing in its glass funnel, was a smooth calf, gleaming very white, and a finger – her finger, with a long, dark, pointed nail – moving absently up and down.

'It's Therese,' said Danilo next to Elena. 'You'll have seen her. Pretty as a picture.' Therese was talking to someone: as they watched, a man's hand came out under the parasol and took hers as it moved, holding it still. Elena had turned away from the window then.

He'd showed her his pictures, one after the other, in a near silence she hadn't liked to break, once or twice simply mentioning where he'd been when he'd painted something. He spent a lot of time in the Maremma, he said. He liked the Etruscan caves. What could she say, anyway? *They're lovely*. She could see him in some underground lair somewhere, painting with a stick.

She didn't know what time it had been when she'd left, but the Palazzo San Giorgio had subsided into silence. The corridor lighting was dimmed, the cream and gold softened to dove grey.

'I'd better take you,' he'd said, carelessly, 'or you'll get lost, and I'll get into trouble again.'

Then what? In the half dark of the early morning, Elena turned from the window to fumble in a bowl on her dressing table for a foil packet of painkillers she knew was there somewhere. She swallowed two dry. She felt cold suddenly, and pulled a sweater at random from a drawer. An awful feeling came over her, the knowledge of having done something really stupid.

The doorman had been nowhere to be seen – it must have been past midnight, although there were still voices from the garden – and Elena wondered if he slept here, or had a home to go to. Lludic had pressed a button to the side of the big door and then he'd just stood there, smiling faintly in the dimmed lights.

The heavy door had closed behind her, noiseless on oiled hinges until it clicked to, and she'd lingered on the street. The flawless façade of the Palazzo San Giorgio loomed, not golden on this side but grey, splashed here and there with the garish streetlighting. It stood blank and closed against her, and Elena had the distinct impression, quite suddenly, that it was hostile. That behind it was a place where violence collected like dust in neglected corners; and with that thought the memory of what it was like to pass through those long, noiseless, cushioned corridors came back to her with a sense of dread. The last thing, the very last thing she would want, Elena realised, was to be locked in there for the night with the wealthy couples, listening to their muffled sounds. She thought of Lludic's shadow on the walls of the corridors as he paced back to his rooms, like the minotaur in his labyrinth, and then, as if on cue, she heard something, inside. No more than the squeak and grind of a shutter being closed, slowly and firmly, but she stood quite still, for some reason her heart pounding as though she'd been witness to something awful.

And then there was silence. As it grew, a kind of relief washed over her like jubilation, that she was on the outside.

There was home, three steps away. It seemed so odd to Elena as she stood there, that her little bedroom and the Palazzo San Giorgio's featureless corridors should be so close, but worlds apart. No wonder John had stood there watching, wondering.

Jingling her keys in her pocket, she'd stood by the dumpster where on her way over to the unveiling she'd dropped the last of John, the CDs. Did she hate him? At that strange hour – one, two? – in the soft darkness nothing had seemed cut and dried. All that she knew was, he had disappeared, and it was all she had left of him. She'd stood on the bar that opened the dumpster's lid, it had come up with a gust of garbage stench and there was the supermarket bag under a couple of pizza boxes. Elena had reached in and pulled it back out, holding it to her as she looked around. No one to see her, fishing around in other people's rubbish.

And now as the dawn brightened, she heard the tortured groan of the garbage truck's lifting mechanism. She turned over at the morning sound, the distant clatter of a dumpster being upended, and buried her face. Another couple of hours and the thing would have been emptied, gone forever. Which was, of course, what should have happened.

There was something about the pre-dawn light: it made you face the worst. John would say he was one place, when he was somewhere else; he would come in after she was in bed and she'd hear him moving around, removing things from his pocket, sending messages. There could have been someone else, while he was with her, and she had just refused to see it. John had used her as a stepping point. Her window was all he wanted.

He found us all so interesting, the Englishwoman – Juliet Fleming – had said, sipping her whisky. John hadn't been her lover, he'd been a sniper commandeering an innocent family's bedroom, or a spy moving in next door to his mark. What had he been after in the Palazzo San Giorgio?

Slowly Elena took off her clothes, and stepped under the shower until the water ran cold.

Chapter Thirteen

THE ALARM SOUNDED IN Sandro's dream, a dream in which he'd been standing with his head back, gazing upwards to a high window from which a woman was letting her hair down for him to climb. She wore rectangular glasses and smiled down at him sadly.

He opened his eyes a crack and winced, putting out a hand to feel for his wife. But Luisa's side of the bed was empty. His head hurt.

Sandro sat up gingerly, and something fell to the floor with a thud. Leaning over, he saw that it was his briefcase.

'Sweetheart?' His mouth felt dry and furry, and he had a nasty feeling in his gut, of dread, or shame. He tried again. 'Darling?'

Luisa appeared in the doorway, in her good suit and stockinged feet, a glass of water in her hand.

'You were snoring,' she said, eyeing him. 'Like a boar.'

'What time is it?' Sandro said, humbly. 'I'm sorry about the snoring. I think I had too much—'

'To drink,' she said, and handed him the water. 'Yes.' But her expression softened, just enough. 'I've got to get in early,' she said, and sighed. 'Frollini has something up his sleeve.'

Sandro realised they hadn't talked all yesterday.

'I heard what happened,' she continued, arms folded. Reading his mind again. 'To your predecessor. Coffee's on.' And she turned and padded into the kitchen.

Sandro drank the water, then refilled the glass, standing in his undershorts at the kitchen tap. He rubbed a hand over his chin. Things to do.

'It all happened very quickly,' he said, sitting down in front of his coffee. 'I'm sorry I didn't talk to you. I needed to get to grips with it myself, and I thought we'd go over it when I got back, but then,' Sandro ended lamely, 'things got away from me.' He felt hollow, and realised he hadn't eaten anything last night except peanuts.

With another sigh that marked the thaw proper, Luisa sat down beside him. Downing the cup, Sandro felt the coffee enter his system. Things were improving.

'How about I tell you what I know,' said Luisa. 'And then you can tell me what you were doing till two this morning.'

He looked at her, hangdog, and took another sip in answer.

'Scardino and his wife were in yesterday, her spending his money. But I wouldn't say she wears the trousers, not by a long chalk. He said something about . . .' She frowned. 'Competition? Vito introducing an element of competition?' She shrugged. 'And Marina Artusi—'

'Not her,' Sandro groaned. He could feel his headache returning.

'Well, if you're not interested . . .' She made as if to stand up again.

'Go on,' he said.

Luisa patted his arm. 'She says that someone over there's not paying his bills. She says that Sir Martin Fleming knows everything, that in the Middle East he always had his ear to the ground. And she said his wife was sick – only I think what she was really saying is, she's a drunk.' Sandro digested this information. Luisa sat back, content. 'Your turn.'

'There was this room-maid there,' he said eventually, looking at his wife sidelong. 'She got fired. Resigned, rather, that was the story, after an accusation of theft. I wanted to talk to her, only she'd gone to work as a cocktail waitress.'

'Oh, yes,' said Luisa, with deep scepticism.

'Long story,' said Sandro, revising what he'd intended to tell her. Truth was, he wasn't entirely sure of things himself. He needed more coffee. And something to eat.

'How about I get dressed and we get some breakfast on your way,' he said. 'Do me good to get started early.' He tried to remember if his office at the San Giorgio offered any opportunity for a lie-down later.

The office. Briefcase. What had he got from Cornell and put in the briefcase? CV, okay. He really needed to get a grip. What had Mariaclara said? He found that trying to remember anything about the statuesque cocktail waitress with Luisa there brought him out in a sweat. She really had been very good-looking.

Luisa looked at her watch. 'Get a move on, then,' she said. 'You need a shave.'

Twenty minutes later they were at a warm corner table in Rivoire, and the elderly waiter was fussing fondly around Luisa. The shop, practically next door, had a tab. She waved him away with affectionate impatience, and pushed the *brioches* and *caffè latte* she'd ordered across to Sandro. He set his briefcase on the table. The pastry was still warm, and full of apricot jam. Sandro paused a moment, eyes closed in bliss. Nothing, it seemed to him, had ever tasted so good: maybe it was worth the hangover.

He paused, suddenly self-conscious. 'You not eating?'

In response Luisa pulled her jacket tight round her. Since the breast reconstruction she'd seemed uncertain about her figure as she never had before. 'You know what I think,' he said, 'about that.' He hoped she did know.

She gave him a quizzical look. 'You're making a mess,' she said.

Brushing crumbs off his suit with one hand, he pulled Giancarlo Vito's CV out of his briefcase with the other and set it on the table. Luisa caught the *caffè latte* before he knocked it on the floor.

'My predecessor,' he said, taking the coffee and giving her the document in exchange. A photograph was clipped to the top; he saw her put a finger to it, tracing the man's jawline. Crew-cut, big chin, that bulge of trapezium muscle Sandro had noticed at the party.

'Good-looking,' she said, and sighed. 'You talked to him at the launch.' She ran her eye down the first page then handed the document back. 'How did he die?'

'They're talking about drugs,' said Sandro, flipping up the photograph. 'The Carabinieri.' He frowned. 'They're being cagey, actually. Even more than usual.' Alessandra Cornell had said they wouldn't tell her anything.

There was a note under the photograph – *This is the one* – and it was signed, *Gastone*. Sandro was not even aware of having been considered and found wanting by Bottai; he'd thought it was Cornell's decision. So Bottai had handpicked the private detective. A young buck. Born 1982 in San Casciano, went into the army. Released on grounds of ill-health in 2007, then he resurfaces as a surveillance expert. One of those boys who fancies himself a mercenary? Or likes guns, or the camaraderie, or the pension, or the Military Academy? Because who signs up for the army, in this day and age? He wondered what kind of ill-health had got Vito an honourable discharge: not so easy to get out of the army. A drug habit would have stuck fast, but his references were glowing.

Transforms himself into a computer whizz – or so his CV said; employed on a freelance contract for four years by the Stella d'Argento. Their address was on the CV. He turned and looked out of the window; Piazza Signoria 36: he could practically see it from here. Sandro pondered how they would receive him if he turned up asking questions. They might think he was looking for a job.

'Maybe I could call Pietro,' he said.

'But it's a Carabinieri case.'

'Yes.' He could see the tiny edging of white at her parting. He put a hand to her cheek. 'You should have been a cop,' he said, with the faintest of smiles, and opened his briefcase to put the CV back inside, thinking, I could call Falco. The *carabiniere* he'd dealt with over the missing girl, three years back. Falco. He paused, looking up at the ceiling. Falco had even hinted then, hadn't he, that he owed Sandro one.

'What's that?' said Luisa sharply, and hearing her tone he jerked his head back and blinked.

'What's what?' He looked down at his briefcase: she was pointing, then her hand was inside it and pulling something out, a fat magazine of glossy pages that he'd never seen before, spilling open in front of them. Horrified, he put both hands out in an attempt to close it, to cover it, but it was too late.

A top-shelf job. A pornographic magazine. A lipglossed blonde, hands splayed against two huge breasts.

He saw Luisa's face. Too late.

*

The sky was overcast and the mothers trudging up to the entrance of the big school in the Via della Chiesa were trailing umbrellas and raincoats as well as their children's overstuffed backpacks. These were the early ones, the protected ones, the children equipped with snacks from the baker's, their mothers bending to kiss them, wipe their noses, straighten their clothing, issue last-minute instructions.

Giuli knew the school well because for a year, in a previous life, she had been temporarily housed in the *casa popolare* opposite. She got out her phone to check the time: eight-fifteen, no messages. Her guess would be that Rosina, for all her good intentions, would take it down to the wire. She would be here eight-forty, unwashed, shouting at the children and at any member of the school staff who challenged her timekeeping.

Two hookers in twelve hours. Maybe someone was trying to tell Giuli something.

Last night, Enzo's reaction to her suspension had startled her with its violence, on the pavement outside the Granduca. 'Don't be stupid,' he'd said. He'd actually been angry – with her, as much as with them. 'Don't be stupid. How can you take it seriously?'

'How can *they*?' she'd said, faltering at the rage she heard in his voice. 'Look, I've been suspended. I've got to take it seriously.'

They'd fallen into silence then, looking up at the hotel's façade. It had once been elegant, with pillars and art-nouveau mosaic, but neglect and decades of pollution from the Via Senese had left the Granduca the worse for wear.

'Come in with me?' said Giuli.

He shrugged. 'If that's what you want.'

She took his hand, looked down. Her engagement ring was loose on her finger, as if it belonged to someone else. 'I've got to talk to a hooker,' she said. 'You think I want to be taken for one myself?'

The look on his face twisted something painfully inside her. Lines of anxiety etched his forehead, weariness – and doubt. But when she turned, still holding his hand, he followed.

The receptionist wore a frogged jacket and cap, even if he was in need of a shave. With a jaundiced look he had directed them through an archway to the bar. The room was still grand – a long curved slab of green marble, soaring ceilings, painted ladies in the Liberty style, with their hands raised to support garlands and arches – but the furniture had seen better days.

They ordered fruit juices and Enzo's unease took on an air

of desperation. Three men in suits, their ties loosened, were standing with their backs against the bar, surveying the room. In the low chairs arranged in groups, an elderly woman was pouring camomile tea very slowly, a middle-aged couple were gazing into each other's eyes over small glasses of something sticky, and a single woman in a red skirt leaned back and looked up at the ceiling. She had a clutch-bag in her lap and her long skinny legs and high sandals were stretched out in front of her; even from a distance, Giuli could see the scuffing on the heels. A coffee cup sat on her low table, its contents long since drunk. She had a star tattoo under one ear.

'See you outside in ten minutes,' Giuli whispered to Enzo, resting her cheek against his. He didn't need telling twice.

'You're Bruna,' she said, sitting down opposite the woman in the red skirt.

Bruna looked down from her examination of the painted ceiling, but she didn't move her long legs. 'So?' she said, sliding a glance across the room.

Giuli followed her gaze to the men at the bar. 'I won't take up much of your time,' she said. 'And that lot need another half-hour, if you ask me. They're still discussing how much you'd charge for all three. And the one on the left is trying to work out how he can cry off without being laughed at.'

Bruna looked at her stonily. 'How much time?' she said. 'It all costs, you know.'

Giuli hesitated: Sandro hadn't authorised payment. She took her business card out of her pocket. 'Come along to the office tomorrow,' she said. 'You want me handing over cash in front of this lot?' Bruna took the card and examined it. 'You know the Palazzo San Giorgio?' said Giuli. 'You saw a client there, maybe this time last week?'

The girl stared at her. Girl. She was thirty, at Giuli's guess, and the next ten years would turn her into an old woman.

'Maybe,' said Bruna. She looked down at the card. 'Why does this . . . Sandro Cellini Investigations want to know?'

'Who was it?' said Giuli. 'Could you describe him to me?'

'I don't kiss and tell,' the girl said. 'Bad for business.' She gave the men at the bar another glance, with a hint of invitation.

'The house detective there,' said Giuli carefully. 'I hear you were on friendly terms. I hear he saw you to the door, just like a gentleman.'

Bruna straightened, drawing in her legs. 'Giancarlo?' she said. 'He's not a bad guy.' Her hand closed around the business card, crumpling it.

'Wasn't,' said Giuli. 'Didn't you hear? He died.'

Outside on the Via Senese, Enzo was standing, hands in pockets, as the cars passed. 'That was eight minutes,' he said when she emerged, and hugged her.

'I don't like to mess around,' said Giuli.

As Giuli had stood up from the table, Bruna had been straightening her skirt studiedly, getting lipstick out of her clutch, but the eyes were dead, concealing fear.

Giuli had got to sleep about three, lying there listening to the rain start. Did Enzo know what it was like, to be judged, never to get away from where you came from? Enzo lived his life looking forwards, and he thought that was how everyone should be – particularly when what was behind you was nasty.

But his parents had loved him, their odd-looking only child; they'd taken him everywhere with them, and had never raised a hand to him.

Eight-twenty-three. A warm drizzle had set up on the Via della Chiesa, and Giuli hadn't brought an umbrella.

Enzo was right; he always was. But there were things she couldn't say, because they'd freak him out. Drugs: he had no idea. Giuli tried to imagine his face if she were to put it into words. *It's not like I haven't been tempted.* Speeding on her *motorino* through the Piazza Santo Spirito at night and turning her head so she didn't see them doing their deals, only to catch the dreamy look on the face of someone who'd just taken a hit.

And when the cold-water shock of betrayal hits you, when someone you trusted and you thought trusted you won't even meet your eye to let you defend yourself – what's the first demon that climbs into your head, as though it was yesterday and not four years since your last fix? That feeling. Like love, that feeling when the chemical unfurls like smoke through your body, when you close your eyes and everything's warm and safe.

Like love, only easier.

There was a flurry of arrivals at the wide steps of the school. Through the glass doors Giuli could see a noticeboard in the hall, artwork stuck up. Still early for Rosina, but all the same, Giuli moved in, closer, so as not to miss anyone. A woman turning from her children gave her a hard look, suspicious of an unaccompanied female hovering at the school gates. Giuli took a step back, bumping into another mother, holding a child by each hand. Her hair was tied back, her coat buttoned, the two children – a girl and a boy – awkward but neatly turned out, each one clutching a greasy paper bag of *schiacciata*. The woman was Rosina.

Tethered as she was by her children, there was no escape. Giuli had only to wait as Rosina bent to kiss them, administered rough instructions about eating their dinners and saw them inside. They looked back at Giuli and their mother together on the steps, and Giuli read the fear in their eyes as clearly as she'd seen it in Bruna's.

'Why did you do it?' Giuli said, under her breath. She was holding on to Rosina by the sleeve. People were looking, and Rosina tried to pull away. 'Let me guess, you wanted a better life. Well, guess what. Me too. Difference is, I'm not going to shit on anyone else to get it.'

The woman stopped pulling. 'I don't know what you mean,' she said sullenly.

'You told Massini – the Director – you told her you'd seen me shooting up.'

From the way Rosina paled, Giuli knew the old cleaner had been right. 'She told you,' Rosina said. 'The Director. She said she wouldn't.'

'You think they're on our side?' said Giuli, suddenly weary. 'Once a junkie, always a junkie, that's how they think. Once a hooker—' She stopped. This wasn't good. She mustn't say this. She mustn't believe this. 'Who told you to say you saw me taking drugs?'

Rosina shook her head. 'I can't tell you,' she said, looking around desperately. 'She said . . . they'd take the kids away.'

'She?' Giuli pulled Rosina closer. 'Nicoletta Farmiga? Is that who hates me that much?'

She saw confusion in Rosina's eyes. 'I don't know who that is,' she said. 'I'll have to tell them you threatened me. I could get witnesses. Anyway,' and she looked down, 'she said you were getting engaged. What do you need a job for?'

Giuli let the sleeve go and for a moment they stood there, eye to eye. Not Farmiga, then. 'Whoever it is,' Giuli said. 'This *she*. You want to live in fear of her?' Softly. 'I've done nothing, Rosina. Remember that. You think about who you can trust.'

But Rosina had turned and fled, her tightly pulled greasy ponytail and narrow shoulders running, running away from her down the street.

Giuli watched her go, almost envious. Run, run, drop everything and run. If only she could.

Chapter Fourteen

'HELLO, HELLO,' SAID ENRICO Frollini with that easy businessman's smile, pulling off one of the gloves he wore until May ended, to ensure, Luisa thought as he took her hand between his again, that his hands were always warm. 'The lovely Mrs Cellini, just the girl I wanted to see.'

Girl. Luisa had caught sight of her own face in the shop's mirrored walls when she'd come in that morning and she had looked about a hundred. And that was after Sandro had talked her down.

Confronted by those breasts, she had felt as though she couldn't breathe. Luisa had made herself believe it didn't matter that one of hers was no longer her own, that it had been scooped hollow and refilled with jelly, that her nipple had gone. She had told herself that no woman should be defined by the disposition of a handful of fat and tissue. The magazine had told her otherwise.

Did she believe him? She had to, didn't she? But he couldn't have faked the shock on his own face, Sandro had never been an actor. He had gibbered, stuffing the magazine back in the briefcase and out of sight. *Someone must have put it in there,* he said, his mouth slack. She'd asked him grimly who would do such a thing. And then he had told her all about what had been going on at the Palazzo San Giorgio. Jewellery missing, shit smeared on skirtings, doors being locked. A woman's pet disappeared – Luisa even remembered the little dog, from the launch. Malicious, nasty stuff, that Giancarlo Vito hadn't been able to get to the bottom of. Vito was dead – and now this.

A magazine slipped into Sandro's briefcase, to let Vito's replacement know it wasn't over? To let him know who was boss? She felt slightly sick.

'Is it jealousy?' she'd said, without knowing exactly why. 'Envy? Seems to me, it's like a waiter spitting in the soup.'

'You think it might be one of the staff?' Sandro's face had smoothed out, abstracted. 'Maybe.' Frowned. 'Maybe.'

Luisa hadn't got around to telling him she was thinking of giving it up. That that was why she had pushed him into this proper job, with the contract and the salary. Because she was getting too old to be standing around a shop waiting on girls young enough to be her granddaughters, girls who walked in carrying Styrofoam cups of coffee, who wore jeans that showed their backsides and got more pocket money than she earned in a year. And the worst of it was she'd always sworn she'd never get that way with customers. She didn't want to be the envious bitter servant.

She'd folded her arms. 'Who do *you* think is doing it?'

Sandro had taken a moment, still far away, and she'd gone on. 'Marina Artusi thinks the guests are no better than they ought to be, either. Drunks and con artists, was more or less her verdict. I told you.'

She'd got his attention then; he'd set the briefcase down. 'And who exactly did she say couldn't pay their bills?'

Now in the shop, Enrico Frollini leaned his head back and called up the stairs, 'Giuseppina?' He'd first employed Giusy, now knocking fifty, as a teenager and still treated her with robust impatience. Overhead they fell silent. Her boss smiled at her, a caressing look, but it only made her feel sick: she could still see that magazine's slippery weight in Sandro's hands. Thirty years on and her boss was still trying it on. Men.

'Enrico,' she said wearily. 'Mr Frollini,' and extracted her hand. 'So why did you want me in so early?'

'Sit down, Luisa,' he said. She sat. 'Look. I know you want to . . . scale back, let's say. Take it easy. Let's not talk about retiring. Please. I have just the thing.' He beamed, leaned down confidentially. 'Personal shopping,' he murmured.

'Personal shopping,' she repeated.

'You know what that is?'

She looked at him deadpan. Personal shoppers came in to the store, sharply dressed young women with hard eyes, bowing and scraping to their wealthy customers, and haggling hard behind their backs. Negotiating discounts, bullying shopgirls, taking kickbacks. Leading the customers round discount malls.

Luisa kept her voice steady. 'I'm just not quite sure how it would work, in my case.'

'I've done a deal with the new outlet,' he said, ridiculously pleased with himself. 'There's a spa there. We can offer the whole service, limousine and everything. You'll be like a queen, Luisa.'

'I don't . . .' Her throat felt constricted. 'I'm not sure . . .'

But Frollini wasn't listening. 'And the Palazzo San Giorgio will be your first customers. I had the management on the phone this morning. Apparently they need distraction today. The residents.' He lowered his voice. 'I expect you've heard? Well, this way, we keep it in the family, so to speak. You and Sandro.'

'You've talked to the attaché?' He looked blank. 'To Miss Cornell?' she said patiently. Her contact, not Frollini's, quietly cultivated, all for nothing.

'No, no,' said Frollini. 'It was Gastone Bottai – my God, do you remember him when he was a boy? Always playing silly tricks.' He tapped his chin. 'He asked me over for a chat, a day or so ago, introduced me to a few people there. Never married, did he?' He gave her a sly glance. 'I think his father set him up at the Palazzo. Has a stake in the place.'

He turned in his handsome camel coat and gazed out at the street; he was going off on one of his reminiscences, or his pet bugbears, Luisa could tell. After more than half an hour's exposure to her boss she often ended up wondering how his wife put up with him. Sandro was deeply suspicious of the man, and not without reason. Luisa supposed she might have ended up as one of his mistresses if she'd been a different sort of woman; it might have been easy. But she wouldn't have wanted to be his wife.

Frollini was smiling to himself. 'There are some charming women at the Palazzo, you know. Really charming. That Professor's wife, such good taste. Bottai introduced me the other day. She did urge me to keep in touch. I have her personal number.'

'Indeed,' said Luisa drily, remembering Magda Scardino in the red dress. He looked at her a little shamefaced and she wondered. How would he have described her to the charming ladies? Poor Luisa, only one breast.

And finally registering her expression, he faltered. 'I thought you might enjoy it.'

Luisa never ceased to be surprised by men's failure to get to grips with what a woman was likely to enjoy. But there was nothing she could do. 'Of course,' she said, and his face cleared, instantly.

That was the thing about Frollini: it was the reason he had so many friends, and the reason he'd live to a hundred if he eased up on the cigars. The clouds passed over so quickly, nothing abided to taint his sunny disposition – or to teach him anything useful.

'Otherwise, of course, I would never waste your expertise out there among the – the . . .' He frowned at his watch again.

'Enrico,' she said warily, 'why do you keep looking at your watch?'

'I ordered the limousine for ten,' he said. 'It'll pick you up here.'

It was nine-thirty-five.

*

Sandro's mobile rang just as Fabio Savino of the Stella d'Argento opened the black and chrome door of his office to admit him. Sandro saw only that it was Pietro before he silenced it.

Pietro? He hadn't heard from his old partner in the Polizia di Stato in weeks. He might have heard about Sandro's new job – his wife and Luisa being thick as thieves – but Pietro's instinct would have been to leave him to it for a bit. He might have heard about Vito's death, too, even if it was a Carabinieri case. Damn, thought Sandro. He'd have liked to be having that conversation right now.

Instead, the Stella d'Argento's Director of Personnel – we're all directors now, thought Sandro – looked at him impatiently as he thrust the cellphone hastily back in his pocket, and turned into his office, leaving Sandro to follow him. Fabio Savino was a slight man in his late thirties in a good suit, and either he was prematurely bald or he shaved his head. A tough guy, but civilised, that would be the idea.

Sandro turned as he went in to nod his thanks to the receptionist. She bobbed back nervously: thirties, slim, dark, anxious. Sandro had had no great hopes of being seen – all he'd said was that he'd stepped into Vito's shoes at the San Giorgio, and could he have a word. But the receptionist must have been on his side, because he was being shown in.

The room was dominated by a wide modern desk at which Savino had seated himself. Sandro lowered himself gingerly into a padded leather chair. He was aware of the briefcase in his lap: the magazine was still in there.

He blinked, trying to get the image out of his head – not the naked woman, but Luisa's face. Who would do that to him? To her? The magazine had been in English, that was all he had registered. Not quite all – there had been something else. Scuffed. A sticker on it from a news distributor.

He hadn't been able to look at it again though, obviously. Not in Rivoire – he would have had to excuse himself to the toilet – and not in the lobby of the Stella d'Argento with the receptionist looking on, even if it did feel like an upmarket men's club.

Savino cleared his throat. 'I don't know what you want,' he said, before Sandro had a chance to open his mouth. 'But Giancarlo Vito ended his professional relationship with us more than a month ago. When he took the job at the Palazzo San Giorgio.'

'I'm sure you've already spoken to the Carabinieri,' Sandro said. 'I don't want to cause trouble.' Was it his imagination or did Savino look distinctly shifty at that? 'You gave him excellent references.' Cautiously he slid the CV out of the briefcase. 'Did he get back in touch? After they . . . fired him?'

Savino sighed. His hands, clasped in front of him on the desk, opened, palms out. 'To be honest,' he said, 'he wasn't a full-time operative for us, ever. He worked on a few jobs. He certainly had impressive technical expertise – army training is very thorough.'

'Do you know why he left the army?' Sandro interjected quickly.

'On health grounds,' said the man, shrugging. 'Leukaemia, I believe. When he came to us he was completely clear of it but he didn't want to go back into the army. A fresh start. Quite understandable.' Savino almost winked. 'And that training is worth quite something in the outside world. Who can blame him?' He resumed his expression of seriousness. 'Anyway. We had what you might call a semi-detached relationship – it's not unusual, in the bigger agencies. It was convenient for him to have the connection with us, the letterhead. He was free to pursue other options in parallel.'

'Other jobs? Competition?'

Savino shrugged. 'As long as he was available when we called him in, the arrangement suited us very well.' He pushed the CV back towards Sandro. 'Needless to say, if we'd had any concerns about his professionalism we'd have terminated the connection.'

Only if there was a chance they'd become public, thought Sandro grimly. He couldn't work this out. He knew there were some odd sorts in private security; there were temptations, after all. Maybe they all had some kind of criminal sideline. Blackmail, drugs, extortion. Illegal surveillance equipment. Arms. What might Vito's have been?

'It's been terminated now, though, hasn't it?' He took the CV back, and held the man's gaze. 'He was murdered,' he said. 'Doesn't that bother you?'

Savino's eyes flickered, and Sandro took his chance, leaning forward across the polished wood. 'What was the last job he did for you?'

The Director considered him in silence. 'Personal protection,' he said finally. 'More than a year ago. An industrialist from Milan and his wife on a business trip to Belarus. He'd worked for them before and they were very satisfied with him. All right?'

It seemed to Sandro he was telling the truth. 'Since then?'

Savino shifted in his chair, looked thoughtful. 'Then he went off on his own business, he might have been on holiday for all I know. Come to think of it he did have a suntan when he turned up again in September. We didn't have anything for him then. I told them. I told the Carabinieri I had no idea what he got up to in his own time. No idea. None of my business.'

He stood abruptly, and automatically Sandro followed suit. Time was up.

Emerging into the warm drizzle on the Piazza Signoria, Sandro already had his mobile in his hand, but he paused. The receptionist had followed him with those soft brown eyes and as the door closed to Savino's office she had come around her desk to see him out.

'Is it true he was murdered?' she whispered.

Sandro inferred a soft spot for Giancarlo Vito, and shrugged apologetically. 'I don't suppose you know where he went on holiday, last year?' he had asked her gently, and with a glance at her boss's closed door her soft eyes had flickered with confusion.

Putting the mobile back in his pocket now, Sandro walked quickly across the big piazza, back to Rivoire, around the side to the tiny dead end of the Piazza Santa Cecilia. The cramped space held the anonymous back entrance to a luxury boutique, ceiling-high stacks of shoe boxes just visible through a linen curtain, and a row of wheelie bins. The bit the customers never saw.

Sandro stood a moment among the overflowing refuse, his back against the wall, then quickly he took out the magazine. He registered that it was dog-eared, and unless it was the alley, that it smelled faintly of garbage. He didn't look at the image, he looked at the line of print across the top. The price in dollars, no euro price. He turned it over and there was the distributor's sticker: *Curtis Circulation*, it said.

The phone rang in his pocket and he pulled it out in a panic, almost dropping the magazine before securing it under his arm, briefcase between his knees. Behind him a door opened and one of the barmen from Rivoire emerged in his black waistcoat, carrying a bucket of slops. He paused, lifting the lid of the nearest bin. Sandro returned his curious look with a contorted smile, praying the magazine was not visible.

An American magazine. And it hadn't been bought at one of Florence's kiosks but in the United States.

At his ear the voice wasn't Pietro's but Giuli's.

'I spoke to your girl last night,' she said. 'Your hooker? She told me who he got her in for . . . in the end.'

He listened to her but he already knew the name.

'The American,' she said. Brett Van Vleet. 'He wanted a threesome.'

'The wife . . . co-operated?' In the humid alley Sandro pulled at his collar. The magazine was sticky in his hand. Just wanting rid of it, he lifted the lid of the bin beside him, but stopped. It was evidence, wasn't it? He grappled with the briefcase between his knees.

'She didn't like it, apparently,' said Giuli. 'She went along with it once and Bruna said she looked like someone was killing her. Only then . . . he wanted the other kind.'

'The other kind?

She sighed. 'The other kind of threesome. Two men.'

He coughed and she went on. 'Another thing. It was him who paid her – Vito, I mean. Because Van Vleet never seemed to have any cash on him. Vito looked after her, she said.' A pause. 'Like a brother, she said.'

Sandro cleared his throat. Something came back to him, from last night. Something the beautiful girl at the Excelsior had said to him, before everything went fuzzy. *There's a word for boys like him.* Mariaclara in a chambermaid's outfit, and Vito hadn't been interested.

Giuli hung up and Sandro stood between the bins holding the mobile up in front of his face, thinking.

Van Vleet. Installed in the biggest suite in the Palazzo and talking about shipping the car back to America. But he brought dirty magazines over in his luggage, and got the house detective to pay his bills. Poor Therese. Luisa would laugh at him, for his pity. Wouldn't she? Did it make any sense at all? Her dog taken – probably dead, he registered absently – the shit still being smeared. Someone was telling her something?

But it wasn't just Therese being targeted. Marjorie Cameron had been locked in the steam room. Athene Morris, whose bracelet had gone. Sandro's head ached. He'd gone to the Excelsior to find out what Mariaclara knew about the damned bracelet and now for the life of him he couldn't get it straight in his head. It occurred to him that he should ask Athene Morris herself who she thought had taken it.

Nothing had happened to Magda Scardino, or Juliet Fleming.

But now Sandro. The magazine had been put in his bag by the same evil spirit, he was sure of it. The malice was the same. Dirty, vindictive. Personal.

Would a man play these tricks? Sandro couldn't conceive of it. The truth was, as he stood in that stinking alley, that it felt very much to him like nothing human at all. It felt to him as if the dog had been swallowed up by the Palazzo's grounds, as if the pale carpeted corridors were growing shit on their own skirtings, the dirty magazine had slid itself into the briefcase Luisa had given him. Something rising up from the building's cellars, like dank air, locking doors and breathing garbage smell.

The phone rang in his hand. His head spun with possibilities, water circling a drain. Who else had thought something nasty was going on at the Palazzo San Giorgio, before it even started?

'Hello?'

The journalist, that's who. John Carlsson.

It was Pietro. He wasn't phoning to congratulate Sandro on his new job, that much was instantly clear. Nor, as it turned out, to talk about his predecessor's murder.

'Hold on,' said Sandro. 'Start again. A suitcase?'

Chapter Fifteen

BEHIND THE BIG COMPUTER screen in the shabby little office Giulietta Sarto started up out of her seat when Elena came through the door. Under the spiky dark hair Sarto's face was ashen.

'I'm sorry,' said Elena. 'I didn't mean . . . I should have buzzed.' Only someone happened to have been emerging from the front entrance when she arrived at the door with the name-plate that said *Sandro Cellini, Investigations*, and Elena had taken her chance and slipped inside.

Sarto sat back down abruptly, the colour returning. 'It's you,' she said.

'You do remember me, then,' said Elena, looking her in the eye.

'Right,' said Giulietta – Giuli, only the teachers had called her Giulietta – her mouth set hard. 'You want to chew over old times? Happy schooldays. My prison reminiscences, my days on the street. That kind of thing?'

Elena felt herself scowl: John had once said it was her

favourite expression. 'I liked you,' she said. 'You looked after me, once.' She looked just the same, thought Elena, a bit rougher round the edges. Maybe she had been born old.

'No one liked me,' said Giuli, grumpily, but her face was clearing. Half her attention, Elena could see, was on the computer screen. Edging round, she saw that she had two windows open – an email with a blown-up attachment, and a page of newsprint. Swiftly Giuli moved to close the email, but not before Elena had seen the photo it contained was of a junkie shooting up in an alley. A subject heading: *Giulietta Sarto*. No other words.

'It's nothing,' Sarto said quickly. 'Someone's idea of a joke.'

'D'you know who it's from?' asked Elena.

Sarto looked at her, musing. 'Maybe,' she said eventually. 'Yeah. Maybe.'

She made no attempt to hide what was on the screen now: she even turned it a little so Elena could see it better. It was an American newspaper, the financial pages, by the look of it. A photograph of a flushed man she recognised from the night before and a headline that said: *Van Vleet Refinances: Hit By Fannie Mae.*

'Funny,' Elena said. 'What's that mean?'

'I think it means he's broke,' said Sarto. 'But not broke like us. Rich broke is different. All you have to do is refinance, apparently.'

'You're checking them out? The guests, I mean?' Elena had a weird feeling in her gut, something occurred to her. 'John must have been doing that too. He knows all about them, apparently.'

'Who's John?' Giuli eyed Elena sideways. 'What did you come here for?'

Elena looked into Giulietta Sarto's pale, weary face, and hesitated. Had this been a bad idea? 'My boyfriend,' she said finally. 'Or maybe he's my ex-boyfriend.' She stopped again.

Giuli eyed her, jaundiced. 'The sculptor? The guy last night? He didn't look very ex to me. Though if you want my advice . . .' She gave a little dry laugh like a cough. 'Scratch that.'

'He's not my boyfriend,' said Elena, flushing.

'Whatever,' said Sarto. 'So which boyfriend are we talking about?'

Elena felt sick. 'His name's John Carlsson,' she said eventually. 'We've been together a couple of months. Then a bit more than a week ago he just went. Disappeared. Didn't answer my messages.' She swallowed. 'I'm not the type to get a private detective out every time I'm dumped.'

'Sure.' Giuli's voice was rough but not unkind. 'Go on.'

Elena told her everything, from when John had first seen her through the window to Juliet Fleming's pitying hand on hers, the night before.

'She told me he'd come back,' she finished. 'He went over there, but he didn't come and find me.'

'Carlsson,' said Giuli slowly. 'Didn't he do a story on the place, early on?' She drew up another tab on her computer screen and there was the headline: *Pleasure Palace*. And a photograph, of faces in the dark, fireworks bursting behind them – and there was John's name, his byline, at the foot of the article.

'Hold on,' she said. 'Before I forget.' As Elena watched, Sarto created an email and drew up photographs, more faces that she recognised from last night. She pasted in one link, then another. *San Giorgio launch pics*. Giuli attached them to an email and sent them to Sandro Cellini, who would be her boss. The subject: *Residents.* She didn't put any message in.

Elena heard her sigh as she opened another window: a photograph of a bridge across a delta in northern Syria. Elena didn't know whether the thing was hideous or magnificent, but it was vast, like some huge dinosaur with its great concrete feet planted in a bleak marsh. Looking closely, the scale became more apparent, a small gaggle of human figures at one end of the bridge were no more than specks. Elena frowned, trying to concentrate on understanding the English. There was a link headed: *Bridge collapse disaster.* Giulietta clicked, and sent.

'Anyone else you'd like to have a look at?' she asked casually. 'That Professor's wife, I imagine she gets about a bit. Your Mr Lludic?' She leaned in to the computer and Elena stepped back, shaking her head.

'No,' said Sarto, 'you're not the type, are you? To spy on other people. But I'd say there's plenty for a journalist to get his teeth into among that lot.' Elena hugged herself, feeling a creep of fear. Where was he? 'You don't know he was using you, though.'

The gruff kindness in her voice was too much. It all spilled out and Sarto listened: she didn't laugh, or sneer. Elena told her how he'd drift in late, smelling of the Palazzo, cigar smoke and women. He'd stand at the window watching; he'd walk out into the street quickly to make calls.

'I think he might have done something, or seen something,' said Elena finally, and she sat, suddenly, on the chair beside Giulietta Sarto's. Sarto put a hand on her shoulder, and Elena smelled nicotine, saw the calloused yellow of a smoker's forefinger.

'He went over there, looking for someone,' said Elena. She hadn't formulated the thought even to herself, but it had been sitting there, since Juliet Fleming had told her last night in the dark that she'd seen him. 'I think John's in trouble.'

*

Sandro had gone straight to his office on arrival at the Palazzo San Giorgio, and shut the door behind him. The laptop he'd left there yesterday sat forlorn on the small desk, the only sign the room was his. Impotently, he'd opened it, shut it again. They'd been around two decades but still Sandro couldn't see the computer as his friend.

He'd left the door unlocked yesterday, and his briefcase in the office. Anyone could have gone in and slipped that magazine into it. He pressed his face to the narrow window and saw a slice of Danilo Lludic's big sculpture, standing there like the Trojan Horse. An outsider. He locked the door behind him and went back to the foyer, looking for Alessandra Cornell. He would have to tell her, sooner or later.

'She's in with Bottai?'

Lino nodded. 'He wants you out,' he said.

'Really,' said Sandro, unsurprised. He still hadn't worked out how much of what Pietro had told him he was going to say to Alessandra Cornell, but he certainly didn't want to say it in front of that buffoon Gastone Bottai.

A suitcase, left unclaimed in the hold of a budget coach at the train station. A big, cheap suitcase, the kind southerners might ship their belongings up and down the country in, everything bar the kitchen sink, tied up with string. Not the kind you'd associate with the Palazzo San Giorgio.

Scardino and Sir Martin Fleming emerged from the corridor, heads down in conversation, and instinctively both Sandro and Lino stepped back, making themselves small.

'I think we might even fly out tomorrow,' Scardino was saying, seeming barely aware of Sandro or the doorman. 'Magda says she'll come too, this time. Funny, she always said she hated Cairo.'

Fleming nodded. They hardly looked up as Lino leaned forward, holding the glass street door open for them. 'I'll be happy to put you in touch with our man over there,' said Fleming, and then the Englishman did look, one eye sliding round to catch Sandro's before flicking back. 'And then we'll see you in London.' And the door closed.

Automatically Sandro registered the information. They were leaving, and soon. The night Vito had been killed the couples had been out together, and after they got back Sir Martin Fleming had stayed outside to smoke his cigar.

Fleming stood there now, hands behind his back, talking to the lean Professor. Thick as thieves. The memory of his conversation with Fleming at the bar the night before came back to him, with the handsome Lauren Tassi drinking beside them in determined silence.

'I often think I should have given her a garden,' Fleming had said. Then, turning to Sandro, 'My wife. We never had a chance, moving around, you see. She'd have loved a garden.'

And something in the man's voice, some insoluble melancholy had made the hairs rise on Sandro's neck; he knew that fear so well. 'There's time now,' he'd said, and the Englishman had just looked at him. Then Lauren Tassi had leaned across and asked them if she had to drink alone, and Fleming had moved off.

He found he was holding his breath; he felt as though he'd been holding it since he'd ended his conversation with Pietro in the garbage stench of the Piazza Santa Cecilia. He needed a coffee, badly.

'We'll need to talk to them in the end,' his old partner had said, with a warning in his voice. 'However much your job is to protect them. It's not the kind of thing you can keep quiet.'

Sandro had half an hour, Pietro said. In which to talk to his boss and gain her permission to take the morning off because he had to get across the city to a low modern building that sat beside the motorway winding up into the Apennines. A building he had become very familiar with during his thirty years as a police officer – the city's morgue and forensic laboratory complex. Sandro needed to go there to look at something they had found in that suitcase.

Vito's body, of course, would be there too. That had only just occurred to him.

'You've missed the ladies,' said Lino, breaking into his thoughts. 'They went off with your wife, I believe.'

Sandro nodded. Luisa had called – not knowing he was still in the Piazza Santa Cecilia, twenty metres from the shop – to tell him what Frollini had let her in for. He'd said, he thought he knew whose the magazine was, at least; he told her about Van Vleet and the hooker too. Registering her stiff silence, he hadn't then told her what Pietro had called to tell him. What would be the point? She'd have freaked out even more. He'd seen the limousine glide past five minutes later but had stayed back in the alley's shade.

Now a figure in a brown and yellow polyester uniform appeared at the glass doors to the Palazzo San Giorgio and stiffly Lino leaned forward to admit him. He looked down at a registered envelope, and signed for it.

'Popular guy,' said the courier. 'Third time this week, isn't it?'

Sandro saw that the slim envelope, plastered with labels, was addressed to Ian Cameron.

'Personal shopping,' said Lino. 'In a limousine. Not all the husbands were delighted.' He flapped the envelope against his knuckles. 'This one, for example.'

'Looks like business,' said Sandro, nodding down at the envelope.

Lino looked at him, impassive. 'I'd stay off that subject if I were you,' he said. 'He likes those letters placed in his hand by me – or the courier – and no one else. I'm not making that mistake again.'

'Mistake?'

'A week or so ago I gave Vito one of the letters – well, he offered. Said he'd seen Cameron on the terrace and he'd take it to him. Half an hour later Cameron comes storming in and threatens to have me fired.' He allowed himself a smile. 'Touchy subject. He calmed down in the end. Miss Cornell . . . well, she defended me.'

Well, thought Sandro. Good for her. 'Quite right too,' he said.

Lino shrugged, still looking ahead, just a shade weary now. 'They're from a legal firm,' he said, in an undertone, then looked back at Sandro. 'That it?'

'You know how it is, Lino,' said Sandro. 'The more you know you shouldn't be asking questions, the more questions you seem to think of.'

There was the sound of hurrying feet in the corridor and both of them turned suddenly, to be faced with the maid Alice, her cheeks pink. When she saw Sandro her hand flew to the crucifix at her neck and then he remembered. Mariaclara.

'You all right?' His voice was gruffer than he intended.

She looked flustered. 'I was going to ask Lino something,' she said. They stood, expectant. 'Did Miss Morris go with the others? So I can let myself in to do her room.'

Lino shook his head. 'I don't know if they even asked her,' he said.

The girl was already backing down the corridor. What was she scared of? Him?

Luisa thought it might be someone who worked there, didn't she? A waiter spitting in the soup. Did Van Vleet put his old magazines out for the trash, did he leave them in his wastepaper basket, for the maid to empty?

'Hey,' Sandro called after her. 'I want to ask you something. About the recycling.'

And then, perhaps with the last of the alcohol departing his system, the fog in his head cleared and what Mariaclara had said returned to him. *He knew*, she'd said. He knew it wasn't me, because he knew who took the bracelet.

The face that appeared in the corridor in response to his call was not the maid's but Alessandra Cornell's, and it was stiff with disapproval. 'You wanted to talk to me,' she said. 'Perhaps somewhere more private?'

*

'Back here at three?' the driver said, squinting up into the sunshine from the leather-padded driver's seat of the limousine, and from where she stood, outside the arched white marble monstrosity that was the Chianti Outlet Village, reluctantly Luisa nodded. The smoked-glass window rose electronically and he disappeared, smile, sunglasses, peaked cap and all. Take me with you, she thought. I'm too old for this.

In the sun Luisa turned to face her clients.

She'd stared at the back of the driver's head for the entire journey, wishing she'd been smart enough to slip into the front seat beside him from the outset, no questions asked. It should have been a nice drive, half an hour down the bumpy potholed Siena *superstrada* under the hills. The green cool of ancient forests, and the handsome old villas looking down through their cypress avenues; a chance not to have to think. About the women behind her, about Sandro walled up in the Palazzo San Giorgio. About who had put that dirty magazine in his briefcase, and why.

But the young one – Mrs Van Vleet – had insisted Luisa sit in the back of the limousine with them. She looked pale and frightened, as if the others might turn on her, and she set herself beside Luisa, who tried not to think about what Sandro had told her, about the husband, and his hookers. No wonder she looked miserable. Luisa wondered if the other women knew.

'It's not like you're our servant,' Therese Van Vleet said, trying to smile.

Luisa had caught a look then from Magda Scardino, settling herself on the leather seat opposite, that implied something quite different. *Don't get any ideas*. Magda Scardino wasn't interested in getting to know other women. It turned out what she was interested in was money – and was careless about disguising it, with only women present. She also wanted Luisa to know her place.

'What kinds of discount can we expect?' she'd asked before they'd even left the city's limits. 'I mean, presumably we have you with us to negotiate a little something extra?'

Lady Fleming – *Juliet*, she'd said, *call me Juliet*, taking Luisa's hand briefly in her small dry paw, but of course Luisa would call her Lady Fleming, even if not out of propriety, for she wasn't a Juliet – also opposite Luisa on the other jump seat, had looked amused.

From Luisa's other side came a small sound almost of distress and Luisa turned in her seat. 'Really, Magda,' the engineer's wife said, tugging nervously at her sleeves. It was a warm day but she had a blouse buttoned to the neck and wrist: a Puritan sort of thing perhaps. Were the Australians Puritans? 'I don't think. . .' before tailing off under Magda Scardino's look of undisguised contempt.

'It's what she's here for, Marjorie,' Magda Scardino said. 'Isn't that right?'

'I suppose I might even treat myself to something,' said Marjorie Cameron, brightening.

'Oh, Marjorie.' What was in the tone? Exasperation? Pity? Magda Scardino didn't seem the pitying kind.

Luisa gave them all her card, to cover the awkward moment. Frollini had had them made for her last year, when they'd gone to New York for the shows, the one and only time. 'It's got my mobile number on it,' she said. 'If you need me once we separate. And you can show it to the *vendeuses* – the saleswomen – if I'm not there. For the discount.'

She didn't catch Magda Scardino's eye.

Carved out of a hillside just north of Siena, the mall was . . . perhaps not grim exactly, to most eyes, but Luisa's heart sank. They were on the edge of a discreet light-industrial area, landscaped with cypresses and box and a few roses about to come into flower, but all of it newly planted, the trees spindly, the box stunted. They went inside through a grandiosely vast arched entrance, a security guard hefty in a black suit and tie hardly giving them a glance. A long hall stretched out in front of them, almost empty, with shops' glassed-in boxes opening to either side. What if Frollini sent her to work in a place like this? Luisa in one of these faked-up cubbyhole shops, Sandro at the door in a cheap black suit. The whole thing horrified her. Was it snobbery?

It had been expensively constructed, of polished marble and speckled terrazzo; the roof was vaulted in a style supposed, Luisa decided, to suggest a cloister. There was at least some natural light, through inset windows high up: a glimpse of the sky, cleared to pale blue after the night's rain.

They entered the first shop, where handbags costing two months' salary were ranged in an interior that was meant to look like an English country house, Luisa guessed. She spotted the manageress and, leaving the four women to wander through the cavernous interior, nabbed her behind a counter full of scarves. Best to sort out the discount before anyone got to the till – and after an hour in the car with them, Luisa found she needed to put some space between herself and the ladies of the Palazzo San Giorgio.

The manageress was agog when she heard where they were from. 'Don't get too excited,' said Luisa. 'You know how the rich get rich. Tight, all of them. Except maybe the Russians.'

Suppose it wasn't a servant of the Palazzo playing dirty tricks. Suppose it was a guest? It might even be one of these women. She watched them move through the shop.

Juliet Fleming was looking at ties, very methodically. It was quite obvious to Luisa that Lady Fleming had not the slightest interest in shopping. Her clothes were transparently bought by mail order and she'd been wearing the same thing since she was twenty years old, but more significantly there was no trace of the chemical response that after thirty years on a shop floor Luisa could almost smell. Nor was she one to follow the herd. So what was she doing here?

To Therese Van Vleet on the other hand, shopping clearly came easily enough: she had separated herself from the others, and was looking through rails and cabinets mechanically. The manageress had fixed on her – the most stylish of the four – as her best hope, but as she watched, Luisa heard the manageress sigh, and silently agreed. Therese Van Vleet's heart wasn't in it. Sandro thought the magazine was her husband's: he'd told Luisa as much on the phone. 'I'll sort it, *cara*,' he'd said, but he'd sounded distracted.

And then Magda Scardino marched up and before they knew it had two saleswomen bringing out bag after bag after bag. Therese Van Vleet wandered away, murmuring something about coffee. Not understanding, as Luisa and certainly Juliet Fleming did, that this was a game, Marjorie Cameron started to offer suggestions – to another look of scalding disdain from Magda Scardino.

'Tell them I'll take those three for an extra ten per cent,' Magda said, her breath on Luisa's cheek, like a lioness's.

Juliet Fleming bought no handbag, nor did she buy a winter coat, a summer coat or a day dress. She didn't even seem bored; she simply evaded attention in each shop while Magda bartered and bullied and the Cameron woman clung obstinately, like an unwanted child. Then, to Luisa's astonishment, in the last shop – which specialised in eveningwear, rails and rails of floor-sweeping chiffon and stiff satin – Marjorie Cameron bought a cocktail dress.

It was dark red and cut low on the bosom, and when she came out of the changing room in it even Magda Scardino was taken aback. Marjorie Cameron had a surprisingly good figure, and her skin looked soft under the lights, even if above the rich fabric her face was too bare, her hair too formless. The dress had chiffon sleeves and, flushing under the gaze of the other women, she was back to tugging at them, as though trying to hide herself. To everyone's surprise, though, when she came back out she hurried to the cash desk with the dress, even before Luisa could negotiate the price with the saleswoman. She paid what was on the ticket, Magda pushing her way to the till too late to insist on her haggling, and Luisa saw something pass between them. Magda annoyed, Marjorie Cameron quietly determined.

'But what will Ian say?' Magda Scardino was being vindictive, no two ways about it. Because the Camerons were a couple for life?

Marjorie squirrelled the bag behind her, flushed. 'It'll be very useful,' she said. 'He likes me in red.' The atmosphere was poisonous.

'I think we need something to eat,' said Luisa hurriedly.

Upstairs, the bar was done up like Florian's in Venice, all wooden panelling and gilt mirrors. Magda parked herself at a table without ceremony. Marjorie Cameron hovered beside her, waiting in vain to be invited to sit, eventually clearing a place for herself among the heaped bags and Scardino's discarded layers. With relief, Luisa went to the bar. It wasn't until she'd placed their order and exchanged a weary smile with the woman behind the bar that she realised Juliet Fleming had followed her.

'Funny, isn't it,' Fleming said, nodding at the table where Marjorie Cameron was leaning forwards, hands in her lap, in an attitude of mute supplication while opposite Magda Scardino ignored her, examining herself instead in a small mirrored compact. Cameron took out a mobile phone and shyly set it on the table. Luisa was surprised to see that it was the most expensive one there was, the top version of the magic phone she and Giuli had talked Sandro into. Everything else about the woman was so modest, so muted; Luisa had had the firm impression Ian Cameron quarrelled with her over every expense. But then she remembered the children, scattered across the globe: it would be how she'd keep in touch. Perhaps he allowed her that.

Juliet Fleming spoke an excellent Italian, although like a certain kind of old-fashioned visitor she made no effort at all with her accent. It was a kind of arrogance, Luisa had always thought, although she supposed that it might also be modesty.

'Funny?'

'Their little sado-masochistic relationship,' Fleming said. 'It looks so one-way, doesn't it? Unrequited love. She wants to *be* Magda, do you see it? But you notice Magda doesn't ever quite dismiss her.'

She held Luisa's eye, mischievous. *Sado-masochistic,* thought Luisa, startled and entertained at once. She wondered, looking at that particular shade of Juliet Fleming's hair – the colour almost completely gone from it, the grey just turning to translucent white – how old she was, to be so bold and curious. The same age as me, almost exactly, Luisa decided.

'Whisky,' said Juliet Fleming to the woman behind the bar. 'Please.' And smiled, becoming unexpectedly charming suddenly. It was just after midday: smelling the alcohol, Luisa became aware of how very different this woman's life must have been from hers, and yet they were the same age. Was Marina Artusi right? Juliet Fleming didn't exactly look like an alcoholic to Luisa, but maybe there were all sorts. Alcoholics were bad news, she knew that much. They were reckless, they were dangerous. They could be vindictive.

'Five years in Saudi Arabia,' said the diplomat's wife, lifting her little glass in salute, giving the bottle's label a quizzical look. 'Not a drop.' Luisa saw something in her eyes that was not about pleasure or nostalgia. It was more as if the alcohol was a regime or a medicine.

'She's like that with men, too, of course,' said Fleming, and Luisa knew they were still talking about Magda Scardino. 'We have a word for it in English. Brazen. *Di ottone,* it means literally, made of brass. But also shameless, also one who can get away with any atrocity.' The smile returned abruptly and with it the charm, lighting up the quiet, anonymous little face. She set down the glass. 'It has a number of associations, and they all fit Magda Scardino.'

Juliet Fleming meant she was a bitch.

'But you're friends?'

Juliet Fleming turned her pale eyes on Luisa, who saw that the whites were dull, sickly. 'Oh, we get along. I admire her, in a way. She's a strong woman. And her husband is very intelligent. Very interesting. He's not well, you know. She can't be all bad, can she?'

Behind the bar the serving woman had loaded their tray: sandwiches, a salad, a bottle of water, two *cappuccini*. Luisa paid; would she be paid back? It occurred to her that Magda Scardino would certainly not hand over any money unless compelled.

'You've known her a long time,' said Luisa, hefting the tray.

Juliet Fleming held on to her whisky, gesturing with her free hand for Luisa to precede her. 'Oh, no,' she said, casually. 'I mean, we've run across each other. Over the years. Her husband, the Professor, well, he travels a great deal, conferences. His expertise is . . . controversial, so we've been aware. . .' She tailed off in a manner that struck Luisa as uncharacteristic, staying carefully out of her line of sight as she spoke.

'Controversial?' Luisa smiled politely, trying not to sound too nosy.

Juliet Fleming waved a hand. 'He's a scientist. A . . . what is it? An organic chemist, developing something or other.' She paused. Luisa didn't believe in this ignorance she professed. 'The diplomat's job is just to look after them, when they visit.'

'But now you're retired?'

Juliet Fleming just gave a little smile. 'Old habits,' she said.

Magda Scardino was leaning across the small table and speaking in a fierce undertone to Marjorie Cameron. Luisa shifted the weight of the tray, feeling the familiar ache along the lymph gland under her right arm, where the scar tissue was still new.

Juliet Fleming half turned. 'Of course, he wasn't married to her when he came to Saudi, he was on his first wife. I believe Magda was his PhD student.'

'His student?'

Juliet Fleming's smile curled up, not quite reaching her eyes, and Luisa knew she would not say any more.

As if she'd heard her name spoken, Scardino looked up and Marjorie Cameron sprang back as if physically released.

'Oh, you English,' said Scardino with sudden spite, sitting back on the buttoned velvet banquette like a kind of queen, Luisa thought, enthroned among her expensive carrier bags, 'and your drinking.'

Juliet Fleming regarded her thoughtfully, her hand curled around the glass, and said nothing. It was as though she was a servant who'd been reminded of her place. Luisa wondered why she deferred to Magda Scardino like that. The English and their drinking – and their good manners?

She laid down the tray and began to set things out on the table, but even with her head down she abruptly became aware of something different among them. She looked up, saw that all three other women had turned towards the mirrored and panelled entrance.

'Therese,' said Juliet Fleming quietly.

Therese Van Vleet was standing in the door: she had no carrier bags with her, and there was no mistaking the fact that she had been crying. She held her handbag out to them, a jumble of lipsticks and tissues. 'It's gone,' she said, her voice a rising wail. 'They took it. They've taken my money now.' And she swayed, and if Luisa hadn't got to her first, would have fallen.

Chapter Sixteen

SITTING IN THE WAITING room of the mortuary in front of a pile of dog-eared magazines – cars, health – Sandro tapped through his phone's address book. Had he put the man's direct line in? It was there. Maresciallo Carmine Falco: a senior officer in the Carabinieri who in a moment of weakness, perhaps, had thanked Sandro for helping solve the disappearance of a foreign girl during the November rains, three years earlier. A case that should, by rights, have been solved by the Carabinieri under whose noses the girl had been abducted, snatched from the Boboli Gardens, where the city's Oltrarno Carabinieri post stood among the landscaped irises and cedars. And Falco had said then, shaking his hand and perhaps thinking it no more than a gesture, *If you need anything.*

Falco had called the Palazzo this morning, and spoken to Cornell.

It was close to eleven-thirty now: Sandro had already been away from the Palazzo forty minutes. The smell was getting to him, layers he was familiar with, chemical freshener over chlorine over the thick farmyard reek of bodies opened. He'd told Cornell he'd be as quick as he could.

Pietro was on his way. The technical staff wouldn't tell Sandro a thing – let alone show him – until he got there, never mind that he recognised at least one of them from his time on the Polizia di Stato, when they used to clump in and out mob-handed to check out this or that case. He'd only been out six years, he sometimes forgot that.

As Alessandra Cornell had closed the office door behind her, Sandro had seen that she had a rash on her neck. It was getting to her. There was something imploring in the way she looked at him, and he'd taken the coward's way out. He had just asked her if there was any news.

Surprisingly there was. 'I had a call this morning from a Maresciallo of the Carabinieri,' she said. 'A courtesy, he said. They're following up leads. A man was seen by a neighbour leaving Vito's building at around one on the night he was killed.' The rash on her neck seemed to be calming a little. 'He – Maresciallo Falco – was keen to reassure me, it seemed. They will not be making any more details of the case public in the short term, there won't be any press conferences for the foreseeable future, so perhaps we can contain it. The bad publicity.'

'Great,' Sandro had said heartily. Falco, he'd thought. Making a special phone call – why? But the man seen leaving the building was presumably not an invention. 'Well, that's progress.'

Unless the man turns out to be someone we know, of course.

'What was it you wanted to talk to me about?' Cornell was suspicious now.

And he'd just told her the truth – or some of it. 'A suitcase has turned up at the train station,' he said. 'An ex-colleague tipped me off. They think it might belong to someone here.' She'd looked faintly alarmed: if she knew what they'd found in it, he thought, it would be more than alarm. 'Best if I have a look, don't you think?'

'If you're sure it's necessary,' Cornell had said, the anxiety still there. The rash was back.

'I'm sure there's nothing to worry about,' he'd lied. And looked away. 'It shouldn't take long.'

Looking like she just didn't want to hear any more bad news, she'd let him go.

Pietro looked harassed when he finally pushed through the door, and he hadn't done a very good job on his morning shave. 'They called me at three,' he said, catching Sandro's look, rubbing his chin. Then, 'It's not pretty.'

And it wasn't. The technician who showed them into the pathology lab was the one Sandro had already recognised, and Sandro felt the man watching for a reaction as he drew back the sheet.

White Caucasian male, dark hair on the torso, extensively discoloured where blood had pooled in the tissues that had sat undermost, principally at the front of the abdomen and chest. The suitcase must have lain with him face-down in it in the baggage compartment.

He had been partially disarticulated. Which meant in this case that the ball and socket joints had been hacked through at the shoulder and the hip. The brief and shocking image of a butcher taking a cleaver to a chicken carcass came into Sandro's head, the crack of bone, sinew yellow against red. The limbs were not fully detached. Which did not mean that the body was whole.

'They did that to get him in the suitcase,' said Pietro.

The face was battered and discoloured, a faint gleam of broken teeth through bloodied lips, of cornea under bruised lids. Sandro wouldn't vomit: that reflex was long gone. He stared at it for some time. He remembered the man's grin, in the dark, on the warm terrace, and he felt something expand in his chest. Fear.

'Where's the suitcase?' he said eventually.

'You know him, don't you?' said Pietro, and Sandro felt his partner's eyes on him, reading him as easily as a mother reads her child. He turned to him.

'First things first,' said Sandro. 'I want a look at the evidence.'

*

Alone in the office now, Giuli stood at the window, looking down into the Via del Leone. The sky was clearing and a girl from the hairdresser's was smoking on the gleaming pavement in a grubby pink cotton coat, the cigarette cupped in her hand to hide it. Just watching her, Giuli wanted one herself. She was down to five a day, on Enzo's orders.

'Did you know the guy who was killed?' she had said when Elena Giovese had finished telling her. Something in the way Elena had described her John Carlsson looking down into the street had sparked the question. She regretted it almost immediately.

'Killed? What guy?' Elena's frown was gone, her arms hanging and eyes wide in the dim room.

'What guy?' Her face was white.

'It's all right,' said Giuli patiently. The girl's fingers dug into her arm.

'The security guy,' Giuli said. 'The one before my boss, before Sandro. His name was Giancarlo Vito. I guess you must have seen him?' She had pushed the crumpled edition of the *Corriere* across the desk. 'Here.'

Elena stared at the page, her knuckles white where she gripped the paper. 'It's not him,' she said. 'It's not John.'

It was Giuli's turn to frown. 'Of course it's not him,' she said. 'Weren't you listening?' She'd taken the paper from her but Elena had gone on staring at it.

'I'm getting married,' Giuli had said. Just blurted it out, before she could think what effect it would have. Another stupid thing to say: had she meant, not all men are bad? Elena had looked at her bewildered. 'I mean, if it can happen to me. . .' Giuli said, feebly, by way of explanation. 'There'll be someone else. You could just walk away.'

Giovese had drawn her thick dark brows together at that. A long pause, and then she spoke. 'You hated that place, too, didn't you?' Bitterly. 'The pleasure palace. The last place he was seen.'

Still watching the girl on the pavement in her little pink uniform, dragging on the last of that cigarette as if her life depended on it, Giuli called Sandro. When he answered he sounded weird, breathless, as if he'd just climbed three flights of stairs. There was traffic in the background. She thought she'd misheard when he told her he was at the morgue. 'I'm still working it out myself,' he'd said when she asked him why. 'You go first.'

'There's this guy,' she said. She told him the whole story, as

Giovese had told it to her.

He said nothing, and she sighed. 'You know, the truth is, Carlsson's probably just done a runner. Trying to get a story, it didn't work out, he's moved on.'

What with the bad line and the traffic noise it took her a while to register the particular quality of Sandro's silence, growing heavier as she spoke.

He'd cleared his throat. 'And what about – ah – your business with the Women's Centre? Best to just put it behind you, don't you think?'

'Maybe,' she said, distracted. She'd deleted the anonymous email. Stupid. Something in the email address had snagged on her memory but she'd put her finger down on the delete button all the same. She sighed. 'There's something you're not telling me, Sandro.'

A silence. Then a sigh. 'I met her boyfriend at the launch,' said Sandro. 'This John Carlsson.'

'Right,' she said, taken aback. 'So what do you think?'

'I liked him,' he said. 'He told me there were a few people he recognised at the Palazzo, and I got the impression he didn't like them much.' She waited, and when he spoke again his voice was low and tired. 'Pietro just called me to say they'd found a body in a suitcase, left on a coach at the station.'

'I don't understand,' said Giuli. 'Why'd he call you?' A silence, a sigh. 'Shit,' she said. 'It's connected, isn't it? Have you told Luisa? Shit.'

'It's the journalist,' said Sandro, and he sounded old. 'It's John Carlsson.'

Shit.

Chapter Seventeen

STANDING BY THE SIDE of the roaring ringroad as he hung up on Giuli, all Sandro could think was, he'd take the bus. The taxi ride there had made him feel uncomfortable, alone and idle in the back seat, unable to converse with the driver for the clamour in his head. He felt like sitting among ordinary people.

There was so much in this case, so much noise, so much distraction, and every time he headed back to the Palazzo San Giorgio it crowded in on him again. The faces, the tricks, the muffled corridors. It was like a bell jar, an isolation tank; invisibly it squeezed his brain until nothing made sense and all he could feel was the fear.

'Do you think there's a killer in there? At the Palazzo?' Pietro had asked him, and with that straight question he had felt the pressure in his head ease. Just the sight of his old partner's face had said it to him. Simplify.

The bus was already crowded. Sandro watched as a stout elderly lady ousted a tourist boy from a seat, got out a mobile phone and began to harangue her son. A little group of Japanese girls came on at the Fortezza da Basso, outlandishly dressed. Circling the city centre on the ringroad, the bus filled up and everyone jostled at eye level; every now and again a glimpse of the Duomo down a long straight road appeared, and Sandro sat and let himself be lulled. The sun came out and shone through the dusty windows.

A killer. They'd looked down at the battered face together, and Sandro had thought of the big façade concealing the closed doors, the underground rooms. 'Yes,' Sandro had said at last, turning to his old friend.

A man had done this: fact. No woman could have heaved the suitcase into the coach's belly. Carlsson had come back from a trip and gone straight to the Palazzo to find someone. And now he was dead.

The suitcase had wheels. The killer might have got it on and off a bus, in and out of a taxi, some way from the station, and innocuously, casually, walked with a thousand others up that ramp. The body had been wrapped in clingfilm inside, and besides, hadn't had much blood left in it, but fluids had oozed, eventually, staining the cheap cloth.

The bus was stuck in traffic to the east of the big Carabinieri barracks by the river. Sandro could see a couple of officers in their peaked caps idling at the barrier.

Frowning, Pietro had laid a plastic bag in front of Sandro: inside it an envelope with the embossed logo of the Palazzo San Giorgio, folded and stained.

'It was in his pocket.' He looked up. 'It's how we made the connection with the place.'

'He was clothed?'

Pietro reached for a large evidence bag under the trolley. Through the plastic Sandro could see a white shirt heavily stained with blood, grey wool trousers. Not casual: the kind of thing you would wear if you needed the doorman to admit you. 'The partial disarticulation was done through the clothing, and efficiently, one stroke for each joint. Someone knew what they were doing.'

Pietro shook the envelope out beside the body, and with a gloved hand delicately extracted its contents.

The bus shifted again, the two *carabinieri* watched it pass. Simplify: every time Sandro tried, another complication turned up.

A bracelet had fallen out of the envelope, a simple antique bangle of gold set all round with dark red stones. Garnets? Luisa would know. Athene Morris's bangle. Where had Carlsson got it?

Pietro had lifted the bangle between gloved forefinger and thumb and held it up to the fluorescent light. On the soft old gold inside, two letters were engraved. M and A.

'Funny way to do it,' Sandro said. 'Backwards? Morris, Athene.'

'You know whose it is?'

Sandro nodded. 'It didn't get there by accident, did it? Someone left it there on purpose, for us to find.' He raised his head and spoke softly, so the technician didn't hear. 'Are you going to pass this on to our brothers in dark blue?' The Carabinieri.

'Not quite yet,' Pietro had said. 'I tried to talk to them about the Vito case yesterday and got nowhere. I'm damned if I'm going to run straight over there with this.'

'You tried to talk to them? Before . . .' Sandro gestured at the body on the gurney. 'Before this?'

Pietro looked exasperated. 'Well, I wanted to know. You're my friend, you got Vito's job. I knew you'd need information. Anyway, the guy – my usual contact there, little guy I did a favour for last year – he wouldn't even take my call.' Shook his head. 'I tell you, there's something odd about this case.'

In the glittering dark of the Excelsior Terrace, Mariaclara had said, leaning down over the bar so he saw a glimpse of cleavage, 'Giancarlo knew exactly who had taken that bracelet. He was biding his time, is all. Working out when he could use the information.' She'd straightened. 'He didn't tell me, so don't bother asking.' And turned her back.

He closed his eyes. A man killed Carlsson. The same man who killed Giancarlo Vito? They were both in the Palazzo San Giorgio to nose out information, the journalist and the detective. Were they both killed for having found out the same thing?

As he considered the physical labour of killing a man, then methodically hacking into his joints like a butcher, for some reason the Palazzo's cellars, which he still had not visited, presented themselves to him. The steam room? And of course there was another place, the room with its dirt floor already stained with blood, that had been bricked up. He pondered a suitcase wheeled up into the elevator and out through the front door: would Lino even notice? Lino wasn't always there.

It would take strength and nervelessness, a certain kind of lunacy. He thought of the men in the Palazzo San Giorgio. Leaving out motive for the moment, concentrating on the physical capacity. Little Mauro, skinny old Lino. No. Brett

Van Vleet, the youngest of them, ex-soldier? Yes. Wiry Ian Cameron, high-minded Scardino? Yes – if they needed to do it badly enough. Sir Martin Fleming? Middle aged, but powerful. Diplomats had all sorts of training, no doubt. The thought set something ticking in his mind.

'Time of death?'

Pietro had just shaken his head at the question. 'With the heat . . . they're not a hundred per cent yet on that yet, and they're refusing to say. Bunch of old women, these scientists.' The technician had looked back at them, affronted.

Off the bus now and walking up the steep cant of the Costa San Giorgio, Sandro fixed his gaze on the sky at the top of the hill. Leaves overhung the walls of a garden, sparkling with the early rain, and something smelled sweet. He dialled Maresciallo Carmine Falco.

'Whom shall I say?' Not quite a direct line, then. The secretary sounded haughty.

Sandro waited. The voice, when it came, was warm, lazy, benign: he needed benign. But it also represented a shift of power: Sandro had helped the man out, but three years had passed and now it was Sandro with his cap out.

'Mr Cellini,' said Maresciallo Falco. The man came back to Sandro: lean and dark in his high-ceilinged office overlooking the neglected Renaissance hedges and paths of the Boboli gardens; a southerner, as many *carabinieri* were. Not stupid, merely with a certain complacency that went with the uniform and the pension, a certain requirement always to begin any negotiation with a smokescreen of politesse and denials. 'What a pleasure.'

'Giancarlo Vito,' said Sandro, not wanting to spin this out. The man remembered him at least, that was something. 'I've got his job. Before he was found dead, as a matter of fact, so I don't want you putting me in the frame.'

'Ah,' said Falco. Not so much interested as calculating. Turning guarded. 'In that case I had the pleasure of speaking with your boss this morning.'

'Very courteous of you,' said Sandro.

'Well, I don't envy you that position,' said Falco, hearty now. 'A high-powered bunch, I bet, and foreigners. Your English improving, is it? But I still don't know what you want, Cellini.'

Sandro stopped walking, just downhill from the Palazzo San Giorgio. It came to him then, it came to him out of the blue spring air, it looked down on him from the shuttered windows of the Palazzo. The danger *was* here.

'A man was seen by a neighbour coming out of Vito's building,' he said. 'Is that right?'

Falco cleared his throat. 'It's one of a number of lines of inquiry,' he said.

'Any physical details on the man?' He made his voice tough: policeman to policeman.

Falco cleared his throat again. 'You know how witnesses are, keen to stick their oar in, but when it comes to details, they go all vague.' A pause. Then, reluctantly, 'Well built, that's all.'

Sandro absorbed that. Vague, all right. 'And what about the drugs angle? Your officer mentioned it yesterday. Asked about drugs.'

'Well . . .' Falco was hedging again.

Sandro calculated that the news that the body in the suitcase was also connected to the Palazzo San Giorgio would reach him by the end of the day. He kept the edge to his voice. 'Well? It's obviously a matter of concern. There was no suggestion of that while he worked here. It's a rumour that could be very damaging.' Sandro was keenly aware that he didn't have a whole lot of leverage, and it might be better to appeal to Falco's better nature. 'You can see my predicament. I have to contain things.'

Falco sighed, acknowledging the favour called in. 'There are other complications, let's say. Domestic. His . . . private life. As for drugs, I don't know. Steroids, maybe, but that's not what you mean, is it?' Cagey: he was giving himself time to think. To throw up some smokescreen.

'How was he found? I know nothing, you see.'

'Oh, the landlady.' Falco almost chuckled. 'She thought he'd gone on holiday, was her cover story, she wanted to be sure he'd turned the gas off. Or something.'

'And what did she find?'

A sigh. 'Blunt head trauma,' said Falco. 'A blow to the back of the neck.' A pause. 'He was naked. On his way to bed, perhaps.'

Sandro digested that. Taken by surprise – a man with Vito's training would have had to have been. 'So, by complications . . . you mean women?' He paused. Could a woman have killed a man built like Vito? It would depend how vulnerable she'd made him. For some reason the image of Magda Scardino drifted into his head, and stuck there.

There was a long pause, that grew. 'Not women,' Falco said abruptly.

'Not women?' Sandro frowned to himself, feeling slow and stupid. 'You mean he was homosexual?' He could hear himself;

he could hear Luisa and Giuli laughing at him. *It happens, Sandro.* Of course it did. It would explain why he hadn't made a move on the gorgeous Mariaclara.

'He was gay?' Sandro lowered his voice to a hiss, and as he did so Lino stepped out on to the doorstep of the Palazzo. 'Who says?' He felt aggrieved, he couldn't help it. It seemed like insult to injury: he couldn't even blame female susceptibility for Vito's employment. His mind turned to those threesomes Giuli had talked about. Van Vleet.

'Oh, the *padrona di casa.*' The landlady. 'She says she's glad he's gone, he was obviously a promiscuous homosexual and she doesn't allow those.'

'Perhaps I should go and talk to her.' Sandro was almost talking to himself, but Falco cut in at once.

'I don't think so, Cellini.' Unmistakably a warning. And Falco barked something away from the phone, his hand over the receiver so Sandro only heard a muffled order.

'I'd like to be of help,' said Sandro, on full alert now for Falco's response.

'If you want to help, stay out of it,' said Falco. And hung up.

*

Luisa was in the marble-tiled washroom of the mall. A Medusa head in mosaic looked down on her from above inlaid mirrors; a stocky Filipina in a pale-green uniform who was wiping out the sinks was watching her like a hawk.

'Let me look,' Luisa had said in the café, while the woman behind the bar pretended not to stare, and she'd taken Therese

Van Vleet's bag from her. 'Are you sure you put your purse in there this morning?'

Van Vleet had looked at her wonderingly. 'I – I . . .' She didn't seem to be able to think. Was she being deliberately tormented? It occurred to Luisa that most of the nasty tricks did seem to centre on the American. Starting with the little dog down the well.

'It was in there, Therese.' Marjorie Cameron had stepped forward. 'I saw it in the foyer. Don't you remember? You were looking for your lipstick.'

Therese focused on her gratefully. Magda Scardino snorted.

'It probably fell out in the limousine,' said Juliet Fleming. She looked tired now, the whisky glass empty in her hand.

'It's too much.' Therese Van Vleet pressed a handkerchief to her mouth. 'It's too much. It's not the purse, it's just the latest; it's all too much. She was gazing at Magda Scardino for reasons Luisa couldn't fathom. 'My little Georgie, my dog, he was taken. The – the mess. And then Giancarlo – Giancarlo's died, doesn't anyone understand that?' She looked pleadingly from one face to another.

In her pocket Luisa's phone thrummed, once, to indicate a message. 'That could be the driver now,' she said, taking it out, although she could see the missed call was from Sandro. 'Mrs Van Vleet, just sit down a moment. I'll go to the mall's help desk, and I'll call the driver. I'm sure there's no need to worry.'

The truth was, Luisa just wanted to get away from them for five minutes. Van Vleet's naked helplessness made her anxious, and the other women clustering round her didn't seem to be helping. A quarter of an hour with the lost property department – a defensive young woman behind a desk, who thought the mall was being accused of something – didn't get her anywhere. The purse hadn't been handed in. The driver – who took so long to answer, she suspected he was sleeping in the car somewhere – told her he couldn't see it in the back of his vehicle. She told him they'd want picking up sooner than expected.

Luisa headed back to the Caffè Barocco. From a hundred metres she could see they were all still sitting there, and she stopped. The restroom door just before the cafe beckoned: the thought of sitting in a cubicle on her own was infinitely preferable to dealing with Magda Scardino's disdain. Five minutes, she told herself. And she needed to talk to Sandro.

In the event she didn't even get a chance to say hello and Sandro was off. Telling her things she could hardly believe, and didn't much want to hear.

A body found in a suitcase.

The disappearance of Therese Van Vleet's purse receded; she forgot where she was. There was a small hard seat in the corner of the restroom and she sat on it. He finally ran out of steam.

'Are you there?' he asked, into the stunned silence.

'Should I tell them?' she asked.

'Time enough for that,' he said. 'Christ knows how the Palazzo will survive it.' A pause. 'How are they reacting? Have they talked about . . . Vito?'

She considered, thinking of the young American woman looking from one face to the next. 'Therese Van Vleet's taking it hardest. Plus she's lost her purse – long story. Nothing's turned up there, has it? She seems to think it's all about her.'

'Really,' said Sandro thoughtfully. 'No, no purse here. I'll ask Lino.'

Something occurred to Luisa. Did Therese Van Vleet crave the attention? 'These people are peculiar,' she said. 'Juliet Fleming follows Magda Scardino around like she's her minder, though she can't seem to stand the woman. As for Vito – Marjorie Cameron seems to be in shock, Magda Scardino doesn't seem to give a damn.' She paused. 'Juliet Fleming is so . . . so English.'

Sandro laughed abruptly. 'I suppose being a diplomatic wife you just have to hide it all, everything. Can't you see her sitting upright in some terrorist video while they prepare to execute her?'

'Sandro!' Luisa was shocked. 'That's actually horrifying.' He was right, though, and now the thought was in her head she couldn't eradicate it. She liked Juliet Fleming. She had admired the woman, for her restraint. But the thought of maintaining that level of self-discipline to her deathbed suddenly seemed terrible.

'They hardly knew Vito,' she said, by way of excuse. 'How long? A month?'

'And yet Therese Van Vleet bursts into tears over it?'

'She's young.' Luisa stood up, suddenly feeling old herself. 'We'll talk about this when we get back,' she said.

The bathroom attendant had stopped pretending to clean and was staring at her. She fished out a coin and put it in the saucer, but the woman didn't move.

'He was gay,' said Sandro, almost in an aside. 'So Falco – the *carabiniere* – says.'

'Gay?' There were voices beyond the door. Luisa didn't know why the fact should astonish her, but it did. 'Sandro? I'd better go. We'll be back this afternoon. Perhaps, well, maybe a bit earlier than we thought.'

Luisa hung up. With the Filipina still giving her that look, she put the phone away and entered one of the stalls, just because that, nominally, was what she was here for. She heard the heavy outer door open and hiss closed: footsteps. Heels. She closed the lid and sat down. Staring at the expensive fake-Roman marble tiling, Luisa found herself suddenly overwhelmed by the claustrophobic awfulness of the place.

'It can hardly have been a surprise. Vito had it coming.'

The voice was Magda Scardino's; she spoke with lazy indifference. 'That man? Knowing what he was like? I could see what he wanted from the beginning.'

Luisa closed her eyes: if she was going to make her presence known she should do it now. She didn't move. They were speaking in English – if the worst came to the worst she could just play the stupid Italian, and feign ignorance. But she understood it all.

'She's not much more than a child.' It was Juliet Fleming.

'Therese? She's certainly behaving like one. She wants the attention. If you ask me, she never had the purse. I certainly didn't see it.' A silence. 'She's been alone most of the morning, she could have done anything with it.'

'It's a possibility.' Juliet Fleming pondered it judiciously.

The door opened with a creak.

'Marjorie.' Magda Scardino's voice was flat. 'You haven't left Therese on her own?'

The tap ran. They, at least, were not pretending to be in there for any reason other than privacy for their conversation. And unlike Luisa, they were practised at ignoring the staff.

'You shouldn't be so hard on her,' said Marjorie Cameron, braver than Luisa had expected.

'You,' said Magda with disdain. 'Always damned well mothering, even when it's not expected of you any more. What a waste of time. Let Therese stand on her own two feet, and deal with what's coming to her.'

'What's that?' said Juliet Fleming quietly.

'Oh, we all know what they were up to, the three of them. Their little threesomes. It'll come out, now Giancarlo's dead.'

'I expect all sorts of things will come out,' said Juliet Fleming.

'What do you mean? What do you mean?' Marjorie Cameron had become agitated.

'Oh, for God's sake, Marjorie. It was your own husband turned him in. Got him sacked. You know exactly what I'm talking about.' Magda Scardino drew breath. 'I expect Giancarlo wanted money, and someone didn't want to pay.'

Magda certainly seemed to know what she was talking about, Luisa reflected from inside her cubicle. Was she talking about herself?

'It all comes down to money, in the end, does it?' said Juliet Fleming softly. 'You don't think he wanted anything more?'

Such as? wondered Luisa. Juliet Fleming knew something.

But Magda Scardino wasn't listening. 'Oh, yes,' she said. 'People are so . . . snobbish about it. I know what they think of us – of me. But take Athene.' There was an indrawn breath, soft. 'You think Athene would appear so marvellous to them all if she were living in an old people's home in some miserable little English town? A wealthy ex-lover is a useful thing.'

A silence. The attendant murmured something and there was a chink of coins.

Luisa simply couldn't do it any more. She stood, flushed, waited the obligatory three seconds, came out. She didn't even have to make eye contact with the women: for them she might as well not have existed. She washed her hands and left.

Chapter Eighteen

IT WAS ALMOST AS though the Professor was blocking Sandro's path. He stood in the foyer where the corridor led down to the library, and to Alessandra Cornell's office. The room smelled of flowers: a big vase of lilies had replaced the orchid and the scent was overpowering.

On his way to Cornell's office Sandro had been looking down at his phone, because he'd just had a message from Pietro. *They're saying seventy-two hours, more or less.* He had looked up, calculating, and there was Scardino. John Carlsson had been dead three days: last seen here three days ago. Who had he come to see?

Sandro pocketed his phone.

'We haven't properly met,' Scardino said, holding out a hand with an odd stiffness.

It wasn't as though Sandro wanted to have that conversation with Alessandra Cornell; he was dreading it. He felt sure that for some obscure reason she would blame him for the discovery of another body connected with the Palazzo San Giorgio.

He took Scardino's hand. 'And I gather you're off tomorrow?' he said.

The Professor's pale grey eyes grew amused. 'You have sharp ears, Mr Cellini,' he said. 'Indeed. We're off to Cairo, my wife and I.' A pause. 'Shall we?'

He gestured towards the garden doors, and Lino obediently stepped forward, poised to open them. Sandro hesitated. He might not want to talk to Alessandra Cornell, but Athene Morris was another matter. He looked up instinctively, imagining the old lady moving slowly through the pale padded corridors above them, peering in at doors.

But Athene Morris might have come down to the garden by now: it was almost one, and warm.

'Why not,' he said.

On the upper terrace the canvas chairs had been set out again, but there was no sign of the old Englishwoman. Scardino looked pale in the sunlight, and insubstantial; he sat down with care, as if something might break.

Standing, Sandro breathed in the fresh scent of rain and earth and early jasmine and looked back up at the façade. Made for one great man, not half a dozen wealthy couples; no Medici would have let himself be squeezed into a luxury apartment. But power took a different shape these days. It bounced between mobile phone masts and satellites, down oil pipelines, virtual money on computer screens transferred at the touch of a pad. Somewhere were there still bank vaults stacked with gold, gleaming underground? Almost certainly there were.

'You were talking to my colleague last night,' said Scardino, breaking into his thoughts.

'I was?' Sandro sat, warily.

The maid Alice appeared, fingering that crucifix nervously. 'Coffee,' said Scardino, without asking Sandro.

'Lauren. Dottoressa Tassi,' Scardino said, when she'd gone. 'Nice girl. Clever.' There was a question in his voice.

Sandro grimaced. 'Truth is, I can't remember what we talked about. I'm not used to these evenings. Cocktails.' He rubbed his head.

'Ah.' Did Scardino sound relieved?

'I think the Dottoressa might have woken up with a similar kind of head this morning,' said Sandro. 'Neither of us will have been making much sense.' Something occurred to him. 'She might have mentioned your work?' he tried.

Scardino smiled, relaxing. 'Enough to send you to sleep without the cocktails,' he said. 'Practically garbage disposal, hardly glamorous. I'm researching biofuels. Generating ethanol from various substances. Algae, for example.'

'Oh.' Sandro was obscurely disappointed: had he hoped for viruses, or nuclear warheads? And if he had been worried about what Tassi might have said to him, it wasn't to do with his research.

The coffee arrived. Sandro tried to catch the girl's eye but she hurried off before he could say anything. He turned back to see Professor Scardino lifting the cup to his lips; oddly, he held it with both hands, and even then seemed to be having difficulty getting it to his lips.

Scardino saw the look. 'Parkinson's,' he said. 'Medication hasn't kicked in yet.'

The calculation that had been silently going on in the back of Sandro's mind shifted, a piece of the puzzle moving into a new place. Fact: Scardino couldn't have lifted that suitcase, couldn't even have got it as far as a waiting taxi.

'It's all right,' Scardino said. 'I'm in a privileged position. I have access to the best medication. They're talking about new treatments, ultrasound deep-brain stimulation. And if that doesn't work, well . . . my job doesn't require manual dexterity these days.' He set the cup down. The city stretched out below them, hazy in the spring sun.

'A lot of travel, though,' said Sandro. 'So you're not retired, after all.'

'My wife wouldn't let me retire,' the Professor said drily. 'Besides, they say I've got at least another ten years' useful life.' It didn't sound like much to Sandro, said like that.

'Are you going with the Flemings, to Cairo? Or did I get that wrong?'

'You got that wrong,' said Scardino. 'Lady Fleming has to be in London for some . . . procedure or other, they're off tomorrow too.' He paused. 'We're all getting old, bits going wrong. It's not that we don't trust the Italian doctors, you understand.'

Scardino with Parkinson's, and Fleming's wife. Marina Artusi had said to Luisa, *They call it a disease.* It came to him that they were both dying, perhaps slowly, perhaps not. He felt the need of a superstitious gesture to ward something off.

Watching him, the Professor smiled again, and Sandro saw calculation. 'What are they saying about Giancarlo, do you know? Are the police keeping you informed?'

A door opened further along the façade.

Was this what he'd been brought out here for? Sandro grimaced apologetically. 'Not much news, I'm afraid. They're talking to his neighbours, a man was seen leaving his apartment late at night, that's all I know.'

'A man,' Scardino murmured. 'They're sure?'

Sandro shrugged. 'The Carabinieri are always sure, especially when they're wrong,' he said, and was rewarded with a smile. 'Did . . . did you ever meet a journalist called John Carlsson?' he asked, casually.

Sandro deliberately looked away as he asked the question, down the terraced garden, to where the soft tumble of blue flowers marked the boundary. He could just about see the old neighbour on her balcony below, a sketchy figure in a pale overall standing in her doorway.

Scardino sat up a little and raised a hand to shade his eyes, and Sandro looked back at him. The man's hand was steady now: the medication must have kicked in.

'Carlsson? Yes, of course. He's often here. I don't much like talking to journalists.' He paused. 'Especially those who consider themselves to be experts on the environment. But he's a sharp guy. Worth talking to – even if you're not quite sure what he's after. But that's journalists for you.' His smile seemed quite untroubled. And he'd used the present tense throughout.

'Recently back from a trip down south, Lady Fleming said.'

'Oh, yes,' said Scardino readily. 'That would figure. He once told me he spent a couple of months down there last year, on a story. Very beautiful, I believe. Bari.' He sat up in the canvas chair, looking over Sandro's shoulder.

Turning, Sandro saw Bottai, with Brett Van Vleet. He got awkwardly to his feet.

Bari.

'The ladies are on their way back,' Bottai said, talking past him to Scardino, who frowned down at his watch. 'So we'd better look busy, wouldn't you say?'

Sandro saw that beside him Brett Van Vleet had the stance of a truculent schoolboy. He held an envelope in one hand, with the Palazzo's crest in one corner, his name handwritten on it. When he saw Sandro looking, he moved his hands behind him and straightened like a soldier. Bottai had moved away, distancing himself. He was sitting now, beside Scardino.

The long doors to the foyer opened and Lino appeared, an old ghost exposed to the sun. He was holding something in his hand. He hesitated a moment, then approached.

I found this,' Lino said nervously, holding it out to Van Vleet. It was a slim black wallet, expensive-looking. 'It was in the foyer. It had fallen behind the table.'

'Van Vleet took it from him roughly. 'Oh, yes?' he said. 'Found it?'

'It's your wife's,' said Lino, lowering his eyes.

'I know that,' the American snapped, and immediately opened it, in front of the doorman. It was obvious that he was checking to see if anything was missing. Over his shoulder Sandro could see a substantial number of banknotes, undisturbed.

Humiliation rose in the doorman's face. 'I haven't looked inside,' he said stiffly.

Sandro looked at Van Vleet's flushed cheeks, his big-knuckled hands going through his wife's purse. His dirty magazines, his threesomes, that crested envelope Bottai had handed him, the man seen leaving Vito's house late the night he died.

'Mr Van Vleet,' he said. 'I wonder if I might—'

But then there was a kind of muted commotion and Alessandra Cornell was there, hurrying along the palace's façade under the bougainvillea. Beside her was the shambling figure of Danilo Lludic, and the maid Alice in their wake. There was something in the way they approached, ungainly in their hurry, that sounded an alarm in the quiet garden.

Cornell came up in front of them, breathless.

'It's Athene,' she said. 'Can you come?'

The rash on her neck had spread.

*

Giuli stood in a doorway on the Piazza Tasso, watching. The cigarette in her hand, the second of the day, was half smoked: she'd lit it from one the hairdresser's girl had held up to her wordlessly as she emerged from the office.

Giuli knew that she should call Elena Giovese and tell her that her boyfriend *was* dead, after all. No one else would, would they? She just couldn't quite think of how you would say it, and desperately she rebelled. Not fair. Thirty years ago she'd sat there listening to the school janitor telling her her mother had been found, dead of an overdose in a doorway. Why should she be the one to do it? She'd ask Sandro. Later.

The wide glazed doors of the Women's Centre had swung open to admit or release the clients – as they'd been taught to call them – half a dozen times since she'd stood there, and still Giuli hadn't seen what she wanted. She didn't know what – or more to the point, *who* – she was waiting for yet, but she had an instinct. Whoever it was that had bullied Rosina into lying about Giuli would reveal herself.

The slightest touch, maybe not even that, maybe only a breath at her shoulder, and she jumped, turning.

'Sweetheart.' He was disappointed in her, the downturned eyes under the straight fringe. 'I know what you're doing.' It was Enzo.

She dropped the cigarette, guiltily. 'What are you doing here?' She heard herself, like a schoolkid caught out.

'I wanted to make sure you were all right,' he said, gesturing at the *motorino* at the kerb. He must have shot over on it to find her.

He'd called, as he always did, to chat over his lunch break and Giuli had told him about Sandro, and his visit to the morgue. She'd heard the intake of breath that said this wasn't their world, that Enzo, who'd come from the quiet grey hills at the foot of Monte Amiata, wanted nothing to do with it. But he'd come to find her.

The trees in the square, scrubby and battered from the children climbing them, were in full flower but not yet in leaf, and the sun shone pale through their branches on to the neglected earth. There was an afternoon lull in the *viale*'s traffic and the old stone wall that surrounded one side of the Piazza Tasso was golden in the afternoon light. Reluctantly Giuli looked back at the Centre's doors.

'You're torturing yourself,' Enzo said quietly, nodding towards the building. 'What if someone sees you?'

Something rose inside Giuli she couldn't subdue and when she turned to him, blazing, he took a step back. 'I don't care if they see me,' she said. 'Someone sent an email this morning. A picture, that was meant to rub my nose in it. Do I just hide?' The address on the email pulsed somewhere just out of reach in her head: it was why she was here. She'd see a face, she'd make a connection. She'd know.

Watching her, Enzo held his ground, and nodded. 'All right, okay,' he said, and turned to look where she was looking. He didn't take her hand but she felt him settle to wait beside her.

'It could take a while,' she warned.

It took a little more than half an hour. Her young replacement as receptionist turned up to take over the afternoon shift, disappeared inside. A *motorino*, flashy but past its best, pulled up at the kerb and Giuli stepped forwards, out of the doorway.

On the other side of the square a woman Giuli knew came out of the glazed doors, discontent even in the way she pulled a raincoat round her thick middle, and looked up at the blue sky. The man on the *motorino* sat surly, a helmet dangling from one finger, and the woman came across to him. As he half turned Giuli saw his profile and something caught on her memory: it must have done once or twice before, but she had developed a habit of saying no to any face that rang a bell, with a past like hers. Just like she'd blanked Elena Giovese.

Vera the English receptionist and her Italian husband the plumber. A marriage not made in heaven.

Giuli stood on the pavement and waited until the woman saw her. Enzo stepped up beside her. 'You can go now,' she said.

*

They came in by Firenze Sud: there'd been an accident around the Certosa, and after twenty uneasy minutes in stationary traffic, the limousine's driver had swung off and diverted. At last they emerged through the hills; the city's red roofs crowded the plain ahead, and Luisa felt herself relax, fractionally.

She still didn't know what to make of it. Luisa had been helping the other women with their bags, helping them one after the other into the limousine's dark interior. Magda Scardino had hung back. Juliet Fleming had been the surprise, her hand suddenly tightening fiercely around Luisa's as if she was afraid of falling as she climbed in. Extracting herself, Luisa had stepped back and Scardino had been there, at her shoulder, leaning close.

'You and your husband should keep your noses out of it,' she had said, quite without inflection, and Luisa was momentarily fascinated to see how completely the attractiveness in her face was gone, abandoned in favour of bare aggression. 'That would be my suggestion.' And then she ducked and was inside, and it almost felt like she had sucked the air in with her. It had been a tense ride.

As the long, ungainly car negotiated the curve of the access road between the long grass of a building plot and a new development, Therese Van Vleet sat abruptly forward in her seat, looking through the window.

'It's here, isn't it?' she said, looking back at Magda Scardino, who returned her gaze with steely exasperation and just shrugged. The younger woman turned to Marjorie Cameron. 'It is, isn't it?'

Luisa looked through the window and saw only a dusty parking lot, and a couple of slightly shabby two-storey villas. Looking closer she saw that a van in the distinctive navy and red livery of the Carabinieri sat in one corner of the lot, and something fluttered from a hedge. Police tape. The limousine glided on and the scene receded behind them.

'I think so,' said Marjorie Cameron hesitantly. 'Juliet?'

Juliet was looking at Luisa. 'It's Giancarlo Vito's house,' she said. 'That's what Therese means.' She patted Van Vleet's hand, her own small as a bird's claw. 'Of course, you're right. Well remembered.' As if she was talking to a child.

'He was always telling us about his landlady,' said Therese Van Vleet, her childish eagerness to please at odds with her trembling lip. Almost in tears, again. 'She used to spy on him, he said. He told visitors to come around the back, he said, to the fire escape, just to annoy her. He would imitate her.'

'Giancarlo accompanied us on a trip to Poppi,' said Juliet Fleming drily, still watching Luisa. 'Another one of Gastone's little treats. Another limousine. And he pointed it out to us.'

'As if we'd be interested,' said Magda, her mouth downturned, looking away from the window and the view of a row of anonymous condominiums. Luisa wondered where she'd grown up, to be so offended by the sight of where ordinary people lived.

'It must have been a shock,' Luisa said. 'His death.'

'We hardly knew him,' said Juliet Fleming briskly. 'Therese . . . Therese's husband was rather friendly with him. Some . . . professional interest, wasn't it?'

'Brett was in the army, when he was a kid,' said Therese Van Vleet in a small voice. 'Before I knew him. Not for long. They talked about the Italian Military Academy, was all.'

'Of course it was a shock,' said Marjorie Cameron abruptly. 'Of course it was. Ian feels dreadful.'

They all stared at her, and fell silent.

The limousine was on the last stretch of the *viale* now, between the great leaning umbrella pines that skirted the slope, and the Duomo revealed itself, floating red-domed over the city, dwarfing every other roof. When the limousine turned through the Porta San Giorgio and headed down, easing its shining bulk through the narrow space, they were all poised, sitting forward, watching.

An ambulance sat at the kerb.

Chapter Nineteen

'I KNOCKED ON HER door this morning,' the maid Alice had said as they hurried along the carpeted corridors for the lift. 'I did.' Her eyes were averted from Sandro.

'I know,' he said. 'It's all right. I heard you say so to Lino.' She darted him a glance.

'There's something wrong,' said Lludic, from the other side of Cornell. 'I heard a noise. A groan. ' He jabbed at the lift's button with a big calloused finger.

'It's all right, Mr Lludic,' said Cornell. 'I think perhaps we should deal with this alone? Miss Morris . . . well. She wouldn't want . . . she might not be dressed.' Her pale face was blank with distress, at what they might find. Alessandra Cornell had led a sheltered life, no doubt.

'She wouldn't mind,' said Lludic. He seemed agitated.

'Miss Cornell might be right,' said Sandro, watching him. 'I think perhaps the fewer of us the better.' The maid fell back too. Sandro took out the bunch of keys Cornell had given him and turned to her. 'Is there a passkey among these?'

The attaché shook her head, just once. 'It's a matter of privacy,' she said, compressing her lips. 'We have one for emergencies, or by prior arrangement. There's no such arrangement with Miss Morris, she only requires one hour a week of cleaning – but . . .' She frowned. She took a silver key from her pocket and held it out. 'I suppose you should have one.' She sighed. 'Vito did.'

Registering that fact, Sandro took the key, looked up at the illuminated numbers indicating where the lift was: it didn't appear to have moved. 'I'm not waiting for that,' he said, and suddenly not caring who followed, took the stairs two at a time.

As he ran, some pulse of adrenaline opened Vito's floorplan in his head: AM. Second floor, next to Lludic. Unerringly, he knew where he was going.

Two men dead. And now the old woman, groaning behind her locked door.

The stairs were of pale soft stone – the same grey *pietra serena* the city was built from, used in every carved window-surround and portico, in the pillars that processed through the great interior of Santo Spirito. His blood pounded in his ears, he could feel his heart through his ribs, and reaching her door he stopped.

Forcing method into his actions, he knocked first. Along the corridor the lift hissed and its doors opened. Cornell stepped out and moved towards him, her steps silent on the carpet.

It was so quiet. No light came from under the door. They might as well have been in the bowels of a vast hotel, in the middle of the night. He looked along the softly lit corridor to gauge the distance between her apartment and the next and remembered that Lludic was the only other inhabitant of this floor. He lifted a hand to indicate to Cornell that she should stand back.

'Signorina Morris?' He pressed his ear to the door. Alessandra Cornell's face, staring at him out of the corridor's gloom, was white. He thought he heard something, a breath, the slightest rasp. He put the key in the lock and turned it.

There was a small anteroom and then an open door to the left; he reached for a switch but found nothing so moved on inside. The bedroom was dark and stifling, and held a smell Sandro didn't like, even though he couldn't pin it down – of something fusty and decaying, with an acrid bottom note, like bad breath, the breath of the hospital ward, of sickness. Cornell took a step behind him into the room and he put up a hand to stall her, he couldn't say why. He didn't want anything touched.

He was aware of Cornell obeying, pausing behind him at the threshold. He was also aware of the shape on the bed, aware that there was something very wrong with it. Sandro crossed to the window and with the cloth of his cuff pulled over his hand manipulated first the inner window then the shutter open.

He might have looked harder for a light switch, but he wanted air as well as light: the stale air was preventing him from concentrating. With the long slice of sun that entered the room, he turned, and looked. He saw Cornell's face first, staring aghast into the room, and only then the bed, the figure on the bed.

He had had in his head before he looked at Athene Morris, Sandro understood, the image of a warrior's statue on a tomb; that was how he'd thought of her, monumentally strong. The shape on the bed was not that at all. He should have known, few suffer trauma without ugliness, not in real life. The shape was humped and twisted; he took a step towards her in horror. The knot of fine silver-white hair was loose and thin, straggling, one shoulder pushed forward as though she had been trying to bury her face in the pillow, one knee drawn up. The sheet was half off her and a dead-white portion of calf protruded from a cotton nightdress, so pale it was the blue-white of skimmed milk, and the skin on it dry. He looked up to the face, willing it to look back.

Dead, was his first thought: he knew he should take her pulse.

'Call an ambulance,' he said to Cornell without turning, and she was gone, her footsteps muffled.

The eye that looked up at him from the bed was like the eye of a dead animal, filmed and opaque. He stepped up to the bed and put a hand to her, meaning to find an arm, a hand, a wrist. He made contact with her humped shoulder.

She was warm: he started back and as he did so half turned, out of some instinct to see if his response had been observed, but they were still alone in the room. He leaned down, his face close to hers, feeling for her pulse with his hand as he did so. Something beat under his fingers, erratic and jumpy.

'I'm sorry,' he said hoarsely, he couldn't have said why. Sorry for the intrusion. The shutter creaked in the faintest breeze and shifted, allowing more light in. 'Miss Morris,' he said. 'Can you hear me? Can you understand?'

Under his hand he felt the vibration of a distant, buried effort; from somewhere in the great stranded body something was struggling against suffocation. The mouth trembled, and slowly a thin strand of drool leaked from it and hung suspended.

'An ambulance is coming, Miss Morris,' he said. 'Can you speak? Can you say what happened?'

He searched her face, but could see nothing that meant anything, only the dry skin in the sunlight, the eyebrows thin from ancient plucking, the good cheekbones intact. Who had said she'd been someone's mistress, long ago?

'I'm sorry,' he said again. Did the eye clear, just a little, of its milkiness? No such thing as miracles. Sandro held her hand. 'They're coming,' he said, and her mouth worked; he thought of all the tiny muscles in a mouth, as it puckers for a kiss. Was it aspirin, after a stroke? He couldn't remember. Aspirin would be for heart attack, wouldn't it? He cursed himself for his uselessness.

In the corridor there were footsteps. 'They're on their way,' said Alessandra Cornell and he saw that there was colour in her face for the first time since he'd encountered her. She was breathing heavily. 'Five minutes, they said.'

It seemed to take hours. They'd stood together in silence in the room, Sandro holding Athene Morris's hand, feeling the life fluttering inside her, as light as a moth. It could just stop, he thought with horror. Like John Carlsson bloody and stiff inside the suitcase, jointed like a carcass; Vito naked and battered in his apartment. With his hand in hers, he squeezed, gently, rhythmically, as if to keep it going.

'Who's down there?' said Sandro almost in a whisper, to distract himself. 'Do they know what's happened? Did anyone say anything? When did they last see her? When did she go to bed?'

This was his case. Carlsson and Vito had died violently, but elsewhere. Athene Morris was his responsibility.

But Cornell just shook her head dumbly.

'At her age,' said Sandro, almost to himself. 'She's close to ninety. Did no one think—'

'It's up to the residents,' said Cornell, faltering. 'If she'd requested care . . . I hadn't thought. She was early to sign up, all paid for. Perhaps we should have a clause—' And she broke off, staring at the slumped figure. Perhaps even, thought Sandro grimly, reflecting on what she had been about to say, no one over seventy-five, in case they die on the premises, and cause upset.

'I left late,' Cornell said, swallowing. 'After midnight. I was on the terrace talking to Gastone and her light was on.'

'You were outside?'

'He was smoking a cigar,' she said absently, leaning back to look down the corridor. 'Smoking's only permitted in the guests' rooms.'

'He has a room,' said Sandro.

'But he's not a guest,' said Cornell shortly. 'It's not a . . . it's a provisional arrangement. He has his office in the city.'

'Is it true his father bought him into the business?' He spoke distractedly. Athene Morris's hand quivered in his, nothing even so strong as an answering squeeze.

'What does it matter?' Cornell said, agitated. 'Yes.'

What did it matter? Sandro wasn't sure. Bottai had the physical strength to dispose of an inquisitive journalist. And what about the envelope that implicated the Palazzo? Containing Athene's bracelet, and those initials.

He couldn't think. 'So some time after midnight Morris

turned off her light and went to bed. It must have happened in the night.' Again the tremor under his hand. 'Where are they?' Sandro muttered to himself, his eyes ranging the room in an agony of impatience. *She could die.*

The room was cluttered: all the pale perfection covered over, decorated. It made Sandro think of one of those little summerhouses in Russia, he must have seen one in a film or a magazine, little stuffed rooms, hung with bright embroidered cloths, shawls and fringing. A life, crowded into this space. One wall was covered with bookshelves, old books, a hundredweight at least that must have been shipped, from somewhere. On a shelf a row of Chinese cups in porcelain so fine it seemed almost transparent in the sun that fell on them. On another a curious little assortment of objects: a gold pillbox, a brooch. A pair of man's cufflinks. Did they mean something? Memories, perhaps.

Beside the bed was a small hexagonal table of dark wood – old, like everything. A teacup with unappetising grey liquid in it, a ring marking the polished surface beside it. A book, with a bookmark just emerging from it. He turned a little, still holding her hand, looking. Bathroom: a door opposite the bookshelves was ajar.

'Did she have a sitting room too?' he asked.

Cornell started at the question. 'Hers is the smallest apartment,' she said haltingly, 'but they all . . . yes. Over there.' She jerked her head back across the anteroom, to what he imagined must be a door opposite. 'She doesn't have cooking facilities, only . . . well as a hotel room. It's one of a range of options we offer. Fully equipped kitchen, down to a kettle and mini-fridge.' She blinked.

Sandro heard the siren then, the sound that he'd been listening for without knowing it.

'You'd better go,' he said. 'Tell them where to come.'

And after all the drawn-out agony of waiting, it seemed that they were inside the building and up the stairs within minutes, their voices loud and echoing along the corridors to where Sandro waited, frozen, her hand in his.

'Hold on,' he heard himself muttering over and over, like an incantation. 'They're coming, hold on.' And still she said nothing.

They had to take her hand from his in the end, and physically move him out of the way: three of them crowding into the room and seeming to fill it with their neon orange jackets.

'Does she speak Italian?' The paramedic addressed herself to Cornell, who just shook her head to indicate that she didn't know.

'Yes,' said Sandro, and Cornell had looked at him with blank surprise. He didn't even bother being offended.

The woman in her fluorescent jacket had leaned over the bed then and talked to Athene Morris softly while the younger of the male paramedics, a gawky youth, had applied some kind of monitor to the old woman's forefinger, a cannula in the back of the blue-veined hand. There was no response that Sandro could detect but by now he had stepped right away from the bed and was standing behind the small bedside table. He looked down at the paperback book: a title in English, Charles Dickens. *Our Mutual Friend*. He found his mouth trying to shape the words, which meant nothing to him, viewed from above, their vowel arrangements too foreign. He stared at the bookmark. Fleming had talked to him about Dickens. Was that only last night?

A mask went over the old woman's face and they manipulated a stretcher under her, with some difficulty. Then there was an awkward shuffling and manoeuvring of the laden stretcher in the enclosed space that knocked over a lamp and propelled Cornell ahead of them out into the corridor. Would it fit in the lift? Sandro found himself wondering. Would they use the stairs? And then abruptly they had gone, leaving him behind with the pieces of the broken lamp in his hand.

The sitting room was larger than the bedroom. At first sight it looked merely rumpled, untidy. A magazine was folded open on a low table, a single tumbler beside it with a sticky varnish of brandy, a small sofa with the indent of its last occupants, and a cushion on the floor. Sandro picked his way to the window and opened the shutter. He looked down on the upper terrace: Bottai stood there, talking to the sandy-haired engineer, Ian Cameron. He turned back to look at the room. At a small writing table an elegant balloon-backed chair lay on its side.

He stared at it.

The apartment held its breath around him, all these odd possessions, these rugs and mirrors and paintings, a red glass ashtray, a silver inkwell – all of them, it suddenly seemed to Sandro, waiting to be disassembled, packed up, sent to nephews or nieces, fingered and sold at auction. Thrown away. A life. *Let her live,* Sandro suddenly, fervently wished, let her live for now, let it not be yet. And he realised they would be waiting for him. She might already have gone.

He closed the door behind him.

Chapter Twenty

AS WAS HIS WAY, Enzo came straight out with it.

'If you're having second thoughts,' he said. 'About getting married. You have to say.'

They were in the office. It struck Giuli as Enzo spoke how provisional everything still looked in it. A single chair for visitors, which Enzo had pulled round to her side of the desk, three books on the shelving unit, and the window dusty. It could all be dismantled in a second. Giuli jumped to her feet, grabbing the cloth they kept on the sink, and began to rub at the glass. She had her back to him.

'Can we not, please,' Giuli said. 'Not talk about that.' She could sense him sitting very still.

'All right,' he said eventually. 'So tell me. You think it was her? Vera. That got the . . . Rosina, to tell lies about you.'

'I need to talk to her,' said Giuli, glancing quickly back over her shoulder.

Enzo was staring at her computer screen, unfocused. She went on rubbing at the glass, slower now. A little way along the backs of the houses of the Via del Leone – their yards filled with junk; here washing hung to dry, there a stack of rabbit hutches – a great overgrown mimosa stood in brilliant yellow frothing flower. It glowed against the blue sky.

'All right, yes, I think it's her. But it'll have to wait.' Dully she remembered Elena Giovese. Who was she kidding? She hadn't forgotten for a minute. The yellow blossom was so bright it left an after-image when she turned away. 'I've got things to do.' She leaned back against the windowsill

'What's more important than sorting this?' said Enzo, looking up at her, then, frowning, back at the screen. 'That is, if you're sure it's her?'

Plonking herself back in her chair beside him with a sigh, Giuli looked Enzo full in the face. Took his hand between hers. 'It's something I have to do on my own, you know that?' she said. Enzo knew she had a past: just because she didn't want to rub his nose in it, did that mean she was shoving it under the carpet?

He looked back at her. 'Yes,' he said. 'I know.' And took a deep breath. 'Is it work that you've got to stay put for?' He gestured at the computer screen, where the picture of Ian Cameron's bridge still sat. 'Because I've got the afternoon. I can help with that, and you can go and talk to her. I can even answer the phone.'

She'd told him what kind of mess Sandro had found himself in. Giuli couldn't get Enzo into that. Could she?

'I was just doing some background for him,' she said slowly. 'On the inmates – I mean, the residents – of the Palazzo San Giorgio. You know what Sandro's like, he can tell if someone's lying to him face to face . . . well, at a hundred metres. But he doesn't have a clue how to do a proper web search. I don't even know if he's got a computer there . . .' She paused.

'*Tesora,*' said Enzo patiently. 'Even you have to agree that's something I can manage.' He frowned. 'Computers. Internet searching.'

She felt shy suddenly at that *tesora*. Could she really be his treasure? 'Well,' she said, awkwardly. She calculated: she could get over to see Elena Giovese on the way. 'Vera does do a shift at the English-language bookshop afternoons.' Then, 'You have to email the links to Sandro, I said I would. I don't know if he's bothering to look at them, you know him.'

Enzo removed his jacket, draping it carefully over the back of the chair, and began to fold his sleeves back with that gesture she loved, meticulous, precise. When he'd done, he stood stiffly.

'So what are you waiting for?'

*

Had Luisa thought for a minute it might be Sandro they were loading into the ambulance? Maybe.

'What is it? Who is it?' It was Marjorie Cameron pressed against the glass this time, inside the limousine. Juliet Fleming sat, small in her corner, so still it seemed to Luisa she was conserving her energy.

'I'm sure it's nothing to worry about,' said Luisa automatically, and Magda Scardino gave her a contemptuous glance.

'Perhaps Alessandra has called the ambulance because she's got a migraine?' Magda said. Professor Scardino wasn't well, Fleming had said. Was this his wife's way of dealing with fear?

They pulled up at the kerb some distance behind the ambulance. Therese Van Vleet, who hadn't said a word, climbed out first, pale and silent. Luisa waited until they were all out before following. Magda Scardino walked straight inside.

There was a moment, a long, long moment when she couldn't see him; she looked from face to face – the doorman, anxious, the paramedic turning as he edged the stretcher out through the doors – and then he was there. Sandro.

He didn't say anything, he barely looked at her, but then he moved his hand, down at hip level, a shushing, calming motion, and she knew he was telling her, wait. She stood back; her clients went inside, and she remained on the pavement. The stretcher came out and then she looked down: it was the old woman. Luisa saw the thin white hair plastered to a pale forehead, the fine profile under a mask. Athene Morris.

'Someone going with her?' The stretcher was inside now and the paramedic looked up from his clipboard, to the two of them.

'I'll go.'

Alessandra Cornell stepped out into the street and they both gazed at her. The attaché looked older, a sharp line between her eyes. She looked weary and her mouth trembled, uncertain. But it was the first time Luisa had liked her.

'Will you . . .' Cornell addressed Sandro, but she didn't seem sure of what to say next.

'I'll sort things here,' he said. 'Don't worry. I'm not going anywhere.'

Cornell climbed in, awkward in heels, and the ambulance set off, its siren beginning uncertainly as it headed down the steep stone street. Uphill, the limousine waited at the kerb for

Luisa: the driver had instructions to take her back to the shop.

Sandro suddenly seemed drained, now that they were alone. In silence they looked down where the ambulance had disappeared with its fragile burden into the red-roofed city: it appeared so serene from here, just the hint of a haze as the temperature rose. They had once dreamed of moving not far from the Palazzo San Giorgio, to a green corner of San Niccolò with a view of a belltower. The afternoon was warm and Luisa could smell damp earth and roses; abruptly the longing for a garden overtook her. Even a balcony would do.

Sandro took her hand. 'Was that grim?' he said. 'How were they?'

'Strange,' said Luisa. 'I wonder about something.' She hesitated. He waited. 'Therese. The other women were gossiping about her in the bathroom; they all seem to know about her husband's involvement with Vito. The . . . games. Magda Scardino certainly hinted that Vito was making money out of them, one way or another. Blackmail? And so many of these . . . mishaps . . . seem to be about her. The dog. The mess. The purse—'

'Lino found the purse.' Sandro interrupted her. 'It was in the foyer, it had fallen behind a table or something.'

Luisa nodded. 'Fallen?' Sandro frowned, waiting. 'Even the magazine in your briefcase, it sort of points in her direction, doesn't it?'

'What are you saying?' he said, but she thought he knew.

'Do you think she might be doing it herself?' But now she'd said it, Luisa felt uncomfortable. 'I . . . well, actually, I like her. I think she's trying to be a good person, and she seems so young. But . . .' She looked around, anxiously. At the wheel of the limousine, the driver had his head down over a newspaper.

'But she's unhappy,' Sandro finished for her.

'Isn't there some kind of medical term? Not self-harm, or that proxy thing. But something like that. She wants the attention, or the sympathy, or something.'

Sandro nodded. Luisa saw him working it through in his head. 'It can't be too much fun in that marriage,' he said, almost to himself. 'And leaving the purse . . . if they're really going broke, that would figure.' Then he looked at her. 'A man was seen coming out of Vito's house,' he said. 'The night he died. Lino didn't see the Van Vleets coming back that night.'

'You think . . . you think . . .' Luisa felt a lurch at the image that appeared in her head of Therese Van Vleet's numb, pale face. Perhaps she should have kept quiet.

'I want you to do something for me,' he said. She waited.

'I want you to go there for me. To Vito's house.' Luisa stared at him, and he looked back at her, his face set. 'The address must be on his CV.'

'I know where he lived,' she said slowly, and it was Sandro's turn to stare.

*

Athene Morris had come up to bed, had sat reading with a nightcap. There had been nothing at that writing table, no pen or paper, no letter of denunciation, no last will and testament. She'd have gone to close her shutters, felt faint, perhaps from standing too quickly, the chair had gone over. She might not have been able to bend to right it, at her age, it might have seemed too much for her, woozy and late at night. She'd gone to lie down: she would do it in the morning.

Was that how it had gone? The overturned chair haunted Sandro. Now it was no longer morning, the day had stretched out to afternoon. Athene Morris should be up and dressed in her linens and shawls and sitting on the terrace in the soft light. Perhaps she wouldn't see another morning.

He hadn't wanted to say goodbye to Luisa. Had he been right to send her there, to Vito's house?

'There's a landlady,' he had said.

'I know that, too,' she'd answered him.

He'd pleaded. 'Try to see the flat. Talk to her. Anything you can find out. About Vito, about the night he died, about what kind of guy he was. Gay, straight, happy, sad – what made him tick.'

'Made him tick.' Luisa had made an exasperated noise.

He'd fallen back on, 'You know what I mean.' And then, because it was true, 'You're better at that kind of thing than I am.' Luisa was used to listening. A woman could get in where a man couldn't. And he was stuck here.

She'd given him that sigh, then the one that meant yes, and then she'd said, out of the blue, 'Would you marry again, if I died?' And that was when he'd hung on to her hand.

'You're not going to die,' he said, in a panic.

And Danilo Lludic had come out then, out through the glass doors with a great explosive sigh. He'd hardly given them a glance, standing there on the pavement, but Sandro had let Luisa go. He had watched her walk up towards the low shiny car, straight-backed, a little thicker at the waist than when they'd first met, but otherwise unchanged.

He'd turned away from the sight of the limousine bouncing, stupidly long and low-slung, on the steep stone street, taking his prize back down into the city. Across the way, Lludic had been peering in at the workshop, tapping on the window.

Sandro stepped out through the French doors on to the terrace.

'Whatever next, eh?' There was no mistaking the pompous boom in that voice, even if it hadn't been preceded by a strong whiff of cigar smoke. Gastone Bottai had been out at the back, on the terrace smoking in the sunshine, as Athene Morris was loaded into the ambulance.

'Still, at that age. . .' He turned away; he wasn't even talking to Sandro, not properly. Gastone Bottai was one of those men who didn't need a reply too often. 'It's hardly premature death.' She's not dead, Sandro wanted to say. 'She takes it all to heart too much.'

'Who?'

Bottai looked at him in surprise. 'Alessandra, of course,' he said urbanely, making sure Sandro understood that they were on first-name terms, and Sandro was still Cellini.

Bottai turned away from Sandro to look down at the river. 'This is a business,' he said. 'Not a charity. And besides, these are foreigners, the Anglo-Saxons don't like interference. It's all about independence and privacy. They don't want us behaving like old peasant women, poking our noses into their ailments, their affairs. Sticking our heads round their doors asking if everything is all right.' He puffed out his chest.

'Miss Cornell is worried,' said Sandro, eyeing him. 'She thinks something is going on here. People have died.'

Bottai sucked on his cigar, eyes narrowed. 'Nonsense,' he said. 'She was ancient.'

'Giancarlo Vito wasn't old, was he? I understand he was your appointment,' said Sandro. 'It must have been a shock. Having to fire him, then his . . . murder.' Bottai's face was thunderous. Yes! thought Sandro. He went on. 'And then there's John Carlsson. The journalist?'

'Who?' A lie: Bottai knew who Carlsson was. The cigar was back in his mouth, and there was a cloud of smoke between them. 'Here today, gone tomorrow, that's journalists for you,' he said. 'Can't be expected to remember them all.'

Sandro thought of that desecrated body, the tendons severed at the joints, and he couldn't help himself, he wanted a reaction. 'People have talked about the room they uncovered, being bad luck. In the cellar. What it might have been used for.'

Bottai turned, squinting through the smoke. 'Don't be stupid,' he said sharply. 'Superstition.'

'It is still there, though, isn't it?' said Sandro. 'Down there somewhere? By the steam room? Or did they let you brick it back up?'

Bottai gave him a long, murderous stare. 'I'm sure there's something you can be getting on with, Cellini,' he said, and walked away.

In the foyer Lino was standing stiff, back at his post. 'Never mind,' said Sandro, pausing. 'Some of these foreigners don't know how to behave, is all. They don't know an honest man when they see one.'

Too proud to relax his pose even fractionally, Lino gave a little nod. 'I remembered,' he said. 'She was standing there by the table, looking in her bag, while they waited for the limousine. I saw her close the bag up. No way it could have fallen out by accident.'

Sandro rested a hand on his arm a second, absorbing the information.

The library was empty save for Mauro, behind the bar. He was reading on his stool, so absorbed he didn't notice Sandro until he leaned across the marble. He set the book down.

Sandro read the flattened paperback's title. Machiavelli, *The Prince*. 'Useful?' he asked.

Mauro smiled. 'Sir Martin recommended it to me,' he said. 'When he found out I'd worked at an embassy. He said it should be required reading.'

'And what have you learned?' said Sandro

'He says men are driven by love or fear,' said the barman.

'And women?' said Sandro.

Mauro just smiled. 'And then he says, better for a ruler to be feared than loved.'

'Sounds like my Luisa,' said Sandro. Mauro got out another glass to polish: Sandro admired a man who didn't like to be idle. 'There was a journalist, a regular in here, I've heard,' he said casually. 'Carlsson? Nice guy?'

Mauro set the glass down, and was still. 'Yeah,' he said slowly. 'Nice guy, up to a point. He seems to be one of the favoured ones. Cornell likes him: her tame journalist, or so she thinks.'

'You disagree?'

'They're like dogs, aren't they? Never quite tame. He was in a few days ago. Chatting to Mr Van Vleet, if that's what you want to know.'

Sandro just nodded, and turned to look into the room. 'Where is everyone?'

'They don't seem to feel much like socialising,' said Mauro, pouring Sandro an inch of gassy water. 'It's probably Miss Morris. They might even be upset.'

'You don't know who might have visited her last night, do you?' Sandro spoke softly.

Mauro looked at him, head tilted. 'If anyone . . . they'd have said, wouldn't they?'

Sandro pursed his lips. 'Of course you're right,' he said.

'Lludic is next door to her,' the barman said slowly. 'He was up late, entertaining visitors of his own.' Sandro remembered: the girl across the way. 'Maybe he saw something.' Mauro rubbed his chin thoughtfully. 'She wanders, when everyone's in bed. Lady Fleming told me that.' Sandro nodded. Mauro went on. 'A free spirit. And keeps her door unlocked, too, I know that. For fear of just this, comes to us all.'

'Fear of what?'

'Of dying alone,' the barman said quietly. 'Lying there for days.'

Sandro stared at him, absorbing this. Athene Morris habitually left her door unlocked – so anyone could have walked in, in the night. She was more afraid of dying alone than of an intruder.

It had been locked at one, when Sandro had knocked. And there had been no key in the lock, or he wouldn't have been able to use the passkey. He hadn't looked for it.

Far off in the great building above them came a sound, distant but unsettling. They both looked up, wondering if they had really heard it. The sound ebbed, but it was still there, in the air. A woman's scream.

They waited a long moment, holding their breath. There were footsteps in the corridor, and Brett Van Vleet, his ruddy face paler than Sandro had seen it, came into the library. He staggered a little.

'You,' he said, staring at Sandro, gesturing. 'We need you.'

Chapter Twenty-One

IN THE DOORWAY OF an artists' suppliers opposite the English-language bookshop, Giuli was waiting. The shop was on the corner of the Via delle Oche and the Via dello Studio, an alleyway in the shadow of the Duomo. At the end of the street the great green-and-white-striped façade loomed, its dome filling the sky, as out of scale as an alien spaceship: maybe, Giuli thought, surprising herself, that had been the intention. Those builders and priests getting together a thousand years ago to scare the living daylights out of us.

Behind Giuli the door opened with a clang and a leggy foreign girl pushed past her with a big canvas, making an annoyed sound.

In the workshop on the Costa San Giorgio, Elena Giovese hadn't been at her bench. Giuli had peered in at the window, shading her eyes. An anglepoise had been left on at the back of the workshop, illuminating a gilded mirror, but the door was locked, and no one answered when she rang. The bell-pull was an old-fashioned iron ring in the wall, and it had set off a clang somewhere inside.

The chair at the bench had been pushed back, as if she had planned to be gone only a minute. In the corner of the window was a little card, handwritten: *If we are away from the shop*, and then a mobile number. Giuli tapped it into her phone, and called. It went straight to answerphone. Her uncle was in the hospital, Elena had said, perhaps that was where she was. Giuli didn't leave a message, because her voice would have betrayed her. If she was going to tell Elena her boyfriend had been murdered, it would have to be face to face.

Across the street the skinny old guy who manned the door at the Palazzo had raised a hand to her. Sandro was in there, and Giuli had to resist the temptation to run in and ask him for help. She had climbed back on her *motorino* instead, and headed for the Via delle Oche.

Now the long-legged art student was giving Giuli a dirty look over her shoulder. Giuli stepped out of the shop's doorway and into the yellow gleam of the streetlights blinking on in the dusk. At her till inside the bookshop, Vera looked up.

Giuli pushed open the door, and it set a bell ringing. She stood and waited until the noise died down, watching Vera's expression. She'd alternated shifts on reception at the Centre with this woman for three years: she'd grown used to her bad temper and her hostility. Something to do with the menopause, something to do with having burned her boats and moved to Italy when she was twenty-five and pretty, only to find the shine on Italian romance wore off at around five months pregnant. Something to do with her idle, seedy husband, a plumber for whom she worked as part-time secretary along with her other jobs.

Vera: yes.

'I've talked to Rosina,' Giuli said, and watched the woman's eyes flicker in her pouchy, expressionless face. English coldness allied with the Italian wife's habit of denial. 'She wouldn't tell me who got her to lie.'

'I'm working,' the Englishwoman said. 'You're harassing me. I'll have to report this.'

'There's no one here but us,' said Giuli softly.

Vera looked over her shoulder into the shop: bookshelves receded into the depths of the building. 'I have customers,' she said, but there was no one to be seen.

Giuli moved up to the desk. 'You made a mistake sending that email,' she said quietly. 'I suppose you counted on my not recognising the address? Not knowing how to find out whose it was? Or maybe you thought I'd be so freaked or ashamed I'd delete it without looking?' Which was exactly what she had done, of course. Only Enzo had got it back.

'I don't know what you're talking about.' Again Vera looked over her shoulder into the ranked shelves.

'Idro@tin.it?' Idro for *idraulico,* plumber. 'All you have to do is type it in to the internet search engine and guess who pops up? Your husband's work email, isn't it?'

Again Vera's eyes flickered. She hunched behind the till, small and bitter. The bookshop was cavernous and chilly, despite the warmth outside.

Giuli remembered the day she'd come in to work with Enzo's ring on her finger and they'd gathered around: Barbara from the Addictions Clinic, old Maria the cleaner, even a client, a regular, a mother of six worn down and exhausted and pregnant again. They'd cooed and smiled down at the modest stone on her thin hand, the haggard, tired faces. You'd have thought they'd be long past getting excited over a ring on a forty-four-year-old's finger. Vera had just stood there, hunched in the coat she'd got on because Giuli's arrival had signified the end of her shift. Giuli had thought nothing of it at the time. *The English*, maybe, if she'd thought anything.

Without a word Vera had turned and left them there with their compliments and exclamations, even though her husband had not turned up to collect her yet and she'd had to stand there on the pavement in full view of the reception desk through the glass doors. Giuli had looked up and seen her, and then someone had asked if they could try the ring on and when she looked back Vera was climbing on the *motorino*.

Had Giuli recognised the man then, or this morning, or years before? Had she said to herself, there's no point looking back, how could you possibly be sure, when there had been so many men and you were out of it half the time anyway?

'I want you to go to Massini and tell her what you've done,' she said. 'From you threatening Rosina her kids will be taken away, right on up.'

Vera's face was frozen. 'And why would I want to do that?' she forced out.

'I'll tell her why you did it,' said Giuli. 'That was your mistake, you see. I've got nothing to lose.'

From the cold depths of the shop came a little cough, and a woman stepped out, clutching a book. Apologetically she looked from Vera to Giuli and back again. 'I'm sorry,' she said, and with those words Giuli realised she knew this woman, she just didn't know how.

*

In the washroom downstairs at Frollini, Luisa peered into the mirror.

You're not going to die, she said silently to herself. Why had she said that to Sandro? About marrying again. No trace of the cancer, last time they looked, and she had her breast back. It didn't really feel like hers, but you couldn't have everything. She rubbed her cheeks to bring some colour back into them. That's better.

I love you, he'd said behind her, as she leaned down to step into the car, but when she'd looked up he was turning away. She thought, *Should I have replied?* Saying I love you was not normal for them. It was not required: it was not welcome.

She came out of the little washroom, and jumped. Enrico Frollini stood at the top of the stairs. Again.

'Is everything all right? I saw that girl working upstairs, what's her name? The whatsit. Intern.' He sounded impatient, and worried.

Typical, thought Luisa; absolutely typical. If they needed him, Frollini was always uncontactable, but just when you wanted to get something done under the radar, there he was.

She had already spoken to Giuseppina about leaving early. They'd arranged for the intern to come in; Luisa had stifled her anxiety. Free help, was what she was. But not bad: the well-educated, sensible daughter of a supplier fallen on hard times, needing to get her a place. It was how the world worked. And with Luisa out of the way, Giusy was promoted to head saleswoman. Was that how it was? You wanted out, she told herself. Did you think you were indispensable?

'Enrico,' she said, climbing the stairs.

Frollini brightened, sidestepping to let her past. 'So how did it go?' he said. As she hesitated, his eyes wandered back to the intern. 'She's Andrea's girl? I suppose she'll do.'

'How did it go?' For a moment she didn't know what he was talking about.

'At the mall,' he said impatiently. 'Bottai's little venture.'

'Oh,' said Luisa, picking up her jacket again casually. 'It was fine. It had to be cut short, because . . . well, it doesn't matter. We got back a little early. But I negotiated their discounts. I'm sure they'll pay up.'

'It was a matter of goodwill, not money,' Frollini said, crestfallen. 'Connections. I wanted to know what you thought of the mall. I thought you might enjoy it.'

Luisa looked at him, expressionless.

'Do you want to know the truth, Enrico?' she said. 'I thought the mall was horrible.'

He opened his mouth, then closed it again.

'I think the last thing you should be doing is getting into a place like that,' she said, gently. 'A place where you'd never dream of working or shopping yourself.'

'They've spent a lot of money on it,' Frollini said, mustering an affronted expression.

'Maybe so,' said Luisa, pulling on one sleeve of her jacket. 'And I'm sure you could make money with an outlet there, too. But it's not your style, Enrico. And personal shopping . . . I don't know if it's me.' She smiled sadly. 'I'm used to my little kingdom. You know that.'

'Where are you going?' he said, automatically helping her into the other sleeve.

'I've got to do something for Sandro. It's to do with the investigation he's on.'

Too late she realised that Frollini knew where Sandro was working, of course he did, and that the whole point of it was it was a steady job, no more investigations. No more trying to still be a police officer, on the side of right against wrong. Turning over stones. She hurried on.

'I've sorted it all. I finish at six anyway, the intern's covering.' Snatching up her bag, Luisa could hear the truculence in her voice. Twenty years ago, ten, five even, she'd never have dared talk to Frollini like this.

Frollini looked around in mute appeal for support, to Giusy on the shop floor, to Beppe who'd appeared on the stairs. They looked faintly abashed, saying nothing.

'Well, I suppose . . .' he said, and stopped. 'I suppose there's nothing I can do about it, is there?' He straightened his shoulders, reasserting his dignity. 'And where exactly is it you're going? On this errand.'

'I've got to go and talk to someone's landlady,' she said with weary patience. 'Out near Firenze Sud. I haven't even called a cab yet.'

'Firenze Sud?' he said with distaste. Frollini lived in a handsome villa below Bellosguardo, everything expensive, everything tasteful; the motorway intersection clustered round with motels and condominiums, the Viale Europa with its supermarkets and dry-cleaners, was somewhere he preferred not to contemplate. 'What kind of a husband is he?'

Luisa said nothing, her expression hardening.

'I'll give you a lift,' he said, and briskly, to save face, he took her elbow and steered her ahead of him. 'Carry on,' he said to Giusy over his shoulder, in an attempt to assert himself.

'I'd rather work on the Viale Europa than in that mall,' said Luisa, as she climbed into the cream leather interior of her boss's huge Alfa Romeo. Enrico Frollini pretended not to hear.

It took more than half an hour: the traffic was building to rush hour and they got stuck in a series of gridlocked arterial interchanges. They were only just beyond the station, wedged between a truck and an airport coach, when Frollini, who'd been working up to it with a succession of sighs and gestures to other drivers, and meaningful looks stolen at Luisa, finally spoke.

'Seriously, though, Luisa,' he said. 'We've known each other long enough. What's he playing at? This is no job for a woman of your . . . of your—' And he broke off under her gaze, apparently unable to say what kind of woman she was.

'I'm helping my husband out, Enrico,' she said, turning to look straight ahead. A *motorino* wove between them and the airport coach, clipping the wing mirror, and Frollini made a pained sound. Up ahead the traffic began to move and he engaged the gears.

From memory she guided them to the dingy villa Therese Van Vleet had pointed out that afternoon. Frollini pulled up in a small parking area, and turned off the ignition.

'Do you want me to come in with you?' he asked reluctantly. 'A landlady, you said?'

'It's fine, Enrico,' she said, turning to look at him. They might have been lovers on an assignation, sitting in a hotel car park before or after their encounter: some element of that dynamic lay dormant between them. Only it would never happen; Luisa knew it, even if Frollini, ever the contented optimist, didn't. 'You can leave now,' she said gently. 'Go back to your wife, have your *aperitivo*, have your dinner. I can get a cab back.'

'No,' he said grumpily. 'I'll wait for you here.'

Chapter Twenty-Two

AHEAD OF HIM, BRETT Van Vleet took the stairs nimbly for a man carrying a bit of extra weight. His shoulders, Sandro noted, were the shoulders of a swimmer or a high-school football star, as wide as a door. These were factors that once he had had to calculate on the spot, as a police officer – things like relative bodyweight, musculature, fitness, as well as concealed weapons and exit points. If there was any possibility you were about to get into what they called a situation.

Exit points had been on Sandro's mind since he first took this job, he realised, puffing in the American's wake. Escape routes.

When they'd come in from the terrace, they had paused at the foot of the stairs, beside the lift doors – Sandro couldn't have said if it had been him or Van Vleet who'd stopped. On the far side, another set of stairs curved down to the basement complex, to the cellars, the steam room. The lift was somewhere above them: had Van Vleet hesitated to decide whether or not to wait for it? Sandro had stepped across the lift doors to glance down, into the soft dark. A gilded sign on the wall with an arrow: *Centro*

Benessere/Spa Complex, it said. And the rest, thought Sandro. The stairs down weren't an escape route, they were its opposite. A place where the condemned would have been led, hundreds of years earlier, with no way back up. There was a faint odour beneath the lily scent, a tang of damp.

Van Vleet had not paused to look down to the cellars, though. When Sandro turned back he was already out of sight, heading up.

The door to the first-floor apartment stood open. She was in the bedroom.

The room was crazy, was Sandro's first thought, like Versailles: the windows so heavily swagged with curtains, the view – the lovely view, down across the gardens to the river and the façade of Santa Croce – was reduced to no more than a sliver of green river and rooftops, the bed crowned with some heavy fabric and piled with brocade cushions. And at the centre of it Therese Van Vleet sat, looking like a child on the vast bed, in stockinged feet, shoes tumbled on the floor. She held something in her hands, and her face was swollen with crying.

Behind him Sandro registered Van Vleet's careful tread, stepping to close the door. He was aware of holding himself very still. A precarious moment, one card set against the next, and a draught, a door opening at the wrong moment and it could all fall. The puzzle, the pattern, and the pulse of excitement that comes with rising certainty: he began.

First things first. Sandro took a step to look at what she held in her hands. A dog's narrow, expensive suede collar, dotted with stones. The original colour would have been a pale sand, only it was heavily stained with dark reddish brown. Probably blood.

'I see,' he said, and cleared his throat. She looked up at him, the eyes no less startlingly large and blue for the puffiness around them. 'But there's still no sign . . . no sign . . .' She shook her head, but he finished the sentence anyway. 'The dog. No sign of the dog.'

'For Christ's sake,' said Van Vleet, and then Sandro heard it, the fakery, the bluff. The lie.

'For Christ's sake, can't you see she's distraught? I should goddamn well sue the ass off this place. You guys. I was warned about Italy. Crooked as they come, and incompetent with it. I didn't want to believe it. The dog, Giancarlo, Therese's purse. My car, goddamn it, they had no right.'

Sandro caught a look in Therese Van Vleet's eye, of panic. Out of her depth.

As one card was laid against the next, Sandro held his breath.

'What happened to the car?' he said quietly, and he saw the same panic reflected in Brett Van Vleet's red face.

'They took it, from the garage,' said Therese, and her fingers tightened around the collar, her chin in the air. 'A mix-up. Over the shipping costs.'

He nodded, holding her gaze, looking at Brett Van Vleet. He knew, and they knew he knew. 'Where did you find the collar?' he asked.

'It was on the door handle,' she said, and her eyes welled again. 'Someone had hung it over the handle, in the corridor.'

He saw that her wallet lay on the bed beside her, open, rifled through. Emptied.

'It's unpleasant,' said Sandro quietly, 'isn't it?' Therese looked at him, not understanding. 'These tricks someone is playing.

The dog. Your wallet.' Her eyes widened, and he frowned. He shouldn't feel sorry for her, but he did.

'Someone put a pornographic magazine in my briefcase,' he said. 'An American one. Did you know my wife had had a mastectomy?'

She was very pale; she looked beseechingly at her husband, whose flush had deepened against the sandy hair. 'What do you mean?' said the American, his voice thick.

'I could show it to you, if you like,' Sandro said. 'The magazine.' And on the bed Therese recoiled. He could see a trace of silk slip at her hem, but when she put a hand down to tug at it he saw her nails were chipped and one was bitten down.

'Mr Van Vleet.' He looked away from the ragged nail, and kept his voice reasonable as he addressed the man. Van Vleet looked as if he was about to explode. 'Your car was taken because you couldn't pay the shipper and your payments on this place,' and Sandro looked around, disbelieving, at the hired luxury, 'are overdue. Your wife hid her wallet so she'd have an excuse not to buy anything at the mall, not to mention getting herself the sympathy vote.'

With each card laid gently down, he saw them flinch. Sandro took a breath, focusing on Therese, who stared as if hypnotised. 'I don't know when you thought of playing all these tricks, to make it look like you were being persecuted – maybe the dog falling down the well gave you the idea. Did you take Athene's bracelet, was it you Giancarlo was protecting? Were you the woman who found the key outside the steam room, when Marjorie Cameron got locked in? Was it going to be your excuse for not paying your rent?'

Therese had her hand to her mouth. 'It wasn't me,' she said faintly. 'I – I . . . you don't think I'd—'

'I don't think you'd kill your little dog, Mrs Van Vleet. But maybe your husband told you he was in a safe place?'

Brett Van Vleet clenched his fists, the knuckles cracking, but his wife only went on staring at Sandro. Who looked at the husband.

'Giancarlo was paying your hookers for you, you were so short of cash. You've just gone through your wife's purse and taken what she had. What did Giancarlo want in exchange?'

Brett Van Vleet was pale too, now, his complexion unpleasant, but the house Sandro was building held. Another card.

'A journalist came around, too, didn't he?' Sandro spoke softly. 'I bet that scared you. Poking around. John Carlsson. Do you know what happened in Bari, Mr Van Vleet? And do you know where Mr Carlsson is now?'

A different look came over Van Vleet's face, giving Sandro pause, but he had to finish this. He pushed.

'Lino said you got back late the night Vito died, after he'd gone off duty. A well-built man was seen leaving Giancarlo's place late. Did he want money? Did it all get to be too much? First Carlsson, you got rid of Carlsson, then you got scared, so you went to see Giancarlo. Your buddy. Did you ask him for help, and instead he told you it was payback time? So you had to kill him too.'

Van Vleet let out a noise, a terrible noise, almost a sob. He put both hands to his face.

'Brett,' said Therese Van Vleet, and her arms came up, hugging herself on the bed, terrified. 'Brett, you didn't.'

'I didn't,' he said, through his hands. 'I didn't.'

The hands came down. As Sandro looked at the man's face he recognised the expression he'd seen earlier, not of guilt, not merely shock, but incomprehension. And he felt it, not that he hadn't already known it was coming: the great deflating rush that laid it all flat. Heavily he sat.

'I didn't,' said Brett Van Vleet again.

*

At a dainty table under Gilli's coffered wooden ceilings Giuli was sitting taking tea with Marjorie Cameron. What a pair, she thought, the odd couple, and she saw the thought reflected in the waiter's eyes as he laid down the apparatus of this foreign ritual. Dishes and jugs and muslin and hinged strainers, an ex-junkie and a menopausal expatriate carrying on a strained roundabout conversation as they sipped and poured. His not to reason why.

'Is it Miss Sarto?'

Giuli had exited the shop in a hurry and with flaming cheeks, at the thought that her conversation with Vera had been overheard, but Marjorie Cameron had followed her out. The wife of that man who built the bridges: the photograph had come back to her on the doorstep, the blind parapets of an endless bridge under a desert sky.

She was clearly upset, and not by the scene she might or might not have witnessed between Giuli and Vera. She barely spoke a word of Italian.

'Mrs Cameron?' She had taken the woman's hand firmly,

hoping it was the right way to behave, under the circumstances. 'How nice to meet you again.'

'I came . . . I came . . .'

The engineer's wife had seemed unable to finish the sentence; her faded hazel eyes looked beseechingly into Giuli's.

'For something to read?' Giuli helped her out.

Marjorie Cameron had stared at her, then turned back to look in the bookshop's window, plastered with historical novels, travel guides showing cypresses and domes. 'My husband told— suggested I come here,' she said. 'Something to read, yes.' She hesitated. 'Culture. He doesn't like me to waste my time. He's in a meeting.'

'A meeting?' Giuli had thought they were all more or less on holiday. But then she remembered the engineer saying something about having to go back out – wherever it was. To the Middle East.

'Oh, lawyers,' Marjorie said vaguely, waving a hand. She gazed at Giuli with her pale eyes like water. 'Letters. But there's been another – did you know? Poor Athene.' And Marjorie Cameron's eyes filled, threatened to overflow. It was then that Giuli had taken her arm, and steered her towards Gilli.

'You're not all right, are you?' said Giuli. She'd ordered tea out of desperation: eight euros each, and she'd never get the money back. Marjorie Cameron put her thin hands in her lap, like a child, and told her what had happened at the Palazzo San Giorgio.

So the big-boned old lady from last night was in hospital – no more than five hundred metres, in fact, from where they sat, because she'd been taken to the big old central hospital of

Santa Maria Nuova just the other side of the Duomo. Athene Morris: the one among them all that Giuli had liked; Athene Morris who had talked to her about love, and independence. It seemed to have upset Marjorie Cameron a great deal.

'Have you come from there?' she asked, and Cameron gave a quick shake of the head, putting a tissue to her pink nose.

'She is very old,' Giuli said tentatively, as the waiter departed. She couldn't get the old woman's face out of her head, though, that look when Giuli had excused herself abruptly. Athene Morris's strong face crumpling just enough to reveal her shameful secret: she was lonely. Afraid of being alone. Me too, Giuli thought, only then with a small pulse of comfort another thought surprised her: but I have Enzo.

'Oh, yes,' said Marjorie Cameron. 'I shouldn't be sentimental, Ian hates sentiment.' She dabbed at her eyes. 'When we got the news about Giancarlo he said, why pretend?' She turned the big pale eyes on Giuli. 'My husband got him fired, you see.' And dabbed again, while Giuli pondered the kind of person that loses another person their job.

'I didn't think I'd miss the children,' Marjorie Cameron said, leaning back against the padded banquette.

'How old are they?'

They were twenty-eight, thirty-one, thirty-three: one in Brisbane, the other two in London.

'I had them young,' she said. 'People don't say that any more, how young I must have been; you get old quite suddenly, you know? They're not surprised. I was twenty when I had Charles. Here is better than Sydney, London's nearer, even if Brisbane isn't. I have three grandchildren in London.'

Giuli let her talk, the colour returning to her pale cheeks. Outside, the light was fading. The waiter hovered: Giuli poured the tea, not sure if she was doing it right, waiting for a moment, and the waiter retreated.

Marjorie Cameron looked down into her empty cup, tipping it. 'My mother used to tell fortunes from tea leaves,' she said. 'Do you do that here? Irish, my mother. Not Scots. She said I should never have married a Scotsman.' Her head bent. 'Perhaps I never should have married anyone.'

'Like Miss Morris,' said Giuli. And Marjorie Cameron looked at her, holding her secret, wondering whether to tell.

'They said she had a stroke.' She turned to Giuli. 'She was alone, and she had a stroke. That's what they said. But why did no one notice, until this afternoon? No one said. She must have been ill last night.'

'I talked to her last night,' said Giuli.

Marjorie Cameron's head turned slowly. 'You did?'

'At the unveiling,' said Giuli. She thought of Athene Morris's stricken face as she had left her: had the old lady been ill, even then? 'She seemed . . . she didn't seem ill.'

Marjorie Cameron's face cleared a little. 'Oh, yes. But that was before. I meant later. After she'd gone to bed. Perhaps you could find out,' she said slowly, almost to herself. 'That's your job, isn't it? You and Mr Cellini?'

'Find out what?' Giuli said patiently.

'They said it was a stroke,' said Marjorie Cameron, 'but he was in her room last night, I'm sure of it.' She leaned down. 'I heard him, you see, very late. Someone must have known she was ill. Or . . .'

'Or what?' Leaning forward, Giuli could feel the thump of her heart. 'Who did you hear in her room?'

But Marjorie Cameron only shook her head.

*

'I used to come up here when I was a kid,' said Elena, looking out through the tiny window. They were in one of the turrets of the Forte di Belvedere, just up the hill from the Palazzo San Giorgio and officially closed for repairs, and it was almost dark.

It was too late to wonder if it had been a mistake, the way she'd started up from her workbench when he'd peered in at the window, now that she and Danilo Lludic were in a space so confined she could smell the chemicals he worked with on his clothes. She could smell his skin beneath them.

'This is what it's really all about, though,' he said, and she could hear the suppressed excitement in his voice in the dark. There were other smells – fusty, stale, the smells of earlier occupation – in the little brick cage that held them suspended over the fort's battlements. 'Can you imagine? The place of power, never mind that puny little palace we're all crammed into. Men dying in battle, dying to defend the greatest city on earth.'

The great fortress looked so peaceful now, grassed over, flowering weeds sprouting from its brickwork. Had it been her idea? She'd let him into the workshop, like a big bear in her space, and he'd begun pacing the room, roaming the walls, inspecting her tools as he talked – small-talk, grumbling, fretful – until she wondered if there might be something wrong with him, attention deficit. She'd asked about the ambulance eventually, and he'd stopped moving about then.

'I must go over there,' he'd said, his mind turning on something she couldn't see. 'To the hospital. If she wakes up . . .' He'd stopped. 'She looked terrible. Do you think she'll die?' He asked the question like a child. Attention deficit – or one of those other syndromes, where you couldn't empathise.

'She's very old,' Elena had said, her heart sinking, but he'd put his face in his hands then.

'Don't say that,' he said, fiercely. She'd prised his hands away. 'It's that place,' he said. 'That bloody place. Eats you alive, being stuck in there; all that money, all that chattering behind closed doors. I don't know what I'll do without her. We were alike. Crazy old bird.'

She'd said, on impulse, 'Let's get out of here.' And once on the steep slope of the hill, she hadn't wanted to go down, back into the city. 'You want to see something secret?' They'd looked at each other then, and it had seemed to her that she was a child again, with this big childlike man in tow.

A heap of rubble half-covered by a tarpaulin and a builders' lorry with an upended wheelbarrow in the dusk meant nothing: the workers left them there just as a sign of their presence. 'They've got funding and a five-year contract to erect the safety equipment,' said Elena as they'd stepped around it. 'So what's the guessing they'll make it last five years?'

Scrubby grass, soft brick walls, a single umbrella pine leaning gently against the yellow villa around which the fort had been built. A few irises planted at random, and a view.

Elena had led him past the link fencing, avoiding the great

door with its Medici escutcheon, the five balls in white marble against grey stone tilted to look down, forbidding them. They'd skirted the massive sloping wall until they located the side entrance, the old route inside, blocked half-heartedly by more building materials and a rusting digger, up a brick-paved ramp and there it was. The view. The sun was going down and the row of statuary along the roofline of the little summer house at the top of the Boboli was silhouetted against the purple sky.

It was just as Elena remembered it: whatever she might have implied to Danilo Lludic, it was years since she'd been up here. The shaded outlines of trees, the blue hills, a distant tower, and laid over it all a soft light refracted through every droplet of moisture seeded in the warm air.

A bleached and battered bunch of artificial flowers sat askew against the low wall. 'Someone fell,' she'd said, when Lludic pointed.

A girl had fallen from the parapets, and the fort had had to be closed. It was easy to see how it had happened: she wouldn't even have needed to be drunk. The walls were no more than knee-high, and the iron rail surmounting them didn't run the full perimeter of the structure. The tops of what Elena knew to be trees, but the girl had taken to be bushes, were just visible, extending up the wall where it abutted the Boboli gardens. She'd simply jumped or climbed over, fallen ten metres and broken her neck.

'Did you know the man that died?' Elena said, at the sight of the dismal little rain-soaked bouquet, and Lludic's head turned sharply.

'What man?' he said, scanning her face. 'You mean Giancarlo?'

She nodded, curious now.

'He was a piece of work,' said Lludic, looking away. 'A nasty little fascist piece of work.'

'Fascist?' Was that just the insult of choice, a word for anyone embedded in the system that artists like Lludic used?

But he had only shrugged in answer and there in front of them had stood the little turret.

Inside it now, Lludic seemed to become aware quite suddenly of her lack of response, and stopped, mid flow. 'Men still like battle, then,' she said, to fill the silence. He took a step towards her, bringing with him the heat of his conversation, and of his big body.

One hand took hers, and she brought the other up instinctively, in defence. John was gone, she was alone, the future had melted away in front of her. But at least this was excitement.

'Do you think I'm going to hurt you?' he said, his voice reasonable, and she held her breath.

'I don't know,' she said, but what she meant was, *I don't care.*

She could only see the gleam of his eyes in the dark as abruptly he dropped her hands, but his voice was ragged when he spoke. 'I have to go,' he said. 'She might wake up.'

Chapter Twenty-Three

AS SHE RECEIVED HIM in her office, Alessandra Cornell looked shattered. A single lamp was on on her desk, throwing light upwards onto the peachy limbs of the frescoed cherubs. Sandro spoke to her mechanically, grateful for the fact that she wouldn't be able to see in his eyes the near-catastrophe of his encounter with Brett Van Vleet upstairs.

'"They'll keep us informed",' he repeated. Beyond the big windows it was twilight. Upstairs he had left Brett Van Vleet packing a bag, his wife standing at the window looking out. 'That's what I'm to say if anyone asks how Miss Morris is doing. I understand.'

Athene Morris would probably die.

Cornell was speaking. 'I tried to tell them at the hospital that she's tough. The English . . .' And as she faltered, Sandro saw that she was struggling with something unfamiliar. Grief? She'd gone on, a frown creasing that perfect face, the line still there when she looked up at him. Alessandra Cornell was becoming a human being. 'But they only said, there's a chance, of course. But at her age. . .'

The next few hours would be crucial. She was already on the phone in search of Athene Morris's next of kin when he let himself out.

In the foyer down the corridor Sandro could hear Lino's voice, courteous but circumspect as he blocked some visitor's enquiry. On impulse he headed the other way, passing through the library but not even pausing to acknowledge Martin Fleming turning from a conversation with Mauro at the bar, and out into the courtyard where Lludic's sculpture stood. Below him the terraced garden was in velvety darkness, and beyond it the city spread out, twinkling. He stepped to the edge of the courtyard and looked along the terrace beneath Cornell's window, an old instinct, to make sure he was alone. It was empty.

He'd known when he'd seen Van Vleet's face: not the whole story, naturally. But Van Vleet hadn't killed anyone, that much was plain. And nor, unless she was capable of dragging a grown man in a suitcase half across the city, had his wife.

'Carlsson? Carlsson? Carlsson's dead?' The man had gone white with unfeigned shock.

And then there had been a silence, during which Sandro had revised his options.

'All right,' he'd said, seeing them poised to break into a cacophony of outrage and bluster and panic that would culminate in his being marched into Cornell's office to be fired. He'd held up his hands, speaking gently. 'Sit down, Mr Van Vleet. The fact is, you're broke. Your wife's purse was never stolen.' Therese gave him a quick glance, but said nothing. 'And you were at Giancarlo's house the night he died.'

He clung to that: a guess, based on no more than Falco's

vague mention of the suspect as well built, and if it turned out to be a bad one, he was done for. But this time he saw in Van Vleet's face that he'd hit home. Reluctantly, the American sat. Beside him on the bed his wife was silent, her face tear-stained, but when it came to it, she spoke first.

'We argued, over dinner that night,' she said. 'I came home alone, at around midnight.' Darting a look at her husband. Not of fear, of what he might have done, but of weariness. 'He got back around two.'

All the bluster gone, Van Vleet spoke then, frightened. 'I was drunk,' he said. 'I wanted . . . I don't know. A girl, maybe.' He didn't meet his wife's eye. 'I'd had a call that day from the States, saying the IRS had been called in, back taxes on top of everything else, and the payroll wasn't being covered by the bank. You get used to doing things with the guys, when you don't want to think. He never asked me for money.' He looked almost tearful. 'It wasn't about money.'

Maybe, maybe not, Sandro had thought, but he'd said nothing. Now he stepped off the paved courtyard and down into the scented dark of the garden. Below him he could see a light on the elderly neighbour's terrace. It occurred to him that he should try to remember where the well was, so as not to go down it.

'Giancarlo wasn't home,' said Van Vleet. 'I rang a couple times, I went round the back, he'd told us his landlady was a – excuse me – a hardass.' Sandro didn't know the word, but he got the gist. 'I thought maybe . . . he didn't want to see me.' His face had changed, Sandro saw. The energy – for a fight, or for business, or a woman – had gone out of it, and he looked scared.

'You didn't hear anything? See anyone else?'

Van Vleet shook his head, white-faced. 'You have to believe me.'

'Well,' said Sandro – who did believe him, even if he wasn't ready to say it. 'Tell it to the Carabinieri, maybe.'

Therese Van Vleet had piped up then, and Van Vleet had looked at her gratefully. 'I did leave the billfold behind,' she said, lifting her chin. 'I just pushed it down behind the table. I didn't think what would happen – I just couldn't face them. What if my card had been declined? All of them would have known. Your wife would have known.'

'She would have looked after you.'

Therese looked up at his voice, slightly hoarse with the mention of Luisa.

'Brett does have those magazines,' she said, holding his gaze. 'It doesn't make him a criminal, though.' She'd drawn herself up and he felt a grudging admiration for her coming to the defence. 'Just like . . . the rest of it. The girls.' She'd given her husband another look. 'I don't like it. To tell you the truth,' and she looked at her husband straight, 'to tell you the truth, I've had enough of it.' She turned to Sandro. 'But hurt my little dog?' Therese turned the stained collar in her hands. 'And it wasn't me let Marjorie out of the steam room, it wasn't me put a magazine in your bag.' Her face was set stubborn, but there was something else in her frown, something of pity. 'I didn't know your wife had a . . . had the cancer.'

Would they go to Cornell? Would he get fired? They might. The further he descended in the dusk, the more remote from his concerns the possibility became: it sat above him in the great house. On her tiny terrace below, the neighbour became visible, looking up from an ancient swingseat with something in her lap. He stopped, not wanting to be seen, below the well now.

He'd reached a small gated area, with fenceposting and hedges planted to disguise it: he caught a whiff of something. This must be where the Palazzo hid its garbage. From her comfortable spot the old neighbour looked up from her work.

The old have excellent long sight, he thought, distracted by a momentary pang. Would he and Luisa ever get to sit in peace on a terrace somewhere? He got out his phone, weighed it in his hand. He should never have sent her across the city to that place. He felt his blood quicken, his sluggish heart stirred. It was dark now, and he didn't know where she was.

He dialled. A man answered.

*

The woman might have been waiting behind the door, she answered so quickly. Thin, with a lined, sour face and hair in stiff grey curls.

The landlady eyed Luisa crossly, then peered over her shoulder, immediately identifying the expensive car in the shabby little lot. Luisa's heart sank. *You know how to do it,* Sandro had said. But now the woman's beady eye was on her, she had no idea. Only the thought of having to scuttle back to Frollini persuaded her to hold her ground.

'It's about Giancarlo,' she said. 'Your tenant.'

The woman continued to stare. Beyond her, Luisa glimpsed a hall, an inner door and through it a heavy piece of dark brown furniture. She calculated that the villa was divided in half: the landlady inhabited the ground floor and let the apartment above.

'You're not the police,' the woman said. 'On first-name terms, were we?' She spoke with a nasty, insinuating tone.

Luisa said the first thing that came into her head, knowing the man's age, knowing he was the right age to be her son – or this woman's, for that matter. 'His mother—' she began, some sketchy plan of being a friend of his parents dying on her lips before she'd even started – but the woman interrupted her, anyway.

The landlady folded her arms across her thin chest. 'Shameful. No other word for it.'

'Well, I did hear . . .' Luisa hesitated. How far was she going to have to sympathise with this woman?

'To have a son like that, grow up like that. It must have broken her heart.' She looked anything but sorrowful; triumphant was more like it.

All the same, she'd stepped back, opening up a space between them. She wants to talk, this one, thought Luisa, glancing quickly back at the car. She could see Frollini's outline. 'You're right,' she said, easing a foot over the threshold. 'Signora . . . ah . . .'

'Maratti,' said the woman, maintaining her position. 'Valeria Maratti.'

And Luisa gasped – not because of the woman's name, but because she felt something that raised the hairs on the back of her neck, the lightest touch of something rubbing against her calf. A mew. She looked down and there was a cat, twining its way between her ankles. Luisa had noticed that the less you liked cats – and this one was a particularly weird-looking specimen, skinny with great bat ears – the more they liked to rub against you. Reluctantly, she made as if to stroke it.

'She doesn't like visitors.' Maratti bent down, between Luisa and the animal, making cooing noises. 'Women especially.' It writhed, pressing its head into the landlady's hand.

'Signora Maratti.' She was forced to speak to the woman's bowed head. 'Do you mind if I . . . it's so warm, suddenly, isn't it?'

The landlady straightened, and the cat fled noiselessly, bounding around the side of the house. Luisa fanned herself with her hand. 'I wonder if it's going to be like last summer? All those people dying. Do you have air-conditioning? You couldn't . . . just a glass of water? It's been. . .' She improvised. 'It's all been such a shock.'

Valeria Maratti moved aside with a tut, and Luisa stepped past her.

The apartment was dark, the green gloom filtering through vegetation just visible beyond half-curtained windows in the twilight. Maratti led Luisa into the room she'd glimpsed from the front door and gestured stiffly to an elderly sofa covered in some kind of scratchy green fabric, flanked by two wing chairs in the same stuff.

'A glass of water,' she said grudgingly. 'One moment.'

The landlady returned almost immediately – because she doesn't trust me, thought Luisa – with a single greasy glass. She set it down on a shiny coffee table in front of Luisa and stood over her with her arms tightly folded.

'I suppose she'll be back for his things. Or is that what she sent you for? I don't know if the police will allow it. They've sealed the rooms. A man from the army came, maybe they won't let her take anything until—' She stopped, indignant rather than afraid. 'It was a murder, you know.'

'So I can't go and look?' Luisa tried to make it sound innocent.

'Nothing to see,' said Signora Maratti tightly. 'A year and a half under my roof and you'd hardly know anyone lived there. Some sort of exercise machine, I suppose that should have told me. They like to . . . work out, don't they?'

'They?' said Luisa wearily. She became aware that on practically every surface in the room – chair backs, tables, sideboard – there was some kind of decorated cloth: embroidered, crocheted, appliquéd.

'Homosexuals,' said the woman, her mouth turning down.

Luisa hadn't even seen a picture of the man beyond the fuzzy mugshot in the paper: what did she know? 'Are you sure?' she said. 'I mean—'

'I'm afraid I got it from the horse's mouth.'

With those words, Maratti sat down in a wing-backed chair, shrunken in the gloom. Over her head on the wall a large black crucifix was prominent. She shook her head.

'He was very good at hiding it from me. Very good. He must have known I'd never have had him under my roof. But I suppose they go elsewhere to do their dirty business. Very well spoken, even if he wasn't proper Italian – only the father, I suppose.' She paused and Luisa wondered if she should ask what she meant, but then she went on. 'And he'd been in the army too. He said he'd been discharged because of illness – but I never believed that.'

'You didn't?'

'He seemed strong as an ox to me. Leukaemia, he said, but as far as I know you die of it.'

'Not always,' said Luisa, but she wasn't heard.

'I expect they found out, don't you?' A grey strand came loose from Maratti's stiff perm as she leaned forward vehemently. 'He had references but he could have made them up, couldn't he?' She settled back again with relish. 'It's only from the tap,' she said defiantly, gesturing at the murky glass. 'I thought you were thirsty?'

With reluctance Luisa sipped, setting the glass back down hurriedly. 'So you didn't know until recently that he was . . . gay.'

Maratti snorted at the word.

'But there were never any women?'

'Well, no girlfriends.' She frowned. 'That makes sense now, doesn't it? He was out in the evenings now and again, came back . . . cheerful. Pleased with himself. The odd army friend round. They didn't look like *finocchi* either.' The coarse term: *gayboys*. She frowned. 'I keep my eyes open.'

'Of course,' said Luisa.

The landlady was still talking. 'I wouldn't have stood for it, do you see? And they only came to talk business with him, that's what I thought. That's what it sounded like. Putting work his way.'

'Sounded like?' Luisa spoke lightly. She wondered what work ex-army colleagues would come round to talk about.

Spots of colour appeared on the landlady's cheeks. She'd have been up there with a glass pressed against the wall, Luisa could see it.

'From what I heard,' Maratti said flatly, and leaned forward again, towards her guest, over the hands folded in her lap; she might have been in pain. 'Who *are* you?' she said, with level dislike. 'You're not a friend of his mother's.'

So she wasn't fooled. Time, thought Luisa. It seemed to her she had no option but to tell Maratti the truth. 'Giancarlo had been working at the Palazzo San Giorgio,' she said carefully.

'I knew that,' said the landlady quickly. 'That's the business they were talking, last time around. A month or so ago. The new job.'

'Right,' said Luisa. 'They?' But the woman clamped her mouth shut.

Luisa went on. 'Giancarlo Vito was fired,' she said. 'My husband replaced him. And now Vito's dead.' She took a breath. 'His death is unexplained. Of course – we want to know more.'

In the dim light the woman's little beady eyes gleamed. 'I thought he'd been fired. He didn't go in on the Tuesday. It was the night before that I caught him at it. He'd been in a terrible temper. Marched past me without a word, then he spent a couple of hours making phone calls.'

'Did you hear any of them?'

Maratti's nostrils pinched, but she ignored the question. 'And then this man came around. Perhaps he needed . . . oh, you know how men are.'

Do I? wondered Luisa. I don't know if I do. 'Caught him at it? You mean, because he'd lost his job he needed . . . someone. You mean, sex.'

Avid, the old woman – as old as me, Luisa reminded herself – leaned forward again. 'Especially them, they're even worse.'

The room seemed stifling, suddenly. 'Are they,' Luisa said without expression. 'I don't quite see – you're sure?'

'He told me so himself,' said the landlady, settling back in the wing chair with satisfaction. 'He told me to my face. I had to knock, you see, they were making so much noise.'

'Noise,' said Luisa slowly. It didn't fit.

'I'm like you,' said Maratti. 'You see, I can tell. We don't want to believe such things go on. We're innocents, really. We give everyone the benefit of the doubt.'

Luisa didn't trust herself to open her mouth.

'He came to the door with this nasty expression on his face, like he wanted to shock me. His shirt was torn. Said it was just a bit of rough play,' Maratti said with relish. 'I knew it was a man in there with him because I'd seen the taxi drop him, bold as brass. Dark.' She sat up a bit straighter. 'Skinny. Perhaps he'd ordered him up. You know, on the internet. They do that, I've heard.'

Luisa ignored her. 'Do the Carabinieri know? About this visitor? Could you describe him?'

'I told them,' said Maratti. 'I have a great respect for the law, I told them that, too.' She hunched her shoulders. 'A shame I didn't get a good look at him, just dark, skinny, was all I could say.' She mused. 'Tallish. Do you suppose Giancarlo might have been . . . what d'you call it? You know, both men and women. Transsexual?'

'Bisexual,' said Luisa, distracted.

The landlady leaned forward again in the chair. 'They found traces of blood in the bathtub,' she said.

'How do you know that?' asked Luisa.

'Oh, these young men,' said Maratti coyly. 'The police technicians. They're just boys. They have respect for their elders – and if you ask, they'll tell you. I brought them coffee. They had the drains up.'

Oh, God, thought Luisa, let me out of here. Had they told Sandro any of this? She took a deep breath.

A violent encounter on Monday, the day he was fired. But Vito didn't die until the following night.

'Did you see Giancarlo again? Before you found . . . his body?'

'I told them,' she said, nostrils sucked in. 'I saw him leaving that afternoon. I thought he was going on holiday, gone back to Bari again, or maybe on a job.'

'On holiday,' Luisa repeated. Something occurred to her then, she'd jumped too far ahead.

'And how about the other guy,' she asked cautiously. 'You must have been curious, I mean . . . it's only natural.' Maratti gave her a beady look, and Luisa felt suddenly claustrophobic, sweaty. But she went on. 'A taxi dropped him, you said.' She stood up out of the chair abruptly, wanting to be gone.

Maratti stood too; she moved across to the front window and raised the roller blind with a practised hand, barely a rattle. 'At nine or so.' She leaned close to the glass, looking out.

Standing beside her, Luisa saw Frollini's car, saw him in the front seat, a tiny light on the screen of the mobile he was lifting to his ear.

'Nine,' said Luisa. The gloomy apartment seemed nothing more than an elaborate hide, with spyholes at every vantage point. She wanted more than anything to be out of there. 'Just one more question,' she said.

In the car outside, Enrico Frollini handed her her mobile in the passenger seat. She could smell his aftershave. 'It rang,' he said. 'Your husband's going to be late, he won't be able to cook. He's booked the Buca, eight o'clock.'

She didn't know if the disbelief in his voice was at the idea of a man cooking, or the fact that Sandro had booked them into a restaurant they couldn't afford.

Frollini leaned down and turned the key in the ignition.

Chapter Twenty-Four

HUNCHED OVER THE COMPUTER, Giuli had been barely aware of the growing darkness beyond the window, but the noisy twilight chatter of the starlings in the trees of the Piazza Tasso had grown deafening. She raised her head in the warm sweet air of evening, thinking.

She'd had to come back to the office; she'd hoped Enzo would have hung around, but she only found a note from him on the desk. *Sent a few things over to Sandro. I'll cook dinner. Give me a call.* She stared down at her phone. Better face to face, she thought.

When she and Marjorie Cameron had come out of Gilli, the afternoon had turned sweaty and oppressive, one of those days when all the freshness and green and sweetness of spring was suddenly gone, and the summer was bearing down already. As she crossed the river the sun had been almost down.

Marjorie Cameron hadn't been alone when Giuli had left her outside Gilli in the Piazza Repubblica. There'd been no sign of her husband yet, but the older woman, Juliet Fleming, had appeared, head down, deep in thought, from the direction of the Duomo. It seemed that she'd been to visit Athene Morris in the hospital – she'd turned to point back in its direction – and that had set Cameron off all of a twitter again. Giuli had made her escape.

It wasn't until Giuli got across the Ponte alla Carraia and the shadowed length of the Via dei Serragli stretched ahead of her into the Oltrarno that she had started to be able to think clearly. Marjorie Cameron had told her someone had been in Athene Morris's room last night: a man, to be more precise. 'I heard a man's voice,' she'd said, uneasy.

'Did you recognise the voice?'

In the soft glow of Gilli's interior, the woman had flushed at Giuli's question, almost pretty with the colour in her pale face, and she'd shaken her head. 'Her neighbour's the sculptor,' she'd said then, and looked down into her lap. 'His door was open, too.'

Giuli took out her phone and set it on the desk beside the computer. Sandro needed to know this, but first she needed to fill out the picture herself. Check the witness's background. Marjorie Cameron's husband had been seeing lawyers. She clicked on the attachments Enzo had sent.

International Herald Tribune, Reuters, Al-Jazeera, all running with the same dire report. *Syrian bridge collapse kills seven. International condemnation. President Assad calls for inquiry.* She clicked at random on an article from *La Repubblica* – at least it was in her own language. She read it as dark fell beyond the window with a vengeance, and just as she lifted her head from the screen her mobile jittered on the desktop beside her.

Enzo, she thought. Damn, damn. I'm late.

But it was Sandro. 'Hello?'

He was ranting: something about Frollini.

'Hold on,' she said. 'You called Luisa, and he answered her phone?'

'What's she up to? Letting the old lecher give her a lift. And what kind of husband am I, sending her out there?' He let out an explosive sound of frustration and she gave up, letting him go on. When he paused for breath she could hear a murmur of voices in the background. She hoped the residents of the Palazzo San Giorgio weren't listening in.

'I hope you didn't shout at him,' said Giuli mildly.

'I should have done,' Sandro growled, going off again. 'He had the cheek to tell me he thought the Buca dell'Orafo had gone downhill.' She let him blow himself out.

'All right,' she said finally. 'Is that it?'

He sighed, deflated. 'Not exactly,' he said.

'Did you see the emails we sent?' she said. Silence. 'Enzo and I did some research,' she went on. 'On the residents. Did you know the engineer's being sued? Maybe the journalist, Carlsson, was after his story.' Silence. She sighed. 'Have you even opened that computer?'

'It's been a busy day,' he said, defensive. 'And I don't like that office.'

'Well, never mind,' Giuli said. 'Just check it later. It could be nothing, anyway. I'll keep looking.'

'All right,' Sandro said, distracted. 'Look, I'd better . . . I've just seen someone. Waiting for me.'

'Don't go,' she said, because suddenly it seemed urgent. 'That's . . . that's not all. I bumped into the engineer's wife this afternoon.' He sighed. 'It's about the old lady who had the stroke,' she went on quickly, hearing his impatience.

That held him. 'How did you know about that?'

Giuli told him what Marjorie Cameron had said.

'The sculptor,' he mused, slowly. 'He's not here. I did see him this afternoon, I can't quite—' His hand went over the mouthpiece as he called something out, then he was back. 'Him, really?'

Outside, the starlings had grown deafening. Aware of the time, and of Enzo waiting for her at home, she stood up abruptly from the desk and crossed to the window, pushing it further open. Cooking smells, and a weary, end-of-day conversation being carried on below her in the street. 'I don't know,' she said, suddenly tired. 'She's one of those women, it was like getting blood out of a stone. She was cagey. Maybe it's that husband of hers, always telling her to shut up.'

Sandro grunted.

She went on. 'Perhaps someone else there saw him, you'd need to corroborate it.'

On the other end of the line Sandro had quickly gone very quiet indeed.

'Sandro?' she said. 'Look, I'll check on the guy, Lludic, how about that? I'll do some research on him, too.'

'Leave it with me,' he said, curtly. 'You hear me, Giuli? Go home. I'll deal with it.'

*

It was Lauren Tassi, the woman who'd made Sandro drink with her the night before, whose face had appeared in his dream, standing square-shouldered in silhouette in front of Lludic's sculpture. Sandro stepped up on to the flagstones, pocketing his phone.

Giuli had emailed him. He'd left the laptop in his office. Christ, had he even locked the door, would he never learn? And where was Lludic? Below them in the garden there were voices, but not the sculptor's.

'I thought it was you, down there,' said Lauren Tassi. 'I hope I didn't interrupt something.' He stared, trying to concentrate. 'Your conversation,' she said, holding her arms tight across her body, and he refocused, looking at her properly. She wore a plain white shirt that made her skin look brown and healthy in the dark. 'It was you I wanted.'

'You did?' he said, momentarily, stupidly flattered. Then hastily he cleared his throat. 'Work,' he said. 'You got home all right? Last night.'

'I came to apologise,' she said. Then, 'What is that thing?'

He turned. 'I'm too old to know what it means,' he said, looking at Danilo Lludic's sculpture in the courtyard. He couldn't remember if it had looked so outlandish – and so threatening – when it had been unveiled last night, like a great rogue boulder left in the aftermath of a landslip.

'You arrived after the unveiling,' he said. 'It's Lludic's. I believe it was commissioned for the residence.' He cleared his throat again. 'You know anything about art?'

Lauren Tassi shook her head impatiently, looking at him from under her thick brows. It seemed to Sandro that she wanted to tell him something.

'Come with me,' he said, steering her ahead of him, feeling

her give in, but not without resistance. 'Get out of earshot,' he explained.

She walked ahead of him, down through the hedged pathways; he watched the thick bell of her hair sway as she moved, streaked with grey, and registered the sturdy grace of her hips.

'You don't have anything to apologise for,' he said, pointing a hand towards the lounger. 'As far as I remember.' He sat. After a moment's hesitation, she gave in and lowered herself to the white canvas.

'I'd drunk too much,' she said, and looked down at her hands, ringless and unadorned.

'I'm sure you had your reasons,' said Sandro. She shrugged, not raising her head. What had she come for? 'You're a – a colleague of Professor Scardino's,' he said, tentatively.

And with her sigh something fell into place.

'I see,' he said. Professor Scardino, who happened to be married. 'You've known him a long time.'

She nodded. How old was she? Ten years younger than Scardino? A year or so older than the Professor's wife.

'I was a graduate student under him at Cambridge,' she said. 'I've known him twenty years.'

She's in love with him. 'I'm sorry,' he said without thinking, and a smile broke across her face, transforming it, then as quickly as it had come, it disappeared.

'It's all right,' she said. 'I know it's hopeless. A woman like Magda doesn't let go too easily.'

Even in the cooling dusk Sandro felt the heat of the southern hillside at his back, and the summer on its way. He thought of

Professor Scardino's hand, stalled and trembling. 'You never know,' he said. 'She might.'

'The Parkinson's?' she said. 'She'll just employ someone to deal with it.'

At the thought of illness, Sandro found himself hoping old Athene Morris was still alive. 'Magda Scardino told my wife I should keep my nose out of their business,' he said.

'I bet she did,' said Lauren Tassi. 'She's quite a number. Maybe that's what he needs. A force of nature.'

'That, too,' Sandro said, and the image of Lludic's boulder came into his head, Magda Scardino like the landslide that had brought it to a halt in the elegant courtyard. 'What is their business, exactly?'

She looked at him askance. 'What do you mean?' Wary.

'Is he . . . that intelligent? I mean, like an Einstein, is that what turns her on?'

Lauren Tassi looked at him, shaking her head a little. 'I guess you wouldn't know,' she said, thoughtfully.

'Wouldn't know what?'

'His research,' she said, and she took off her glasses in a moment of unselfconscious eagerness. Her eyes were large and grey, but without the glasses she looked vulnerable.

'It's the next big thing. He plays it down – but it's huge.' She put the glasses back on.

Sandro frowned. 'Garbage?' he said with an effort. 'Something like . . . recycling?'

'Biofuels,' said Lauren, smiling faintly. 'He's working on algae that produce a fuel oil. You can grow them offshore. Obviously it has all sorts of implications.'

'Ecological implications?' He spoke cautiously.

'Think of the wars that have been fought over oil,' said Lauren Tassi, looking off into the great city, slumbering in the velvet dark.

Above them on the upper terrace something was happening, heads moving to and fro, as though ferrying props. Lludic? No.

She turned back to him, intent. 'Think of Russian oligarchs and Texan billionaires and Gulf sheikhs. That's the level Charles – I mean, Professor Scardino – is operating at, though he's quite keen not to make it too public. Nor's Magda.'

'She's involved?'

Lauren laughed, a brief, bitter sound. 'Involved?' she said. 'She's in charge. Magda's not just his wife, she's his minder, his agent. She negotiates his contracts and decides where they go, who their friends are. Whose money they take.'

'Whose money?'

'Governments pursue him,' she said carefully. 'He's out of my league.' She took a deep breath, and stood up from the lounger. He saw her eyes gleam. 'She's not even faithful to him.'

'She's not?' Sandro was on his feet too, eye to eye with her. 'How do you know?'

Lauren Tassi held his gaze, suddenly weary. 'It's a small world,' she said. 'The scientific community. We look very busy, we go to conferences thousands of miles apart, we look like our minds are always on higher things maybe, in our labs. In our cloisters.' She looked away.

'Anyone in particular?' said Sandro, picking up on something in her voice.

Tassi looked up at the façade of the palace above them. A champagne cork popped and there was a little spatter of applause. Any excuse. 'She likes them . . . rough-cut, if you know what I mean. Disposable types. Picks them up, puts them down, moves on. So. You want his name?'

'I have to phone my wife,' said Sandro, knowing how ridiculous that would sound but not wanting to hear what she was about to say, suddenly. Not wanting this woman – decent, clever, unhappy – to turn malicious before his eyes. *I don't want to know.*

'I think you do,' she said, answering her own question.

Chapter Twenty-Five

ENRICO FROLLINI'S TAIL-LIGHTS DISAPPEARED off down the Via dei Macci, the big car moving gingerly in the narrow, littered street. Luisa felt nothing but relief.

Sexual harassment, she supposed it might be called. Poor Enrico: he wasn't used to rejection, and it wasn't like he'd even put a hand on her. Just the sheer persistence of it tired her, the offers, the suggestions, the banter and the pleading look that was replaced with a mournful one. All he wanted from her was an acknowledgement that she harboured a kind of love – more or less any kind, she divined, would do – for him. And she refused.

It was ungrateful, she supposed. It had been nice of him to take her out there and bring her back, but she could have managed, there were taxis. Had it been unfair of Sandro to send her out there, as Frollini had been implying since he made her take the lift? No. She was his partner, she was his co-worker. She wanted that, she didn't want Frollini's air-conditioned car and the mistress's standard pair of diamond earrings every birthday.

'Your husband said he'd get the car and meet you there.' He'd looked at her, expectant.

A husband who wouldn't even pick her up to take her to dinner, had been his subtext. A husband whose car was parked on the ringroad covered in birdshit.

It was quite possible in any case that Frollini had made that bit up himself so he could press her into taking another lift in his leather-lined car. When she'd said no, she needed to go home and change, he'd said, I'll wait. Quickly adding, outside. *No*, she'd snapped then. *No*. And getting inside her own flat, pushing open the kitchen window and breathing in the ripe, overheated street, Luisa realised that in all the years she'd worked for him she *had* considered the possibility, had comforted herself with the thought of those diamond earrings and his admiration. Or at least, she hadn't ruled it out – until now.

The Maratti woman had turned her pretty sour: those doilies and traycloths and the stale-smelling kitchen, the effort of trying to make sense of what the woman had said and trying to remember it, and all the time with the awful feeling that something more urgent was nagging for her attention. Something in her gut, that pulled and twisted.

And to have opened the car door and seen Frollini's expression as he hung up on her husband was the last straw. The thought of what Sandro might have read into the situation made her want to scream at both of them.

Leave me alone. I've got more important things to think about than two grown men – old men – bickering like children.

Enzo had called Luisa that afternoon, and left a message.

Do you think she wants out? I'm trying. But she's here, then she disappears.

And that was the thing in her gut: Giuli.

Wet from the shower, looking at the kitchen clock – it was seven, she'd need ten minutes in a cab to Fiesole, plenty of time – she called Giuli again. Engaged. She called the house phone, and got Enzo.

'She's here,' he said, sounding ragged. 'She's trying to get hold of someone. Some old schoolfriend.' Luisa was taken aback – who? Enzo went on. 'She's having trouble getting through and she's got a bee in her bonnet, the usual. Look,' he lowered his voice, 'don't tell her I called you this afternoon, all right? Don't tell her I was worried.' Then his hand went over the receiver and she heard him call, 'It's Luisa, sweetheart.' Then Giuli was on the phone.

'Jesus, what a day,' Giuli said, loud and breathless into the receiver, but there was exhilaration as well as urgency in her voice. 'Have you talked to Sandro?'

Luisa felt a pulse of panic. 'Why?'

'What *were* you doing with Frollini? Out late with him?'

'Oh, for God's sake,' said Luisa. 'Has anything actually happened? Who's this friend you're trying to get hold of?'

Giuli made a sound of frustration Luisa recognised. 'It might be nothing,' she said. 'I was so busy trying to get things straight in my head. I got hung up looking up all the residents in that place online, trying to help Sandro. What a bunch. Vipers, the lot of them.'

'You're telling me,' said Luisa. 'I was with them all day.'

Giuli wasn't listening. 'It's the girl from last night.'

'Girl?'

Giuli's voice was impatient. 'I never told you. A girl I was at school with was at the unveiling. Elena, her boyfriend . . . oh, never mind. It's just that she's not answering her phone, and I wanted to warn her about someone. A guy who's got a thing for her. An artist. I found something out about him.'

The voice went muffled and Luisa heard her call over her shoulder to placate Enzo, her tone suddenly soft and gentle. Then abruptly she was back, sharp and brisk as ever.

'It's probably nothing, like I said. She can look after herself.' She was distracted.

'Are you okay?' Luisa said cautiously. 'Has something happened? At the Centre?'

'I haven't told Enzo yet,' said Giuli. 'But I know who's been telling lies about me.'

Luisa heard the exhilaration in her voice again, and she wasn't sure if it was a good thing.

'And what are you going to do?' She felt suddenly sick with anxiety.

'I don't know.' Her voice was lowered, and Luisa didn't like it. There were things Enzo didn't want Giuli to hear, and vice versa.

Again her hand went over the receiver and Luisa heard her say, light and loving, 'I'll be right there, sweetheart.' And she hung up.

*

Where was it? Stopping, perplexed and sweaty in the hot darkness under the ringroad's trees, Sandro swore softly.

It was three weeks since he'd last used the car. Below the Piazza Beccaria, four lanes of late rush-hour traffic streamed, tail-lights and exhaust fumes spooling their glinting filament around and around the city. He always left the car here, in the same place give or take, because here you didn't need to move it for road-cleaning, and the *vigili* – the traffic police – left the cars alone on this stretch.

Which was significant, as his resident's permit had expired. Sandro's stomach tightened with self-reproach: why am I so useless? *Can't renew my permits in time, can't even remember where I left my own car.* What must have happened was, he'd managed to get himself towed, of course he had, even where no one's been towed in years, because, like all his country's many and various unspoken agreements, this one could be rescinded at no notice.

Under his feet in the dark last autumn's dead leaves rustled, waste paper and dogshit, the hot dry smell of summer approaching. And then Sandro stopped and his heart lifted, quite unexpectedly; it soared. A reprieve. The spattered brown roof of his unglamorous, unlauded 1986 Fiat 600 sat humbly patient, between a camper van and an elderly BMW canted over with a flat tyre, waiting for him.

The little engine coughed, turned over and started first time. Sandro resisted the urge to lean and kiss the cracked dashboard in gratitude. The car's interior breathed out the day's heat, the crumbs of something long staled on the back seat, warm leatherette, ancient cigarette smoke from the last time he'd given Giuli a lift; he always told her not to, but she would lean out of the window and ignore him. He wished she'd give up.

Craning his neck to see, Sandro pulled into the heavy evening traffic. A pair of headlights moved out for him and, turning back, he let the day out with a long sigh.

Winding down his window, Sandro almost wished for a cigarette himself, as if taking up smoking again after twenty years could bring back that sudden cool clear-headedness of his younger self, that ability to set out his evidence in a row and make sense of it.

Out of uneasy politeness he'd taken half a glass of champagne – the real deal, curved script on an orange label, all the way from the low white hills of northern France – before finally slipping away from the Palazzo, and it had gone to his head. Softened all his thinking, all the order he'd spent the day fighting for, into a sludge.

Therese Van Vleet anxious for her husband. Marjorie Cameron, whose husband was being sued, and who said she'd heard someone in Athene Morris's room. Sir Martin Fleming, who'd suggested Mauro read Machiavelli.

Magda Scardino, who bartered and haggled over her husband's brain. What did Parkinson's do to you? The circuits sparking and flaring, the blood vessels congesting, the nerves hardening like coral?

Magda, who'd been sleeping with Giancarlo Vito.

Lauren Tassi had slipped away quickly. Sandro had seen the sideways glance she'd given Charles Scardino as she'd gone, edging round the small crowd gathered on the terrace. He'd seen a faint smudge of colour appear in the Professor's sallow face as she passed: Magda had barely turned her head, but she'd registered Tassi's departure all right. Had she won? At least Lauren Tassi got to escape from the Palazzo San Giorgio.

The champagne had been for Alessandra Cornell. The man in the silver-framed photograph on her desk had proposed to her, it seemed, that afternoon. He stood there at her side on the terrace, tall, pale, well bred. Alessandra Cornell had had enough. It seemed to Sandro that her decision to jump had a lot to do with climbing into the back of that ambulance with Athene Morris. On the other side of the attaché stood Gastone Bottai, looking murderous.

Cornell was apologising, talking about her notice period, gazing blindly up at her fiancé. Sandro hoped she knew what she was doing. As if on cue, Magda Scardino had nudged into him: had it been her breast that had pushed against his upper arm? He'd smelled her perfume and stepped back, on his guard. Her breast was far enough distant for him not to know, but he'd been caught looking at it. She was wearing a red silk dress whose reflection made her skin glow and gleamed in her hair. She smiled, but it wasn't friendly.

'I know what you think of me,' she said, lightly, not looking at him. 'Does that surprise you? You and your wife.'

'Mrs Scardino,' he said, scenting danger. 'I am only here to be at your service.'

'Of course you are,' she said, turning to him, and she laughed. Sandro had not blushed, he felt, in fifty years. The heat rose under his collar and he remembered all the women last night. Maybe it was the male menopause. A bit late. 'I didn't have to pay him, you know. Whatever that little bitch might have said. And we believe in freedom, my husband and I.'

Freedom. Sandro pondered the word. It meant, he realised, almost nothing to him. No such thing. She must have seen his expression.

'You don't believe in sexual freedom,' Magda said. 'I can see that. But it isn't against the law, not in this country.'

He bowed just a little. 'Perhaps I'm just too old,' he said, 'to find the idea of freedom exciting.'

'Oh dear.' Magda Scardino's laugh was scornful. 'How sad. But then you're a man; men are always so much more . . . timid.' Was that true? Maybe. 'Look at Athene – well, even Athene's old now. But she was worse than me, in her time. More *free*, let's say. She started with old men and moved on to younger ones.'

'But without the security of a husband.'

'Someone paid for her apartment,' said Magda, shrugging. He wondered if she knew who: he decided she did. 'We all have a price. Even you, Mr Honest and Upright.'

Sandro looked at her, but she didn't return his gaze, suddenly busy instead with arranging her dress at the neckline, looking down approvingly at herself. The fact that Athene Morris was lying in a hospital bed, unable to speak or move, was obviously not her concern.

It came to Sandro that Athene Morris had known something, and that was why she was in hospital now. That was why she would soon be dead. 'Someone told my colleague that Danilo Lludic went to see Miss Morris last night,' he said.

Magda pulled her head back to get a look at him. 'Your colleague?' she said, letting out an abrupt little laugh. Had he made her nervous? 'You have a whole team at your service?' Her voice lowered, husky. 'Are you investigating us?'

For a split second he wondered if he might conceivably have unsettled her, but then she smiled her cat smile, her little sharp teeth showing. 'Oh, you mean the woman you brought last night.'

'Giulietta,' he said. Let her underestimate Giuli if she liked.

'Well, clever her. Yes, he was up there; I saw him from here.' She turned and looked up at the façade, Athene Morris's big second-floor window closed and shuttered now. 'So I suppose it came on in the middle of the night, after he'd gone. The stroke, or whatever.'

'Perhaps,' he said, quietly. 'Have you heard how she is?

Magda turned back to him, her gaze briefly snagging on someone beyond them. 'She's still alive, if that's what you mean,' she said, carelessly brutal. Then, more vaguely, 'Someone visited this afternoon, I think. Apparently the next twenty-four hours will be crucial.' She shrugged. 'But really, at her age . . . I mean, you could see it as merciful.'

From someone else's mouth it might have been acceptable, or to someone else's ears, but Magda Scardino was one of those women: you wanted to make her pay attention. You wanted to take her by the throat. You wanted to hurt her.

'Did Vito try to blackmail you, after he'd slept with you?' Sandro said, trying to keep the anger out of his voice but hearing it thicken.

'I could have you fired,' she said, her flecked eyes dark. 'I didn't need to pay him for it. Although he did want something from me.'

'Something more than sex.' She kept her gaze steady. 'And did he get it?'

'He might have done, if Ian Cameron hadn't got him fired. I was considering my options.'

'What did he want?' She just shook her head, so he probed. 'So you had no reason to wish him . . . ill.' Dead, was what he meant.

'Wish Giancarlo ill?' She laughed lightly and her hair tumbled around her face as her head moved. 'He was just a baby. Did your wife tell you we didn't like him?' A sigh. 'We adored him. Poor Giancarlo.'

'And what about that handsome journalist, what was his name, John Carlsson?' He watched her for a reaction, but there was none. 'Did you adore him, too?' She pulled back a little, fixing him, amused. 'He came here looking for someone a few days ago, didn't he? Sniffing around. Would you know who he wanted?'

Magda Scardino regarded him. 'Yes,' she said. 'Sniffing around is about right. He asked me if Giancarlo was off the scene. I told him he wasn't my type. He is good-looking, isn't he?'

Was, thought Sandro. And asking about Giancarlo.

She leaned in. 'Do you think he might know something, you know, for your *investigation*?'

And she had looked over his shoulder. 'Darling,' she said smoothly to her husband, who had arrived beside them, and taking him firmly by the elbow she steered them both away without another word.

Ahead of him now on the ringroad, lights blinked, moved, the blockage easing. A figure was moving through the traffic, selling something. Nifty, these rush-hour vendors, one eye on the lights changing, the other scanning the cars for movement. He wondered what the death and injury rate was: half of them looked maimed already.

Negotiating a path through the crowd of guests – a raft of younger people had turned up, no doubt friends of the happy couple – Sandro had had to track Alessandra Cornell down before he left. She might be abandoning ship, but he'd be damned if he'd ask Bottai if it was all right if he went home. Cornell's fiancé was holding court on the terrace, but the bride-to-be was nowhere to be seen. Remembering his laptop, Sandro had headed to his office, in through the courtyard, a quick sidestep at the wide staircase, past the lifts. To his relief he found that he had locked it after all, and even managed to locate the bunch of keys in his briefcase.

It had been coming back that he'd found Alessandra Cornell, frowning down at her mobile at the top of the stairs that led to the cellars.

Sandro was all too aware that he still hadn't said a word to her about what he'd seen at the morgue that morning. Fortunately for him she seemed to have forgotten his errand: the suitcase that might have belonged to someone at the Palazzo. Other things on her mind. That cat would be amongst the pigeons soon enough, and in the meantime it was simply easier to say nothing.

Of course, she might have just stepped out of the lift, or come down from the upper floors, but what Sandro said to her, before he could stop himself was, 'Been paying a last visit to the torture chamber?'

Her head snapped up instantly, eyes wide. Trying to make a joke of it, Sandro said, 'That'll be good practice for marriage.'

'You'd better not let Gastone hear you talking like that,' Alessandra Cornell said.

'Once you're gone he'll get rid of me, won't he?' said Sandro. She smiled wearily, but said nothing. 'Because he's got something to hide?'

She snorted. 'Gastone?' She shook her head. 'He hasn't the brains.' She put the mobile away. 'A message,' she said. 'The Carabinieri want to talk to me.' She sighed. 'You wouldn't know what about?'

Sandro shrugged. 'Search me.' Not exactly a lie. He hesitated. 'I could call them, if you like? I was about to ask if I could leave, but . . .'

Alessandra looked at him a long moment: tired like that, you could almost imagine her a mother. 'I'll call them back in the morning,' she said. 'If I feel like it.'

'He's a lucky man,' said Sandro, sincere. 'You're doing the right thing.'

'Running away?' She shivered. 'I thought I – you and I – I thought we could bring it under control. I thought it was just coincidence. Or – or mischief.'

'But it's not, is it?' said Sandro.

'It's evil,' she said, and although he didn't like the word, he didn't correct her. 'Athene,' she said, and he saw the distress on her face. 'An old woman. In the ambulance she was trying to tell me something and she couldn't make me understand. Her eyes—' She broke off.

'I know,' said Sandro. 'I saw.'

She straightened her collar, rubbed her eyes. 'I just have this – this feeling.' She glanced over her shoulder, down the stairs, then quickly back at him. 'That there's worse to come.'

Something occurred to him. 'Who was it,' he said, 'who found Marjorie Cameron in the steam room? Who let her out?'

The colour was returning to her cheeks, she seemed unburdened. 'Who? Oh, I see.' She frowned at him. 'I believe it was Mrs Scardino, as a matter of fact. Magda.'

The vendor was beside his car now and through the window Sandro handed him a coin and took the paper. He thought with longing of the restaurant table, and his wife sitting there in the soft light waiting for him.

His phone went: *Giuli*, it said. He juggled the phone and the paper; the traffic was stationary and he set the paper down.

Gay Slaying: Man Sought, it said.

He answered the phone. 'Giuli,' he said, and sighed.

Chapter Twenty-Six

MARESCIALLO FALCO HAD BEEN raging behind the door of his office. 'Where the Jesus fucking Christ did this come from?' his secretary Carlotta Franchi heard, through the flimsy partitioning. Followed by, 'Well I sure as hell didn't say anything.' Then, 'Christ. I suppose I'm going to have to talk to Cellini, if Cornell's not answering.'

He'd asked her to put him through to Gastone Bottai at the Palazzo San Giorgio. The man had come in to the office that afternoon, and it had been all very civilised then: coffee and a chat, two gentlemen looking pleased with themselves and shaking hands at the door.

Before the clatter of the receiver going down had died away, Falco was storming towards her through the door, his face like thunder. For a minute Carlotta thought he was going to accuse her of feeding the story to the evening newspaper. She didn't have the balls to ask, *Is it true?* He stopped in his tracks at the sight of her, glaring.

'Get me the names of the officers first on the scene,' he said.

'And the forensic team. Now.'

One look at his face was enough to prevent Carlotta saying, they'll be at home eating dinner by now, I should have been gone an hour ago myself. As if he'd read her thoughts, he went on, rigid with anger, 'I don't care if they're bathing their newborn children or burying their mothers. Get them in here.'

But five minutes later he was out of his office again, and miraculously calm. All smiles, in fact. 'Get me Cellini, would you?' he said.

*

'Talk to me,' pleaded Enzo at last, all his resolve gone. Dinner was eaten, the kitchen was dark and he and Giuli were sitting – together but not feeling like it, not at all – in the tiny sitting room, the TV flickering with some idiotic gameshow neither of them was paying any attention to.

She'd come in close to an hour later than he'd expected her, pale, her eyes somewhere else entirely. She'd kissed him, muttered *sorry* into the side of his face, but offered no further explanation. He'd listened, while trying not to look like he was, to one side of the conversation with Luisa. *She loves you,* Luisa had said to him earlier, but he'd heard something in her voice that unsettled him. *She wants this,* Luisa had said. In dull despair, he didn't believe her.

He'd cooked dinner while Giuli sat at the computer, raising his head from the pan when he heard a hiss of triumph, but only to see her lean down again and tap in another set of characters.

He'd heard the message Giuli had left on the answering

machine of the girl she'd been at school with. Elena: she'd worried him, for a start. The way Giuli had disappeared this afternoon, her failure to answer his calls, now this Elena, this woman from the past, stirring things up.

'I don't think you should get too close to Danilo Lludic,' Giuli had said into the phone, and he'd heard the panic in her voice. 'I don't think you should see him again. It's not safe. Call me, Elena?'

She'd sat staring at the phone for a good ten minutes then, almost catatonic with tension, and she hadn't looked at him standing over her.

Now she did look up, at last, reluctant, the TV remote loosely in her hands. Slowly she raised it and clicked: the noisy screen died. She looked a long moment into his face and, seeing only desolation, he thought grimly, that's it.

'Is it over?' he said. 'I mean, you and me?'

And her face flared into infuriated life. '*What?*'

'This girl,' he said helplessly. 'This woman, this Elena.' He didn't know how to explain. 'The Centre – it's the past, coming back to clobber us. I always thought I could wipe it out for you, the past.' He wasn't making much sense, not even to himself, but Giuli leaned forward, closer, and courage flickered inside him.

'You can't wipe it out,' she said, with an impatient sideways brush of her hand. 'I don't care about the Centre any more. I can sort that.'

'You can?' He waited for her to explain.

'As long as you believed me,' she said, which wasn't an explanation, but set a pulse of hope up inside him.

'I believed you,' he stated flatly. He didn't need to sell her that, surely.

She nodded, just once. 'I know.'

'So what—' He broke off because she'd bent over, her face in her hands, trying to hold something back. When she took the hands away he saw that it was all right, that she'd tell him now. Her face had softened, crumpled: it was giving way, and he waited.

'Her boyfriend's dead,' she said, tonelessly. 'Elena's boyfriend's dead. Murdered. I was so . . . offhand with her, I thought he'd just done a runner, you know what guys are like.'

'Not me,' Enzo said, but she didn't seem to hear.

'I thought she'd be fine, because she already had this other man, this sculptor, chasing after her. And I find out the boyfriend's dead but I'm too chicken to tell her.'

'Poor woman,' said Enzo, frowning.

She nodded fiercely. 'And the other man—' She broke off, looking right through him, fixed on something worse.

'What?' he said, but she didn't answer, only got to her feet and retrieved her laptop from the kitchen.

He was patient while it started up, watching her face illuminated by the screen. She set it on his lap and he saw a page of newsprint, the *New York Post*. It was in English: he shrugged helplessly, having no more than a handful of words in the language. Giuli edged up next to him and he felt the heat in her body. It could be just the humid evening, the stifling apartment, but it seemed unhealthy.

'You're burning up,' he said.

She didn't seem to hear. She raised a finger to a paragraph

headed: *Sculptor Lludic: Charges Dropped.* There was a small photograph of a bulky, bear-like man, haggard beneath a beard, being jostled in a small crowd on the steps of some city building.

'This is the other man,' she said. 'I was even ribbing her about him, called him her boyfriend.' Giuli stopped abruptly, as if she'd run out of breath. 'He was accused of violent rape.'

Enzo stared at her, and in her closed white face he saw that other world he'd spent three years trying to shut them away from: all the men before him, the men who'd damaged her and stolen from her and used her body. Helpless, useless, wrong – that was how he felt.

'I think you'd better call Sandro,' he said.

*

He had phoned from the hospital. 'They won't let me see her,' he said, and she could hear tears in his voice. 'Can I come over?'

'All right,' said Elena, weary. 'All right.' And if she was making a mistake, well, it wouldn't be the first time.

Chapter Twenty-Seven

QUITE COMPOSED, LUISA SAT alone at her table in the restaurant. At the bar the waiter was eyeing her as he waited for a trayful of drinks. She'd been there twenty minutes and he'd brought her an *aperitivo*. 'I'm waiting for my husband.'

They never came here. It was too expensive: it was the kind of place where Luisa might spot clients, and Sandro would squirm in his seat because his jacket was too shabby.

The information had seemed to cheer the waiter, who was about her age, but now he was worried about her, she could tell. She watched him cross the room, glancing back at her. He appeared at her table with a folded newspaper and a plate of *crostini*. 'While you wait,' he said.

Should she have returned the missed call? He might have been running late, he might have been cancelling.

The waiter retreated, and she unfolded the paper. The headline jumped at her, but at the same time the door into the restaurant opened and, primed as she had been to watch for Sandro, she looked, the image of the newsprint sitting unprocessed on her retina. Because there he was.

Looking worried. 'What's up?' she said. At the back of her mind she tried to fix on her mission, what Maratti had told her. It occurred to her that she should have written it down, or something.

'Giuli just called me,' he said, and seemed to deflate into his seat. 'She's in a state.'

'Not Enzo? The wedding?'

He took a breath, shook his head.

Luisa listened, in dread. If anything was going to get to Giuli, it was the thought of putting another woman in the way of that kind of danger. Violent men was something Giuli knew all about.

Sandro passed a hand over his face. 'And Magda Scardino says she saw Lludic in Athene Morris's room last night.'

'Her.' Luisa made a sound in her throat.

'Lludic lives next door to Athene Morris, and Magda says she saw him closing her shutters.' He sighed. 'I told Giuli. Mistake.'

'Well, it's hardly keeping a low profile,' said Luisa, thinking hard. 'The worst case scenario, let's say the sculptor did rape his ex-girlfriend, and got off. He's been accused of rape once, he's not going to risk it happening again. Is he?'

Sandro just looked at her: she could see something gnawing. 'I don't know,' he said.

She sat and thought. 'Do you think he's a psychopath?' He looked startled. 'Because he would have to be. Wouldn't he?'

Sandro frowned. 'No,' he said finally. 'I don't think so. But I hardly know him.'

He looked old, and worried. Luisa leaned forward and put a hand on his. 'You always had that instinct,' she said. 'You can still trust it.' He looked at her, unconvinced. 'Don't you want to know how it went?' she said. 'I talked to the landlady, you know. Or are you too hung up on Enrico having given me a lift?'

She raised a hand for the waiter, and gave their orders. She knew what Sandro would eat too, after all this time. Minestrone and grilled chicken. She saw the waiter glance down and it was only after he'd gone she realised she still had the newspaper on her lap. She set it on the table.

'She was a monster, the *padrona di casa,*' she said. 'The landlady. Sharp-eyed, though. And sounds like she worked on the *carabinieri*, too.'

'So what did you find out?' said Sandro.

The waiter was back, setting down the dishes. Beans flecked with parsley and black pepper, gleaming with oil, chicken deliciously blackened from the griddle, ribboned pasta with artichokes for Luisa. It smelled good: it smelled like heaven. Luisa realised she hadn't eaten all day.

But first things first. She left her knife and fork where they were; at the sight of the food her head had cleared and it was all there.

'He was doing business with some old army friends. It was them he called when he got fired, that's number one. The first thing she knew he was gay was that same night, when a man came round to see him. For a bit of rough play, that's what he told her when she complained about the noise.'

'Hold on,' said Sandro. 'Which night is this? The night he died? What man? Vito had been sleeping with Magda Scardino.'

'That,' said Luisa drily, 'doesn't surprise me.' She cocked her head. 'Although if Maratti didn't know about it, it wasn't at his place. Do you think he used her apartment?'

Sandro didn't seem to hear. 'She said he wanted something from her. But could you – he – a gay man do that, whatever he had to gain from it?'

Luisa looked at him, wondering how her dear husband, with thirty years in the police force, sometimes seemed to know so much less about the world than she did. 'You'd be surprised,' she said.

'I don't believe he was gay,' he repeated stubbornly.

'Nor do I,' Luisa said. 'For the record. Magda would have known. And it wasn't the night he died, because Maratti – the landlady – she saw him the next day, and she thought he was going on holiday. Back to Bari, is what she thought.'

'Bari?' He was on full alert now. 'John Carlsson was on a case in Bari too, last year.'

'Yes,' Luisa said, and she picked up her knife and fork thoughtfully. 'Maratti said they had the drains up. They found blood in the bathtub.' She nodded down at the newspaper headline. 'What's the betting it's her has been talking to the papers?' She twisted some pasta round her fork. 'She said his mother hadn't been to get his things, that the Carabinieri wouldn't let anyone touch his place.'

'His mother?'

'He must have been forced to introduce them,' said Luisa, pondering. 'She spent her life looking out for his visitors. She said a man from the army came and the Carabinieri sealed his rooms off.'

'Right,' said Sandro, beginning to see something. Wondering why it had taken him so long. 'He never looked like he'd had leukaemia to me.'

'Maratti said that, too,' said Luisa. 'And I always thought it was only kids survived it. What's that got to do with it, though?'

'Nothing,' he said. 'Not yet, anyway. A theory.'

She frowned at him. 'Do you know what I was wondering?' Sandro just gazed at her. 'What do you think made Maratti think he was going on holiday?'

'On holiday.' Sandro stared.

'The next day, she thought he was going on holiday, saw him go out in the afternoon. It's why she used her passkey to poke around in his room the following morning. What would make you assume someone was going on holiday, not just out?'

He looked at her.

'If he had a suitcase with him,' he said slowly. 'A big suitcase.'

'And the man he was having rough sex with,' Luisa said. 'Tallish, skinny, dark?'

'You saw him, at the launch, too, didn't you?' said Sandro. 'You saw John Carlsson. Skinny guy, dark eyes. I guess he was taller than me.'

Luisa looked down at the expensive pasta on her fork, but suddenly her appetite was gone. She laid it down. 'Vito's landlady never saw him leave.'

'It was Vito,' said Sandro. 'Vito killed him, hacked him, folded him into the suitcase and hauled him to the station. Yes.' He took a breath. 'Christ. He must have been wired. He must have been angry.'

On the table Sandro's mobile jittered. Looking down she read the caller's name upside down. *Falco.*

*

Elena lay awake, staring into the dark. He was asleep at last. He lay there in her bed like a felled animal, a big one at that, looking out of place, alien, immovable. He had cried and cried; she hadn't been able to ask him to go, after that. Was he dangerous? Not asleep, he wasn't. She sat up and put out a hand tentatively, feeling his warmth through the sheet, thinking how odd it was that she'd been the one who'd ended up giving comfort.

Whatever had happened at the hospital, it had worn him out. He must have loved the old woman.

She squeezed her eyes shut, thinking of the shape of John in her bed and how different it was. He'd slept restlessly, feverish to the touch, not this big steady warmth. He'd come to bed after her, he'd disappear in the night.

Downstairs she'd heard her phone blip some time back, telling her there was a message, but she would look at it in the morning. After all, what else was there that could happen? What else to be afraid of? She lay back down, stared at the ceiling and waited for sleep to come.

*

The intensive care ward hummed quietly with machines in the dark, the small glow of bedside examination lamps on standby punctuating the long, warm room. The patients on intensive care were not in a position to complain about the noise their neighbours made, to ask for the lights to be put out, or to cause any kind of trouble at all, apart from dying. It was a nice safe billet and it suited Ginevra Craxi, the ward sister, very well. You had to stay on your toes, but it was medical, not people management, not wailing relatives – at least, not until the end.

An alarm bleeped discreetly on the panel behind the desk. The old woman was ninety-odd, and this wasn't so bad a way to go. The nurse who'd been attending to her came, unhurried and silent on rubber soles out of the darkness, with the old lady's chart on its clipboard in her hand.

Ginevra looked at her and in answer to the unspoken question the junior nurse shook her head. 'Not yet,' she said. 'But I don't think it'll be long. Her stats are all dropping.'

The ward sister seesawed her head. 'It happens,' she said, taking the chart and looking down it. 'Started falling off this afternoon, after the visitors. Sometimes that's what does it, they wait for the loved ones to come and then they just let go. Even if they seem totally out of it. I wonder if we shouldn't keep the loved ones away.'

'Only they have to go sometime,' chimed the younger woman, as they agreed on this.

'This the next of kin?' Ginevra frowned at the name at the top of the chart. 'No children?'

'No children, no husband.'

'So he's . . . something else.' Ginevra nodded judiciously. 'Did he come and visit her this afternoon? Was he one of them? Foreigners.'

The young nurse tipped her head sideways to see the name. 'Don't know,' she said. 'I came on after. I got the impression it had been women, from the girl going off duty.'

'Interesting,' said Ginevra. 'You look at them when they come in and you can't tell, though she did look . . . distinguished. She must have been well connected.' Neither of them remarked on the use of the past tense, even though Athene Morris was still alive.

'Interesting,' said Ginevra again, handing the clipboard back to the girl.

And bowing over her week's timetable behind the desk as the junior nurse retreated, she thought, around half-three in the morning, that's when she'd likely enough go, just before dawn. You got an instinct for these things, like being a midwife, only instead of ushering them into the world, you're helping them leave. The body has its rhythms, it's when the will dips, deep in another world. She'd phone the next of kin when the sun was up, though, no point bothering him in the middle of the night: she wondered if he was lying awake now, wondered if he would grieve or be relieved.

Must be important, titled anyway. Sir Martin Fleming.

Chapter Twenty-Eight

CLOUD HAD MOVED DOWN in the night, from the mountains between Italy and Austria, down from Russia. Along the northern horizon a line of purple had bubbled up ominously over the Apennines.

Sandro stood in a car park and shivered. He'd left the house somewhere between six and seven, unable to lie still any longer. Awake since three, by around four the light had begun to filter thin and grey through the shutters. The days were getting longer, and he was too old to enjoy it.

Luisa had sat up blearily as he came to the bedroom door, ready to make him coffee, but he'd shushed her back under the covers. He'd rested a hand on her hair, and gone.

On the ringroad the traffic roared already, and somewhere off in the distance the siren of an ambulance sounded. A road accident, or an overdose, or a middle-aged man with chest pain, collapsed in his own bathroom.

Sandro had walked to the car in the cold morning, a wind whipping his ankles and setting the pigeons up into the air as he crossed the Piazza Santa Croce. He'd sat a while before starting the engine, looking down at his messages. One from Giuli, sent last night, around one in the morning. Unable to sleep. *You think it was Lludic?* it said. He sat back in the seat. How to answer that? With the truth. *No, I don't think it was Lludic.* Which didn't quite cover it.

John Carlsson had got a taxi to Giancarlo Vito's place. He could have gone from the Palazzo San Giorgio straight there, after he'd talked to Magda Scardino. She'd thought he'd been chatting her up, asking her if Vito was off the scene, but he wanted Vito.

What had he gone to see him about? Sandro was beginning to think he knew.

The newspaper report had said Giancarlo's murder was a gay thing. Naked or near enough, a handweight to the back of the head. Bondage gone wrong, rough sex gone wrong. 'Is that right?' he'd asked Falco on the phone last night, sitting at the table in the Buca, his chicken congealing on the plate in front of him.

The man's voice had been studiedly sombre. 'It does rather look like it,' he'd said. 'Of course I regret very much that it's been made public.' Under the serious tone he didn't sound regretful at all.

'The landlady, was it?' Sandro said. 'She does like to talk. So my wife says.' There was a silence as he allowed Falco to register that. 'So it's likely enough it will have been the man the neighbour saw leaving early that morning?' Brett Van Vleet. Had Falco already identified him?

'Unlikely we'll ever trace him,' said Falco, as if reading his mind. 'That little square kilometre's been up for development the last ten years, they want to knock the villas down and build some condominium development. It's all been left to get run down and so there are no security cameras till the one coming off the ringroad. It was dark, the neighbour's not sure of detail. . .'

The message was clear enough, and familiar enough: let sleeping dogs lie. It's in all our interests. The Palazzo San Giorgio's dark cellars had been closed back up. Only dogshit kept appearing on the skirtings. And John Carlsson was dead and mutilated in the morgue.

'And the blood and tissue you found in the drains,' he'd said to Falco then. 'You know whose it is, yet?'

'I don't know what you're talking about, Cellini.' The warning was unmistakable.

There'd been nothing about it in the newspaper report. 'Ah, I must have got that wrong,' Sandro said. 'You know how rumours fly.'

Luisa had been watching him like a hawk across the table throughout the conversation, but when he hung up all she said was, 'Eat it. Before it gets cold.'

Vito had killed John Carlsson. Why? And Falco might not know yet that the body had turned up, but he knew there was a body. And he was ready to cover it up. And why was that?

The answer was in there somewhere. Along with whoever killed Giancarlo Vito.

The little car park in front of the villa where both men had died was empty: the building was shuttered up as if the landlady had already had a warning from the Carabinieri. Sandro turned, three hundred and sixty degrees. There was a down at heel condo backing on to the car park that must have contained the neighbour who saw Van Vleet, but there was no sign of anyone watching now. There was the overhead section of the ringroad, the distant illuminated sign of a Holiday Inn, the tops of umbrella pines leading towards the river. Slowly he skirted the villa, keeping his footsteps soft. The shutters remained closed. Sandro kept walking round.

At the corner, out of sight of the shuttered windows, he paused. He could see the fire escape: a metal stair leading up to a balcony. Carlsson had come in by the front door. A strip of scrubby grass and some arthritic plum trees, petals turning brown on the grass underneath them. Out of the corner of his eye Sandro saw something move under the trees, an animal, and he knelt to get a better view. It was a cat, one of those odd, thin, big-eared creatures, like a sphinx. He held out a hand and rubbed fingers and thumb together. It hesitated, stepped towards him delicately, paws crossing. In his pocket the phone vibrated and slowly he extracted it.

'Hello?' The cat paused, then resumed its dancer's walk towards him.

'Why are you whispering?' It was Luisa. 'Someone called from the Palazzo San Giorgio.' He looked at his watch: to his surprise it was close to eight o'clock.

'At home?' In front of him now the cat raised its bony triangular face to his, wide-spaced eyes with that devil's slit in them. He held his hand out, as much to keep the thing away as to show he meant no harm.

'She said she couldn't get you on the cellphone.' No surprise there: in half the city there was no mobile reception. Her voice strained with its burden of fatigue and bad news. 'It was Cornell. The old lady who had the stroke. Or whatever. She died.'

And the cat swiped, claws extended. It caught him above the thumb, a long scratch that drew blood, welling immediately along its length. He jerked back, shocked beyond reason.

'Died? Died?' He heard his voice stupidly repeating the words. He saw the woman's old, slack face, her pleading single eye. Her little stash of treasures. Men's cufflinks. Her bracelet, with the initials, still in its evidence bag at the morgue, and who would get it now?

The cat lolloped away from him back under the trees, a tiny rustle beneath its paws, its damage inflicted.

'Did she say—' he began, but before he could finish he registered that Luisa sounded more than just tired. It was too much for her, he could hear it. 'Don't worry, sweetheart,' he said. 'I'm going.'

He sent the message to Giuli as he trudged down the Viale Europa towards another bus stop. *Athene Morris died. I'm sorry.*

*

As she urged the *motorino* up the hill in the cold morning there was a painful feeling in Giuli's chest, like burning. Guilt. She'd lain all night feeling it, feverish with waiting for a message to come back, with wondering if she should call. Danilo Lludic had been the man in Athene Morris's room late last night. Sandro didn't think he'd done it – but he didn't say why. And what if he was wrong?

Giuli had felt hysteria mounting in her, thinking of the old woman. Beside her on the sofa she'd sensed Enzo's distress. 'She knew something. Why didn't I stop and talk to her? She knew something about why Vito was fired, if only I'd waited and asked her what she was getting at, there'd have been no need to hurt her.' She took a breath. 'To keep her quiet.'

'And if she'd told you, don't you think you might be the one in danger?' Enzo was on the edge of the sofa now. 'This isn't all your responsibility, *cara*. There are so many unknowns, it's not easy to do the right thing. You need to sleep.'

She hadn't slept.

The second message came in as she removed her helmet. Staring down at it, her hair standing up stiff, she wanted to cry. Old, she told herself. She was old. But still.

Her eyes blurred, it took Giuli a while to find the bell-push for the apartment over the workshop. The wind whipped at her legs in the blue-grey morning. She put her hand to the dusty glass and looked inside: it was in darkness, only where the pale early light fell did it bring into relief this end of the workbench, the shapes of tools dimly hanging. Something sharp lay on the ground on its side, with a worn handle; there were puddles of shadow among the shavings on the workshop floor. Had something happened in there?

No answer. She stepped back off the pavement, feeling the pressure in her chest rise higher to choke her, listening to her heart speed up. Did something move up there? She stepped back, pressed the bell again, back into the road to look. A light came on in the workshop and then Elena was at the door, pale, hair down in a wild tangle, holding her mobile in her hand and frowning down at it.

'Elena,' she said. 'I'm so sorry. I didn't know. I didn't think. It was in the back of my mind, that there were rumours about him—' She didn't even know what she was saying.

Under her tight embrace she felt a squirm of resistance that released. The wild hair felt strange and scratchy against her cheek and then she felt Elena's hand on her back, patting tentatively, as if Giuli were the one who needed comforting. They pulled apart, and Giuli felt her cheeks burn.

'Sorry,' she said again. Elena looked up and down the steep grey street: no one. They both looked across at the Palazzo San Giorgio, all shuttered and the great arched doorway firmly closed.

'Christ, it's cold,' said Elena, her face pinched in the wind. 'Come inside.'

She held a finger to her lips as Giuli stepped into the gloom. Warmer at least, in here, and that smell, that lovely smell of wood and paint. Could anything bad have happened in here? Elena was pointing upstairs, finger still to her lips. Giuli understood something, at least, and nodded. She followed Elena through the workshop and out the back door. There, to her a surprise, was a tiny, neat kitchen, like the kitchen on a boat, filled with a long shaft of the clean white light of a just-risen sun.

Someone had constructed it painstakingly, by hand, measuring and positioning and planning until everything fitted. A unit of old wood with an aluminium cooking ring, the little flap of a folding table built into the wall, a single stool. And a door onto a minuscule courtyard where the bright yellow-green leaves of a climbing plant trembled in the wind. Rubbing her eyes with one hand, Elena reached for a coffee pot.

'He's upstairs,' she said, yawning over her shoulder. 'He's asleep.'

'Did you see my message? About what he did?' Giuli corrected herself, 'What they said he did?'

'Who? I – I didn't look at my phone,' she said, and then suddenly awake, 'Do you mean John? Have you found John?'

Giuli looked into her face. 'No,' she said. 'You'd better sit down.'

But Elena remained standing. Giuli knew that feeling, and she was back in the janitor's office at school. Sit down and they'll get you with it, they'll tell you the thing you don't want to hear.

Elena's small face was set stubborn. 'Yes, I know. I know what Danilo was accused of. As a matter of fact he spent most of the night crying about it.'

On the stove the little pot bubbled and spat. She set out two small thick china cups, a bag of sugar, poured. There was no sound from upstairs.

Elena studied her hands. 'He couldn't do anything . . . last night. He was too frightened.'

'*He* was frightened of *you*?'

Elena shook her head fiercely. 'Who knows?' she said. 'What happens between two people? No witnesses. He said they had a row, he wasn't kind to her, in fact, he was horrible to her. But he didn't lay a finger on her.' She frowned down fiercely, mouth set. 'She retracted it in the end. Do women do that, if they've really been raped?' She looked up into Giuli's face.

'Yes,' said Giuli. 'Sometimes.'

'And do women sometimes make it up?'

'Less often,' said Giuli, uneasily. 'Much less often. But yes.'

'He can never get away from it now,' said Elena, raising the small cup to her lips. 'It's a nightmare. He's being punished. That much is true.' Her eyes were inward, remembering something. 'I wouldn't want to be his lawyer but I don't think he did anything to her.'

'They must have already known? At the Palazzo?'

'They knew,' said Elena slowly. 'It's how they got him, he was desperate to get away from the US, the case had been dismissed. A little bit of notoriety was fine with them.'

Overhead there was movement, heavy-footed. A groan.

In alarm, Giuli pushed herself off the stool she'd been sitting on. The little room, suddenly, seemed like a trap, the comforting smell of coffee and the sunlight the lures.

Elena put a hand to her arm. '*Tranquilla*,' she said wearily. 'It's okay.' She stepped into the doorway and stood at the foot of the narrow stairs. 'Danilo?' Silence. 'We're down here. There's some coffee.'

'There's something I've got to tell you,' said Giuli, and Elena's eyes flashed, then she turned away. She knows, Giuli thought.

The man who appeared in the kitchen doorway behind Elena gave off nothing to raise Giuli's defence mechanisms.

'Hey,' he said, ducking his head sheepishly. His eyes were sore-looking, his beard unruly. He looked at a hand, then held it out to Giuli; it felt tentative as it closed around hers, wary. 'Danilo Lludic. I saw you the other night.'

'Giuli works with Sandro Cellini,' said Elena. She held a cup of coffee out to him. 'We're old friends, Giuli and me. Sort of.'

Lludic closed his eyes, leaning against the doorpost, then abruptly opened them. 'Do I have to go back?' he asked, of no one in particular. 'That place, God almighty. Does your Sandro know what he's getting into?'

'Were you in Athene Morris's room when she got ill?' Giuli said abruptly.

He frowned. 'What do you mean? I closed her shutters for her; she gave me some whisky.' The look he gave Giuli was level. She became aware of Elena beside them, poised to intervene. 'She was fine when I left her,' he said. 'Rearranging her treasures. Plotting something.'

'Plotting,' said Giuli, thinking of the look on Athene Morris's face when she'd last seen her, bewildered, crafty, wounded. Thinking of what it must be like to be old, and losing your powers: what would be left but plotting?

'I don't know what you're saying,' said Lludic. 'Are you saying I'd hurt Athene?'

'Did she know about your . . . past?' She took a breath. 'Did Giancarlo Vito?'

'He went to see her in the hospital yesterday,' blurted Elena. They both turned to her. '*What?*' she said, in response to Giuli's warning look. 'He's her friend.'

'Sandro thinks – I think, too – that Athene Morris knew something about why Giancarlo Vito was killed,' said Giuli. 'There was something. Plotting, you said, right? Gossip. She was hinting to me, about all sorts of things. I – I was in too much of a hurry. I had things on my mind—' She stopped. They aren't interested, she told herself.

'Sandro thinks,' she went on slowly, 'that something happened in Athene Morris's room that night she died. Someone helped that stroke along.'

Elena looked from one to the other, bewildered. 'But Danilo . . . he went back to see her,' she said, pleading for him. 'In the hospital.'

'Did he,' said Giuli.

Lludic gazed at her, pain in his eyes. Don't ease up now, Giuli told herself, even though she felt Elena at her elbow, ready to cry.

'They wouldn't let me see her,' said Danilo Lludic slowly. 'In the hospital. You can ask them. They wouldn't let me see her, they said she was . . . she was sleeping.'

Giuli's phone blipped in her pocket, and she got it out and looked at it. Something heavy seemed to descend on her shoulders. She looked up.

'And I wasn't the last one to see her, anyway,' Lludic said, his voice higher now and insistent, like a child wrongly accused. Sullen, defiant. 'After – after. He was in there, that spook, Mr Suave. I could hear him droning on, in that self-satisfied voice of his, sent me right off to sleep.'

'Spook?' said Elena.

Giuli stared at her blankly, the word ringing in her ears too. 'She died,' she said. 'In her sleep, early this morning. If she had anything to tell anyone, it's too late now. Athene Morris is dead.'

Chapter Twenty-Nine

IN A LITTLE SQUARE just off the foot of the Costa San Giorgio there was a bar, and Sandro was in it.

He was well aware that he'd been summoned back to the Palazzo, but he knew just as well that once across that threshold his capacity to think straight would be impaired – if it didn't evaporate altogether. Besides, it was to the old woman he felt the tug of duty, and Athene Morris was beyond caring if he got to work on time or not.

The bar had loud music and a TV screen dancing in the corner of his eye, but he could think through that. Besides, coffee before work was a human right – or if it wasn't, it should be. The girl – black hair in a ponytail, kohl-rimmed eyes – brought him his *caffè lungo*, leaning down with a smile. Why did women suddenly all look wondrous to him? Middle age, maybe. He corrected himself, nothing middle about it, at sixty-five. Old age.

Something was forming, more an instinct than a thought, more emotion than logic, but it needed the outside world if it was to develop.

It was a feeling that had on several occasions in his life as a policeman raised the hairs on the back of his neck. A middle-aged woman neatly bisected, the two halves of her body retrieved from a drainage ditch, had been perhaps the first time. As Sandro, thirty-one years old but feeling like a virgin as he vomited over his shoes, had stared at the horrible puzzle of her death, it had been inescapable: somewhere else the consequences of this violence were still unfolding. His job, then as now, to follow the trail, find the end of the fuse, stamp on the embers.

On that occasion the woman, it turned out, had been murdered by her violent younger lover, who'd decided she'd cheated on him. When Sandro caught up with him he was living with another middle-aged divorcee, who'd started missing days at work, turning up with bruises on her arms. Sandro had got there in time. Maybe thirty per cent of cases he – they, he and Pietro – had managed that. Not enough.

Carlsson was dead, killed by Giancarlo Vito. Twenty-four hours later Vito was dead. Athene Morris was dead. Was that the end?

He knew with certainty that it was not.

His old friend appeared in the door. He was in uniform, his cap under his arm: Sandro had caught him on the way to work. He looked tired out. Sandro wondered if Pietro was remembering the woman found in two halves in the drainage ditch. Red hair, she'd had. More likely it was John Carlsson's murder that had kept him up – and the solution Sandro had presented to him on the phone.

He gestured to the bar girl for another, Pietro pinching finger and thumb to tell her, *ristretto*, not *lungo*. The hard-core single shot, to jumpstart the brain. Sandro smiled, nostalgic for the old double-act they used to pull before a working day.

Pietro grimaced: the music was deafening. He looked pleadingly at the girl as she set down the coffee and she nodded. He and Pietro must stick out a mile in this place, he thought. The other customers – a few long-hairs, a moony couple who'd obviously just hauled themselves out of bed – were decades younger, but they didn't seem bothered when the music subsided.

Sandro watched him take a sip. 'Well,' he said. 'I've solved your case, how about you solve mine?'

Pietro downed the coffee, and gestured for another. 'So, tell me again,' he said.

'The landlady will identify Carlsson as the man who visited Vito the night he was fired – and the suitcase Carlsson was found in as the one he left with the next day. Vito was an ex-soldier, he worked out.' He paused. 'It was bugging me, trying to get my head around which of my old guys in the Palazzo San Giorgio could have hauled that body across town.'

Pietro nodded. 'There was a – a crusty, a rough sleeper, said he saw a man with broad shoulders coming up the ramp at the station with a big wheeled case, at dusk,' he said slowly. 'The witness – and his girlfriend, and his dogs – smelled so strongly of weed, I took what he said with a pinch of salt.' He sighed. 'And the envelope? The bracelet?'

'Stolen from a guest. One of the dirty tricks Giancarlo never quite cleared up,' said Sandro. 'The maid said he knew who stole it.'

'Do you?' asked Pietro, interrupting his flow.

Sandro sighed. 'You always ask the hard questions,' he said. 'That one's on the back burner.' Was that true? The inversion of the initials was bothering him: Athene Morris should be AM, not MA. Marjorie Cameron locked in the steam room was bothering him. Released by Magda Scardino. What had she been doing down there? Marjorie Cameron didn't seem like the steam room type.

Sandro went on. 'But I think he wanted that envelope to be found, he wanted the body to be traced back to the Palazzo San Giorgio – maybe he wanted to send a message too, to the person who stole it? To Athene? Did he want to scare somebody, or was he just angry because he'd been fired, and wanted to cause trouble?'

Pietro groaned. 'I can't say I'm looking forward to talking to the Carabinieri on this one,' he said. 'Call it an intuition.'

'I can tell you what they'll say,' said Sandro. 'The story's already out there. Gay sex. Bondage gone wrong, or something, plus spite at his former employers maybe. Things get out of hand with Carlsson then the following night he gets himself killed by a bit of rough trade, maybe reckless out of remorse.'

Pietro was silent. When he spoke he sounded guarded. 'Ties it up nicely. Shit stops piling up. Everyone's happy.' He sucked his cheeks. 'Except the dead men, obviously.'

'Only trouble is,' said Sandro, 'It isn't true, is it? Because outside the landlady – and he fed her the story to cover up the fact that he'd just murdered a journalist in his own bathroom – there's absolutely no evidence Giancarlo Vito was gay: rather the contrary. And John Carlsson wasn't either.' He shrugged. 'Which kind of puts a spoke in it.'

Pietro stood, his face set. He looked old in the bar's lurid lighting; Sandro had always thought of him as a kid brother, and now they were both old.

'What happened at Bari, last year?' Sandro said, almost to himself.

Pietro frowned. 'Bari?'

Sandro became aware of the bargirl hovering over a table inside the room, watching them. He cleared his throat. 'The Carabinieri are obviously having to ring-fence information on this,' he said stiffly, hearing the change in his own voice as the explanation dawned on him. Outlandish? Maybe. 'For whatever reason.' Because a clock somewhere could be ticking now, his voice registering on a screen in jumps and dips, in a nondescript house in a dusty suburb, or an unmarked surveillance van parked in a sidestreet. Sandro on the radar. Paranoia?

'So we keep our noses out, and our mouths shut,' said Pietro, wearily.

Sandro smiled: they were both old and tired, a quiet life was probably the way to go. He put out a hand, and with the other held his friend's head a moment against his. 'I have to go to work, now,' he said. 'You do your thing, and I'll do mine.'

Pietro stepped back. 'Watch yourself,' he said.

*

'You'll have to set up for us outside,' the Professor's wife said, turning her back on him before she'd even finished the sentence.

Mauro liked strong women. He had a fierce mother he

worshipped, bossy sisters he loved, a quietly determined fiancée he would lay down his life for, but there was something about Magda Scardino that made his skin prickle.

'Outside?' he echoed in hollow dismay.

Magda Scardino looked back at him over her shoulder with a kind of imperious blankness, her eyes turned dark. The other women clustered behind her in the library like a small flock of sheep. Well, perhaps not all sheep. The small white-haired Englishwoman, Lady Juliet Fleming, might be able to act docile when required, but Mauro knew there was an awful lot more to that sharp clever little face than just following the lead of other people. She wasn't well, that was the rumour.

'But it's turned very cold, Signora Scardino,' Mauro protested, shooting a glance at Lady Fleming.

'We didn't come to Italy to hide inside,' said the Englishwoman with gentle persistence. 'It's May.'

Precisely, thought Mauro, puzzled. It's only May. Why did they so urgently want to be out on the terrace? The lower terrace, Scardino had specified. He looked around the large, echoing library, his fiefdom. He had to admit he hated it in here himself. Was it claustrophobia? Or the need for privacy?

'You've got those big heaters,' said Magda Scardino. 'I know, I've seen them. Patio heaters. Just bring one out.' She turned away briskly at his pained glance and said to her small audience, 'All this rubbish about them being bad for the environment. It's a myth, did you know that? Charles says so. A drop in the ocean, he says.'

It took a good ten minutes' shuffling, with the women standing on the upper terrace watching them, and another five minutes finding the extension lead. Mauro had looked around for Sandro Cellini, a good man, he felt, in this situation; he might be getting on a bit but he was solid where Lino was frail and more importantly he was a man who understood. But Lino said Cellini wasn't in yet. Just late, Mauro had thought at the time, but now it stopped him in his tracks. He hoped nothing had happened to Sandro Cellini.

Should he have told him outright what he knew about Giancarlo Vito? Cellini would work it out: he'd given him enough. And it was a dangerous business, besides. Cellini didn't want to get involved, not if he could help it. What good would it do, after all? The authorities would divide it up between them, the Carabinieri, the army, the Polizia di Stato, a little bit of responsibility each, and no one carries the can.

A friend in the Polizia di Stato had slipped him another little piece of information that morning, about a body in a suitcase. Mauro would wait and see about that one. Dead bodies did tend to attract all sorts of rumours, not all of them reliable.

'Ladies,' he said, with a bow, back on the top terrace. 'Your table is ready for you.' Magda Scardino was already walking away: Marjorie Cameron shot him an apologetic glance, Therese Van Vleet blushed, Juliet Fleming just gave him that gentle smile. *I know you*, it said. *I know what you know, I know how much you understand*. Mauro looked up at the sky; the few heavy drops had evaporated, but there was no knowing how long it would hold off.

Coming back down with his tray of drinks – *I'll take them*, he'd said to Alice, who'd been hovering in the library, *I spend enough time stuck in here*, and she'd looked at him, wonderingly

– the sight of the women's heads all bent towards each other aroused something queasy in Mauro. He leaned down, setting a tall glass of milky coffee in front of Magda Scardino. She didn't even look up.

'But surely,' Marjorie Cameron was saying, with what seemed like alarm, 'they won't let us just leave the country?' Mauro slid her tea – strong, with milk – carefully on to the table, where her thin hands fidgeted with her phone, bare of rings, nails unpainted.

'You mean me?' said Magda Scardino with amusement. 'What do you think they're going to do to stop me?' She leaned forwards. 'You know what's his name's been poking around?' She clicked her tongue in exasperation. 'Our new Director of Security, the old fool. Cellini. I spoke to his wife yesterday. I told her not to poke her nose in.'

'Magda.' It was Juliet Fleming, weary, exasperated. 'Why did you think that was a good idea?'

Mauro put the Englishwoman's mint tea on the table. She'd told him she'd got the taste for it in the Middle East; the only thing that settled her stomach, she said. Perhaps that was where her trouble lay, in the stomach. The whites of her eyes, he saw, were yellow.

Looking sidelong he saw Magda Scardino's expression harden.

'Well,' she said, her mouth set in a line, no big full flashing smile wasted on this lot. 'I didn't like her . . . manner. Looking at me as though . . . well. She clearly wasn't listening, anyway. A little bird told me she went out to Vito's house to poke about, last night.'

'A little bird?' It was Marjorie Cameron again, like a bird herself, bobbing anxiously at every word. Behind her, Mauro hung back.

'Another old fool,' said Magda, the smile of self-satisfaction returning. 'Her boss, what's his name? The man who owns the boutique, Frollini. He telephoned me this morning to ask how it had gone yesterday, our little jaunt. He said he hoped we weren't all too distressed by it, then let slip he'd taken her to see the landlady. Vito's. Oh, he got flustered at having said anything, but I got it out of him.'

The sigh Juliet Fleming let out held something of weary calculation, like a mother surveying some mess her child has made behind her back.

'They're just being nosy,' said Magda, in defiance of the sound. 'She's a nosy bitch.' She shrugged. 'Let them try to stop me leaving. A weekend in Cairo's just what I need after all this – this stress. And if I don't come straight back here . . . well. It's hardly going to come to extradition now, is it?' Her laugh was hard and ringing. 'And we're pretty much all off out of here, aren't we? Ian's going to . . . where is it? Dubai? He'd better be careful, hadn't he, talking of extradition?'

'I don't know what you mean,' whispered Marjorie Cameron, tears coming to her eyes, pulling at her sleeves. Mauro wondered why she defended him. He'd seen the marks he left. 'And it's Bahrain.'

'Leaving you behind to face the music?'

'I could go if I wanted,' Cameron said, turning away under the onslaught. Mauro stood at her elbow, holding his breath. But she just turned to Therese Van Vleet, stubbornly sticking to her subject. Made of stronger stuff than she seemed. 'Are you going, too?

'Just for a week or two,' said Therese Van Vleet. She turned her heart-shaped face up to Mauro as he gave her her black coffee, and in the grey cold light he saw fine lines around her great blue eyes. 'Thank you,' she said, and reluctantly turned back to the others. 'Brett has some business to sort out. Financial.' Her lip trembled. 'He says he wants me along this time; moral support.'

Mauro saw Magda Scardino's hand come out briskly and settle on Van Vleet's delicate, china-white forearm. He thought he saw the American flinch.

A bit late for that, he thought. A bit late to get squeamish about who your friends are. Were.

Mauro turned his back on them and walked away up the gravel path towards the Palazzo San Giorgio.

*

He had to leave the car at the foot of the hill. Watching the old woman toil up ahead of him, it wasn't until she turned off into a gate in the wall below the Palazzo San Giorgio that Sandro realised it was the foreigners' neighbour. He was almost at the big front door when a familiar figure darted out of the little workshop opposite.

Sandro couldn't work out what she was doing there. 'Giuli?'

Pale but determined, Giuli looked back over her shoulder, up at the window over the workshop. Belatedly he spotted her little battered *motorino* at the kerb, unmistakably Giuli's. 'I saw you,' she said. 'Elena said it's where her boyfriend used to stand, watching. I was standing there and I saw you coming.' She paused. 'Who are you looking at?'

The old lady was at her door, where the road curved away from them out of sight. 'Nothing,' he said. 'Just the neighbour.' He could see the strain in Giuli's face. 'Have you told her yet?' he said quietly. 'Do you want me to do it?'

She shook her head. 'It's Lludic,' she said. 'He spent the night with her. I can't . . . I need to get her alone.'

'Is that an excuse?' Her face was stubborn as she shook her head. 'He didn't hurt her, then? The sculptor.'

She looked uncomfortable. 'If you'd had my life, Sandro,' she said, 'you would have freaked too, reading that. Rape?' She folded her arms tight across her chest and he could see goosepimples coming up on them in the cool breeze: it wasn't summer yet. 'Although you didn't have to read too far into it to see it wasn't true. He's just . . . a bit of a dolt. Where women are concerned. I think Elena feels sorry for him.' Her eyes were dark.

'What is it?' said Sandro.

Giuli took a deep breath. 'The old lady.' For a moment he frowned, his mind still on the neighbour watering her pots. 'Athene Morris. Lludic told me someone else was in there, after him. He closed the shutters for her after he'd seen Elena out. But he heard another voice in there, as he was going to sleep.' On the sloping street Sandro turned a little and saw Lino watching him through the glass of the door. 'A man.'

'And you believed him?' he said quietly.

Giuli shifted uncomfortably. 'Yes,' she said eventually.

'Did he say who it was?'

She nodded.

Lino watched as he came in to the Palazzo.

'You haven't seen me,' said Sandro. And he entered the long, sloping corridor, almost jogging through the empty library, past the stairs and into his office without a word. He closed the door behind him, took his laptop from his briefcase and set it on the desk. He hadn't looked at his mailbox in twenty-four hours: he opened it and fifty-nine messages came in. He scrolled down, deleting all except those from Giuli's email address, with their picture attachments. The first one that came up was from the launch. It was of Gastone Bottai and Giancarlo Vito, and another man between them.

Only then, it seemed, did he take a breath.

Chapter Thirty

WITH TEN MINUTES BEFORE she had to be at work, Luisa was drinking coffee in Rivoire and thinking about Giancarlo Vito's mother. A doter, a spoiler, that had been the landlady's implication. Luisa imagined old Maratti standing on that gloomy doorstep sticky with whatever her unpruned trees had dropped, waiting jealously for Vito's mother to come around to collect his belongings so she could talk poison under the guise of condolence. Something about it troubled Luisa: she couldn't quite believe in that scenario. Why hadn't the mother already come?

Two old ladies on the next table were looking at her. She nodded at them. Uncertainly they smiled back. One even lifted a shaky hand in greeting and then said, meaningfully, 'You're looking well.'

Luisa's smile stiffened. She was resigned to the fact that everyone knew she'd had a breast removed, but she certainly wasn't going to go around updating them. *I'm in remission. I'll be clear next year, God willing. I've had the reconstruction.* Sandro still hadn't gone near the new breast, not even now the scarring was close to invisible and the swelling all gone. Had he jumped out of bed this morning and shot out of the door just to avoid rolling over in the dark and brushing against it? Abruptly Luisa stood. 'Sorry,' she said. 'Late for work.'

*

At the foot of the stairs Alessandra Cornell and Gastone Bottai were waiting when Sandro emerged.

'A word,' said Bottai, with a smile that went nowhere near his eyes.

Having been fired before, Sandro was surprised he hadn't seen it coming. But then maybe Alessandra Cornell herself hadn't known what she was going to say until it came out of her mouth. That was what her blank, startled expression said, although Bottai's face – crafty, self-satisfied – told Sandro he at least had got what he came for. And it had been nothing like being fired from the state police after thirty-five years' service, either; even though they hadn't called that being fired – they'd called it early retirement.

The way they marched him through the bar as though escorting a prisoner should have told him something. But he'd been distracted by the sight of the women, back inside now, their heads bent over a newspaper at one of the library's tables. Therese Van Vleet off to one side, distancing herself, looking much less empty-headed, it occurred to him, than he'd ever thought. Magda Scardino standing tense with her arms crossed. Marjorie Cameron seated in front of the paper, and the most absorbed, with a finger moving along the newsprint, her lips moving. Juliet Fleming lifting her silver head to watch him go. They were reading about Giancarlo Vito's death, in a gay bondage session.

'Look here, Cellini,' Bottai had started straight in, the door barely shut behind them, but Alessandra Cornell had silenced him with a hand raised.

'Sandro,' she said, in a tone he imagined was supposed to be softer, but sounded no less threatening.

And suddenly Sandro thought, damn this. Damn them. 'You need to be very careful,' he said. 'Aren't you even the slightest bit curious about the stories they're putting out about Giancarlo Vito? And his gay sex sessions. There's more to come, do you know that? A body in a suitcase, one of Vito's lovers, or so they're saying. With an envelope from this place in his pocket.'

He saw Cornell look towards Bottai.

'What do you think, Alessandra?' said Sandro, and at the use of her first name she turned to him. 'Do you think he was gay? Do you, Gastone?' Bottai puffed up with outrage at the familiarity. 'What was he up to here?'

Cornell looked pleadingly at Bottai.

'Yes,' Sandro said, abandoning caution and taking Cornell by the wrist. 'He knows, doesn't he? He knows why Vito came, why he was employed here with such a skimpy CV – and the agency who recommended him so highly hardly knew him, it turns out. All *I* know is, he was involved in something pretty fishy in Bari last year. Did you know that, Mr Bottai? Perhaps you didn't. Perhaps your father doesn't tell you everything: if you were my son I certainly wouldn't.' Bottai's face turned wooden with rage in front of him. Watch it, Sandro told himself, but it was too late for that. 'Nice picture, by the way, of you and Giancarlo and your father at the launch. Very cosy. A picture is worth a thousand words, isn't that what they say?'

'Bari?' said Alessandra Cornell wonderingly. That hadn't been on the CV, had it?

Bottai shifted his position slightly, stepping away. Sandro held Cornell's bewildered gaze: could her innocence be fake? Only one way to find out.

'A Greenpeace boat investigating a government research project was scuppered,' he said. 'It went down, two activists died. The project was top secret; the word was it was investigating wave power, but there was a Syrian connection, and rumours of pollutants being released into the sea.'

It was easy: all you did was type *Bari* and *security services* into a search engine; he might even have done it on his phone. It wasn't magic. He'd called the detective agency and the girl behind reception had confirmed it, in a whisper. Vito had spent that holiday in Bari, last summer. Several months was a long holiday.

'I don't understand,' said Cornell, looking from Sandro to Bottai's turned back. 'Why would Giancarlo . . . why would a private detective be investigating a government project? Employed by whom?' Bottai didn't turn, just stood looking out of the window at the livid sky.

Sandro used his advantage to change tack. He took a step towards Bottai's sleekly jacketed back, a light mustard tweed, just that fraction small enough to be fashionable and at the same time . . . ridiculous. A hint of fat creeping in as middle age established a foothold, despite the tennis and the rowing. Marvelling with a blink that it had been a while since he'd thought about his own waistline, Sandro addressed the man's shoulders.

'You must have been furious when Cameron got him fired. You took such trouble to get him the job, Cameron must have really been rubbed up the wrong way. Was it just the question of the prostitute? He must be very strait-laced – or his wife must be very sensitive.'

Bottai didn't turn but Sandro detected something in the contraction of the shoulders, the carefully cultivated man becoming a sullen boy in a tweed jacket. At his side Cornell, aghast, cleared her throat, trying to work out how to break this up, and at the same time, what exactly was going on. Sandro took another step away from her and towards Bottai, his face only centimetres away from the man's tanned chin.

'What – what were you talking about, another body?' said Cornell. 'Connected with us?'

'A body with Athene Morris's bracelet in his pocket, in an envelope with the Palazzo's crest on it.' Sandro didn't turn to face her, still addressing Bottai's shoulders. 'They've identified the dead man, now. It was John Carlsson.' He heard her gasp. 'A man who'd been entertained here, who wrote that nice little piece about the San Giorgio even though he had seen the things that were happening here. A man who'd recognised Vito, who knew what he was. Knew perhaps what he was doing here, because he'd seen him in Bari.'

'*What* was Vito doing here?' said Alessandra Cornell, pleadingly. 'And what was he doing in Bari?'

No, she doesn't know, thought Sandro. And finally Bottai

turned to face them, haughty, defiant, pulling the Florentine aristocrat card over them both, over Alessandra Cornell and her mixed parentage, over Sandro and his peasant parents.

'Don't be stupid,' Gastone Bottai said sharply. Cornell's hands flew to her mouth in protest, and Sandro tipped his head on one side, waiting.

'That pompous old bore Cameron, that bullying small-minded Puritan from nowhere, with his dreary wife, no wonder he took against Vito. As if it were some great crime, to enjoy oneself with women.' He was puffed up with outrage, maybe real, maybe feigned. Sandro suddenly felt stifled in the room, as if the heavy cloud beyond the window was pressing against the glass.

'That wasn't all,' said Alessandra Cornell, interposing herself at last, facing Bottai, her chin high. 'You know that.'

'It wasn't your place to fire him,' said Bottai turning to her in fury, almost spitting it out. 'You know that. I hired him. It should have been my – my judgement.'

Cornell held her ground. 'Ian Cameron said Giancarlo had intercepted his mail. Legal documents, quite clearly confidential. He said Vito had opened the mail before giving it to him. He talked about blackmail. He was convinced Vito was planning to use the information he'd obtained.' She was quite calm.

'You talked to Vito about it?'

'He laughed,' Alessandra Cornell said, and her eyes, so pale and cool, turned dark. 'He denied opening the envelope, and then he laughed when I suggested he might have been planning to blackmail Ian Cameron. He called me a stupid woman.' Sandro saw her look flicker in Bottai's direction, challenging him, and saw Bottai's lip lift and curl. 'I had to fire him,' she said, and her eyes flashed.

'John Carlsson knew what Vito was doing here,' said Sandro, looking at Bottai. 'That's why he died. Did Vito do it? Or did they wash their hands of him and get rid of Carlsson first, then Vito?'

'But who is *they*?' said Alessandra Cornell stubbornly.

'Are you going to tell her, or am I?' said Sandro, looking at Gastone Bottai.

The man gave him a look, a look cultivated since boyhood, Sandro deduced, to get himself out of trouble, a look of boredom and disgust . . . and said nothing.

Sandro turned back to Cornell. 'Vito worked for the . . . ah, security services,' he said. 'Military intelligence.' And Sandro turned to Bottai in mock appeal. 'I don't even know what their acronym is these days, it changes so often. It used to be SISMI and now it's AISE. Agenzia Informazioni e Sicurezza Esterna.'

'He was a – a—'

'He was a spy,' said Bottai, sonorous and bored.

Alessandra Cornell's eyes were wide.

Bottai regarded them both with heavy-lidded disdain. 'He was an undercover agent. A floater. Professor Scardino is a big fish, you see, and they thought Vito was the man to reel him in.' Alessandra Cornell made a small sound, of dismay, but Sandro could see Bottai was enjoying himself. Showing off, pretending he was a spy himself, rather than just a PR man. 'But this place has other big fish, too. Everyone wants a piece of biofuels, there are huge sums involved.' He smiled with lazy greed. 'The Gulf states in particular, and the man's an academic, he's an intellectual, not worldly wise. It was just a matter of getting in first.'

Don't know about that, thought Sandro – had Bottai seen Magda Scardino? But then he began to see. Where Vito's skills might be useful: those strong shoulders, those good teeth. A very good-looking ex-soldier.

Bottai looked at Cornell and Sandro with equal contempt. 'And don't think there's any point in getting worked up over it, it's how the world works.'

Sandro was taken aback by the man's sudden disregard for discretion; he could see Cornell's growing alarm. Bottai was getting into his stride now, disdainful of Sandro's ignorance, wanting to show him how much he knew, how naive they were.

'Gastone,' began Cornell, then turned to Sandro. 'You'd better go,' she said. 'This is something I need to discuss with Gastone privately.'

'It's not as though he was the only one,' Bottai went on, ignoring her. 'It's war, you know. Information is power. Admittedly, Vito turned out not to have been quite the man for the job.' That lazy smile again. 'And don't think you can talk about it outside these four walls, either,' he said. 'National security is involved, they'll have you banged up before you can open your mouth, ex-policeman or not.'

At that moment the great glaring masses of cloud beyond the window, moving all this time unnoticed, thickening and merging, split; light spilled through, flooding the earth below like God making his presence known, travelling across the far hills like the beam of a searchlight.

Sandro turned away from the sight, the image of glory still dancing behind his eyes. 'Have you seen the picture from the launch, your father between you and Vito, his hand on the man's shoulder? I would get that taken down off the internet, if I were you. Your father asked – or did he instruct? – you to give Vito the job here. Barman would have done, but security man was a dream. How did you get it past Signorina Cornell here? Did he use his famous charms?' Sandro was aware of something then, of an intake of breath from Alessandra Cornell that indicated he'd made an error, but it was too late.

Bottai, lordly still as he chose to ignore the implied slight, his father's lackey, waved a hand. 'Apparently it was a matter of urgency. There was competition.'

'Competition?' The word sparked something: Professor Scardino had said it about his wife, Luisa had told him so. *She liked an element of competition.*

'Another agency, moving in on Scardino.'

Sandro turned the phrase over in his mind. What did that mean? Another agency. It meant another country's spy, in the Palazzo San Giorgio. And then something Giuli had said returned to him, a word she hadn't understood. *The old spook,* Lludic had said.

He had been talking about Sir Martin Fleming, the man who'd visited Athene Morris's room as Lludic went to sleep, the smooth-talking old spook. Spook meant spy. He thought of Dickens on the old woman's bedside table, the calm Englishman who'd recommended Dickens to him before telling him poetry was good for policemen. The couple who'd made so many cosy foursomes with the Scardinos, who'd signed up on the same day for their tenancy at the Palazzo.

'Fleming,' Sandro said quietly. 'The Brit. Fleming's a . . . an undercover operative, too. He's a spy too.'

And then, quite suddenly, Alessandra Cornell lost her cool. 'Enough,' she said, and they both turned at the sound of her voice. 'That's enough. Gastone . . .' He looked at her, expressionless. 'A moment alone, I think.'

'Alessandra,' said Bottai, his voice velvety, 'I don't think there's anything we need to discuss. You have other priorities now, after all, and I'm sure we all hope you'll be very happy.'

Her eyes flickered in panic as it dawned on her that she had renounced her authority.

Bottai turned to Sandro. 'I am afraid I simply cannot permit you to discuss our residents in this way, Mr Cellini,' he said calmly. 'Under the circumstances,' and as Alessandra Cornell looked away, Sandro knew his time was up, 'I don't think your employment here could be said to have worked out.' He smiled. 'Do you?'

*

'Looks like the rats are leaving the sinking ship,' said Danilo Lludic, walking into the bright little kitchen where Giuli and Elena sat, each warming their hands around a cup, saying nothing. Giuli felt weary, as if she'd climbed a mountain; she didn't have the energy to ask him what he meant.

She hadn't climbed a mountain: she'd told Elena Giovese that her boyfriend was dead. They'd left Lludic looking into the street. He'd seemed to know not to follow them into the kitchen, to know that Giuli needed to talk to Elena alone once she'd come back inside. She didn't know if he'd been waiting for their voices behind the closed door to fall silent, but they were done.

'Sinking ship?' said Giuli. 'Who's leaving?' She felt completely wiped out: a night of no sleep, and this. Elena.

'The American and his lovely wife,' said Lludic gruffly. He looked at Elena from under lowered brows; she seemed to be miles away, cup to her lips. 'No stamina. Just saw them getting into a big car, private hire. With a lot of luggage. I hope no one's got them down as suspects in all this: it would be embarrassing to be turned back at border control.'

By 'no one', he meant Sandro; by 'all this' he probably meant Vito. Giuli imagined he knew nothing about Carlsson yet, not even he would be so crass. Maybe he wasn't so much crass, as inept.

Giuli had shut the door behind her carefully. The kitchen had suddenly seemed very small indeed, as Elena looked at her, knowing what was about to happen. Time stood still.

'John Carlsson's dead,' she said. 'Your John. They found his body in a suitcase. He was murdered.'

She didn't know if it was shock or stoicism, or if Elena hadn't heard, but she didn't blink or speak. Giuli had to repeat it.

'Murdered.' Elena was expressionless, as if she didn't recognise the word. She was very pale. 'People always say they'd rather know,' she said, looking up through the glazed kitchen window to the grey sky, the reflection in her eyes turning them opaque. 'Don't they? When people disappear, and they don't know if they're alive or dead. They say they just want to know.'

Giuli cleared her throat. 'It's what they say. It's not always true.'

'Murdered.' Elena rubbed her eyes then and turned to fill the coffee pot. 'I only knew him a couple of months,' she said, head down over the sink, not turning round. 'I'll be fine.' She sounded choked, and when she turned, her face was bleak.

'Murdered,' she said, for a third time, and her eyelids trembled. Her eyes were like dark stones at the bottom of a river. 'I've never . . . murder. It's not something that happens to ordinary people.'

'Was he ordinary, though?' said Giuli. And raising her head abruptly, Elena seemed to really see her for the first time that day. 'Sandro is pretty sure John was killed by Vito, the security man over the road.'

Elena fixed on her, hungrily, waiting.

Giuli went on. 'Perhaps because he knew something about him. Or worked something out.' She looked away. 'They found traces of blood in Vito's bathtub. In the drains.' She held Elena's gaze, thinking of the lurid headline on the newspaper stashed in her backpack: *Gay Killing*. 'At the moment they – the authorities – seem to be working on the theory that he killed John, then . . .' She hesitated. 'Killed himself, or sort of. Engaged in risky behaviour, out of remorse.'

'I don't know what you mean by that,' said Elena, frowning. 'That doesn't make sense.'

'No,' said Giuli. And slowly she withdrew last night's paper from her backpack. 'Not to Sandro it doesn't, either.'

Elena studied the front page in silence for a moment that turned into five minutes, and eventually she raised her head. 'Oh, I see,' she said. 'They're saying John was gay?' She tilted her head. 'I suppose it's possible. That I knew him so little.' And to Giuli's astonishment she laughed, with an edge of hysteria. 'It's surreal,' she said when she'd finished, quite calm.

'Do they think anyone will believe it?'

'It's in the paper, isn't it?' said Giuli, and putting her arms around Elena drew her close.

The new pot of coffee began to bubble, and the room filled with the smell – of morning and comfort, of a thousand bars Giuli had walked into for breakfast and company. She opened the door, and at the front of the shop Lludic turned, and it was as if life creaked back into painful motion.

Elena lifted the coffee pot in weary invitation. Edging apologetically into the small space, he settled against the sink. On the little wooden counter where she'd set it down, Giuli's phone jiggled with an incoming call. She lifted it hastily and pressed *Reject call*, only registering as she set the phone back down where it had come from. *Centre*, it said: the Women's Centre calling.

Lludic swallowed the coffee in a gulp and set the cup down. 'Not that I'll be sad to see them go,' he said. 'Van Vleet was a sleaze.' He rubbed his arms, his pouchy face thoughtful. 'Don't know if I'd miss any of them, come to think of it.' He tipped his head on one side.

'None of them?' said Elena. She refilled his cup.

'Your boyfriend,' he said. 'Carlsson. He was after Cameron: that's who he came for, did you know that? He was investigating some bridge collapse in the Middle East somewhere; people died, negligence. He asked me about Cameron, that first night, the night of the launch. Only I think he maybe got sidetracked when he recognised Giancarlo and worked out what he was up to.'

'He recognised Vito,' said Elena.

'And what was Vito up to?' said Giuli.

Lludic downed the second cup. 'Dunno,' he said, chewing his lip. 'I think he was in the business of getting information. On whoever, just in case. Finding out secrets. He knew mine, all right, and he made sure I knew he knew. He knew who'd stolen Athene's bracelet, and got rid of Therese's dog, he knew who paid for Athene's room and what Magda Scardino liked in bed.'

'So they all might have wanted to get rid of him,' said Giuli. 'Do *you* know anyone's secrets, Danilo?'

There was something appraising in the look he gave her, something shrewd. Not unfriendly. 'I'm just a hack,' he said, wiping his mouth. 'Hack artist. What do I know?' But he smiled. 'I suppose I've got eyes,' he said, shrugging. 'I know Van Vleet liked threesomes. I know Ian Cameron left marks on his wife's arms. And I know,' and he sighed, 'I know poor old Athene liked to stay up late. Who knew what she saw?'

Giuli felt her mouth tighten. Lonely old woman, with that expression when Giuli had walked away from her. Athene Morris couldn't have killed him. But perhaps she knew who had.

'You said it was the Englishman,' said Giuli slowly. 'Sir Martin Fleming, in there with her, the night she died.'

'Was he at the hospital?' It was Elena again, and they both turned to look at her. 'When you went in to look for her. Did you see him in there?'

Danilo Lludic was pale under the beard. 'They said she'd had enough visitors,' he said slowly. 'Enough visitors for one day.'

'So there'd been others,' she said.

*

They hadn't insisted on escorting him from the building, at least, although Sandro had witnessed a little tussle between Bottai and Cornell even over that, muttering over by the window while Sandro stood there. The attaché eventually turned to him to say, 'If your departure could be accomplished in a civilised manner, please, Mr Cellini. There's been enough drama in this place.'

'You can call me Sandro, Alessandra,' he'd said. 'After all, we're both civilians now.' Bottai looked put out. 'I'll gather my things,' he added, and at her nod, he had left the room.

He put away the laptop and locked the door of the tiny office behind him.

Hugging his briefcase, Sandro didn't even pause before turning – not back towards the library, where Ian Cameron sat at the bar, nor via the doors outside to where the cold wind ruffled the neat hedges, but down the stairs. It would be his last chance, after all, and the building's cellars had sat there all this time, waiting for him.

He smelled the damp, leaching up through the earth and stone into the expensive carpet, as he took the first step into the gloom. He could hear voices, maybe Bottai and Cornell coming in search of him, and he hurried down, two steps, five; he groped for a light switch as he went, but found nothing. The deep chill of the underground came up to meet him, and at the foot of the stairs Sandro stopped, feeling his heart pound in his chest. There were only so many more years he could get away with doing this to himself. He breathed steadily, waiting for his eyes to adjust, moved his hand along the wall, up, down, and there was the switch.

The wall lights were muted, part no doubt of the spa atmosphere they were trying to create down here, but it felt like nothing so much as a tomb to Sandro. A wide, deep corridor led away from him, a door to his right with a plaque, an etched icon of waves and steam in Art Deco style. *Centro Benessere/ Spa Complex*, it read: a discreet slot beneath the door handle for a keycard.

Slowly he reached into his pocket for the bunch of keys. He'd decided to leave them with Lino rather than return to Cornell's office; had it been at the back of his mind that he might find a last use for them? A metal and plastic key to his office, a large brass one to the front door of the building, the passkey he'd opened Athene's door with, the plastic card marked *Spa*. Another, smaller, brass key. He turned it over in his hand, wondering. A cupboard? Lino's cubbyhole in the foyer?

He slid the plastic card into the slot beside the steam room door without much expectation, but it sprang open with a soft click. Inside, it was dark, a smell of chlorine overlaid with eucalyptus, a dripping from further in. There was another slot inside the door, for the lights; he pushed the keycard in and saw dark slate walls, downlit, some glass panels. Out of habit he went after the source of the dripping and found a shower head, turned it tight off, came back to the door as quickly as he could.

Magda Scardino had heard Marjorie Cameron, locked in there. What had the Professor's wife been doing down here?

Overhead, feet moved, muffled voices filtered down, a woman pleading with a man, although he couldn't have said which man and woman, nor even which language they were speaking. Sandro became aware, with a sense of dread, of the great weight of stone above him, the massive cornices and lintels and slabs imprisoning the sounds, turning them inhuman. And he saw something.

They were here and there around the city, allowing access to the ground floor and subterranean part of great palaces, carved or painted to resemble stonework but visible if you knew how and where to look. Another door, disguised in the marbled paintwork, at what Sandro had taken to be the dead end of the corridor. Reluctantly he took a step, and saw a tiny keyhole. Not bricked back up, after all. He looked down at the bunch in his hand.

Chapter Thirty-One

THE SUITCASES HAD BEEN in the hall for a good hour already: Magda Scardino had recruited Mauro, poor sap, into lugging them down for her. The others had managed their own, even Juliet Fleming. Lino had offered to help her – the woman looked smaller and greyer every time he saw her. She'd shaken her head with a wintry little smile and turned to find her husband.

Lino had been widowed too long: what did he know? But when you looked at the Flemings together, to think he'd been the ambassador and she just the wife – she seemed like the one holding the reins. Maybe that was women for you.

The Americans were gone. Lino looked at his watch. They would be in the air, on their way to St Louis, Missouri. She'd tipped him as he opened the car door for them and he'd almost shaken his head, no; only came to his senses at the last moment. Did she know they knew? The Van Vleets wouldn't be back, the lease would be re-sold. It was all an illusion, masters and servants, Lino knew that better than anyone, but a tip was a tip. The notes rustled in his pocket.

There'd be no tip from Magda Scardino. Mauro had helped her only because he was a gentleman, not in the expectation of reward. A Sardinian.

The stacked suitcases had taken over the foyer now. Lino looked at them with a curious mixture of emotions. He wanted them out, cluttering up the cool marble perfection of his workspace; if he admitted it, he wanted the guests out too, all their murmuring in corridors. Perhaps he was in the wrong job. He had the feeling Cornell thought he was. But it was all a bit sudden; they were running, all right. And it wasn't Lino's job to stop them at the border, ask questions. Look what had happened to Sandro Cellini when he tried it. In the corridor Lino could hear voices.

It had been not much more than an hour since, no suitcases yet piled by the door, Sandro Cellini had come into the foyer with his briefcase under his arm, a funny look in his eyes.

He'd held out a hand, and Lino had taken it in confusion. 'You all right?' he said. 'You look like you've seen a ghost.'

Cellini had just shaken his head and pulled a bunch of keys from his pocket. 'See these get back to Miss Cornell, will you? They're Vito's keys. I'm done here. Going.'

'Going?' Lino hardly knew the guy, but he felt it like a thump in the chest. 'No,' he said feebly.

The keys sat in Cellini's upturned palm. 'Didn't work out,' the detective said, looking down then up into his face. 'Have you ever been down in the basement, Lino? Seen the room down there?'

Oh, that, thought Lino. 'It's old wives' tales,' he said, uncertainly. 'Superstition. It's just a room, they bricked it back up, I heard.' He paused. 'Someone said something about bloodstains, but I think . . . say it had been used as a cellar, once upon a time? A broken bottle of wine, is all.'

'So no one goes down there now? Uses it . . . for anything? Storage, anything like that?'

Lino felt a prickle. 'I don't think so,' he said. 'Why?'

'Vito had a key to it,' said Cellini, and he picked up Lino's hand, turned his own palm over and dropped the keys into it. 'There was a chair, that's all, nothing more. But I wouldn't go down there again, not if you paid me. Never mind.'

Cellini turned away, but he didn't go. He paused, then turned back.

'That night,' he said, and Lino knew straight away, which night. 'Vito died between eleven and midnight. Van Vleet and Lludic were the only ones unaccounted for, you said.'

Lino shrugged uncomfortably, and despite himself he glanced over at the door to his little cubbyhole.

'So you saw the others come in?' said Cellini lightly.

'Well, saw. . .' Lino said uneasily. 'I heard them. I was having a little . . . I was resting. It's permitted. When I heard voices, I came out. Lady Fleming was talking to Mr Cameron, they were going inside. She said her husband was on the doorstep with his cigar.'

'And did you see him?'

Lino wondered if Cornell might suddenly appear, or Bottai, to see Cellini off the premises, but there was no sign of them. He shook his head. 'I was so tired,' he said, suddenly not caring. 'So I went back in.' He nodded over to his cubbyhole. 'In there. I only meant to close my eyes a moment, but when I woke up again it was after twelve, no one was there.' He sighed. 'Except Miss Morris, I heard her down the corridor, talking to someone.'

Sandro Cellini looked at him then, weary, and in his gut Lino knew what he wanted to know.

'I don't suppose . . .' said the detective, and Lino shook his head.

'I didn't see who she was talking to,' he said. 'I was dead beat. I got my things, and I went home.'

Cellini held his gaze, forgiving him. 'We're too old for this,' he said. 'Aren't we?'

Chapter Thirty-Two

THE MESSAGE CAME IN at ten-thirteen, and Luisa, who as a rule left her mobile behind the till, out of courtesy – she'd seen too many girls busily clicking away in shops, heads down while customers idled or left – saw it at ten-thirty when Giusy handed it to her in silence.

I'm sorry

She stared at it. Of course there were mornings when there'd be something for Sandro to apologise for, but this wasn't one of them. Not even a full stop: a draft sent by mistake, a message interrupted. The lack of full stop upset her. He'd gone while she was still asleep; she tried to recall his tone when she'd told him, some time around eight, that Athene Morris had died. Urgent and distracted. Frightened? Maybe.

She turned away from Giusy's inquisitive gaze. Her place was behind the till, and it was part of the etiquette that when Luisa's mobile sounded down below the counter, Giusy wouldn't look at what it said before handing it to Luisa at the earliest possible opportunity.

Upstairs there were footsteps, and the murmur of male voices. It was menswear, after all, but they weren't customers. Frollini was up there, talking to Beppe.

He'd come in with a gleam in his eye, all puffed up with assuaged vanity. He had been talking to Magda Scardino at the Palazzo San Giorgio, he announced. Didn't take you long, thought Luisa. Chew him up and spit him out, that one. 'They had a lovely time yesterday. She was interested in *you*,' he'd said pointedly, to Luisa. 'Interested in you and Sandro. Married to a private eye. I said you were his right-hand woman.'

She'd stared at him then, expressionless, remembering last night. *You better not have told her anything else.* Enrico Frollini had flushed as though reading her mind, and Luisa had turned her back. That woman: Magda Scardino was a witch.

She pocketed the mobile instead of putting it back behind the till, and walked away from Giusy's curious look, walked to the window that looked out over the Por Santa Maria. She dialled Sandro's number.

It rang three times, then went to answerphone. Luisa didn't know much about technology, but she knew it took six rings for Sandro's phone to go to messages. He'd cut her off. Stay calm, she thought. He'll have his reasons. She looked up and a customer was there on the other side of the glass door, looking at her angrily. She stepped back, smiled, put the phone away. Frollini's face appeared at the top of the stairs and she turned her back on him.

Waiting outside the changing room, Luisa tried to still the unreasoning anger she felt against the customer, and at the same time to diffuse the silly panic that rose in her every time she thought of that message, without its full stop. In her pocket she pressed redial: it went straight to answerphone this time.

From behind the door of the changing room came sounds of dissatisfaction: an ill-tempered sigh, a tut, an elbow banging against the partition. Women. Luisa felt a wave of tiredness at the thought of women – the fretting, the anxiety, the competition, the sheer labour of it. The answer, it came to her, the answer to Giancarlo Vito's death lay between the women. And add to them Valeria Maratti, Vito's landlady.

Somewhere between them, they knew. Why he'd died.

Therese Van Vleet: no. Too young, too unhappy – not guilty. Magda Scardino: she'd slept with Vito, said Sandro. Well, of course she had. Luisa thought of her in the limo heading for the mall, chasing her discount like a dog with a bone; she was a woman who felt it her duty to take what she wanted without hesitation. If someone stood in her way, how far would she go? If Vito threatened, say, to tell her husband? Something ticked in the back of Luisa's mind, stalling that line of thought. Even if Magda Scardino was the strongest of them, wouldn't she just walk away? Not her problem.

What nagged at her, an inconsistency half-formed, had to do with Maratti, and that mother she'd invented for her lodger. Because Vito's CV had had his parents down as deceased.

Did you invent that kind of thing out of thin air? No.

The changing room door thumped open and the woman thrust a handful of garments at Luisa, her face pouchy and unattractive with disappointment. As Luisa looked into her face, she wasn't quite seeing her customer but the vengeful features of Valeria Maratti, peering through the green gloom of her backyard, spying, and Giancarlo Vito finding an explanation for something his nosy landlady had seen. Just like he explained away the sounds of his struggle with a man.

She's my mother.

'No good then?' she said automatically to the client. 'I'm so sorry. Can I show you—'

'I wouldn't trust you to show me anything,' the woman snapped. 'Are you an idiot? The sizes were all wrong.' There was movement at the other end of the shop and Luisa looked, and saw Enrico Frollini at the foot of the stairs eyeing her, turning his most treacherous placatory smile on the customer.

An older woman had come to visit Vito. She pictured them together, in the parking lot, in the garden. She thought of Juliet Fleming, watchful when the news was broken of Vito's death, and remembered the sickness in the woman's own face when Luisa had told them Athene Morris had been taken ill. An older woman.

Why would Juliet Fleming have gone to Vito's house? Luisa didn't know why.

The door closed behind the customer and Frollini was looking at her. Something calculating in his look, something colder. 'Really, Luisa,' he said. 'Didn't you recognise her? I'm beginning to think—'

But she turned her back on him and she heard an intake of breath. She walked away, to the stairs down to the stock room, retrieved her jacket and her bag and came back up to find him still there, standing at the foot of the stairs. Behind the till, oblivious, Giusy was struck dumb and pale with startlement.

'I'm finished,' said Luisa quietly. Did he actually look relieved? 'I mean, Enrico,' she amplified, 'that I resign.'

After thirty-five years. He couldn't even complete a response. 'Well, Luisa, if you think . . .' He cleared his throat and fell silent.

The soft sound of the door as it closed behind her, her bag clasped against her newly awkward chest, seemed to Luisa like a little rush of wind, as though she had stepped off a ledge and the air was all that would hold her up. The brightness of the street and the passers-by whirled about her for a moment, and then the world steadied, and she was out.

She turned to walk towards the river.

*

Carlotta could see them clamping the little car from where she stood on the Carabinieri station's terrace: leaning out you could see right down into the Via Romana. The sound of the truck's beeping reverse alarm had brought her out; her own very smart and shiny new Vespa was parked legally, as far as she remembered, but when the *comune* was running out of cash they'd have the *vigili* out clamping anything a centimetre over the line. From what Carlotta could see of a bird-spattered brown roof just visible through the canopy of leaves, the car they were fixing the clamp to probably wasn't worth much more than the removal charge.

It was cold, and raindrops still stood on the long-bladed leaves of the iris beds from the morning's shower. Turning to go back in, Carlotta heard voices. Falco had opened his window.

The man had been in there five minutes. Carlotta didn't know him to look at – an unprepossessing, stocky man in a shabby coat, but with a weary sort of authority that had stopped her from fobbing him right off when he'd appeared in the doorway. Sandro Cellini.

'He'll see me,' said Sandro Cellini, and he'd sat, without asking, lifting the old raincoat aside as he lowered himself, in a gesture that made Carlotta think of her father, a bus driver all his life. She didn't think this man drove a bus.

He'd taken out a mobile phone and looked at it, holding it far away from him in his lap. To Carlotta, hesitating, it seemed as though he wanted to throw the thing away, but perhaps he just didn't have his glasses on. He smoothed the screen with a thumb, then reluctantly stabbed at it. One word, two. He looked up and she went; when she turned back at the door, the mobile phone had gone.

'He said you'd see him.' Falco had looked at Carlotta with eyes narrowed. She knew the name: Sandro Cellini had phoned, yesterday. And knew it from somewhere else too, some old story, some old case.

Falco had sighed. 'He did, did he?' And to her surprise said, 'Show him in.' He'd closed the door behind them.

Carlotta leaned forward a little and saw the ironwork of Falco's tiny balcony.

'This is confidential,' he was saying. 'This is a matter of internal security. You've been in the service, Cellini, you know we can't make things public.' Carlotta was surprised by the pleading edge to Falco's voice. No wonder he'd wanted the doors closed.

'You know they've fired me?' said the other voice. 'What am I going to say to my wife?'

'So you don't owe them anything,' said her boss. 'Just let it drop.'

'Owe them nothing?' The voice was weary. 'What about public safety, Falco? Two men dead. Both murdered, beyond a doubt. Don't you want to know what Carlsson discovered? Unless you know already, that is. And of course if you go talking to his girlfriend you'd have to admit he wasn't gay, wouldn't you?'

'I don't know anything about girlfriends,' said Falco. 'Who is this girl?'

'Oh, no,' said Cellini, grimly triumphant. 'You're covering this up; how do I know you won't go after her yourselves? Vito killed Carlsson, that seems beyond a doubt. But Vito wasn't gay and he wasn't a psychopath – that murder was sanctioned, officially or unofficially, by the intelligence services. Would she get the same treatment?'

'I don't know what you're talking about,' said Falco stiffly.

Hardly daring to breathe, Carlotta moved closer. She could see the open shutters on Falco's balcony from here: if he stepped out he would see her.

'Giancarlo Vito was murdered,' said Sandro Cellini, and although the words were spoken quietly she could hear perfectly. They must be standing right in the window. 'What interests me is how. Are we talking trained killer? Just between us. You've had access to the autopsy reports by now.'

There was a sigh. 'It's a mess,' muttered Falco. 'Conspiracy? It's the usual cock-up.'

'I'm sorry?' Cellini's voice was sharp. 'Is that an admission?'

'You won't believe me,' said Falco, although Carlotta knew her boss well enough to know he was speaking the truth, for once. 'But I don't know why Vito killed this journalist. By the sound of it, he was a loose cannon, to say the least. Maybe he was angry because he'd been fired, angry he'd been uncovered by some hack. Angry his career was certainly over.'

A pause. In the silence Carlotta could almost hear Cellini working out what he could trust. Holding his fire. Falco went on.

'And no, that's not an admission of anything. But everything points to Vito's killing being an amateur job. He was taken absolutely by surprise, he'd let the killer in, no sign of forced entry. One blow to the head and the killer didn't wait around to make sure he was dead, just wiped down the handweight he'd used and threw it into the grass.'

'A lucky strike,' said Cellini, thoughtfully.

'But of course I would indeed like to talk to Carlsson's female friend.'

There was a silence in which the note of sly calculation that had crept into her boss's voice still sounded in Carlotta's head. She wondered if Sandro Cellini was right: she knew who she'd trust on a dark night. The tired-looking man who spread his raincoat as he sat.

Falco went on trying to sound superior, but only sounded crafty to Carlotta. How could she work for this creep? 'Trained killers leave no evidence. You can't have it both ways, Cellini.'

Another silence, and when Sandro Cellini spoke he sounded weary. 'I don't know who it was,' he said. 'I just don't like the way it's being handled, and I don't want anyone else hurt, if it's in my power to prevent that. Although as you will have observed, I have almost no power, these days.'

'I'll contact the girlfriend,' said Falco, urgently. 'Let me have the details, I'll get after her, I'll have protection for her.'

It occurred to Carlotta that she had better get back inside, and she stepped back, feeling a shower of cold raindrops hit her cheek from a hanging rose. Below her the Via Romana was silent. The clampers had gone. She waited, just one last moment, to hear Cellini's answer.

'No,' he said. 'I don't trust you.'

*

Behind Lino's back, at the door, someone cleared their throat, and he turned, expecting the limo driver. It was the spiky-haired girl – young woman. Cellini's colleague. She smiled, but she looked nervous. 'I need Sandro,' she said.

'Oh,' said Lino, realising he would have to explain. At the back of his mind things were shifting. One of this lot, he thought, eyeing the residents gathered in his foyer, waiting for their transport. Fleming, glancing down at his wife, looked like he'd had a late night – at the hospital, Lino'd heard.

'He's gone,' he said in an undertone to Signorina Sarto.

'Gone?'

He jerked a thumb over his shoulder into the street. 'Must have been something he said. They fired him.' She stared.

'Where's that car?' The voice, insistent in Lino's ear, was Magda Scardino's. 'The flight's in less than two hours.'

'Just one moment, madam,' said Lino, with dignity. Turning back to Giuli, 'I can't tell you much more than that,' he said. 'He left an hour ago. I saw him get into his car, down at the bottom of the hill. He didn't say where he was going.'

Giulietta Sarto was looking at Magda Scardino, who had her hand on Sir Martin Fleming's arm in a gesture that would have made Lino nervous if it had been his body she was touching. 'They're leaving?' Sarto muttered, wondering. 'They're just allowed to go?'

'This isn't a prison,' said Lino, trying for a laugh. But she was frowning down at her mobile, punching in numbers, turning away from him already, and out of the door.

'I'm sorry, madam,' he said, addressing Magda Scardino's profile. 'I'll step outside and give them a call for you. It won't be long, I'm sure.'

But Giulietta Sarto was halfway down the Costa San Giorgio, perched small and proud and upright on her *motorino*, by the time he'd got his mobile out and was in the street.

Chapter Thirty-Three

Merda.

He should have known better, than to drive in this city. Of all the cars parked illegally on the Via Romana right under the looming façade of the Boboli's Carabinieri post, Sandro's was the only one with a fat yellow clamp attached to it. He looked from the car up to the Carabinieri station: someone up there didn't like him.

He took out his phone. As he looked at it, it rang. He didn't want to talk to anyone, no one. Except maybe Pietro. It would be Luisa, wanting to know what he'd meant by the text he'd sent abortively from the *carabiniere*'s office. *I'm sorry*. Ah, shit.

It was Giuli. Reluctantly, he answered. She launched into it.

'Yes,' he said, when she stopped. 'I've been fired.'

She let off another round.

'They're what? Slow down, Giuli.' He looked up and down the street: there was no sign of the clamper van. From the doorway of an antique shop opposite, a man watched him with mild interest. Sandro nodded to him.

'They're going,' she said. 'The foursome, the Flemings and the Scardinos. They're going to the airport, together. They were waiting for their car when I went over looking for you. Why were you fired?'

'Together,' repeated Sandro, ignoring the question. 'You're sure?'

'Pretty sure. You should have talked to Danilo, the sculptor. He knew what Carlsson was there for – he wanted to find out about Cameron and his bridge. And he's certain Fleming was in the old lady's room that night. D'you think he hurt her?'

'I think someone frightened her,' said Sandro, picturing the chair overturned in her room. Hold on. Did you say . . . yesterday, didn't you say Juliet Fleming went to see her in the hospital?' He felt a sweat bead on his upper lip, despite the leaden sky. The antique dealer in his doorway was wearing tweeds, so it must be cold. The weather was odd: his city felt strange. Was he ill? He pulled at his collar.

'Marjorie Cameron saw her,' said Giuli. 'Yes.'

Something prickled at the nape of his neck. 'Is the girl all right?' he said. 'You told her?'

'Elena?' Giuli's voice sounded distant now. 'She's all right, I think. He didn't tell her anything, he didn't leave anything behind, as far as I know. Maybe he was protecting her.' More remote, or was there something the matter with his ears? 'Lludic's with her. She's okay.'

'What's up, Giuli?' he said, trying to bring things into focus. 'Something's the matter.'

'I've got to go over to the Centre,' she said.

'Right,' said Sandro, but his mind was somewhere else.

'Have you told Luisa you've been fired?' she said, and he heard the sigh, as if far away. 'You haven't, have you?'

'I'll talk to you later,' he said. It was only after he'd hung up that he remembered that Giuli didn't work at the Centre any more.

'Bastards,' said the antique dealer, stepping into the road. Sandro looked at him: the man nodded up at the Carabinieri post. 'Bastards. They just love to throw their weight about.'

Sandro just grunted agreement; he was dialling a cab. *Incoming call, divert?* said his phone. It was Luisa. With guilty impatience he told the phone, *Reject.*

The cab arrived in three minutes. The driver looked at the clamp from behind reflective aviator glasses and said, 'Bastards.'

He asked to be taken to the airport. He felt the driver take in his crumpled jacket. No suitcase, no passport – no tip, was what he was thinking. He engaged gear slowly.

'As quick as you can,' said Sandro. 'That all right?'

The fare was thirty-two euros in the end. In his wallet Sandro had thirty-five in crumpled notes: he waited for his change. Around him, as he stood on the airport forecourt, the world still felt strange. He seemed to see the people moving in and out of the ghostly sliding glass doors as if in a dream. A young couple kissed as if they were never going to see each other again. Hand out for his three euros, Sandro's stomach soured with apprehension.

Inside, people milled around, looking up at screens. A check-in queue snaked around the edge of the departures hall; must be some Third World airline, he realised – most people checked in online these days. The other desks were manned but largely idle. He scanned the signs above each one.

Where had they been going?

The Flemings to London, for her health. The Scardinos to Cairo.

He located Cairo: twelve-fifteen. Looked back at the departures screens. The London flight would already be boarding, an hour earlier. The sickness rose in him. He thought of Athene Morris dead in a foreign hospital – was that how she'd imagined it would end? He didn't care too much about Vito, he found. He thought of Juliet and Martin Fleming disappearing into London, folded back into the arms of the home country to hide from whatever it was that they'd done, and felt a chemical surge that he realised was anger.

Sandro turned, full circle, looking. Toilets, handbags, newsstand, VIP lounge. Security, Passports. He ran, feeling the flesh on his ageing body shift heavily as he moved, as if it might pull from the bones. The official checking tickets looked up at him expressionless as he came up to the cordon, panting, and he realised, too late, his absolute powerlessness. The man shook his head. Without a ticket? No. Sandro tried to explain that it was a police matter, no longer caring about taking Pietro's name – his badge – in vain. Adrenaline, he tried to recall, was it good for you, or bad? At his age, most things were bad. He was sweating.

The official pursed his lips, a small queue of impatient travellers beginning to form, jostling. The man nodded towards a door marked *Polizia di Frontiera*, and turned away.

There was no one behind the door: the chair, even, was pushed up against the table as if no one had been there for some time.

As he stood in the doorway, looking back into the concourse, Sandro felt the adrenaline begin to ebb and remembered, that was the dangerous bit, the crash.

The illuminated signs around the thronged space blurred as he tried to regroup his thoughts. Car hire, Information. VIP lounge.

VIP Lounge. Something stopped inside him. There.

The door was manned, of course: not a bouncer in a suit but a young woman in a tilted old-style stewardess's cap, very stylish, turning to look at Sandro as he approached.

The space opened behind her, partitioned off under the high-beamed roof of the concourse, and he saw them off to one side. Sitting on upholstered bucket seats in bright colours, a laptop open between them on a low table. Four of them.

'I'm from their hotel,' he said, mustering as honest and open an expression as he could. 'There's . . . something was left behind. I have to hand it over in person.'

She looked at him a long moment. I could be your grandfather, he thought, and in that moment she stepped back. From inside the partitioned space that didn't resemble a real room, only a makeshift attempt at luxury, Juliet Fleming turned in her low seat and looked up at him.

*

Giuli took a breath and stepped through the grubby glass doors of the Women's Centre. The clammy cool of the overcast morning gave way to the usual fug of the too-crowded space. She registered that the receptionist on duty was a newcomer, a temp, by the look of muted panic in her eyes, and the low-grade discontent among the waiting patients. Maybe they already know, she thought.

The temp looked up, hostile already. 'I'm here to see the Director,' said Giuli. 'I got a call, I'm expected. Giulietta Sarto.' And walked past as the girl lifted the telephone receiver.

She didn't feel any fear any more. Massini might have summoned her because Vera had confessed, or she might be telling her it was all over, they couldn't take the risk on her, there'd been other complaints, she was damaged goods. Giuli didn't care, she just wanted it done with.

She sat on the bench outside Massini's office. There were voices inside. In her pocket her phone blipped and she took it out, half on her feet again, ready to run back into the outside world. Coward.

The message was from Luisa: *Have you heard from Sandro? I'm worried.*

The door opened.

I'm going over there.

Massini stood in the doorway. Behind her, inside the office, Giuli could see the squat figure in quarter profile hunched in a seat in front of the desk. Vera.

'If you'd like to come in, Giulietta,' said her boss.

*

'What's this?' Danilo was kneeling by the door of her bedroom.

Since Giulietta Sarto had gone, Elena had felt as though she'd gone half deaf, in the aftermath of some blast.

'What?' she said. John was dead. John had been killed. She'd sat in a daze while Danilo and Giulietta had argued insistently over people she hardly knew, would never care about: the old woman who'd died of a stroke. She'd been so old, how could it matter? Somewhere inside her, Elena knew it always mattered, she wished she could care. All she could think about was that before Giuli had walked in, the worst she could imagine was another woman in John's life.

Danilo Lludic stood up, frowning, right in front of her in the bedroom. Holding an open CD case. 'Tell me you've got a computer,' he said. 'That can read this.'

She looked down, and saw the case. *Now That's What I Call Music*, it said. He held it up to her and she saw the disc that was inside it, only it wasn't a music CD, it had something written on it in indelible felt-tip, John's neat writing. She looked from the silver disc to Lludic.

'I've got a laptop,' Elena said. It took her a moment to locate it, under a chair, behind a heap of clothes, another moment to locate the cable, to plug it in. It was slow to boot up. 'I don't use it much,' she said, apologising. 'It's a distraction. Don't you find? All that noise out there, in the universe.' She was talking nonsense, but anyway he wasn't paying attention, he was holding the writeable disc in his hands like some religious relic.

The words written on it were: *Giancarlo Vito.*

Little windows opened on her screen, over the screensaver of a hundred-year-old olive tree in Vinci. *Storage disc. Read files.* She watched Danilo Lludic's big hands turn deft over the mousepad, opening the file. She held her breath, as though she would see him again. But the words were in Italian. Frowning over Lludic's shoulder at the screen, with a knot in her chest it came to her that John hadn't written this, he'd stolen it.

It was a list, notes, abbreviations, names. Dates.

Danilo's big head followed the screen down, and she felt the excitement radiating off him like heat. Abruptly he turned to look at her.

'It's Vito,' he said, breathless. 'I told you, didn't I, that your John made himself at home in the Palazzo? Maybe he found his way into Giancarlo's office one day. Vito wrote this.'

She looked from him to the screen.

The names of residents: at the top, *Charles Scardino, Magda Scardino*. A dossier on each resident – perhaps in order of importance. Dates of birth, places of education, photographs, taken in the street and through hotel windows. A couple of racy ones of Magda posing in underwear, from years back by the look of them. Newspaper reports, abbreviations, names of informants and meetings and betrayals.

She looked at Danilo, mystified by the language on the screen. 'What was he doing?' she said.

Lludic just shook his head, absorbed. He scrolled down.

Martin Fleming, British Foreign Office 1962 – retirement 2005. A list of places and dates: Elena tried to conjure the life that accompanied them. *Zagreb 1964–66, Kenya 1966–69, Rome 1969–72, Egypt 1972–77, Syria, Jordan, Yemen, Kuwait. Trade envoy, aide, liaison, vice-consul, ambassador.*

Rome, she thought. That must have been good.

And then, in capitals: *JULIET FLEMING née HARDEN. Probably recruited Cambridge 1962.*

Juliet Fleming was the little grey-haired woman who drank

whisky while her husband watched her from across the room, half proud, half anxious. Who'd said the secret was to pace yourself, and had used John's words when she said that Elena looked like a Vermeer through her workshop window.

'Recruited?' she said, wonderingly.

Danilo Lludic tipped back his head to look at her. Without thinking, he took one of her hands in his and rested his lips on it.

'I might have been wrong about him, then,' he said, thoughtfully.

Elena looked at him levelly, then removed her hand.

Chapter Thirty-Four

STICK TO CERTAINTIES, REPEATED Sandro doggedly to himself like a mantra as he looked from one face to another, all four turned towards him. At his shoulder he could sense that the woman on the door of the VIP lounge was poised to eject him. He chose Martin Fleming. Stick to certainties.

'Please,' he said. 'It's about Athene.'

And Juliet Fleming's head moved up and back so she could fix him in her sights, the movement echoing an animal's reflex, some clever reptile. Her husband was on his feet: he looked haggard under the airport lighting, confirming Sandro's instinct. Fleming was the one suffering, the weak link.

'The night she . . . collapsed,' he began, and Juliet Fleming was standing too. Beyond them, he saw Charles Scardino's head turning, calculating, to gauge the situation, and Magda Scardino putting a hand out to his arm to deflect him. What gave Scardino the right, wondered Sandro in that instant, to protection from this messy business? His brains? His earning potential? And then Juliet Fleming blocked them out.

'Darling,' she said quickly, voice raised just enough for the Scardinos to overhear, 'I think we should be making a move, don't you? Look at the time.'

And she turned back, leaning down to the other couple, talking swiftly and easily about catching up in Cairo, about a restaurant, about hotels, while Sandro looked into Sir Martin Fleming's face and saw, variously, fatigue, fear, misery.

Juliet Fleming's hand on his arm, then in the small of his back, was light but unerring, impossible to resist. They moved back past the woman on the door, whose head turned to follow them. The soft insistent pressure of her hand on his back eased only when they were out of sight and earshot, between a newsstand and the small queue for Security.

Sandro spoke immediately: give this woman an entry point and she would deflect him, stun him. 'You were in Athene Morris's room the night before last,' he said. He spoke in Italian; for now they were still in his country, and they both knew the language. 'What did she see? What did she know?' He thought of Dickens on the bedside table, and the little pile of treasures, and something slid into its place in his head. 'She was the one in and out of other residents' rooms, wasn't she? Did she find something she shouldn't have? Did she know you were resident at the Palazzo San Giorgio on behalf of the British security services? Did she know you had a reason to want Giancarlo Vito disposed of?'

'What reason?' Juliet Fleming's voice was sharp. Martin Fleming's face looked slack as rubber. 'My husband is a retired diplomat. His connection with Athene goes back a long way. They were friends.' The words were crisply delivered but they seemed abruptly to have left her without breath.

Her husband looked at her, and set a hand on her shoulder.

MA, thought Sandro. Martin, Athene.

'Athene and I were lovers,' he said. 'A long time ago. I went to see her that night – because I was worried about her.'

'Athene was in Florence because of my husband,' said Juliet Fleming. 'He paid her lease.' Her face was sallow, with tension, or sickness. 'He wanted to look after her.'

'That's nice,' said Sandro, looking from her to Martin Fleming. 'And you thought you'd sign up yourselves, just to keep an eye on her? Or did she turn into a bit of an inconvenience? Did you spot Scardino on the list of other residents and decide jostling a few old lovers wouldn't do any harm when the stakes were so high – snaring a stratospheric scientist for Britain? So you signed up too, imagining you would be able to manage Athene. Only then Giancarlo Vito seemed to be after the same thing. So you had to deal with him. And maybe Athene, being an old woman, being still in love even at her age, started to get indiscreet?'

'It's business,' said Juliet Fleming, and then, at last, Sandro understood.

'He really is just a retired diplomat,' he said. 'It's not him who's the spy, it's you, isn't it?' It whirled. He'd always known it, hadn't he? That it would be a woman. A woman's touch in the nasty tricks: was it bitterness, or strategy, or alcoholism? 'Did you steal the bracelet back, because you hated Athene Morris after all these years?'

She stared, haughty.

'And did Vito find it in your room, or maybe the maid did and told him?' Had he tried to use it to get leverage, then sent it back to her, on Carlsson's body after he was fired, as a message? Only it never arrived. 'Did you put that magazine in my briefcase?'

Juliet Fleming frowned and he thought, in panic – no. She knows nothing about it. Could she have trained herself to deliver that response? And then her face loosened, and he smelled just the ghost of whisky on her breath.

'What do you think this is?' she said. 'You and Vito both, you men, this Italy. It isn't a boys' game of spies and sex and flashes of brilliance, it isn't about ego. It's business. Negotiation. Incentivising.' She held her head very still and straight. 'It's about hard work.' She drew herself upright, her eyes bright. 'Has it occurred to you that you might consider putting women in charge in this country, now and again?'

Sandro looked at her, thought of Luisa and Giuli and how long it was since he'd spoken to them. The call he'd rejected from Luisa: it occurred to him that the odds were they'd been quietly making their own deductions. Humbly, he persisted. 'Who killed Giancarlo Vito?'

Her head bowed, Juliet Fleming was unzipping a flat leather bag slung across her body, extracting passports and plane tickets. 'A licence to kill, is that what you imagine?' She handed Martin Fleming his ticket as she spoke, not bothering to look at Sandro. Fleming's face was stony, guarded.

'Vito clearly thought he had one. Such idiocy. Almost always an error, to take extreme measures. Almost never necessary. You seriously think that I or my husband,' she spoke proudly, 'would have made such a mess? Do you think we could have thought of no other way of stopping Vito getting Scardino's business than to kill him? He only had his handsome face, his honeytrap; he couldn't offer Magda Eton or Westminster for her sons.' She shrugged. Sandro realised he had had no idea the Scardinos had children. She went on. '*My* husband having to terrify Athene into a fit because she might or might not have seen something wandering the corridors late at night?'

Then she looked at him. 'If my husband had killed Vito it would only have been to *protect* Athene.' And laughed shortly. 'Vito was an unnecessarily manipulative and unpleasant man. He was clever enough to find out secrets, but not clever enough to use them properly, and too stupid to know when he was playing with fire. Dropping hints to Martin that he'd let people know about their affair. Stupid enough to think it was worth keeping that idiot Van Vleet supplied with girls. That fool Bottai, and his father almost as bad, throwing their weight around, pretending to be men of influence.' She stopped briefly, her face grey, to take a quick shallow breath. 'No wonder AISE only used him as a floater: I don't suppose they'll be regretting the loss so much as concentrating on cleaning up afterwards.'

But Sandro was looking at the husband.

'Juliet insisted,' he said, weary. 'I told her it would be too much. I'd retired, she could have left it to someone else, this time. Particularly with Athene here, I didn't want to . . . get involved. But Scardino was such a prize, apparently.' He didn't look at his wife. 'It's made her ill.'

Ill. She was dying: Sandro saw that with sudden clarity. And Juliet Fleming confirmed it. 'It's liver cancer, darling,' she said wearily. 'It was already there. It's not the job that did it, it was me.'

As if the words were a talisman, Sandro stepped back, to let them go; not that he had any power to detain them, nor ever did have. Juliet Fleming stepped between them, holding a thin yellow hand out to her husband, who took it, like a prize. But Fleming didn't walk away, not yet.

'She was happy when I left her,' he said. 'Athene.' Grief, thought Sandro, just sounded like exhaustion in this man. 'I never went near the damned man, bloody Vito, not for her or anyone else, and she knew I hadn't. I went to warn her. She never could resist gossip, she never could resist stirring things up: it got worse as she got older, if anything.'

'Less to lose,' said his wife. One hand still in his, she raised the other to his upper arm to steer him towards their departure.

'Athene knew,' said Sandro, hearing his own voice hoarsen. 'She knew who killed Giancarlo Vito.'

From over her shoulder Juliet Fleming said in her dry, rusty little voice, throwing it away without breaking step, 'I think we all knew.'

Sandro had no power to keep them. As he watched her narrow upright figure disappear through the security gates he understood that he would not see Juliet Fleming – nothing like a Juliet, except in her husband's eyes – again.

We all knew.

*

Heading east along the river, under the high yellow arcades that held up the Vasari corridor in its last stretch before it met the grey arches and pillars of the Uffizi, it seemed to Luisa that this must be what it was like to have failing sight restored at a stroke, or hearing: everything suddenly sharp and bright and loud and new. Overhead, she imagined the gilded and varnished galleries, the long windows, the murmuring of guides. The Africans laid out their cheap prints at her feet and chattered at her. Looking down, she saw wire figurines, little wooden letters; the usual stream of tourists walked towards her in their shorts and hats and as if in a dream of dancing, unerring Luisa sidestepped every obstacle.

If Sandro wouldn't answer, she certainly wouldn't leave him a message. Standing at the foot of the Ponte Vecchio while the crowd parted to stream around her, she had left a message for Giuli, instead. The phone had rung again almost immediately and her heart had leapt, but it was neither of them, the number was unfamiliar and so, for some time, was the voice.

She looked across the river and saw the Palazzo San Giorgio silhouetted on its slope against the low dark sky. She could see that all but one set of its shutters were closed, like a fortress battening down. A gust blew as she came out from under the arcades, and below her on the rowing club's green terrace something beat and flapped with a cracking sound. Spring storms were the worst, the most violent: they could wreak havoc.

On the mobile the voice had whispered half of what it said – in English – incomprehensible to Luisa. It had echoed like the simulated voices of the spirits at a séance her mother had dragged her to, fifty years earlier, rising and falling and sobbing and pleading, ectoplasm and fakery, making her feel slightly sick, then and now. What was the woman trying to tell her? *I'm sorry. Help me.*

'All right,' she'd ended up saying, just to terminate the conversation. 'I'm coming anyway. I was on my way.'

'I'm so sorry,' were the words she remembered from the call, echoing Sandro's. 'I was so sorry about your husband.'

*

As Giuli walked out, she passed a woman waiting on the bench seats of the STD Clinic: a woman not young. Her face turned to follow Giuli, and she had the same look in her eye as Vera had had, turning from the seat. Shamed, wrong, defiant, hopeless.

'I'm so sorry,' Massini had said, immediately the door had closed behind her. 'I should have believed you, Giulietta.'

There had been justifications, excuses. Giuli had merely sat there waiting for it to finish, staring straight ahead.

'Of course,' Massini had said, 'we would never have taken it at face value, and when she couldn't come up with these supposed witnesses—' She stopped. 'Are you all right?'

'I'm glad to know,' said Giuli, distantly. *Just let me out of here*, she thought, Vera's sullen face imprinted on her retina. 'She's explained to you why she did it?'

Massini was properly uncomfortable. 'Something to do with her husband—'

'He was one of my customers,' said Giuli. 'Twenty years ago. You see enough women like me in here to know, we're not in it for kicks.' She turned her head and looked Vera in the eye. In her pocket the phone vibrated again. *Let me out of here*, she thought once more, *I've got things to do.*

She blinked, looked into Massini's face and tried to focus. She could make out sincerity, she saw remorse.

'So under the circumstances, naturally we would lift the suspension with immediate effect, that is, if you—'

'I need to think about it,' said Giuli, standing abruptly. 'Under the circumstances.'

Massini cleared her throat, got to her feet. 'Well I—'

'How long can you give me? To decide.'

'As long as you need, Giulietta,' Massini said, and if she had been going on to say, *within reason,* she swallowed it with a stiff little movement.

'I have to get to work now,' said Giuli, thinking with longing of the haven of the little office. Could she ever come back here?

As Giuli walked back through reception, the temp was too harassed even to register her return and she carried on, stopped only on the threshold by the sight of the trees of the Piazza Tasso under a teeming downpour.

Of course she had seen that look before, the look on Vera's face, on the woman outside the STD Clinic. A look so undiluted that you could almost smell it, like burning: shame, fear, the stubborn residue of desire. It's the weak, Sandro had once told her. It's the weak that kill, because they have no other options.

Chapter Thirty-Five

'Darling,' said Magda Scardino, leaning back in the bright bucket seat to address her husband before Sandro, back in the flimsy stage-set doorway of the VIP lounge, could even open his mouth. The woman on the door barely gave him a glance this time. 'Darling, I'm gasping for another coffee. Would you mind?' And she gestured with a toss of her head to the bar at the far end, as makeshift as the rest of the place, with its meagre row of bottles and plastic barstools.

Charles Scardino looked up from the journal he was reading, and got to his feet without a word. He was a man, thought Sandro, for whom everything was calculated moment by moment and without sentiment: when he'd had enough of Magda, he might not even pause to say why he wanted her gone. But for the time being, it seemed, she was what he wanted. He walked away.

Magda pointed at the seat beside her and the instant Sandro was close enough she spoke, rapidly. 'I told your wife to tell you to stay out of it,' she said, leaning in, making him do the same. 'If you don't have the brains, she certainly does. What's to be gained? Vito was a fool. Was it because he was Italian? Are you all like that? Trying to provoke me, to make me jealous, as if sex would do it.'

She rolled her eyes, then tipped her head to look across the room. Her husband seemed to know what was expected of him, and was taking his time.

'And with *her*, of all of them, with that husband. Controlling doesn't describe that man adequately.'

Sandro grappled with what Magda was telling him, her face half turned away from him still as she kept an eye on the Professor.

'He only wanted a wife who'd listen to him and make children and shut up. Barefoot in the bush – the number of times I've heard him say that! Can you imagine what he'd do?' Outraged. 'If he found out she was. . .' And she hesitated, at last. 'Enjoying herself with another man?'

'I'm sorry,' said Sandro. 'Are you talking about the engineer? Cameron? He got Vito fired. I knew that. He accused him of looking at his post.'

'And the rest,' said Magda Scardino. 'Getting him fired wasn't enough, was it? The strange thing was,' she tapped a long fingernail to her plump lip, 'Giancarlo never did look at his post. He was actually trying to be helpful for once, taking him the letter. But from then on Cameron had it in for him. Everything about him, he hated.'

Pimp, seducer, player. What's not to hate, thought Sandro. And yet. He didn't quite hate Vito.

'And Vito thought . . .' She glanced over at her husband, taking the coffee from the barman, turning to walk back. 'Well,

I was holding out on him – he thought he could kill two birds with one stone. Make me jealous and at the same time sweeten Marjorie up, get her to bring her husband round.' She leaned her head back, exposing her long throat, and closed her eyes a moment. Nothing accidental about Magda's gestures.

Sandro stared at her. 'Jealous? Of . . . he was . . .'

'You should have seen her,' said Magda. Perhaps, thought Sandro, this is what pity looks like, in her, this scornful mouth. 'Oh, God, no fool like an old fool, a virtuous old fool. She's only ever slept with her husband and Giancarlo turns those eyes on her and touches her. . .' She put a finger with deliberate sensuality to the inside of her own elbow. 'I was on the other side of the library and I could see it happening. Do you think her own husband couldn't see?'

Sandro could feel Charles Scardino's approach, slow and deliberate – he must have taken his medication for the journey – balancing the coffee. Magda turned and smiled at her husband, out of earshot, and spoke under her breath.

'Athene said, she came back without him that night. Marjorie and Ian went out for a romantic dinner, the night Vito died. Athene said, Marjorie came back without him.'

Sandro frowned, trying to remember what Lino had said. Something wasn't quite right.

Then Magda lifted her head towards her husband. 'Darling,' she said, calmly. 'We were talking about Ian Cameron.' Beyond the single wide VIP window onto the tarmac, the light changed as she spoke, and the glass shuddered in a sudden gust of wind.

Scardino lowered the coffee to the table between them. 'An excellent engineer, by all accounts,' he said, his face concealed.

'Single-minded. That's what it takes. So what if he took the lowest bid for materials? Sometimes that's what it takes.' And raising his head he smiled, perhaps the first time Sandro had seen it, before speaking again. 'Wouldn't want to be on the wrong side of him, mind you. Did you see the bruises on her? That scratch?'

'Oh, she probably likes it,' said Magda, startling Sandro. 'Drawing attention to herself. Locked in the steam room – I don't think so. I found the keycard lying on the floor in the corridor. She did it herself. And does a man inflict scratches?'

'What scratch?' But before Scardino could say anything they were all distracted by a sudden rattle overhead, like rain only harder, followed by a series of sharp cracks against the window glass. For a wild second it made Sandro think of gunfire, as if they were in some Third World airport under siege, and then he realised it was hail. Beyond the window on the runway a plane was pushing to take off into the wind with what seemed like some difficulty. Watching it, Sandro thought of Juliet Fleming strapped into her seat, facing her end.

But when he turned back, Magda Scardino's face had faded, frozen, looking towards the door. In a dull beige suit, sand-coloured shirt, attaché case, the new arrival to the VIP lounge was eyeing the greeter in her smart hat with grim distaste. It was Ian Cameron.

*

A fanatic, Vito had written, and you could almost read disbelief in the word, underlined and in bold. *Borderline sociopath, controlling in extreme.* And like an alarm bell ringing too late. *Mistake.*

A man called Ian Cameron. Danilo had leaned down and said, 'Well, of course, he's the one got Vito fired. Obviously it was a mistake to wind him up.' Then he'd stepped back.

Sitting so intent at the computer screen, Elena hardly noticed Lludic leaving. Last time she looked he'd been standing at the window as John used to do, gazing down into the street.

Was it wrong to pore over Giancarlo Vito's last words, searching through the CDs for any more evidence? Looking for what he might have said about John. About her. As if there'd be anything on these CDs that would say what she wanted to hear, that John had felt for her what he'd said he felt, all those weeks ago, reaching to touch her cheek: that he'd loved her. Perhaps she didn't need to hear the words again. Perhaps once was enough. And when she looked up, the sculptor was gone.

*

A tall, startlingly good-looking woman was standing in the street outside the front door in the Via del Leone, so handsome she almost had a force field, and Giuli found herself stepping off the kerb as she reached the spot.

'Ah, can I help you?'

The woman was looking up at the building. Giuli had her key in her hand: all she'd planned to do was sit a moment in her safe place, check the messages. Hide. Fight the weakness she felt overcoming her, the desire to cry. Think, instead. Think.

The woman looked down at her, standing in the gutter. 'I'm

looking for Sandro,' she said, frowning. 'I'm Mariaclara. I used to work at the Palazzo San Giorgio.'

'He's my boss,' said Giuli. 'They fired him.' She wondered what it must be like, to look like Mariaclara. The power.

'I know,' said Mariaclara. 'I called.'

'He's off somewhere,' said Giuli. 'I think maybe he went to the airport.' She hesitated. 'Do you want to come up?'

Once again Mariaclara looked up at the building, her long dark hair falling back from her white throat, then back at Giuli. 'I liked him,' she said. 'Shit. There was something I wanted to tell him.' And when she shivered suddenly, hunching her shoulders, Giuli saw that the power was a veneer. Just like it was with everyone. 'He's well out of there,' said Mariaclara as an afterthought.

'What was it you wanted to tell him?' said Giuli.

'There's someone,' said Mariaclara slowly. 'I think she could tell him who's been playing those nasty games. She sees everything that goes on up there. It's her he needs to talk to.'

*

'Hello?' said Luisa. '*Permesso*?' She pushed at the glass and it gave under her hand. 'Is anybody there?'

Was it the weather? Since turning to walk uphill she hadn't seen a soul. As the sky darkened and the wind rose, it was as though they'd all scuttled inside, tourists, locals, waiters and all. Something followed her up the street, a hard pattering, and she stepped inside the Palazzo San Giorgio to escape the hail that flung itself against the glass at her back.

The doorman was nowhere to be seen. Through a long window the great canopy of a tree was being buffeted by the wind. Lower down the slope there was a flash of white as a big canvas umbrella inverted itself.

'Hello?' There were doors: one of them, Luisa knew, was her husband's office, but they were all closed. She turned down the only other avenue, a wide grey corridor, a glimpse of books at the end, a library, tables with chairs. *I've come to see my husband,* Luisa rehearsed as she came into the big room. But it was empty as well, the long bar polished and clean, flowers at one end, and not a human soul. It was like a dream, or a nightmare: the big house with many rooms, the wind battering at the walls and the absolute silence inside. Or was it silent? Luisa felt something creep and draw tight inside her, closing her throat.

From somewhere a soft sound moved in the cavernous quiet, a padded footfall. She turned in the centre of the big windowless room, trying to find its source, and stopped. Beyond the bar at the far end of the library another door stood open, framed in cut grey stone, light falling across the space beyond it. Luisa held her breath. She heard nothing but as she watched the light a shadow moved in it.

Chapter Thirty-Six

ON THE LOWER TERRACE Lino and Mauro sheltered inadequately under the collapsed umbrella. He might be my son, Lino thought. If he weren't too dark, too short, too Sardinian.

'I don't know who was firing who,' he said, looking sidelong at the barman. A great deal of shouting from Cornell's office, and then a silence that had grown.

'It was, you go or I do,' said Mauro, ducking his head to look out over the city. The purple pall of cloud stretched into the hills to the north.

'And then she went,' said Lino gloomily.

'She was leaving anyway,' said Mauro. Alessandra Cornell had departed in a whirl of coat and bag and heels, without addressing a word to either of them. 'And Bottai goes out for an early lunch,' said Mauro, thoughtful. 'It won't last. They'll make it up.'

They looked down. The old woman who lived below the palace's garden was standing in the glazed door that opened onto her terrace, looking anxiously out at her bedraggled plants under the downpour. A plumbago was on its side on the terracotta, its pale blue flowers scattered. As they watched there was the sound of a doorbell and the old woman turned and went inside.

'And meanwhile we're holding the baby.' Lino glimpsed something on the stone and knelt, raising it in triumph. 'Here it is,' he said. 'I thought she said further down.'

Mauro looked at him. 'I thought it was a wild goose chase,' he said, eyes narrowed. 'Who knows what goes through that one's head.' He reached for the mobile – brand new, top of the range – and Lino handed it to him.

The younger man weighed it, lightly touched the gleaming screen and it lit up. The screensaver was a family group, three grown children, all looking warily back against a wide red landscape. He slid back the cursor to see the icons: a map sprang on to the screen. 'She doesn't keep it locked,' he said. 'Not a practised deceiver then.'

Lino looked at him sharply. 'Signora Cameron?' he said, disbelieving.

Mauro looked back into his face, expressionless, just a little shake of the head, then stared back down at the screen. They both looked.

'Isn't that . . . where is that?' Mauro said, tilting his head to see the map, a red thumbtack highlighting the tight hairpin of a sliproad leading down from the motorway. Mauro moved finger and thumb apart over the screen, looking for street names. Firenze Sud. He raised his head. 'Ah,' he said. The hail peppered them. 'Someone needed to find their way home.'

*

'*Permesso.*'

The old woman – whose name, according to the plaque on her door, was Bertelli – looked at Giuli expectantly as she hovered on the threshold.

Mariaclara had said, *I wanted to tell him, ask old Bertelli, she sees everything*. The old lady's building was close to the bottom of the hill, she said, at the foot of the Palazzo's garden. It was overgrown with something tangled and unkempt.

There'd been four bells and she'd rung all of them, having no idea which had admitted her. She'd just come straight up to the top floor and Signora Bertelli had been standing there, like a grandmother from a fairytale, white hair escaping from a bun. Giuli noticed earth under her fingernails, an apron, red lipstick in the cracks around her old mouth. A smile.

Tentatively Giuli handed over her card. The old lady looked at it with interest.

'I wonder,' said Giuli, 'if I might look at your terrace.'

But even as she stepped into the old lady's dim, cluttered apartment, felt the cool breeze shifting the long muslin curtains at the window and saw through them the terraces that tumbled below the great façade of the Palazzo San Giorgio, it was already forming in Giuli's mind. The face over the teacups in Gilli, the figure hovering in the corridor outside old Athene Morris's room: the reason Marjorie Cameron knew a man had been in Athene Morris's room her last conscious night on earth, was because she had been waiting in the corridor herself. Waiting for him to leave.

'Is it about the dog?' said Signora Bertelli. 'Poor creature.

She put it in one of the bins, where they keep the paper, the old magazines, all that. I didn't know who to tell, you see? They're hardly neighbourly, up there.'

*

She was standing between the glazed doors and some steps leading down, in the light that suddenly flooded in from outside, haloed by that frizz of colourless hair. Marjorie Cameron.

'Oh, you came,' she said and her voice was reedy and lost. She put out a hand.

Luisa's heart was still thumping on alert, but without thinking she put out her own hand in response. The fingers fastened on her wrist. Luisa looked down in surprise, tried to pull away, but the thin hand was strong. The sleeve fell back and there above the wrist was a long, deep scratch, no more than a couple of days old. She looked up at Cameron's face, indignant, but protest died on her lips.

'She told you, didn't she?' said Cameron, and pulled.

Luisa stumbled forwards at the sudden force and was abruptly only centimetres from the other woman's face.

'That woman. His awful old landlady. You were there last night.'

Frollini must have told Magda Scardino, thought Luisa grimly. No fool like an old fool.

Marjorie Cameron was examining her. 'She must have told you.'

So close, Luisa could see the softness under her chin, the lines around her eyes. She had thin northern skin and not enough flesh to resist ageing. This close, Marjorie Cameron might have been Maratti's age, the awful old landlady. Absently she was rubbing at the scratch on her forearm.

'Told me?' managed Luisa. Her eyes were drawn to the moving fingers, the dark beaded blood along the scratch: a cat might have done it. *She doesn't like strangers,* Maratti had said. *Particularly women.*

'About me,' said Marjorie, and abruptly released her hand. Her face faded, the eyes filled. 'I'm sorry,' she said. 'I went to see him before, you see. I'm married, of course. He was trying to protect me. That's what he said. No one should know about how he felt about me, it had to be platonic.'

The eyes widened, brimming. 'I told Ian he was wrong. Ian said he never wanted me, he said, who would want me if they could have *her*. I had to go back and make sure. I never meant—' And she stopped.

The big pale tear-filled eyes seemed quite blank to Luisa, empty of all understanding. I'm stronger, Luisa thought. She's asked for my help. *He told the landlady you were his mother.* She felt pity bubbling up in her, dangerous. 'It's all right,' she said, rubbing her wrist. 'Your husband . . . where is everybody?'

'They've gone,' said Marjorie Cameron. 'I wonder if they'll come back?' It was not clear if she included her husband. They were right on the edge of the short flight of stairs and Cameron looked down. 'I need to show you something,' she said. 'Is that all right? If I show you maybe you'll understand.'

Luisa could feel her on the brink of hysteria, and wanted to keep her calm. 'All right,' she said. 'Show me.'

Marjorie Cameron took a step away.

'Down there?' said Luisa, and looking down to where the stairs narrowed, she felt a sudden ridiculous vertigo. She set a hand to the wall to steady herself, and didn't move.

Cameron turned to look back, colour in her faded cheek at last, raising her head like a hopeful child. 'It's all right. I'll go first.'

At the foot of the stairs the corridor opened out ahead of them, wide and dark. Luisa knew it was a mistake. Was it some absurd kind of politeness that was keeping her here? 'What . . . where are we going?' she said, a hand to the wall.

Cameron glanced back at her again. 'Don't you want to see?' she said, and she was smiling but her eyes were distant, wild. 'They were in there,' her head bobbing as if in agreement, 'Giancarlo and . . . that woman. I went into the steam room, I wasn't spying on them—' She broke off, and Luisa heard a hiss, from between clenched teeth. 'But when I heard them . . .'

Cameron drew a breath; she took hold of Luisa's arm again, her hand felt hard, like a claw. Luisa looked back at the stairs: she could always run. Just not yet.

'He used to meet her down here,' said Marjorie Cameron. 'He had the key, you see. It . . . he said she liked it. It excited her.' Her eyes were huge. 'The killing room. Did you know about it?' She tilted her head like a bird, searching Luisa's face. 'They kept an unfaithful wife down here. Her husband had her chained and tortured till she gave her lover's name.' Her fingers insistent on Luisa's arm, Marjorie Cameron whispered, 'They used instruments.'

How could she know all this, thought Luisa, hypnotised; then she saw it blooming behind the woman's pale, mad eyes, a mess of the real and the imagined. The skin on her face seemed stretched, drawn back over the bones of her skull, as she turned towards Luisa. 'Don't you think she might have started making names up, in the end? They left her in her own filth. They left her to starve.'

A mistake, a mistake: it clamoured in Luisa's head even as she followed Marjorie Cameron down to the dead end of the corridor.

'Look,' said Marjorie Cameron, pushing at the wall. 'Look, someone's left it open.'

'There was a magazine in my husband's briefcase,' said Luisa, and Marjorie Cameron turned in the black rectangle of the doorway. It was cold, suddenly, a deep chill came from inside the room: she saw something illuminated in there in the dim light of the corridor. It looked like a chair, its seat padded with cloth she had first thought was black, but that was only the light. It was red.

'I found it in the garbage,' Cameron said, with satisfaction. 'The magazine.' And then she turned, her face close to Luisa's. 'But not you. You mustn't think . . . I just wanted to . . . to show your husband, all men are the same. I didn't know, when I put the magazine there. About your – your operation.'

She turned and ducked her head under the door's low lintel. 'Come on,' she said.

Mistake. But Luisa stepped inside, because she had to see. And the door closed behind her.

*

Sandro had had to run: in the doorway to the VIP lounge Ian Cameron had taken in their faces, turned so hard he'd knocked the greeter sideways with his attaché case, and disappeared. Sandro caught up with him outside the men's room and blocked him, feeling a burning in his chest. The adrenaline wouldn't be enough, he realised as he looked into Cameron's face, if he had to fight this man.

'Get out of my way,' Cameron said with level fury. 'What do you think you're doing?'

Sandro shouldered the door open on a gust of disinfectant and lavatory fug. 'In here,' he said. 'If you don't want this to become a police matter, here and now.'

One man was in there, a North African washing his hands: at one look from Sandro he left. Cameron set his case down, and Sandro could feel the rage coming off him, incandescent. 'Have you left her behind?' he said. 'Your wife?'

'She never comes with me,' said Cameron, white-lipped. 'It's work.'

Sandro stared at him, feeling with sudden force how much he disliked this man. Since when? And he knew quite instantly: since he'd seen a small, distinct movement of Cameron's across a crowded room, removing Athene Morris's hand from his arm with distaste – hatred on his cold, fanatic's face. She'd stood up to him. She was dead.

'Giancarlo Vito,' he said, and he saw Cameron's Adam's apple bob and subside. A slight sideways movement of the head. Sandro went on, quietly, almost with respect, considering what he was saying. 'He seduced your wife. Did he actually sleep with her? Perhaps he thought she would talk you round, when he saw you'd got it in for him.' Sandro had to speak in English: he couldn't be sure he'd got it right. 'You got him fired, but that wasn't enough, was it? You went out to dinner with your wife, the night Giancarlo Vito was murdered. What did your wife say to make you feel that firing him wasn't enough?'

The eyes Cameron turned on him were like pale stones: Sandro almost faltered. He had to go on. 'Did you make her tell you where he lived?'

'Marjorie hardly said anything,' he said, and his smile was thin. 'She told me she wanted a divorce, of course, she told me she was in love with another man.' He made a small prissy movement with his shoulders, imitating a woman. 'She seemed rather pleased with herself, I believe she thought she'd done something courageous. But after that I did most of the talking. I told her, for example, that Vito had slept with that . . . woman, Magda Scardino. She said she already knew, it was just business.' He laughed, and Sandro imagined him laughing at his wife. 'I told her he'd arranged prostitutes for the Van Vleets.'

His grey face in the smeared mirror was a picture of disgust: he clenched both fists at once, then looked down and released them. 'I told her I had no intention of giving her a divorce. I told her if she thought Vito would rather have her than Magda Scardino, she must need her head seeing to. And she walked out of the restaurant.'

There was a flush on his cheek now: Sandro imagined the waiters watching him finish his meal, alone. He wouldn't have hurried.

'Athene Morris saw her coming back without you,' he said, very softly.

Ian Cameron looked down, brushed at his shirt. Sandro remembered the time he'd first seen the engineer and his wife by candlelight on the terraces of the San Giorgio, Cameron examining something in her eye. Even then Sandro had thought, tenderness, or something else? Something else.

'Ah yes,' Ian Cameron said. 'Did Miss Morris tell you that personally? She didn't like me. And now she's dead of course.' Sandro said nothing. 'So she can't tell you that she also saw me, coming back without Marjorie. The problem, for your theory, would be that I returned first, some two hours earlier than Marjorie, at approximately. . .' He looked down at an imaginary watch. 'Eleven-thirty. Marjorie returned closer to one, in a taxi. I expect a minimal amount of investigation would trace the taxi – oh, and of course Juliet Fleming saw me come in, the doorman saw me come in – without Marjorie, or didn't he notice?' He sneered. 'Whatever his name is.' And he swung the attaché case down to his side.

'I don't suppose any of this is admissible in a court of law,' he went on, turning at the door. 'Not even in Italy. But I may be prepared to take it further. I haven't spoken to Marjorie yet.' And he was gone.

The message from Giuli came in as, stunned, Sandro emerged on to the crowded concourse, a family group parting around him as he ground to a halt. *Missed call* – no signal in the men's room – immediately followed by *Message received.*

Marjorie Cameron, it's her? And Luisa's up there, looking for you.

Chapter Thirty-Seven

AS THE DOOR CLOSED behind Luisa, all she could think was, this is a terrible place. It had been built deep into the rock and stretched away into shadows, and there was a smell. Of something ancient and filthy, something that seeped and sat. A single bulb suspended at the centre of its low ceiling illuminated a dark spreading stain on a dusty dirt floor, and heavy stone rings set in a back wall – and the chair.

'I knew whose magazine it was,' said Marjorie Cameron. 'That disgusting man. The American.'

'Why did you want to hurt *her*, though?' said Luisa. 'She never did you any harm. Therese Van Vleet.'

'Hurt her?' Marjorie Cameron spoke wonderingly. 'But why should everyone protect her, because she's young, and pretty? She's dirty. I wanted her to know, that someone knew.'

'You smeared . . . mess.' Luisa tried not to make her revulsion audible.

'It made me feel better,' said Marjorie Cameron simply. She looked at the chair. 'I married Ian at nineteen,' she said. 'I wanted to kill him, there and then at the table in the restaurant, when he said that to me.' She sat on the velvet seat, and looked up.

I could run, now, thought Luisa, but she didn't.

Cameron pushed her sleeves up unconsciously and there was the scratch again. Looking higher up the bare arm Luisa saw bruises.

'Does he hurt you?' she said. Was she constructing a case for the defence? But Marjorie Cameron hadn't killed her husband.

'Ian?' Saying his name, Marjorie Cameron's upturned face was childlike, or perhaps the light was kinder. You could see she would once have been pretty, when the hair had been a child's silky gold, and the soft mouth had been hopeful. 'Ian never touches me.' She looked down at the arms, as if seeing the bruises for the first time, touched them tenderly. 'He did that. Giancarlo did that. I thought he wanted to – to make love.' She looked around herself. 'I thought Ian must have been . . . wrong. But it hurt, I said, that hurts, and Giancarlo laughed and then I – I knew. That it had been true, what Ian said.'

'Did you understand that you were in danger?' Again, the case for the defence.

'Danger? I didn't care. Was I in danger?' Her eyes were wild. 'I just thought, he doesn't love me. He's had enough of me. He wants *her*.' In a white, drawn face.

In the limousine, in the mall, Marjorie Cameron had followed Magda like a dog: what had Juliet Fleming called it? Something about masochism, and unrequited love. With Vito dead, all she had left was Magda. To long for, and to hate. Luisa shifted, a step back, her head turned towards the door Marjorie Cameron had closed behind them. She swallowed down, the tiniest reflex of fear, but suddenly Marjorie Cameron was on her feet beside her and that hard small hand had fastened again around Luisa's wrist.

'He wasn't dressed. He was ready for bed, he said. His face . . . I tried to explain to him, it wasn't my fault, if I'd known Ian was going to have him fired I'd have tried to stop him . . .' She faltered. 'But he just looked at me as if I was nothing. All those years, alone, mending fences, fixing the pick-up. I always thought there'd be someone to rescue me.' She looked up. 'And then he said – Giancarlo said – go away. You're a stupid ugly old woman. And I saw the – the little thing, the dumbbell, just sitting on the shelf, it was so small but it was so heavy in my hand. It felt like . . . power. When I lifted it.'

Under the swinging bulb Luisa hardly dared breathe, and Marjorie Cameron went on.

'Do you know what it's like to be married to a man who only uses you? Do you know what it's like to have only that for nearly forty years, until he's sure you're no good for anyone else, and then suddenly there is someone else?'

Stiff-necked, Luisa shook her head, *no*, knowing there was no answer that would get her out of there. *Sandro*. Still holding her wrist, Marjorie Cameron's other hand crept up to Luisa's face, touching it with a thin finger, stroking. Luisa tried to breathe: under the woman's touch her body felt old and heavy and useless.

'I didn't mean to hurt Athene, you know. I didn't touch her. I tried to ask her not to . . . not to say she'd seen me. But . . . she was laughing at me. She's another one of those women. With her lovers.' She stroked. 'I should have gone and got someone, an ambulance, when she stopped being able to talk. But I just left her, on the bed.' A shuddering breath. 'I locked the door and threw away the key.'

Overhead came muffled sounds, footsteps on the corridor's soft carpet. Marjorie Cameron looked up, then down. 'Would you tell?' Sorrowfully, looking around. 'He brought me down here, too. It's where I kissed him.'

Involuntarily Luisa closed her eyes against the sight of the red chair, for shame.

Marjorie Cameron sighed, final. 'You would, wouldn't you? You'd tell.'

*

He's still here then, thought Lino. Danilo Lludic was standing among the library's tables like an escaped bull when they came back in, dripping and dishevelled from the terrace, Mauro holding Marjorie Cameron's mobile phone away from him as if it might be dangerous.

'I saw her come in,' said Lludic, looking around, jumpy as hell. 'I saw her.'

'Signora Cameron?' said Lino.

'Weren't you on the door?' said Lludic. 'No. Not Cameron. The detective's wife. Black hair. I saw her come over, I watched for her, but she didn't come back out again.'

The wife, thought widowed Lino, remembering the black hair, and something tightened in his chest. 'I couldn't . . . I wasn't . . . I had to help Mauro.'

'So where did she go?' said the sculptor, and just as the bewilderment in his face turned to something else, they all heard a noise. They all turned in search of it, the sound of something crashing over underground, a crump and a splintering, beneath their feet.

Mauro moved first, with certainty. Of course, thought Lino afterwards, it's his place, his territory, he must have known all along. The cellar.

*

Christ, thought Sandro in the taxi. Christ, for a squad car and a blue light.

Close to halfway back, staring at the meter in the gridlocked Piazzale Donatello, he'd realised that he didn't have any cash left on him. He muttered and pleaded under his breath, sweating, until the taxi driver turned to look at him, and he had to keep quiet or risk being turfed out into the traffic.

Before they even came to a halt outside the Palazzo San Giorgio he had thrown open the door and bolted; the taxi driver had no time to grab him. 'A minute,' he managed over his shoulder, anything to slow the man's pursuit, anything to get in there, anything to find her, *please God*, he begged, and then he was inside.

He heard them before he saw them, voices clamouring in unmistakable panic. Around him the luxurious space with its stairways and high ceilings echoed and taunted him. He ran, down the wide corridor's incline, the books of the library ahead of him. Someone was screaming. Someone was crying. They were clustered in the door at the far end, Giuli with her hands to her face and two men standing, one with his arms tight around someone, another kneeling, a woman on the floor, he could see her feet. Her bare feet, turned in like a child's. He blundered, knocking his knee against a chair, he almost fell. Behind him someone shouted but he stumbled back upright and kept moving, trying to decipher the configuration of bodies.

The woman on the floor was not dead, the big kneeling man was holding her hands across her body to keep her still and talking into her face – but the woman who wasn't dead wasn't Luisa, either, he'd known even from the bare feet, not her. Sandro slowed, his eyes travelled up, and there was Lino, there was the doorman in his ill-fitting suit and it was his arms around her. A strand of black hair was across her cheek and between her body and Lino's, one arm was folded against the breast. Luisa turned and saw him, and the space narrowed to a tunnel between them. As if in slow motion he righted the chair and went for her.

Behind them the taxi driver was shouting about calling the police.

Epilogue

'WHO'D HAVE THOUGHT HE'D have so many friends,' said Pietro in wonderment. At the back of the small square they sat in the shade on plastic chairs. On a precarious-looking stage, on the other side of several rows of trestles, four scruffy musicians were playing something deafening.

They looked at Enzo. Giuli's husband of six hours was sitting beside the remains of the wedding meal – a *porchetta* roasted by his father, of which only the pig's golden head remained, on its side like a drunken uncle, and the teetering fruit and meringue shambles of the *torta nuziale*. The bridegroom was leaning forward with his elbows on his knees in earnest conversation with six or seven cheerfully sweating men in suits. There'd been close to seventy guests at the height of the evening: the hardcore remained, those who'd hung the streamers and the photographs of the happy couple on every telegraph pole and lamppost between here and the town hall at Monte San Savino where they'd been married.

'Yes,' said Sandro. 'From school, apparently.' Which was a good sign – not that he'd had any real doubts about Enzo, not for some time. The shyness and the dodgy haircut disguised determination. And Giuli had had the clippers to him: his shorn forehead looked naked and new and pleasantly surprised.

Even at close to eight in the evening, even up here in the shade of Monte Amiata, it was hot and the men had removed their ties. Sandro mopped at his forehead, and looked around for Luisa. The square wasn't square, and it wasn't a city *piazza*: it more closely resembled a farmyard below a belltower, with one side occupied by an open barn filled to the corrugated roof with straw, and it was among the rolled bales that he spotted her, talking to the girl Elena who was Giuli's friend from school. The only one – but one was something. They might have been mother and daughter themselves, both dark, both compact and prickly, though tonight in the summer dusk Luisa's expression was anything but fierce.

'Any consolation that you left Falco with a nice mess to sort out?' said Pietro, looking sidelong.

Sandro grunted, still watching Luisa. 'Ah, they'll cover it up,' he said. 'They'll say he went rogue.' Brushed his hands together in a motion of dismissal. 'Sleeping around's not against the law. Not yet. And crimes of passion . . . well. It might turn out to be a pretty useful smokescreen.'

Gingerly he adjusted his waistband; even after the gargantuan feast of meat he felt pretty comfortable. Luisa had had him on fruit for breakfast for a month. She'd made it up with Frollini and had returned to work, two days a week and the best two at that, Thursday and Friday. It left her with time on her hands to keep tabs on his diet.

'If it ever gets to court. I don't suppose anyone in the service is enjoying the press coverage, though.'

It could be worse. Marjorie Cameron was not young and if she'd once been pretty, the photographs of her now, wild-eyed and dishevelled as she was hustled in and out of one hearing room after another, showed no evidence of it. It was being spun as menopausal madness, possibly even fantasy.

'She seems to want to be put away, though,' he went on, ruminatively. 'Luisa says, with a husband like that, she's not surprised. She thinks she's . . . well, not enjoying it exactly. But Ian Cameron's on the hook, all right. He's back in Australia, keeping his head down, but it's not just a matter of embarrassment. The Gulf Arabs don't like this kind of scandal, and it must be keeping attention on his collapsed bridge, too.' He didn't like Cameron, but did he deserve this? Just for being a cold bastard. Forty years of loveless marriage. Luisa thought he did.

'It's a pretty good mess,' said Pietro. 'Try to untangle the justice of it, even if Falco knows what justice is, which I doubt. Vipers, the lot of them, rich foreigners plus security services. Lock them all up in that killing room and throw away the key.'

'Falco's not so bad,' said Sandro, wearily.

'Vito must have been nuts,' said Pietro ruminatively. 'Maybe it's something they don't teach you in the army – or the secret service for that matter. Not to mess about with women of a certain age.'

Despite himself, Sandro smiled. 'Falco's learned that lesson, too,' he said. 'We could have covered it up ourselves, you know? Luisa and me. I didn't want Marjorie Cameron put away. She hardly knew what she was doing.' Uneasily he passed the handkerchief over his forehead again and sat up, scenting coffee. A stout woman emerged from the small restaurant beside the barn, carrying a tray.

'Locking the door on Athene Morris was something else, though.' He took the coffee and leaned back, sobered. 'She had to answer for that.'

'Just like someone has to answer for Carlsson,' said Pietro grimly. 'Or not, as the case may be. They'll hand that one on.' Falco was holding on to the gay secret life theory for grim death: the security services so far had not been mentioned in the media.

Sandro grunted. 'If they keep going with him being a promiscuous homosexual they're going to have trouble when Elena comes forward as a witness. Convincing the magistrates Marjorie Cameron is delusional is one thing, but Carlsson didn't even have a gay high-school crush to his name.'

He drained his coffee and stood: seeking Giuli. The band had quietened down; dimly he might even have recognised what they were playing, and people were moving forward to dance. Enzo was on his feet too, and looking, and there she was, coming shyly around the side of the stage. Afterwards, when people asked curiously, knowing Giuli, about her dress, all he could say helplessly was, it was sort of white.

*

When she saw Giuli was going to speak, Luisa's heart was in her mouth. At her side under the barn roof, Elena – Giuli's old, new, only friend – turned towards the stage too, a hand to her cheek. The music stopped.

The microphone gave out an amplified rustle and suddenly everyone was still. Giuli turned from one side to the other. 'I . . .' she said. 'I . . .' Holding the microphone in both hands, small in white as if she was at the first communion she'd never in a million years have had, and Luisa held her breath. Don't say too much, she found herself thinking, don't . . . don't. Her own wedding to Sandro swam behind her eyes. Her parents fussing and fretting; an awful stiff dress of nylon lace. Sandro doggedly determined: never one minute of hesitation. Never one single minute of doubt in forty years.

Across the crowd she saw his head turn and he was looking at her and it seemed to Luisa that something like her real wedding had taken place only that morning as she'd stood, tears in her eyes, in front of the mirror in her bedroom in her slip and her outfit waiting on the bed. 'You were lovely then, and you're lovely now,' he'd said, and taking the strap on the right side down over her shoulder, he'd leaned and put his lips to it, scars and all, and made it hers.

The crowd stirred, expectant, and Giuli spoke.

'I love him,' she said, tears in her voice that no one in the crowd would have recognised because Giuli never cried. And then the microphone dropped and Enzo was there at her side, gently leaning to retrieve it. The clapping and cheering and calling out drowned what he had to say when he lifted it and spoke, but it didn't matter because they all knew, anyway.

Across the heads Luisa looked at her husband, and he looked back at her, and nearly forty years narrowed to a long warm afternoon, under a belltower and a barn.